Praise for
MARY ALICE MONROE

THE BOOK CLUB

"Monroe offers up believable characters in a
well-crafted story."
—*Publishers Weekly*

"*The Book Club* skillfully weaves the individual story
threads into a warm, unified whole that will appeal to
readers who enjoy multifaceted relationship novels
with strong women protagonists."
—*Library Journal*

"Having the courage to start over and forge ahead in
tough times are themes that run eloquently through
author Mary Alice Monroe's very special new novel.
The Book Club is a dynamic snapshot of life, with all its
joys and sorrows. A very special book!"
—*Romantic Times*

GIRL IN THE MIRROR

"What price beauty? Mary Alice Monroe's
Girl in the Mirror reflects the shadows and shapes of
a woman's painful and illuminating journey of
self-discovery, of choice, of loves."
—*New York Times* bestselling author Nora Roberts

"What would you do if the career you cherished
threatened to cost you your life?
Mary Alice Monroe draws you into an absorbing tale
of hard-won success, devastating choices and the
triumphant power of love."
—Bestselling author Diane Chamberlain

"In a gripping story dealing with a sensitive issue,
Ms. Monroe will grab your heart...her character's
choices are tough ones we will all be thankful
we don't have to make."
—*Romantic Times*

Also available from MIRA Books and
MARY ALICE MONROE

GIRL IN THE MIRROR
THE BOOK CLUB

MARY ALICE MONROE

THE FOUR SEASONS

MIRA

ISBN 1-55166-789-4

THE FOUR SEASONS

Copyright © 2001 by Mary Alice Kruesi.

Visit us at www.mirabooks.com

Printed in U.S.A.

For my sisters,
Marguerite, Ruth, Maureen and Nuola
And to mothers and sisters everywhere.

I am grateful to many people for their generous help and support in the writing of this book.

Heartfelt thanks to Judith Stoewe, M.D. for helping me separate fact from fiction about homes for unwed mothers during the 1970s. Her professional experiences were invaluable as was her extraordinary sensitivity. I could have written a book just on this one aspect of the story. Janet Grossman, DNSc deserves special thanks for helping me develop a profile of classic sister roles in families, and a big hug for being one of my biggest cheerleaders. Thank you, David and Linda Kravitz, for timely input on the world of motel management and little dogs that steal scraps and hearts.

For reading the manuscript in the early stages and providing razor-sharp comments I thank Martha Powers. Julie Beard came through for me again when the draft was completed and provided worthy insights. I'm also grateful to Diane Chamberlain for pounding out plot points with me—and for that fabulous dinner at the Indian restaurant that was such an inspiration. Sincere thanks to Martha Keenan for her insightful editing and above and beyond efforts in the eleventh hour. And to all the MIRA gang for their support during the past year. Finally, thanks to Markus Kruesi for his invaluable help in every aspect of this work.

I also appreciate the cooperation and knowledge shared by the Soundex Reunion Registry, a unique organization that helps miracles happen every day. Finally, I extend my sincere thanks and appreciation to all the courageous, loving women who willingly shared their personal stories on the Internet so that other birth mothers would learn from their experiences and triumphs.

All things have their season,
And a season for every purpose under heaven.
                                        —*Ecclesiastes* 3:1

One

Rose Season stood at the threshold of her sister's bedroom and silently watched the shadows of an oncoming storm stretch like plum-colored talons across the empty bed. A great gust of icy wind from Lake Michigan howled at the windows.

"Merry," she whispered with longing. Rose resisted the urge to open the window and call out to her in the vast darkness. Merry's presence was palpable tonight. Rose had read somewhere that the spirit lingered for three days after death. Merry had been dead for four. Did she tarry to be sure her last request was honored?

Her last request. Why had she agreed to it? Rose asked herself, wringing her hands. The request was crazy, intrusive, maybe even hurtful. No one would ever go along with it. What would her sisters do when they read Merry's letter? Especially Jilly. She'd never spoken of that time, not once in over twenty-five years. It was as though it had never happened. She'll be furious, Rose worried. But secrets in families always had a way of coming out in the end, didn't they?

The hall clock chimed the hour. Rose tilted her head, thinking to herself that she should be calling Merry for dinner now, telling her to wash up. A pang of loneliness howled

through her like the wind outside. She wandered into Merry's
lavender room, idly running her fingers along the girlish
white dresser, the dainty vanity table and the silver-plated
brush, comb and mirror set. Strawberry-blond hairs still clung
to the bristles. Across the room, she bent to pick up the ratty
red-haired baby doll lying in the center of the pristine four-
poster bed. How Merry had loved the baby doll. Spring,
she'd called it, and never once in twenty-six years slept without it. Rose brought the doll to her cheek, catching Merry's
scent still lingering in the fabric. Then, with a loving pat, she
placed the doll back on the bed, careful to prop it against the
pillow. Rose's hands felt uncomfortably idle. She smoothed
the wrinkles from the comforter with agitated strokes, then
moved to the bedside stand to straighten the lace doily, adjust
the pleated lampshade and line up the many small bottles of
prescription drugs that she was so familiar with. She couldn't
part with anything of Merry's yet, not even these useless
medicines.

Without Merry to take care of, she felt so useless and de-
tached in the old house, like the shell of a cicada clinging
worthlessly to the bark. She needed work to keep her going,
some focus to draw her attention from her mourning. With a
discipline that was the backbone of her nature, Rose walked
swiftly from the gloomy bedroom to the wide, curving staircase of the old Victorian that had been her home since she
was born.

The walls along the stairs were covered with dozens of
photographs of the Season sisters at various moments of
glory and achievement in their lives. For comfort, she
glanced at the familiar photographs, treasuring the faces captured in them: Jilly, Birdie, Rose and Merry. The Four Seasons, their father had called them. The largest numbers of
photographs were of Jilly and Birdie, the eldest two. There
were fewer pictures of Rose, and hardly any of Merry, the
baby. She longed for her sisters; it had been nearly ten years

since they had all been together. How sad that it took a funeral to bring them together again.

Who would arrive home first? she wondered. Birdie was extremely busy with her medical practice in Wisconsin, but Jilly had the farthest to come—all the way from France.

Rose paused at a framed 1978 Paris *Vogue* magazine cover that showcased a young Jillian at twenty-one years of age, looking sex-kittenish in a fabulous pink gown that clashed in a chic way with her vibrant red hair. It was her first cover. Rose studied her eldest sister's full red lips pursed in an innocent pout, her deep-set eyes of emerald-green and the come-hither pose exposing one long, shimmering leg that seemed to go on forever. She couldn't imagine herself ever standing in front of so many people, in the glare of the lights, while men snapped her photograph. For that matter, Rose couldn't imagine ever looking so seductive or desirable.

Jilly was born at 12:01 a.m. on November 1, 1955. All Souls' Day. Mother always told of how she'd squeezed herself shut because she didn't want a child of hers born on Halloween. Who knew what nickname father would have chosen then? Their father, William, claimed it was a family tradition to play with their unusual last name. After all, he was nicknamed Bill Season. But their mother, Ann, a petite beauty with a will of iron, swore no child of hers was going to be tagged for life with a name people laughed at. As a compromise, Ann Season gave her daughters strong, sensible names, allowing their father full rein with the nicknames. Thus for his first daughter, Jillian, born in a Chicago autumn, he thought himself clever to name her "Jilly Season."

Moving down the stairs, Rose perused the large collection of photographs of Beatrice. Jilly liked to be first, but in most things Birdie came through for the prize. "The early bird catches the worm," their father used to say with a wink of pride at his second daughter. Birdie was his favorite, everyone knew that. Jilly would tease her and say Birdie was the

son he never had. She was a tall, broad-shouldered girl with
a powerful intellect and an even more powerful, competitive
spirit. Even the name "Birdie" seemed to mock her tom-
boyish body.

Bill Season had chosen the nickname because she was
born in early summer and was insatiable, howling for more
food like a hungry bird in the nest. And she'd certainly
caught the worms, Rose thought as her gaze wandered over
the photographs. The first was Birdie at sixteen, beaming into
the camera, dripping wet and clutching an enormous silver
trophy for the state championship swimming team. She'd
been the captain, of course. And there were more photographs, of Birdie as class valedictorian, of Birdie winning
trophies for swimming, lacrosse and the science fair. Birdie
receiving a diploma from medical school. Birdie dazzling in
white lace and tulle smiling at her handsome groom, Dennis,
the biggest trophy of all.

There were fewer pictures of herself, the third child. This
section of wall seemed almost barren when compared to
Birdie's. Rose felt the usual flush of embarrassment that the
scarcity of photographs was an accurate—if pitiful—statement about her life. It was all very well that Jilly was a
famous model, on magazine covers all over Europe, and that
Birdie was a successful doctor, wife and mother. But what
about her own life? There was neither a photograph of her
graduating from college, nor a picture of a radiant Rose on
her wedding day. Her mile-marker was a high school graduation photograph that showed a thin, shy girl looking much
like she did today.

Rose's hair was a paler, washed-out version of the Season
red that her father playfully called "pumpkin" and her
mother optimistically called "strawberry blond." She still
wore it in the same long, straight style of high school and
her body was every bit as lean and shapeless as it been then.
"Sticks," the other children had called her. In all the pic-

tures, her eyes were the dominant feature. Enormous hazel eyes with brows and lashes so pale they were seemingly not there. They peered out from her pale face, large and wary, like a cat's when poised to leap away.

Rose was born in the dog days of August when her mother's roses were blooming. Thus she was called Rose, the only one of the four Season girls without a nickname. Rose was a fine, plain name, her father had always said. And it suited her, she thought with a sigh of resignation.

As with most families, the baby had the fewest photographs. Which was too bad, she thought, since Merry was arguably the most beautiful of all the Season girls. Their parents had been older when they married and had had children late. Thus, their father liked to say that Merry was his last hurrah. *The fourth Season.* Meredith was born in December, a season ripe with nickname potential, but Bill had settled on "Merry" because she was such a cheerful baby. Rose traced a finger across a picture of a precocious, impish Merry at two years of age. The pictures stopped then.

Rose turned her head away from the photographs, closing her mind from the memory, and wandered from room to room, feeling that edginess that comes when one is aimlessly looking for something to do. Each of the twelve rooms of the Victorian was immaculate, a savory dinner was waiting in the oven and flowers were beautifully arranged in the bedrooms. She turned on the television, then as quickly flicked it off again. She picked up a book and settled into a comfortable chair, but no sooner had she read a paragraph than her mind wandered again. She closed the book in defeat and laid her head back against the chair. With a heavy sigh, she reached into her apron pocket and pulled out a pale blue envelope.

Merry's letter.

She'd carried this letter in her pocket all day wondering whether to burn it or send it to the family lawyer. The mo-

ment of decision had come; the funeral was tomorrow. Rose
closed her eyes and recalled how Merry's pink tongue had
worked her lip as she'd struggled with the letter, wanting it
to be her best. Merry couldn't have comprehended how those
brief sentences, written in her childlike script, would send
thundering repercussions in her sisters' minds and hearts—
as it had hers when she read them.

She looked down at the envelope in her hand and was
moved to tears by the sight of the address painstakingly written in Merry's handwriting, encircled by a big heart: *To Jilly,
Birdie and Rose.*

She would give the letter to the lawyer, Rose decided. It
was the right thing to do. Merry needed her—trusted her—
to deliver it. This time she would not fail her.

Beatrice Season Connor looked up into the April sky and
cursed.

"Look, it's snowing!" Hannah called, stepping out from
the car. Her fifteen-year-old daughter's face turned upward,
and with a delighted grin, she darted her tongue out to catch
the soft, moist flakes as they tumbled gracefully from the sky.

"That's just what we need. A snowstorm on top of everything else."

"It's just a few flakes." Hannah's voice was full of reproach.

"From the looks of it, we're going to get a dump. Damn
snow," Birdie muttered, grabbing the bags full of last-minute
shopping items from the car and hoisting them into her strong
arms. "I'm sick of snow. Hasn't Milwaukee had enough for
one year? It's April, for crying out loud. Well, that's it," she
said with the quick decision typical of her. Slamming the
door, she headed toward the house. "We're going to have to
hustle and leave for Evanston earlier than we'd planned if
we expect to get everything done by the funeral." She

stopped at the door and turned to face her daughter. "I'm counting on you, Hannah. I'm going to need your help."

"I don't see why *we* have to do everything." Hannah crossed her arms over her chest.

"We do if we want it done right." Birdie privately groaned at the prospect. The notion of pushing forward her departure when her schedule was already jammed full thrummed in her temples. She was squeaking out of town as it was. Sometimes she felt like a circus performer twirling countless plates: she had had to arrange coverage for her medical practice, calm her patients, take the dog to the kennel, cancel the housecleaning service, pack... The list went on and on. On top of all that, the funeral was tomorrow and it was up to her to make certain everything ran smoothly.

"When you need something done, ask a busy woman," she murmured with a heavy sigh, though secretly she felt a superior conceit. To her mind, all it took to succeed was discipline, setting goals and lots of hard work. And she worked harder than most. She could list her achievements readily: she was a pediatrician with a thriving practice, a wife for nineteen years, the mother of a healthy daughter and the mistress of a large, well-managed home. If there was such a thing as a supermom, Birdie thought with pride, then she was it.

But today was a test of her abilities. She lifted her wrist to check her watch and her lips tightened with annoyance. God, look at the time. Where was Dennis? And Hannah? Peering outside, she saw Hannah still leaning against the rear fender, gazing at the twirling flakes of snow. Frustration brought the pounding in her head to a painful pace.

"Didn't you hear me say we were leaving early?" she called from the back door.

Hannah's smile fell but she remained motionless, resolutely staring out.

"Don't pull that passive-aggressive act on me, young

lady," she called, raising her voice as she walked nearer the car. She could feel her anger growing with each step. "I've asked you to get your packing done for twenty-four hours and so far you haven't done a thing. I'm not going to do it for you."

"Who's asking you to?" Hannah swung her head around. "You'd just pack the wrong things, anyway."

"This isn't a prom we're talking about. It's my sister's funeral. My baby sister! It's hard enough for me to deal with the fact that she's gone without having to argue about meaningless things like your dress."

"At least you have a sister."

Birdie felt the weight of that reply start to drag her under. How many years had she had this thrown in her face like a broken promise? "Hannah, please. We don't have time to argue. Just go upstairs and pack a black dress," she ground out with finality.

"You never ask me to do something, you order me. Yes, you do! I hate you!" she shouted when Birdie opened her mouth to object. Hannah fled into the house, slamming the door behind her.

Birdie knew that those words were spoken in the white-hot fire of teenage anger and flung at her to burn—and burn they did. A mother never hears the words "I hate you" without cringing and feeling like a hopeless failure.

She followed Hannah back into the house with a heavy tread. Closed doors were a way of life between them now. Why did push always come to shove between them? And when had she started to feel the need to win these senseless battles? Not so long ago, she'd let trivial arguments slide by because all the parenting articles she'd read had a unified rallying cry: *choose your battles!* With teenagers, however, *everything* was a battle.

She walked to the small desk in the kitchen and worked away her frustration by cleaning up the day's disorder. When all was spotless and organized, she reached for a stack of patient messages awaiting her. Clearing her mind of personal problems, she picked up the first one and dialed.

An hour later, she was just finishing up her last call when her husband walked in from the garage. She turned her head to see Dennis shake off a covering of powdery snow from his lambskin jacket. He was five foot ten, just an inch taller than she was, but his build was slight in line and breadth of bone. With his long, thoughtful face, his dark brown eyes behind round, tortoiseshell glasses, his blond hair worn shaggy to the collar and his rumpled corduroy trousers worn with a sweater rather than a jacket, he looked every inch the university professor that he was.

He kicked the snow from his shoes, but when he looked up, she noted that his face was pale and pinched from fatigue. He used to smile and call out a cheery "I'm home!" Lately, however, he entered the house in silence. Birdie frowned with concern, then turned her focus back to the patient on the phone.

"No, Mrs. Sandler, Tommy doesn't need an antibiotic. Yes, I'm sure. He doesn't have a bacterial infection. It's a virus, though a nasty one. No, an antibiotic won't help. In fact, it would weaken his natural resistance." Birdie caught Dennis's eye and held up her finger for him to wait a minute. Dennis nodded, flung his coat over the edge of the kitchen chair, then reached into the fridge for a beer.

"Keep a close eye on him, and if he takes a turn for the worse or spikes another fever, then call my office. Dr. Martin is covering for me. What? Ninety-eight point six is normal." She rolled her eyes and reached out for Dennis's beer. "Yes, very good. Bye now."

Birdie sighed with relief, placed the receiver back on the hook, then tossed back her head and took a long swig of the beer. "Diagnosis—worried parent," she muttered.

"Tough day?"

"The worst. It started off with the dog being sick. He's so damn neurotic every time he has to go to the kennel. Hannah's been her usual petulant self. Then the patients started in." She lifted the thick stack of yellow messages.

"I thought you arranged coverage."

"I did, but you know there are always those patients who panic when I leave town. It's just easier for everyone if I call them."

"You don't have to go that extra mile. No one else's patients expect such service. I don't know why you have to push yourself so hard. You're already better than most docs out there."

"I'm better because I'm compulsive about such things. It's who I am. Anyway, the point's moot because I'm all done. That was the last of the calls, thank God." She tossed the yellow slips into the trash.

"So, you're free."

She smirked. "Free to go home and run a funeral."

Dennis set his beer down on the counter and lifted his hands to her shoulders, a familiar gesture that Birdie welcomed. She sighed and leaned into him, slumping in relief the moment his hands began massaging. He had wonderful hands, long-fingered and strong; he could knead knots out of her shoulders like no one else. They'd started dating in college when she was a champion swimmer for the team. He used to massage her shoulders after her swim meets. She still teased him that she married him for his hands.

"God, that feels good," she groaned.

"You're all knotted up. You need to relax." He leaned closer and said in a seductive tone by her ear, "I know what will loosen you up. When do we have to leave?"

Birdie cringed and moved out from under his hands. The last thing she was interested in right then was sex and she was irked that Dennis would even think she would be. "For God's sake, Dennis, we have to leave in forty minutes."

Dennis held his hands in the air for a moment, then let them drop to his sides with resignation. When he spoke, his voice was lackluster. "I thought we weren't leaving till four."

"Did you forget we're supposed to pick up Jilly from O'Hare?" Her exasperation rang in her voice. He could remember the dates of every foreign war the United States was ever in, but he never seemed capable of remembering one family date on the calendar. "If this front becomes the storm the weathermen predict, traffic will be snarled up all along the interstate and Jilly's flight will be delayed, if not canceled. Who knows what time she'll get in? It's crazy for us to pick her up. We could sit there for hours."

"So why doesn't Rose pick her up?"

Birdie snorted and shook her head. "I'm not even sure Rose knows how to get to the airport. She never leaves Evanston, and as far as I can tell she rarely leaves the house! She doesn't much care for talking on the phone, either. She screens calls on the answering machine before picking up. Who does she think is going to call her, anyway? She doesn't have any friends. Rose is a dear heart but I swear she's becoming more and more isolated every year."

Birdie rubbed the stiffness in her neck. After the funeral was over and the family house was sold, she'd have to have a serious talk with her sister about her future. Rose had to face up to leaving the house, and she'd have to get a full-time job, one that would support her. At least she had her computer skills. But Rose was such a stay-at-home she'd have a hard time making new friends and a new life. It wasn't good that she had locked herself away as caretaker for Merry all those years.

"Tell Jilly to take a cab."

"What? Oh yeah...well, I suggested that to her on the phone but she complained and reminded me how long it'd been since she'd been home and told me how much luggage she had and so on and so on. Get this. She wanted to be picked up by a family member—at the gate!''

His shook his head. "And you relented...."

"Who doesn't with Jilly?"

"Well, even you can't order a blizzard around."

Birdie chuckled then pursed her lips, considering her options. Her first priority was to get to Evanston and make certain the funeral arrangements she'd spent hours—days—on the phone making were going smoothly. She rested her hands on the counter and leaned against them. "God, this is going to be a nightmare. Who knows what to expect from her? Do you remember the scene Jillian made at Mother's funeral?"

He shrugged. "Jillian lives to make a scene. I don't see what the commotion is about. She'll arrive in a state, stay long enough to make another scene, then leave and we won't see her for another ten years. God willing."

"I don't see why you dislike her so. She's never done anything to you."

"She doesn't have to. It's what she does to *you* that makes me dislike her."

"What do you mean?" Birdie replied, genuinely surprised. Dennis never made any pretense over the fact that he didn't like her more glamorous sister.

"She puts you on edge," he replied, looking Birdie directly in the eye. "She makes you feel somehow less." He lowered his gaze. "You're not the same whenever she's around."

Birdie wanted to tell him that was because *he* was never the same when she was around. Dennis had dated Jilly for a brief period in high school, something Birdie never felt comfortable about. Neither of them ever mentioned it, but sometimes, when he didn't think anyone was looking, she caught him gazing at Jilly with an odd expression on his face. She'd wondered if the gaze was merely speculative, or, and she shuddered to think this, if it was lust she saw under his heavy, hooded eyes.

"If she makes me feel less," she replied, loading ice blocks into the cooler, "it's only in the arena of beauty. Let's face it. Jilly is gorgeous."

"So are you."

"No, I'm not." She wasn't being coy. Birdie knew that age and the additional twenty pounds that crept on over the past decade had not improved her already large frame. In the looks department, nothing she had could compare to Jilly. Birdie's eyes were pale blue, not a vivid green like Jilly's. All she had of the famous red Season hair were a few red highlights in the dull brown. Worst of all, she had her father's nose. He told her to be proud of the aristocratic though slightly askew family inheritance, and in fact, she was. But it did nothing to enhance her beauty.

"You are to me."

When he said things like that Birdie's heart did a quick flip and she felt a sudden gush of love for him. She turned and busied her hands rinsing a few cups in the sink, flustered. "That's sweet. But really, Dennis, I'm over forty years old and a success in my own right. I don't need to pretend I'm beautiful for my self-esteem."

Dennis just shook his head sadly.

She turned off the water and made a snap decision. "We'll skip the airport. I'll call Rose and see what else can be arranged. But we'll still have to leave early in this storm. Where were you, anyway?" she asked, turning to face Dennis. "You said you'd be home by twelve."

"What time is it now?"

"It's almost three."

He shrugged and raised his brows in a gesture of innocence. "I had a lot to do to leave town for several days. Midterm grades need to be averaged before spring break. Then there was an emergency meeting with the chairman."

He loosened his tie and tugged it off with a frustrated yank. "I got out as quickly as I could."

"Didn't it occur to you that I've got a lot to do, too? While you were arranging your schedule, I was doing the same *plus* shopping for the trip, packing up and taking the dog to the kennel."

He turned his back to her and grabbed the beer bottle from the counter along with the stack of mail. "Well, we can't all be as efficient as you."

She felt the sting of his words as she watched him lean casually against the counter and sift through the mail as though he had all the time in the world. He could be oblivious to everyone's needs but his own, she thought. Hannah may not have inherited his lean physique, but she had certainly inherited his temperament.

"Where's Hannah?" he asked, as though reading her mind.

"She'd better be upstairs packing. Would you go up and check on her? I've asked her to pack for two days and she hasn't done it. Now we've run out of time and if she's not done I guess I'll have to do it."

"No you don't," he replied, looking up from his mail. "If she leaves something out, then she'll have to live with it."

"Oh, Dennis, don't be ridiculous. If I don't get after her who knows what she'll wear?"

"Then she'll be embarrassed. You're the one who's always preaching about natural consequences."

Birdie fumed. She knew he was right, but she just couldn't bring herself to allow her daughter to be poorly turned out for her sister's funeral. "Whenever someone sees a poorly dressed child, or walks into a messy house, they never blame the father. It's always the mother who's thought of as a slacker."

"Who cares what anyone thinks?"

"I care!"

"You might as well relax and let her be. She's fifteen. She's not going to listen to anything you say, anyway."

She put her hands up in an arresting position, cutting him off. "We're *not* going to get into this right now. I've simply too much to do. Could you *please* just go upstairs and finish your own packing without this big discussion? I already packed your dark blue suit for the funeral. Just pick out some casual clothes. That's *all* you have to do," she said with exaggeration.

"You never like what I pick out, anyway, so why not finish it yourself?" he muttered, but he shuffled up the stairs, anyway.

She bit back a retort and turned on her heel to head for the phone. If she didn't get some space between them quickly the fuse they'd lit would explode. Lately, anytime they were in a room together it was like putting a match near a powder keg. The tension had really started heating up again in the past few days. Ever since Merry's death.

Birdie paused to think, *Was it only four days ago that Merry had died?*

It was a night much like any other night. There had been no premonition of trouble to come. Birdie had always thought she would somehow *sense* when a loved one was dying, especially someone as close as a sister. She was a physician, after all. She expected that she'd develop some intuition as to when death was imminent. Apparently not, she thought, chagrined. She hadn't suspected a thing as she crept under the sheets, yawned and murmured good-night to her husband before falling into a deep, undisturbed sleep.

The call from Rose woke her just after 11:00 p.m. Merry's lungs had filled again with the current bout of flu and she was having trouble breathing. Complications weren't unusual for Merry. Her lungs had been damaged as a child, making her a high-risk patient. Her doctor had upped her medication and was on his way but Rose wanted to call Birdie for help.

Birdie had risen promptly, dressed, made a pot of coffee and placed a call to her colleague to cover her morning appointments in case she was late getting back. It didn't take long, not more than forty minutes, to get on the road. When she knocked on the door of the Season family home not even four hours later, Birdie had known instantly that she was too late. Rose met her with grief etched across her drawn face and red-rimmed eyes. Even in her shock, Birdie noticed the calm, even serene cadence to Rose's voice.

Birdie, our Merry is gone. I know, I know... It was all very sudden and there was nothing that could be done. It caught all of us by surprise. It was her time and she was ready. There, there... It was peaceful, really it was. You know our Merry.... She died with a smile on her face.

Birdie reached a shaky hand up to wipe the tears from her cheek. That was four days ago and she still couldn't believe her sister was dead. In her opinion, she *was allowed* to slip away. Rose should have called her to Evanston the minute Merry's flu worsened. The doctor should have admitted her to the hospital at the first sign of fluid in the lungs. Fury, guilt and sorrow twisted in Birdie's heart as she wrestled with the issue that kept her awake at night and shortened her temper during the day.

If only she had been faster—perhaps skipped making the phone call or that pot of coffee, if she'd pushed the speed limit on the way down—she might have been able to save her.

Jillian DuPres Cavatelli Rothschild Season reached above her head with a shaky hand and buzzed for the steward. Most of the other passengers were slowly becoming alert, having eaten and napped. But the plane was a mess. The stewards had done their best, but eight hours of togetherness was getting very old and the interior of the enormous plane looked as tired as the 178 passengers felt.

She buzzed for the steward once again.

A handsome blond young man in a horrid navy-and-burgundy striped shirt sauntered down the narrow aisle to her seat and mustered a tired smile. He had long, curly lashes that any model would kill for, but from the looks of the circles under his eyes and his bored expression, he was more eager for this plane to land than she was.

"I'd like a Scotch, please," she said, handing him money. "And some water and ice."

He paused, furrowing his brows, seemingly trying to gather his last vestige of polite intervention. "We'll be landing soon, ma'am. Perhaps some coffee?"

Jilly straightened in her seat and delivered one of her famous megawatt smiles. "If I wanted coffee," she said in a honeyed voice, "I'd have asked for it. What I want is one of those cute, itty-bitty bottles of Scotch and a glass of ice with just a smidgen of water. Please."

The steward looked severely uncomfortable now, glancing furtively at the old woman in the next seat who was hanging on every word. He stretched across the backs of the row ahead and said in a low, conspiratorial whisper, "You've had three already and you didn't touch your dinner."

Jilly leaned forward and replied in a staged whisper, "I know. I never eat anything I can't identify."

"Are you sure you wouldn't want some coffee, or perhaps some tea?"

It was embarrassing enough to have to ride in coach again. In first class they wouldn't have questioned her request. More Scotch? Right away!

Jilly dropped all pretense of friendliness. "What I'd like, young man, is a cigarette. But since you fucking well won't let me have that, I'll settle for a Scotch." She turned to the elderly woman. "Excuse my French."

She could tell from the way the steward's lashes fluttered that the slim young man wanted to tell her what she could

do with her fucking cigarette and Scotch. Jilly steeled herself,
ready for a fight when the little bell went off and the pilot's
voice informed them that he was sorry but that there was
heavy snowfall in Chicago and that there would be long delays. This was met with a chorus of groans from the passengers. The steward closed his eyes for a moment and took a
breath. When he opened them again, he proffered a perfect
steward's polite smile that said, *Forget it, it's just not worth
the aggravation.*

"Right away, ma'am."

Jilly watched him retreat down the aisle as a dozen more
lights lit up and hands flagged him as he passed. She hated
to be called ma'am, madam, frau or any other sobriquet that
implied she was old. Still, she felt a twinge of regret for
making such a fuss, but not so much that she didn't want her
drink.

A short while later the little bottle of Scotch was delivered,
along with her five-dollar bill. Apparently the flight was in a
holding pattern and drinks were on the house. Grumbles were
still audible throughout the cabin but the gesture of goodwill
went a long way to settle the passengers. "Thank you," she
said sweetly as she tucked the five-dollar bill into her purse.
These days, every dollar counted.

"It's been a long trip, hasn't it," the old woman beside
her said in a sympathetic voice. She'd introduced herself as
Netta. She was doll-like and positively ancient with waxy
skin rouged in small circles over her cheekbones. Her eyes,
however, were an animated blue that rivaled the sky Jilly had
left in Paris.

Jilly could only nod, thinking how it would take longer
than the endless eight-hour flight to explain to this woman
the journey she'd traveled since she'd received the telephone
call from Rose. Hell, just since her last smoke. Until the last
boarding call she'd stood in the bar, puffing like a locomo-
tive, storing up nicotine in her cells for the long trip like a

camel would water. She'd been in agony anticipating her return to the old Victorian loaded with memories as ancient and musty as the velvet curtains and bric-a-brac. *You can't go home again,* the old adage said. She wished it were true. For twenty-six years, she'd tried not to. But here she was, on a Boeing 747, doing just that. Everything she owned was squeezed into two large Louis Vuitton bags and stored in the belly of this plane. She'd had to borrow the money from a friend to purchase the ticket to Chicago—one-way coach.

"Are you all right?" the old woman asked kindly.

Jillian turned her head. She saw genuine concern in the bright blue eyes, not curiosity or annoyance at her fidgety behavior.

"I'm just tired," she replied, taking her glass of Scotch in hand. "Thanks."

"Is it your job? I read about stress on working women all the time."

A short laugh escaped as Jilly shook her head. "No, not the job. Unfortunately."

"What do you do, if you don't mind my asking?"

"I'm a model." She shrugged lightly. "And I was in a few foreign films."

The women's eyes crinkled with pleasure. "I thought so. You're very beautiful."

The compliment washed warmly over Jilly and she smiled for the first time that day. "Not so 'very' anymore. I'm... retired."

Her smile fell as she heard again the comments of the agencies. *You are still a beautiful woman, but... You're over forty. You know how it is.... Look at them, they are nineteen! So young!* She couldn't blame them. Age was an occupational hazard of the beauty business.

"I'm too old," Jillian said, finding it easy to confess to a stranger.

The elderly woman laughed lightly and shook her head.

"How amusing. I was just thinking how I wished I was as young as you!" She reached out to pat Jilly's hand. "You see how Einstein was right, my dear. Everything is relative."

"By that you mean the grass is always greener, I suppose." She didn't want to add that she didn't find that the least bit comforting.

"No," the woman replied. "Actually I was referring literally to the theory of relativity. How different observers can describe the same event differently. From my position in the universe, my dear, you *are* young. And vibrant and beautiful. From your position, let's see…" She raised a crooked finger with a tiny, yellowed nail and pointed.

"I suppose you see that child over there as young and beautiful, am I right?"

Across the aisle sat a twenty-some-year-old woman in jeans and a clinging shirt, devoid of makeup, with dewy skin and the firm muscle tone Jilly had lost long ago. Mouth pulling in a wry smile, Jilly nodded.

"You see? It's all relative. Why do you think older women like to stick together? Because we see one another as beautiful and vibrant. I guess you could say we're traveling at the same speed." She laughed softly again, then added wistfully, "I wish someone had explained Einstein's theory of relativity to me when I was young. It would have taught me to be more accepting, and probably more compassionate, to others' points of view. That would have prevented a few troubles in the past, I can assure you. Take my word and remember this—how you see the world may not agree with how others see it. But you have to accept that their observations are valid. So," she said with a light tap of her nimble fingers on Jilly's hand, "you *are* young and beautiful, my dear, and nothing you say will convince me otherwise."

Jilly smiled, conceding the point. "For me, *relative* means my sisters. And let me tell you, do we ever see the world from different positions."

"Ah, you're going to see your sisters?"

Jilly nodded. "Yes. Well, two of them. My third sister just passed away. It's her funeral that brings me home."

"Your older sister?"

"The youngest. She was the baby, just thirty-two when she died. She had bad lungs and they gave out."

"Oh, that is sad. Death is always so, but an early death is more tragic. You have my sympathy. Funerals can be very emotional, you know. Use this time to gather your strength." With another gentle pat, the older woman turned her attention back to her book.

Jilly shifted in her seat. As she watched the amber-colored fluid swirl around little chunks of ice, her mind stumbled over thoughts of Merry. Dear little Merry, gone. She swallowed the Scotch and relished the smooth burn. It was strange to think of her thirty-two-year-old sister as *little,* but that's how she always thought of Merry. Poor, poor Merry... Whenever Jilly looked into those sparkling, childlike eyes, she felt a stab of guilt in her abdomen so painful it drove her an ocean away.

Yet here she was, crossing that same ocean again. It was poetic justice that she was stuck in a holding pattern over O'Hare, she thought, twirling the ice, since her mind was going round and round the same old stories, the same old issues. Thirty years of circling...

Her thoughts were interrupted by the voice of the captain.

"Ladies and gentlemen, good news. The runway at O'Hare has been cleared and we've been given permission to land. Thank you for your patience. Please return to your seats and fasten your seat belts. Stewards, prepare for landing."

The sigh of relief was audible in the plane. Taking a deep breath, Jilly pulled her large Prada bag from under the seat and reached for her makeup. Polishing her face was second nature to her. It was an armor against an unfriendly world. In her compact mirror she saw the familiar green eyes staring back at her. They were once described as bedroom eyes, but now they were simply tired and hardened by experience. She dabbed at the mascara smudges under her eyes and smoothed blush onto her cheeks. Though still creamy and smooth, her skin was far from dewy. She stared at her face a moment longer, hating it.

Her move to Europe may have lessened the emotional intensity with distance, but it was never the cure. Each mile closer, each moment nearer to landing, she could feel the turbulence of her emotions rise closer to the surface.

After thirty years, Jillian Season was coming home to stay.

Two

A hello burst from Rose's lips as she swung the door wide to see Birdie, her nose red and her head tucked into her coat collar like a turtle.

"Come in! Come in, at last!" Rose cried out, feeling a heady joy and hugging Birdie tightly, relishing the feel of her sister's arms around her, padded as they were by her thick coat. Birdie dwarfed Rose as she engulfed her in a long, firm embrace. Instantly they were ageless, bound by a shared childhood and years of history.

"Mother, I'm freezing!"

The sisters laughed and stepped aside as the wind gusted, sending a spray of icy crystals in their faces. Rose shivered but held the door for Hannah, then waited for Dennis as he huffed and puffed up the stairs with the suitcases. Rose thought their faces were travel-weary as they filed past and she sensed a tension between them, as though they'd been arguing. She notched up her cheeriness, closing the heavy oak door behind them against the cold. They stomped the snow from their boots and slipped out of their coats and gloves, all the while delivering bullets of reports on the journey. *Boy-oh-boy what a trip...back-to-back traffic...one ac-*

*cident after another...slippery...damn tollbooth backed up
for miles.*

Rose led them into the living room, where soft halos of
yellow light from the lamps created a welcoming warmth and
the scent of her roast beef and garlic permeated the wintry
air. Vivaldi's *Four Seasons* played softly in the background—a family favorite.

On the table cheese, crackers and crudités, looking a bit
tired after the long wait, awaited on silver trays. She was
proud of her efforts to make the house comfortable, pleased
to see the tension ease from their faces and color suffuse their
cheeks.

"So many flowers!" Birdie exclaimed, eyes wide as she
walked from table to table admiring the arrangements and
pausing to read the cards.

"More come every day. Merry's doctors, the neighbors,
old friends of Mom and Dad's, they all sent something. I
didn't know so many people cared about her. She didn't see
people much, but she obviously made an impression. I only
wish she were here to enjoy them," Rose added wistfully.

"Aunt Merry loved flowers," Hannah ventured solemnly.

Rose nodded, noting the sullen expression on her niece's
face.

Birdie's face was passive as she walked around the large
living room, taking in the familiar twelve-foot ceilings, tur-
rets, molding, quaint panes of glass and gorgeous woodwork.
It was a shame, she thought, how far from grace this room
had fallen. Growing up, the room had been a showcase of
the craftsmanship of an age past. Now it was a gloomy house,
muted, shuttered, even shabby. It was far too big a house—
too expensive—for Rose and Merry to have lived in alone.
It all but bled Merry's trust fund dry. Several times she'd
suggested that they sell it and move into a small, more man-
ageable house. But that was unthinkable to Rose. She'd
claimed Merry would be too upset to move and argued, right-

fully, that private hospitals or homes would be as expensive, if not more. In truth, she knew the prospect of leaving the family home filled Rose with as much horror as it did Merry.

And Rose deserved every consideration. She certainly took her duty as caretaker to heart. The house, though falling down around their ears, was spotlessly clean. The brass fixtures gleamed, the wood was polished and smelled of soap, and all the beveled glass on the cabinets and the grand crystal chandelier sparkled. Yet with her mind on putting the house on the market, Birdie was looking at it with a cold and practical eye. They'd certainly have a lot of work to do before selling it.

"Would you like a glass of wine?" Rose asked, eager to make them comfortable. "Water? You all must be parched. Hannah, how about a Coke? Dennis?"

"A beer would be great if you've got it," he replied, rubbing his hands.

"Nothing for me. I'm going upstairs," Hannah called out, retreating as usual. "Where am I sleeping, Aunt Rose?"

"I put your parents in the guest room, so you can either sleep on the sofa bed in the library or in Merry's room."

"I'll take the sofa bed."

"I thought you might. You'll find linen and blankets all ready for you."

"You put me in the guest room?" Birdie asked, her brows raised in obvious pique.

Rose's toes curled, but she nodded firmly and looked Birdie in the eyes. "Yes. I put Jilly in her old room." Then to Dennis, "I'll get your beer."

Birdie's lips pursed in annoyance, but she didn't reply. She tucked her hands in her slacks' pockets and followed Rose into the kitchen. It was an immense room, old-fashioned, with the same white cabinets and appliances that were there when their mother cooked in the room. Only in the pantry did a large new refrigerator hum. Rose headed straight for it.

"Have you heard from Jilly yet?" Birdie asked.

"No. It's a good thing you didn't go to the airport," Rose replied, pulling ice from the freezer. "You were right, as usual. The news reported delays galore and they might even shut down the airport."

"I hadn't heard that. But I'm not surprised. It's really getting nasty out there."

"I know and I'm worried. I've called the airline a million times but they can't tell me anything other than that her flight is in a holding pattern. They think it will be allowed to land, which is a relief." She yanked the cork from the bottle of cabernet she'd chosen while Birdie hunted in the cabinet for a few glasses. "We're lucky. I gather other flights are being redirected. That would've been a disaster. She'd be late for the funeral."

"Jilly does love to make an exciting entrance...."

Rose filled a glass with wine while her lips curved in a teasing smile. "That's not fair."

"I know, I know. I didn't mean it." Birdie took a long swallow of her wine. Over the glass her eyes glistened with humor. "Much. Can't you just imagine her in that plane? She must be beside herself. You know how she hates being trapped. Remember how she was on a Chicago bus in rush hour?"

Rose shared her first laugh in days, remembering. Jilly would leap to her feet, yank the buzzer and demand to be let off the bus. Then she'd march off in a huff, her flame-red hair like ribbons of fire fluttering behind. Birdie and Rose would track her through the bus window till a break came in traffic, then they'd point and laugh at her as they sped past her. But she never looked their way. She kept her glance stubbornly straight ahead.

"Pity the poor stewardess," Birdie said, rolling her eyes. "But I have to admit, circling up there in a confined space for hours is hell. She'll be exhausted and cranky when she gets here. I shouldn't be talking. It was a real push getting out of town by car and I was a total bitch, I admit it. I thought I'd kill my daughter before we arrived here.'' She swirled the wine in her glass. "Be forewarned. Hannah is in one of her moods.''

"Poor baby,'' replied Rose with sympathy. "She looks unhappy.''

"She is,'' she replied, then added flippantly, "perpetually.''

"Is she okay?''

"Oh, yes, she's fine.'' Birdie cut off further inquiry. She didn't like anyone to think there was any problem with her family.

"This is probably the first death she's really experiencing. She was so young when Mom died.''

"That's true. She's seemed so remote, but I hadn't thought of it that way.'' She rubbed her temple and said in a low voice, "To be honest, I can't accept it, either. It's so hard. I keep going over it in my mind, how quickly she went downhill. If only I could have been here…''

"No, Birdie,'' Rose said firmly. "Don't go there. It isn't healthy. Her doctor was here with her. Really, there was nothing you could have done.''

"You don't know that!''

Rose grabbed her hand to still it and looked directly into her sister's eyes. "I know what you're thinking,'' she said in her quiet voice that could be surprisingly firm. "That you could have saved her.''

Rose had nailed it. Birdie squirmed in discomfort and tried to snatch back her hand, but Rose held on tight.

"You couldn't have done anything to save her, Birdie. Not this time.''

Birdie stared into her hazel eyes, blazing with intent, until the message slowly, reluctantly sunk in. When she indicated her understanding, if not acceptance, with a nod, Rose released her hand then smiled faintly and looked away, a little embarrassed about the intense exchange. Birdie took a long, deep breath and said in a robust manner, "So now we're planning her funeral."

"Yes."

"Yes." Birdie paused. "I'm sorry you got dumped with checking all the funeral details. I tried to get here early today but the traffic was unbelievable and…"

"Don't be silly. I needed something to do."

"I have to tell you, I'm concerned about the luncheon at Alfredo's. I telephoned them before I left Milwaukee just to check on our reservation and see if there was anything else that needed taking care of. The idiot girl I spoke to said we didn't have one! Can you believe that? I didn't have time to talk to the manager, but I told her to look into it and I'd follow up when I got here. She probably just got something mixed up in her book but I worried the whole way down. Do you have the number handy? I'll give them a quick call. If they've screwed up…"

"Birdie," Rose said hesitatingly. She plucked at the loose threads of the oven mitt, then took a deep breath. She hadn't meant to get into this before Birdie had a chance to relax, maybe had a second glass of wine. "They didn't screw up. I…I never made the reservation."

Birdie's eyes widened with disbelief. "What?"

"Don't worry, I've taken care of everything," Rose rushed to say.

"What do you mean you didn't make the reservation? Why? We discussed this in detail. My God, Rose, what were you thinking? Did you forget? Why didn't you tell me? Damn, I don't know if we can reserve a room for tomorrow on such short notice." Her voice was high and she placed her hand to her forehead as she paced across the linoleum.

"I didn't tell you because I knew you'd react like this. You'd drive in from Milwaukee and take over like you always do.'' At the surprise on Birdie's face she softened her tone. ''I wanted to do something special for Merry. For all of us—you, Jilly and me. We hardly know one another any-more, Birdie. We need to remember Merry and the good times we had together. I didn't think we could do that in a restaurant.''

Birdie spread out her palms in a futile gesture. ''We can spend all the time we want together, just the three of us. Here at home. But we still could have had the funeral lunch at a restaurant. Oh, Rose, what have you done? It would have been so much easier.''

''For whom?'' she replied sharply, nettled by the all-knowing tone in Birdie's voice. ''I *want* to do this. And it's really not so difficult. I've planned for a light lunch here in this wonderful home where we all grew up. It's much more personal, and with all the flowers already here, it will be beautiful. It just didn't seem right to have the funeral lunch for Merry at a restaurant that she'd never even been to.''

''Oh, come on, Rose, this has nothing to do with Merry,'' Birdie fired out. ''You're the one who wants it here. It's you who can't stand the idea of leaving the house.''

Rose sucked in her breath, stung by the truth in the com-ment. She clasped her hands tightly in front of her. ''That's only partly true,'' she replied, looking away. ''Just because I don't like leaving the house doesn't mean I can't. I truly believe Merry would want it here, too.'' Rose raised her eyes and held her sister's gaze. ''And I know—better than you or anyone else—what Merry would want.''

Birdie had the grace to concede. ''No one could ever dis-pute that.''

The tension eased a bit between them and Rose spoke from the heart. ''Merry and I used to dream all the time about having parties. But we never did. It's kind of sad when I think of that. The last time this house saw a party was your wedding and that was...what? Twenty years ago? Mom has so many pretty things crammed into boxes that no one ever uses. Platters and urns, punch bowls and coffee urns, china and silver. You wouldn't believe half of what's stored in these chests and cabinets." She stepped closer, eager to assure Birdie that all would be well. "What are we saving it for? Let's use it, all of it! I only wish I'd done something special for Merry while she was alive."

Birdie frowned, but it was more with worry. "It's a lot of work."

"It's all under control. I've ordered sandwich meat and all sorts of things from the deli and two cakes from Mueller's bakery. Custard cream and angel food, Merry's favorites. And cookies, too, chocolate chip and four-pounds-of-butter ones. We'll have hot coffee and tea with fresh cream. Really, Birdie, it will be lovely."

"You could have told me."

Rose took heart at the tone of resignation. "I know, I know. I'm sorry."

Hannah burst into the kitchen, coming to a halt as her eyes shifted back and forth between her mother and her aunt. "Is everything okay in here? Should I leave?"

"Yes, everything is okay and no, of course you shouldn't leave," Rose replied easily. She looked at Birdie and smiled. "We're just having a disagreement about the plans for tomorrow."

"Watch out, Aunt Rose. Mom is in one of her moods."

Rose's lips twitched at the echo to Birdie's earlier comment about Hannah. She was pleased to see Birdie's lips curve into a smile as well.

"Like mother like daughter," Birdie said, surprising Hannah by wrapping an arm around her shoulder and giving her a squeeze. Hannah wriggled out of the embrace and reached for a cracker to nibble. Birdie grabbed a cracker, too, and after a bite she said in an offhand manner, "The church service is still on, at least? I had to duke it out with Hannah to wear her black dress. I'd like to think the bruises were worth it.'' She winked at Hannah.

''Very funny.'' Hannah rolled her eyes.

''Father Frank is saying mass and Kathleen Murdoch is all set to sing,'' Rose said. ''She has such a lovely voice.'' She poured the crackers onto a plate. ''Merry loved to listen to her on Sundays.''

''Good. And everything is as I arranged it at the funeral parlor?''

Rose hesitated, seemingly busy arranging the crackers.

Birdie leaned forward so her face was close to hers. ''Please, Rose, tell me. What did you do now?''

''Nothing major. It's all taken care of.''

''What?''

Rose raised her head, flinching at the pair of eyes trained on her. There was nothing left for her to do now but jump right in. ''I ordered a different casket, okay? I saved a great deal of money by shopping on the Internet.''

Hannah's hand stopped midair en route to delivering a cracker to her mouth. ''You shopped on the Internet...for a casket?''

Birdie looked stunned. ''You've got to be kidding.'' When Rose didn't respond Birdie's eyes widened further. ''You're killing me, Rose. I spent hours on this! I had everything ordered at Krause's Funeral Home. Why did you have to change it?''

''Birdie, I don't know why you're so upset just because everything is not exactly the way you ordered it.'' Rose's voice was clipped. ''You never once asked me what I wanted to do for the funeral. You just called up and told me what to do. I went along with it, as I usually do. But for heaven's sake, this isn't a change as much as, well, a better deal.''

Birdie put her face in her palms. ''Please tell me there's a casket for my sister tomorrow.''

''Of course there is. You ordered an oak casket, and

though it was lovely, it cost two thousand dollars. I found one almost identical for nine hundred dollars.'' Her pride couldn't be disguised.

''Mom,'' Hannah said in that teenage know-it-all voice, ''you can buy anything on the Internet these days.''

Rose shrugged. ''I'm on the computer a lot for my word processing job. When I need a break I surf the Net. It's fun, relaxing. In fact, it's how I keep in touch with the world out there. I find it absolutely fascinating. When I'm on the Net, I feel so connected.''

Hannah waggled her brows. ''Are you doing those chat rooms?''

Rose didn't answer, but she could feel the blood rushing to her cheeks.

''Oh, no,'' Birdie groaned. ''You are, aren't you.''

''What if I am?'' Rose laughed lightly but her color heightened.

''You do know there are a lot of creeps out there that prey on lonely women like yourself.''

''They're not all creeps. There are some very nice people looking for someone to talk to.''

Birdie released a short, sarcastic laugh.

''Lots of people are in chat rooms,'' Hannah said in Rose's defense.

''Not you, too, I hope,'' Birdie replied with narrowed eyes.

''Sure I am.''

Birdie leaned back against the counter. ''Good God, is there anything else I don't know? My sister and my child are hanging out in chat rooms, we've got some casket coming in the mail and, as far as I'm concerned, we're having a damn picnic in the house tomorrow.''

Dennis stuck his head around the corner. ''Hey, in case you're interested, there's a chauffeur at the door.''

Three

Birdie and Rose looked at each other for a brief instant, then in a flash, Rose darted from the table and tore off to open the front door as eager as a nine-year-old girl. A tall, blond man with a bodybuilder's physique squeezed into a black chauffeur suit smiled uncertainly.

"Excuse me, ma'am, but is this the Season residence?"

Rose looked beyond the man's massive shoulders into the darkness but didn't see her sister. Only the sleek red lights that trimmed the limo were visible along the curb. A shiver of worry shot through her as she nodded.

The chauffeur pinched back a smile and said, "My passenger told me to tell you to meet her in the side yard."

Rose wasn't sure she'd heard right. Behind her, Birdie stepped forward to ask in her imperious voice, "Where is Miss Season?"

The chauffeur cleared his throat and leaned forward in a confidential manner. "In the side yard. She should really come inside. She's...well, she's had a bit too much to drink."

Rose heard Birdie mutter an oath. Dennis stepped forward and shook the chauffeur's hand in a man-to-man manner.

"Why don't you bring her luggage right inside." He looked over his shoulder, jerking his head at Birdie.

"Come on, Rose, let's go get her," Birdie said. They hurried into their coats and out the door into the night. Hannah was right behind them.

The snow had finally stopped and the full moon was as white as a large plate in the inky black sky. The light illuminated the clean, virginal snow in breathtaking beauty. Rose had always felt a particular thrill stepping into a stretch of new snow, akin to being an explorer discovering uncharted territory. Ahead, the path of her sisters' deep footprints in the nearly foot-deep snow were the only marks scarring the frosty white. She followed them, trying to step in their prints, with a curious excitement in her chest. Around the wide front porch she could hear high-pitched laughing and shrieking.

Turning the corner, she saw in the moonlight a flash of vivid red hair and lush black mink against a sea of white. Blinking in the cold air, she moved closer. Birdie was standing a few feet away from the blur of motion, her hands on her hips. Rose saw Jillian lying in the snow, laughing with delight, as her mink-clad arms and her long, slender legs in dainty spiked heels moved back and forth, carving out a snow angel.

"Jilly!" Rose cried out with joy.

Jilly stopped laughing, cocked her head up and waved her arm, beckoning Rose closer.

"Rosie!" she shouted. "Look at all this snow! Isn't it beautiful? I haven't seen snow like this since we were kids. It's so damn wonderful. Come on, Rosie! Birdie! Remember how we used to make snow angels? Look, I've made two already!"

Sure enough, Rose spied two snow angel outlines looking somewhat ethereal and magical in the moonlight. Rose ran to Jilly's side, bubbling with anticipation. Except, she couldn't remember how to make the angel. Suddenly Hannah appeared beside her, grinning with delight.

"So cool," she exclaimed joyously. Spreading her arms out, she simply fell back into the soft snow, then began to thrash her arms up and down in an arc.

"Hannah, get out of there!" Birdie called, exasperated. "Oh, no, Rose, don't you dare. Rose!"

With a squeal, Rose shut her eyes, spread out her arms and fell back. It was deliriously delicious, like free-falling, then finding herself deeply enveloped in the snow, face up to the moonlight.

"Aw, come on, Birdie, you ol' stick in the mud," Jilly called out. "Nobody's looking."

Birdie stood a few feet away, feeling every inch of the distance.

"Jilly, you'll catch your death of cold," she scolded. "You all will. No boots, no gloves, no hats. You're all behaving like children. Jilly, come on, give me your hand."

Jilly lifted her hand as gracefully as a queen's. When Birdie stepped forward to take it, Jilly whipped up her other hand, clasped Birdie's tightly and pulled her down with a laugh. Birdie shouted in surprise and tumbled face first into the snow beside her sister.

The snow was icy on her cheeks but nothing was hurt, except maybe her pride. The sound of hilarious laughter filled her ears. Birdie sputtered and felt ready to throttle her older sister, who was obviously drunk. She could smell the Scotch mixed with perfume. She struggled to raise herself to her knees and wipe the snow off her cheeks, scowling, ready to light into her sister.

But then she saw Jilly's face, inches from her own, lit up with laughter. Birdie could only stare into that beautiful face, beautiful not for the reasons fashion magazines had clamored for her picture, but because it was the face she remembered from their childhood. Jilly's eyes were bright with a childlike joy and that incomparable pleasure of just being alive that she hadn't seen in her since they were kids. Birdie wasn't sure if Jilly was happy, or merely drunk.

"Missed you, sis," Jilly said soberly, still looking into her eyes with a wistfulness that was endearing. She reached up to swipe away a chunk of snow from Birdie's collar. "You always made the best snow angels, remember? The snow was just like this, too. Soft, like powder. Remember?" Then with a cocky smirk she added, "But I always had to drag you out here, even then."

Though the words were slurred, Birdie smiled and nodded, remembering it all.

Hannah sat up and howled with laughter at seeing her mother dumped in the snow. There was a look of awe on her face; she couldn't believe anyone would really dare to do that to her mother. Beside her, Rose, the traitor, was laughing so hard tears were icing on her lashes and she clapped her hands in the same spontaneous manner she used to when she was little.

Something deep within Birdie pinged; she could hear the sound in her mind as clearly as she heard the laughing of the three women she loved most in the world. It was a rare moment of intense beauty and joy. Their world, their senses, felt heightened. She breathed in the cool air, slowly and deeply, feeling the moisture slide down her throat and enter her lungs. The snow made her cheeks burn with cold. She imagined they were cherry red, like Hannah's, and the sting made her feel alive.

What small miracle had transpired that allowed her to be kneeling in the new-fallen snow in the moonlight with her sisters, laughing like children. Playing, rather than fussing over details of the funeral?

She knew the answer, of course. Jilly. It had always been Jilly who started the games.

Ah, but it was cold, and late, her mind rushed to warn her.

They couldn't stay out here forever. Reality interfered. Suddenly, she was no longer a child but a grown-up, with an adult's sensibilities. She knew that a drunk could get hypothermia and not even know it. She knew that there were countless details to be sorted out before the funeral tomorrow. The dinner had to be served. Jilly probably needed to get some food in her. And unlike her sisters, Birdie was a mother. A wife. A doctor. She had responsibilities.

In a flash, she felt herself projected out from the scene, becoming an outsider, looking in. She couldn't play. She pushed a hand through her hair and looked again at Jilly, then at Rose, and finally her own daughter, Hannah, still making snow angels. Birdie felt very cold. Her fingertips were flaming red and her toes were numb. "Okay, everybody, time to go in."

"Okay, Mom," Rose called back, giggling at her own joke.

Birdie wanted to shout back that she wasn't her mother. She didn't want to be the mother. Slowly, she dragged herself to her feet, feeling every one of her forty-one years.

"I said, everybody up. Time to go in."

Ever the cooperative one, Rose climbed to her feet and offered her hand to Jilly. This time, Jilly went along, allowing Rose to take one hand and Hannah the other as they hauled her to her feet. She rose like a beautifully plumed bird, graceful, arms outstretched. A phoenix, Birdie thought with a wry smile.

"I think I'm going to be sick," Jilly moaned once she was on her feet, weaving.

"Too much booze," Birdie said matter-of-factly as she stepped forward to grab hold of Jilly's arm. "Can you walk?"

"I'm a model, *chérie*. I've strolled down runways in a lot worse condition than this."

"Spare me the details. Okay then, one foot after another."

Like a trooper, Jilly straightened her shoulders, fixed her direction. Then, releasing her sister's hand, she paced through the snow with remarkable grace.

"You didn't tell me your sister was so cool," Hannah said, coming to her side.

Birdie saw the admiration in Hannah's eyes and felt a sting of jealousy. She couldn't remember the last time she had seen anything but scorn in her daughter's eyes.

A squeal caught her attention. She looked up in time to see Jilly wobble on some ice in the ridiculous spiked heels, then fall flat back into a snowdrift. Birdie hated herself for it, but a part of her was glad to see Jilly knocked off the pedestal a notch. She stifled her smile and hurried to help Jilly to her feet with Rose catching the slack. Jilly seemed to have used the last of her steam to make the distance to the porch; she was like a rag doll now.

In the light of the front porch, Birdie studied her sister with a physician's eye. It had been ten years since she'd last seen her. Jilly still possessed a sultry sexiness that even women turned their heads to admire. She was still a beauty. Her hair was the color of flame and as thick and wild as ever. She wore much less makeup now so her face appeared more pleasing and natural. But Birdie didn't like its pallor and gauntness, nor the puffy eyelids and the blueness of her lips. And Jilly was thinner. The bones of her face and even her hands appeared sharp under blue-veined skin. Intuition bred from years of training and experience recognized excessive fatigue and possible illness.

"Help me get her up, Rose," she murmured.

Rose and Hannah both responded to the serious tone in Birdie's request. The sisters each shouldered part of Jilly's weight while Hannah opened the front door.

"I'm okay...." Jilly muttered.

"Sure you are. Now, take another step. Up, up, up," and so on as they made their way up the front steps,

"Welcome home, Jilly," Rose murmured as they ushered her into the warmth of their old family house.

Hours later, the dishes were washed and put away, the lights turned off and everyone settled into their respective rooms. The whole house seemed to sigh in peace. Rose sat before her computer, wide-awake. Coffee had been served when they all came in from the cold. Though she didn't usually drink caffeine at night, that wasn't what stirred her blood. There had been too much excitement and tomorrow promised more.

These dark hours were her favorite, when no one needed her or called her name. They were hers alone. Merry had always fallen asleep quickly and early and slept untroubled through the night. Occasionally illness would rouse her, but usually her breath purred and she dreamed of happy things. Rose knew this because she'd sit by her bed and watch her, envious of the gentle smile that curved Merry's lips.

Her bedroom had once been their parents' room. Rose had offered this largest bedroom to Merry after their mother died but Merry had rejected it, preferring the familiarity of her own lavender-and-lace-filled room. So Rose had moved in, using her old room as an office for her part-time job as a word processor. There were twelve rooms in the house, but her office was hers alone, filled with things that she had chosen for herself rather than inherited. Her desk was designed for her new computer. The bookshelves were installed to house her personal library. Everything here was here only because she wished it to be. She could come into this room, close the door and be free to explore her own interests, either through books or, more recently, the Internet.

She turned on the computer and, as she waited for it to boot, thought that Birdie was wrong to say chat rooms were only for lonely shut-ins. She knew this wasn't true because her Internet friend, DannyBoy, traveled all across the country as a trucker. They didn't go into personal details, didn't exchange pictures or such, but she gleaned from what he wrote that being on the road so much was the reason he couldn't meet nice young ladies. He wasn't some pervert. He was kind and caring. A real gentleman who never was vulgar, or stupid, or chauvinistic. In fact, he was the nicest man she'd ever met, if only in cyberspace. They'd met months ago in a chat room for stamp collectors, and their conversations had soon drifted from stamps to whatever was on their minds. They'd liked what each other had to say and she wasn't surprised when he e-mailed her privately.

As she clicked to her mail, she felt the familiar thrill to see his e-mail waiting for her. DannyBoy had been her greatest ally when she'd decided to buck Birdie's directives and have her luncheon. He'd been the one to write words of condolences, sincere and heartfelt. Though she'd never seen his face, Rose could honestly believe DannyBoy was her best friend. She clicked open the e-mail.

Dear Rosebud,
All day I kept thinking and wondering if your sisters had come yet. I know how excited you are and how sad that the occasion for this get-together is your youngest sister's funeral. I heard on the weather report about all that snow you folks in Chicago got. What bad luck. Hope it all goes okay. Let me know.
    I'm in Texas now. The weather is pretty good, but the clouds are collecting and in these parts in this season, we all keep our eyes on the sky and our ears tuned to the radio. Moving on soon, though, to the Midwest.
DannyBoy

She smiled, wondering as she always did what he looked like, how old he was, and if he was tall or short, fat or thin, balding or wore his hair in a ponytail. Not that it mattered,

of course, though she couldn't help but be curious. She put
her fingers to the keyboard.

Dear DannyBoy,
Yes, they're here! We had a terrible snowstorm but
we're lucky. Birdie and her family made it down and
Jilly's plane got in, though late. It's so very wonderful!
I really should go to sleep. Tomorrow is a busy day.
I've a million things to do. I'll have to get up early and
polish the silver, set the tables, make the sandwiches.
Oh Lord, the list never ends. But I can't sleep. My blood
feels like it's racing yet my eyelids are so heavy. I
haven't slept well lately. I hate the darkness. I lie in bed
staring at the ceiling until I see red spots before my eyes.
I don't know what I'm waiting for, but I have this sense
something is going to happen. Maybe Merry is hovering
nearby. Who knows? I hope I don't sound crazy. I probably just need some sleep. But my sisters are here!
                                            Take care,
                                            Rosebud

She sent the letter. While she was scanning the Net, she
was surprised to see another letter come in. Clicking over,
she saw it was from DannyBoy. He must be online, she
thought, feeling a sudden, almost intimate connection with
him.

Dear Rosebud,
Go to sleep!
                                            DannyBoy

Four

❧✦❧

Jilly awoke to a persistent stripe of bright light seeping in from behind the curtains. It spread across the room playing with the shadows. She lay flat on her back, disoriented, dry-mouthed, in that limbo space between wakefulness and deep sleep. She was aware only of being very cold, and not knowing where she was. Blinking, she thought the bed was different. The walls…the smells.

Then suddenly in a rush, she knew.

She was in her old room, the one she'd shared with Birdie so many years before. She blinked again, then wiped her face with her palms. Her brain was awake now, absolutely, but her body wasn't. Perhaps it was the jet lag, perhaps just the excitement of being home again after all these years, but she knew there would be no closing her eyes and falling back asleep. And for that, there'd be hell to pay. She'd had too much to drink last night. Her head was already pounding with a hangover and lack of sufficient sleep. A bad combination, and one all too familiar.

She licked her dry lips and dragged herself up to her elbows to take stock. She was wearing only a bra and undies. Rose and Birdie must have helped her out of her clothes. If she were in her own apartment in Paris she'd get up, boost the heat a bit, slip thick socks on her feet, then search around the kitchen for something to eat and perhaps something hot to drink. Maybe even listen to some music. But she didn't want to wake anyone up, especially not Merry.

Jilly rubbed her eyes, waking further. No, she thought with a pang, she couldn't wake Merry.

She dragged herself to a sitting position and took stock of the room. Nothing had changed. Her square white dresser was still covered with her collection of miniature boxes, each undoubtedly filled with the same costume earrings, buttons, pins and rings she'd carelessly tossed in eons ago. Birdie's was topped with swimming trophies and medals attached to blue ribbons. There were two twin beds with matching swirling white wrought-iron headboards. On Birdie's bed lay her favorite teddy bear, a big white one that was now as dirty and gray as the morning light. She looked down by her feet then cracked a smile, feeling more delight than she thought she would on finding her own teddy bear still there. It was a ratty, old-fashioned brown bear with stuffing sticking out from the roughly repaired seams.

"Hello, Mr. President," she said, reaching out to pull the bear close, oddly comforted by it.

It was so eerie to see everything as she'd left it years ago. She hadn't expected it to be the same. Rather, she'd thought all traces of the big bad sister would have been weeded out. It felt nice to see some trace of the young Jillian Season still remained. Rose was a sweetheart for putting her back in her old room. Oh, the dreams she'd had sleeping in this bed!

And the nightmares.

The last time she'd slept in here was in her senior year of high school, before she left for Marion House. When she'd returned, her mother had moved her to the guest room. It was all part of her mother's infinite plan. Marian House was *never* to be discussed. Not even with—especially not with—her sisters. Her mother had arranged for Jilly to leave for a year's study at the Sorbonne immediately after graduation. After all, she had painstakingly explained to Jilly, by going so far away, she wouldn't have to deal with all those prying questions about where she'd been the previous months.

"It's over Jillian," her mother had said. "We never have to talk of this again. Everything can be just as it had been before. And you look so well. So slim!"

That was when Jilly knew the pretending had already begun. So, she went to France in the spring, upsetting her mother's plan the following fall when she was discovered and hired as a Paris runway model and had refused to return home.

"But here I am again," Jilly said to the stuffed bear, shaking the memories from her head. "I keep coming back. What is the matter with me? I thought I'd left it all behind. "In anguish, she squeezed the bear. "Why can't I just let it go? Am I like you, you bear? Torn and badly mended at the seams, hmm?"

Ready or not, here I come, she thought as she crawled from the bed. She went first to her closet and, opening it, found it stuffed with her old clothes from the 1970s. Everything was still there. She grabbed a short lavender silk kimono, a favorite in high school, and slipped it on.

She moved slowly through the hall and down the stairs, cautiously, sniffing the air like a long-lost dog finding its way home. She paused to study a photograph or two on the stairwell wall, then paused again at the landing that overlooked the foyer and the front room. Dust motes floated in the sunbeam that poured in through the tall, gracious beveled glass windows. Jilly clutched the railing and stood, blinking, taking in the sight. Time could have stood still in this house. Last night she'd been too drunk to notice. But now, as she took in the heavy brocade curtains, the antique coatrack by the door, the crystal chandelier in the foyer, her mind slipped back once again to when she was seventeen years old and coming down these stairs for the last time.

It was the day she had left home for France.

"Jilly, come down!" her mother had called. "It's almost time to leave!"

She'd felt rooted to the edge of the bed, her ankles together, hands clasped in her lap. She was so thin the smart navy suit her mother had purchased for her hung shapelessly from her shoulders as though from a mannequin.

The lies and the secrecy of the past weeks had worn her out. She took a last, desperate look around the room, terrified, committing to memory the details, knowing instinctively that it would be a long, long time before she saw this room again.

"Jilly!" Her mother's voice was strident.

Jilly rose, pausing to stroke her favorite stuffed bear, then she silently came down the wide staircase, beginning her long journey of isolation from her family. She held her shoulders back and her chin high. Her eyes appeared glazed and directed inward. Already, she was unconsciously assuming the trademark walk that would later place her in high demand in the European fashion world.

Downstairs, her father moved silently from the garage to the foyer, shoulders stooped, carrying her suitcases back out into the car. He appeared saddened that she was leaving for Europe, but she couldn't be sure. He wasn't one to share his private feelings, and in the past weeks he'd taken pains to avoid her, spending long hours at the courthouse or in his den.

Birdie and Rose, fifteen and eleven, slouched against the door frame, whispering to each other. She offered them the briefest of smiles. She coveted their innocence.

Then, suddenly, it was time to go. The family moved quickly, as though caught by surprise.

"I want a picture!" her mother cried out, frantically waving her hands. She was clumsy, tottering, which meant she'd been drinking again. Jilly felt a wave of sadness, then, looking at her sisters, concern. She wouldn't be there to draw their mother's ire anymore.

"Bill, get the camera!"

"I will, I will."

Jilly felt the press of the bodies as they crowded together for the photograph. Her sisters crowded close with a kind of silent desperation. Birdie put her arm around her shoulder and Jilly caught a quick scent of her emerging body odor, strong and pungent, not yet masked with deodorant. Birdie was squeezing her shoulder hard, firmly hanging on. Rose, smaller, stood in front of her, silently but determinedly nudging Merry away with her elbow in order to stay close to Jilly. Merry clung tenaciously to Jilly's arm.

"Merry, Rose, stop wriggling," their father ordered. "Look here, everyone. Okay, Four Seasons, smile for the photograph. Say, *fromage!*"

Jilly smiled wide, shoulder to shoulder with her sisters, feeling one of the family again in that frozen moment in time captured on film. This would be the memory she'd take with her to Europe, she decided. The four of them, close together. It ended too quickly. Bodies separated and Mother began directing again.

Have a good time! We'll miss you! Bring me back a bottle of French perfume!

"Say goodbye, Merry," her mother said, nudging her forward. "Jilly has to go now."

"I don't want her to go!" Merry wailed, shaking her head so violently her long pigtails swung around her neck.

Jilly turned her head away, not wanting to see the sorrow swimming in her sister's eyes lest it break her own fragile hold on composure. "Bye, sweetheart," she called out in a tight voice as she headed out the front door. If she could make it down to the car, she told herself, she could escape into the private darkness and end this charade forever.

Merry, however, burst into tears and tore after her, clinging to Jilly's arm at the car and tugging her back toward the house. Their parents rushed forward and wrapped their arms around their youngest daughter.

"Jilly has to leave," they said in singsong tones.

Jilly stood ramrod straight at the curb, clutching the car door handle and struggling not to cry. She'd vowed she'd play her role in her mother's plan without fail. She'd failed her family enough already; it was the least she could do.

"No, she doesn't!" Merry cried belligerently. "She doesn't have to go. Make her stay! Ple-e-ase, Mama! Make her stay!"

Jilly held those cries in her heart like a talisman, loving her poor little shaman sister all the more. She let go of the car and slowly walked to her baby sister, kissing her cheek and hugging her, hard, all the while looking over the small, bony shoulder at her father with a gaze that challenged. *You can let me stay if you want to.*

"Jilly! You're up!"

Jilly blinked and turned her head to the voice calling her name, dragging her back to the present.

"Rose!" Jilly's voice squeaked out of her dry throat. She opened her arms to the slender, smaller sister as she hurried up the stairs to hug her, fiercely, in her surprisingly strong arms. They hugged for a long time, rocking back and forth in tender glee. *No more yesterdays. This is now,* she told herself, relishing the familiar scent of sweet roses in her sister's hair.

"You were daydreaming," Rose said. "Miles away."

"More like years away," she replied, then cast a sweeping glance at the house. "It's being back here again."

"I didn't want to wake you," Rose said, pulling back yet keeping their arms linked. "I've read all about jet lag and thought you might want to sleep straight up until the funeral. But oh, Jilly, I'm so glad you're awake. I've missed you."

"I've missed you, too." Jilly's hungry gaze devoured her sister. Although Rose was only six years younger, Jillian still felt a twinge of envy that Rose looked much the same as she did in high school.

"You look tired," Rose said, her eyes searching with concern. "Are you sure you had enough sleep?"

Tired and old, she thought to herself. "I'm sure I haven't, but I'll catch up later. Besides, who could sleep? Such racket! The birds were relentless and I swear I heard bells all morning."

"That must have been the deliveries. We're having a light luncheon here after the funeral."

"What a charming idea," Jilly replied, yawning. "I thought we were going to some stuffy old restaurant. Much nicer this way."

Rose beamed. "Do you think so, Jilly?" She turned and led the way down the stairs, through the wide foyer to the dining room. She pointed out the stacks of china plates, bowls, cups and platters, tableware and silver bowls desperately blackened and in need of polish.

"Mom had all these lovely dishes stashed away. And there's more in the attic. We have to sort through them, anyway, so we can divide them. Think about the ones you'd like."

"Doesn't matter to me in the least."

"You'll have to have some! You're the eldest. You get first pick."

"Tell you what, *chérie*. You pick for me, and then you can keep them."

Rose was taken aback by her generosity. "I want to use the china for the luncheon, but it'll mean a lot to wash and polish, I'm afraid. Do...do you want to help?"

"Sure. Of course," Jilly replied, looking with longing at the kitchen door. "But have mercy on me. I smell the tempting aroma of coffee and if I don't get some of that, a few aspirins and a gallon of water down my throat soon I swear I'll drop right here and be useless to anyone."

Rose tilted her head and laughed brightly, excited by Jilly's willingness to back her luncheon. "Come on, then. I've made a *petit déjeuner*," she said, emphasizing the French. "Nothing special, just a few things I picked out that I thought you might especially like."

Jilly appreciated not only the breakfast but the obvious effort Rose extended to make her feel welcome, down to the use of a few common French phrases. She touched her shoulder, delaying her for a moment before joining the others in the kitchen.

"Rose, thanks for the flowers in the bedroom," she said in a soft voice. "You remembered how much I love yellow roses." Then with a crooked smile she added, "For that matter, thanks for putting me in my old room. It meant a lot."

"I thought it might," Rose replied in a conspiratorial whisper. Then, in a swift change of mood, she smiled brightly and said, "You'd better grab something to eat before Dennis devours everything."

Dennis... Jilly reached up to smooth her hair with her palms, straighten her shoulders and mark her entrance.

The kitchen was warm, bustling and smelled deliciously of hot coffee and rolls. Here, too, there was chaos. White bakery boxes were stacked high on the counters, plastic bags of fresh vegetables lay beside cutting boards and knives, ready for free hands, and there were dozens of plastic containers filled with all sorts of deli items. Nonetheless, at the table she found Dennis and Hannah sitting back in their chairs, leisurely munching croissants as though they had nothing in the world to do.

"Good morning to all," she murmured, heading straight for the sink.

Hannah's eyes widened at the sight of her exotic aunt whose legs seemed to go on forever under the short, sexy kimono.

"Good morning, Aunt Jillian."

Jilly held up one finger to indicate that everyone should wait while she drank the water thirstily. Then, after a lusty "Ah," she peered over at the pale, dark-eyed, rather plump teenager slouched in the chair across the room. Her red hair was the mark of a Season.

"Hannah?"

The girl nodded, eager.

"I wouldn't have recognized you if not for the hair. You've grown!" She caught the nanosecond of anguish in the eyes and the faint blushing of her cheeks and instantly understood, as one woman does with another, that this was a teenager sensitive about her weight. "You've become a woman!" she amended smoothly.

Hannah's face relaxed. "I'm fifteen, Aunt Jillian. Almost sixteen."

"You must call me Jilly. We're all adults here," she replied, winking before sipping more water.

Dennis lowered his Chicago *Tribune*. His was a considerably cooler gaze than his daughter's. He masked it with a politely rigid smile of greeting. The house suddenly felt several degrees colder. Jilly tightened the kimono about her neck.

"So, the prodigal sister returns," he said, more as a pronouncement, folding the paper and placing it in his lap.

Jilly felt a stab of annoyance. How like Dennis Connor to pull some biblical quote laced with criticism as his greeting after ten years. She wasn't hungry, but to mask how upset she was, she casually reached out for a croissant.

"Prodigal?" she replied, with an arch to her brow.

"Prodigal is apt," he replied, crossing his arms. "The long-lost child returning to the fold from her wanderings."

Jilly picked a corner from her croissant and delicately put it between her lips. "I wasn't aware that I was wandering."

"She lives in Paris, Daddy," Hannah said, as though he were a dolt.

"In this family, living anywhere beyond a day's drive is clearly exploring the wilds." His countenance lightened. Then with a crooked smile he added, "And we do rejoice that you've returned."

She cracked a smile, forgiving him a little.

Rose set a cup of coffee at the table beside a pitcher of fresh cream and a bowl of sugar. She clasped her hands, studying her table anxiously. "I know this isn't as good as what you're used to, but…"

Jilly gratefully accepted the steaming cup of coffee and ignored the cream. "Mmm, Rose," she said with an appreciative groan. "It's better."

Rose's chest swelled.

While she sipped, Jilly discreetly eyed Dennis as he returned to his paper.

Dennis Connor… He had aged exactly like she thought he would. He was always handsome, even in high school, in a mature, intellectual way that she'd once found attractive. Back then he'd worn his blond hair long to the shoulders and parted down the middle. His heavy eyeglass frames were a statement over his dark and piercing eyes and thick, arched brows. And that cleft in his chin. Lord, that dimple had turned quite a few heads back in high school. Hannah had his eyes and the cleft in her chin, she realized, amazed at genetics.

His hair might have thinned at the crown, his body thickened at the waist, but he'd aged very well indeed. She might even say he was more attractive now, having grown into his mature appeal. There was no denying that Birdie was a lucky woman.

"I can't imagine living in Paris," Hannah said with her chin in her palm. "How can you stand to come back to boring old Chicago? Or Milwaukee?" She rolled her eyes and reached for another croissant.

"Are you sure you want that?" Dennis asked his daughter from over the newspaper.

Hannah's arm stiffened and she furtively glanced at Jilly. A faint red blush crept up her neck and ears. She slid her hand back into her lap, slumping her shoulders forward as though to somehow make herself smaller.

Jilly's heart cringed for her. She knew Dennis was trying to be helpful, but men could be such idiots! The last thing he needed to do to an overweight teenager was draw attention to that horrid fact.

"Hannah," Jilly said in a breezy manner, "pass me some of that grapefruit, would you? One of the first things I learned in modeling was to eat lots of fruit and drink gallons and gallons of water. It flushes out the system and leaves your skin glowing. It's *de rigueur.* Here, darling, won't you split a grapefruit with me? You know," she continued, slicing through the fruit, "when I'm exhausted like I am now, I tend to pick at food all day without thinking. And I am absolutely exhausted now. So be my friend, would you? When you see me nibble, tell me to stop. I swear I won't bite your head off." She laughed, pleased to see Hannah's frown lift to a shy smile. Lifting her spoon, Jilly dug into the grapefruit with relish.

Hannah's dark eyes lost their dullness as she reached for the other half of the grapefruit.

Jilly was well aware of the lure modeling held for teenage girls. Her career gave her status. Eyeing Hannah, she thought her niece wasn't so much fat as she was *big,* much as Birdie had been at that age. Except that Birdie was a champion swimmer with long, defined muscles as sleek and smooth as an otter's. With her physique, coupled with her blazing confidence, she was magnificent. In contrast, Hannah was soft, slumped-shouldered and recalcitrant. That glorious sparkle of confidence that was such a hallmark of girls at this age was missing in this child.

Looking up she was caught by surprise to see Dennis leaning back in his chair looking at her intently. The disapproval she had seen in his eyes was replaced by open gratitude for her rescue. She smiled briefly, acknowledging.

The back door swung open and Birdie swept in with a gust of cool air. Her arms were overflowing with plastic bags and she was fired up with a sense of accomplishment.

"What a morning I've had!" she announced, her voice as blustery as the wind. "The sun is shining and melting the snow. Nobody will have a problem making it to the funeral. Come see. I've bought all sorts of paper products: plates, napkins and cups. And tons of plastic tableware.''

"Paper products?" Rose went directly to the bags and began sifting through them.

"Take a look at the pattern, Rose. The gray is somber but not too dark, don't you think?" She wasn't asking as much as thinking out loud. She came up for air, looking around the room.

Everyone sitting at the kitchen table stared back at her in silence. One face caught her attention.

"Jilly!" she exclaimed, catching sight of her sister at last. "You're up!"

Birdie's face registered delight, surprise, then maybe a hint of disapproval at seeing her so scantily clad and barefoot. Her gaze darted to Dennis, but she regrouped quickly, set down her bundles and hurried to Jilly's side. They hugged a bit awkwardly, what with Jilly still seated and Birdie bending low. The wind had chilled Birdie's cheeks and the ice on her woolen coat soaked straight through Jilly's silk. Yet it was the chill in her greeting that Jilly wondered about.

"You were three sheets to the wind last night," Birdie said in a scolding manner. While she spoke, her eyes studied Jilly with a clinical thoroughness. "And you're pale as a ghost this morning."

Jilly immediately brought her hand to her face, smoothing it. "It was a horrible flight, followed by a horrible drive from the airport." She was gratified to see a flash of guilt in Birdie's eyes for not having picked her up as promised. "Then, of course, there was the jet lag. But Rose took care of me, as always the perfect hostess. I've had coffee and fruit and feel much more myself."

She wanted to ask Birdie what *her* excuse was for looking so bad. She hoped her face didn't reflect shock at seeing how much her sister had aged since she last saw her. She looked ten years older than her forty-one years, more bulky and

pasty. The vivid red highlights in her brown hair had faded
and competed now with a new crop of gray. And to make
matters worse, the hair was cut in an unflattering, mannish
style. Birdie had always been bigger than the other Season
girls but she'd been lithe and strong and had carried herself
like a queen. Now she was so changed. Was it age or food
or just no longer caring that led her to let herself go? She
watched as Birdie unwound a brightly patterned fleece scarf
and slipped out of her navy pea coat, tossing it over the back
of a chair. Crossing the room to Rose, she unconsciously
stretched her Fair Isle sweater over her wide rump.

Rose looked up from the bags, her face crumpled with
worry. "But, Birdie, we don't need all this."

"Of course we do," Birdie replied decisively, coming to
her side. She reached in the bag and began unloading the
contents.

Dennis sighed deeply and lifted the paper high to block
his view.

"Really, Rose," Birdie continued, oblivious. "We'll go
along with the luncheon at home. We have no choice. But
this notion of yours to use china and crystal is far too romantic. This is a funeral and we don't need to be theatrical.
It's too much work to set up, then wash up after all those
people. If you're worried about the expense of paper, don't
be. I'm happy to cover it."

Rose's back was ramrod straight and she had laid her
hands over the bags as though to forcibly keep the contents
in. "But..." She swallowed hard. "I've already unpacked
the china."

"Rose, be sensible. We cannot use Mother's dishes."

Jilly glanced at Hannah and saw her face set in fury, the
same as her father's, as they listened.

"Why not?" Rose wasn't backing down.

Birdie stopped unpacking and rested her hands on the
counter. After an exaggerated pause she said, "For one thing,
there isn't enough of any one set of china to serve this size

a crowd. For another, there are not enough salad forks or matching wineglasses. It would all be an embarrassing mishmash of patterns. And it's much too late to call for rentals."

"Who the hell cares?" Dennis snapped, obviously fed up with his wife's interference. "If she wants to use the damn dishes, let her."

"Dennis," Birdie said in controlled fury, furtively checking Jilly's reaction to his outburst. "Would you go out and get the rest of the bags from the car, please?"

Dennis tossed down his newspaper with an angry flip of the wrist, then rose abruptly from the table, pushing back his chair so hard it almost toppled over. He took pains to allow a wide berth between himself and Birdie.

Jilly sensed the tension escalating in the room. Daggers flowed in the gazes between Dennis and Birdie, and again between Rose and Birdie. Jilly sipped her coffee, narrowing her eyes. She'd never seen this side of Birdie before. She'd always been bossy growing up, but now she was more of a bully. In contrast, Rose caved in, staring absently at some point across the room.

"If Rose has planned to use Mother's dishes," Jilly began cautiously, "then that's what we should do. We don't have time to argue over the point, so let's just pitch in and do what she wants." She put down her cup and lifted her chin. "It *is*, after all, her call."

No one missed the steel in Jilly's voice. Birdie drew her shoulders back and met her gaze. "*Her* call?" She took a breath, then said in a controlled voice that fooled no one, "Jilly, I know you just arrived. Perhaps you don't appreciate all I've done to organize this funeral. Everything was set until Rose decided entirely on her own to change everything. Imagine, a luncheon here! You don't have any idea...."

"But of course I do!" Jilly replied with a light laugh. "This isn't a formal sit-down dinner, darling. It's a *petite soirée*. You're making entirely too big a fuss over it. I've thrown lunches bigger than this on a moment's notice. It's

all in the attitude. I think it's fabulous that Rose is finally
going to use all this stuff. Mother hardly ever entertained.''

"That's because she was a perfectionist," Birdie said,
drawing herself up. "It mattered to her that things were properly done, or not done at all."

"Oh, come on, Birdie," Jilly countered, waving her hand.
"Mother was so intimidated by Emily Post and things like
matching china, menus, which side to serve on and which
side to take away, that she was simply overwhelmed by it
all. The truth is she was afraid nothing was ever good
enough.'' Her eyes flashed. "She was always so damn worried about what other people thought. That's why she never
entertained."

Hannah watched her mother summarily silenced by this
mysterious aunt and sat back in her chair. Birdie appeared to
be holding on to her position, for the sole purpose of winning
in the eyes of her daughter.

"Come on, Birdie," Jilly said, rising from the table.
"Rose has done all the preparation, let's have fun putting it
together."

"Jilly," Birdie said, thoroughly frustrated at having to de-
fend the only sensible position on the matter. "This is not
another game. You can't fly in after all these years and expect
us to pick up where we left off as children. I'm sure your
life in Europe is very exciting and glamorous," she said in
a stuffy manner, "but here in America, everything is not
always fun."

Jilly shook her head, seeing clearly the woman Birdie had
become. "Why can't it be? Birdie, listen to yourself. When
did you get so old and sour?"

Birdie stiffened as though slapped and Jilly regretted her
words instantly.

"We can do this," said Jilly soothingly. "We'll make this
the most charming, delightful luncheon imaginable. We'll
have china and silver, pink tablecloths trimmed with lace and
ribbon, tea sandwiches and flowers everywhere."

"Exactly," Rose exclaimed, her face glowing. "I'm sure that's the way Merry would have wanted it."

It was the first time that morning that Merry's name was mentioned. Merry, who was already gone from them. Merry, whose presence was suddenly overwhelming. They had been tiptoeing around their grief, trained as they were since childhood to tuck away emotion. But now that her name was spoken she sprang to life in their thoughts.

Rose's eyes were bright with tears. Jilly went to her side to wrap an arm around her.

Birdie did the same. "Glad you're home," she said in Jilly's ear. "Missed you."

"Me, too," Jilly replied, relishing the heartfelt hug from Birdie she'd missed with the first hello.

Dennis pushed through the door, his arms filled with bags of paper products.

"Okay then," Birdie called out, releasing her sisters to face Dennis. "All this stuff goes back in the car!"

Dennis stopped short, looking confused.

"Don't ask!" Birdie swooped up the bags from the counter and proceeded out the door. "I'll take them back— but I still think I'm right," she called over her shoulder.

Dennis shrugged, shook his head and followed.

Jilly met Rose's gaze and smiled as the mood shot skyward.

Outside the garage Birdie paused to take a deep breath and stare at the yard. The sun shone brilliantly in a clear blue sky. Cheery heads of crocuses were emerging through the sparkling snow, valiantly promising spring would come, even if a bit late. Beyond, in the side yard, the hot sun had melted the snow on the rectangle of sidewalk that bordered a forty-foot expanse. That space had been an in-ground swimming pool, long ago.

She saw in her mind's eye the brilliant blue of the pool's water. Bahama Blue, it was called. Every other summer the girls had to help paint that color on the sloping cement walls, looking like Smurfs when the job was done. The pool was the family's playground. In happier times, Dad would come home from work and jump in like a "bomb," splashing his girls while they squealed with delight. They'd take turns being hurled from his shoulders, pretending to be mermaids diving off a cliff. *One more time, Dad!*

They'd spend the day playing mermaids in the pool and wouldn't come out until their fingers were pruned and their lips were blue. Especially Birdie. She loved to swim and was a natural, able to hold her breath longer than anyone she knew.

Mermaids... Birdie's lips turned up in a smile. She hadn't thought of that in, oh, so many years. It was their favorite game. Jilly made it up, of course, though she herself had thought up most of the game's rules, like holding their breaths under Iceland and being dead if they ever touched the drain. That's how things worked between her and Jilly. Imagination and rules. Right brain and left. They were a good team. They were best friends. Rose had loved the game, too. And Merry.

Birdie cringed at the vision of a girl's small limbs kicking beneath Bahama Blue water. She blinked it away and looking out, saw again the rectangle of earth in the yard that was once the swimming pool. Snow piled high over it, creating a mound. It occurred to Birdie with a shudder how much it looked like a gravesite.

Five

The "May Ball" funeral luncheon, as it was known in later years, succeeded in dispelling the usual gloom and doom Birdie dreaded at such occasions, even if it did rouse the ridicule she'd predicted. She overheard a few smirking comments on the pink damask tablecloths and the yards of lace trim. But overall, Birdie was moved by how many people really loved Merry. Though her sister hadn't seen people often, the impression she'd made was deep and permanent. Perhaps it was her innocence, or perhaps it was her joy that elicited devotion from everyone she met. All in all, Merry's memory had been properly honored, even if in pink and lace.

The final stragglers were clustered in the foyer, gathering their coats and saying their goodbyes. With her red hair pulled severely back in a chignon at the neck, Jilly stood at the door with the poise and straight shoulders of a dancer, sending off strangers and family alike with a grace that Birdie both envied and was proud of. Birdie might have attributed her skill to her training as a model and actress, except that she knew better. Jilly always was the swan in the pond.

In contrast, she hardly saw Rose all afternoon. Her shy sister had skirted through the rooms like Jeeves, quietly attending the buffet, discreetly collecting dishes and scurrying

them off to wash. To the guests, she undoubtedly appeared
the perfect hostess, but Birdie knew her sister would rather
scrub the floor with her tongue than wag it in small talk with
all these people.

As the last of the guests were leaving, Mrs. Kasparov, the
real estate agent she'd selected, came forward to discreetly
hand her a sales portfolio. She was a diminutive woman with
gray-and-black hair and an overbite. With her aggressive
manner, she reminded Birdie of a terrier.

"Here is the list of sales comps and the other information
you requested."

"Thank you. I should imagine we'll put the house on the
market right away, to take advantage of the spring market.
We'll call you," Birdie said, nudging her toward the door.
Blessedly, Mrs. Kasparov nodded then signaled her husband,
who sighed in relief and rose with a cumbersome effort. The
couple shook Jilly's hand warmly at the door, then, after her
gaze took a final, hawklike sweep of the room, Mrs. Kasparov left.

The whole house seemed to sigh when the door clicked
shut. Birdie rubbed her neck, thinking she'd love nothing
more than to prop her feet up and collapse. She caught Jilly's
eye and they shared a commiserating smile. Their lawyer,
Mr. Collins, who had been sitting patiently in a wing chair
by the front window, rose on cue.

"I think we're all ready now," she announced. "Mr. Collins, thank you for your patience. Shall we move to the dining
room?"

Reaching out her arm, she placed it around Rose's shoulder as she passed, and together they went to sit at the dining
room table which had been cleared of the luncheon, linen
and lace.

Mother's mahogany table gleamed under the crystal chandelier. As Birdie sat, she idly wondered who would get the
dining room furniture. The heavy wood would look lovely in

her Tudor house. And who else would need such a big set? Jilly wouldn't want to lug it to France and Rose would probably get a small condo.

Jilly took a seat at one end of the table, directly across from Mr. Collins, who was busy laying out papers. Her hands were folded neatly and she sat straight, her green eyes wide and alert, as though on stage. They waited patiently for Rose to take her seat. Her face stilled pensively when she caught sight of Mrs. Kasparov's real estate portfolio on the table.

When at last they were all settled, Mr. Collins folded his hands on the table and smiled benignly at them. He was a tall, dignified gentleman who had been their father's best friend. "Uncle George," they'd once called him, though only Merry continued calling him that into adulthood. Today was a formal setting, however, and as he was acting as their legal adviser, he maintained a respectful reserve. Adjusting his eyeglasses, he proceeded.

"Your sister was a very special person to me, and your father was a dear friend. It was my pleasure, and my honor, to act as the co-executor of your father's will and Meredith's trust fund, as it has been to serve the interests of the entire Season family throughout the years." He glanced briefly at Jilly, who met his eyes with equal reserve.

"You are all well aware of how your father wished his property handled and distributed after his death?"

The three sisters nodded to indicate their understanding.

"At the time he wrote his will, back in August of 1977, his chief concern was for the care and welfare of his youngest daughter, Meredith, once it became established that she would not be capable of providing for herself after he and your mother were gone. Your mother willingly chose to accept one-third of the estate for her own support, thus leaving the bulk of their joint estate in a trust fund in Meredith's name. If you recall, after her death in 1990, what little was left of your mother's estate was distributed equally to all four daughters. I believe the amount was forty thousand dollars?''

Jilly's face remained impassive as she nodded. Birdie recalled her phone call from Europe, full of doubt and disappointment to learn how little was left from their mother's estate. Birdie had been filled with resentment and her attitude toward her sister had changed that day.

Mr. Collins adjusted his glasses as he checked a figure on the paper. ''It was also stipulated that, upon the occasion of Meredith's death, the residue of the estate should be distributed equally among the remaining Season issue. As of this date, that would be Jillian, Beatrice and Rose Season. The estate includes all remaining monies, assets and real property, or in this case, this house, the summer home in Indiana having been sold in 1984. I've frozen the bank accounts and sold the few remaining stocks, and after the estimated taxes and funeral expenses, excluding the sale of the house, of course, I'm calculating approximately twenty thousand dollars will be left in the trust fund to be dispersed.''

''Is that all?'' Jilly asked, sitting straighter. ''I thought my father had left a considerable estate.''

''Oh, for heaven's sake,'' Birdie muttered, furious that Jilly was disappointed again.

''Your father left a fair-size estate,'' Mr. Collins replied calmly. ''One that diminished over time, considering the expense of upkeep for a house and property of this size, not to mention Merry's considerable medical and educational expenses. If you wish, I can give you a detailed accounting afterward.''

''We were very careful with the spending,'' Rose interjected, worried.

''That won't be necessary,'' Jilly replied to Mr. Collins. ''I'm sure everything is in order, I'm just…surprised. How much would you say the house is worth?''

Birdie promptly opened the portfolio and sifted through

the papers. "According to Mrs. Kasparov, the fair market value would be somewhere around five hundred fifty thousand dollars. Less the real estate commission, transfer taxes and such."

"You can't be serious." Jilly looked devastated. "In this area? That can't be right. It seems very low."

Here we go again, Birdie thought. She cast a quick glance at Rose, not wanting to offend her with what she was about to say. "Mrs. Kasparov believes the house and property need quite a bit of work. Things she itemized in particular include the porch, which is rotting in places, pipes that have broken, and the walls haven't been properly repaired. The paint and wallpaper need to be freshened. The grounds are completely overgrown and the filled-in pool detracts from the land value. And of course the kitchen and bathrooms are terribly outdated and would need to be totally redone. The bottom line is, the place is architecturally lovely and in a great location, but it's what's known as a handyman's special." She set down the papers and folded her hands over them. "I quite agree with the estimate. Under the circumstances, we can't expect top dollar."

"Regardless of the condition, it's a double lot," Jilly argued. "Within walking distance of the lake! The land alone is worth that much. Why, the house down the block is up for over a million."

"Walk through the house, Jilly. You can't compare the two." Birdie hesitated. "There's some question as to whether the house should be torn down."

"No," Rose gasped.

Jilly was indignant. "I want another opinion."

"You can look at the comps," Birdie said, handing the folder to Jilly. "We have to consider if we really want to do the work ourselves to fix the place up, or just sell it as is as quickly as possible. Frankly, I vote for the latter."

Rose was shifting in her seat, wringing her hands. She

stared at Mr. Collins in silence, then glanced at her sisters, cringing under the question shining in their eyes.

Mr. Collins cleared his throat. "Well, now, that is an issue that should be discussed between the three of you, privately. I wouldn't presume to interfere, but I am at your service should you need my professional advice or—" he ventured a smile that revealed the affection accrued from a lifetime of association "—if you just want the advice of an old friend."

"Thank you, Mr. Collins," Birdie said.

Jilly echoed this but Rose remained silent, seemingly distracted.

"Is that everything, then?" Birdie was deeply flustered by Jilly's disappointment. She began tucking back papers and closing up the real estate portfolio. She couldn't imagine why Mr. Collins requested this meeting after the funeral when everything was perfunctory. They could have just as readily handled it between a phone call and a FedEx. Dear man, he was probably being thoughtful. She really didn't know what she would have done without him all these years.

"There is one more rather delicate matter to discuss," he replied.

Birdie looked up, surprised. Mr. Collins's tone altered and he appeared to be treading on softer ground. "Oh? And what would that be?"

He slowly removed his glasses and tucked them into his breast pocket. He seemed to be collecting his thoughts. "I called this meeting today because I wanted to discuss something with you while all of you were still together, under this roof. This is a unique situation." He cleared his throat and began again, glancing briefly at Rose.

"I've known Merry from the time she was born. She would, from time to time, come down the street to visit Mrs. Collins and me. As you know, your sister was not legally competent, but during this last illness, she had a remarkable intuition that her time was limited." He looked at Rose for confirmation. She was sitting straighter in her chair, pale and still.

"We had several long conversations. Merry was quite concerned about one issue in particular." He cleared his throat again and pulled from under the sheaf of papers a videotape. On top, taped to it, was a small envelope, a young girl's blue stationery adorned with pastel flowers.

Birdie narrowed her eyes, noticing that the writing on the envelope was large and childlike—Merry's.

Rose stood and, in the manner of one who had anticipated this event, took the videotape from Mr. Collins's hand and carried it to the living room television, which was set up and ready to receive the tape.

"Won't you make yourselves comfortable on the sofa?" he said, indicating that they should all move to the other room.

Birdie and Jilly rose without exchanging glances and followed him to the living room. The mood was uneasy; no one knew quite what to expect. They sat opposite each other in the two wing chairs. Rose fiddled with the television and Mr. Collins remained standing, apparently eager to begin.

"What's this all about?" Birdie asked.

"Be patient," he replied. "It will all become perfectly clear."

"All set." At his nod, Rose pushed the play button, then seated herself in front of the television.

The room settled into silence as the video ran, beginning with a short strip of blank tape. Suddenly, there was Merry, full of life. There were gasps from the sisters at the shock of seeing her beautiful face fill the screen, smiling, giggling and covering her mouth when she laughed.

"Oh, my God," Birdie gasped, bringing her fist to her lips. "Merry…"

It was almost too much to bear. Merry was a breathtakingly beautiful woman, without any outward sign of mental disability. Beyond her delicate bones, her tiny waist, her brilliant blue eyes that lit up her face when she smiled, there was another, more elusive quality to her charm. For all that she was thirty-two years old, Merry still possessed the coquettish, utterly beguiling innocence of a child.

As the camera zoomed in, Birdie saw signs of Merry's illness in the dark smudges of fatigue under her eyes, the whiteness of her skin and the blue cast to her lips. And she looked so much like Rose. The younger two Seasons were both small with delicate frames and the same red-gold hair worn long and straight. Except that Merry was obviously frail and weak, where Rose was physically strong. The invalid and the caretaker.

Mr. Collins's voice could be heard on the screen. "Hello, Merry, how are you today?"

Merry grew suddenly coy, turning and lifting one shoulder. "Fine." Then tilting her head, she asked, "Are you making pictures now?"

"Yes, I am."

"Like the ones of Jack and Ali?"

"Your picture will look just the same," the off-camera voice of Mr. Collins assured her.

Merry nodded, accepting this, seemingly distracted by something over his shoulder.

"What do you want to tell us today?"

"Nothing."

"Nothing?" He chuckled. "I thought you had something you wanted to say." When Merry frowned and shook her head, apparently confused, he prodded,

"To your sisters? Rose and Birdie and..."

"Jilly!" she exclaimed, sitting up in her chair. He had her full attention now. "Will Jilly see this?"

"Yes, I'll make certain she does. Now, tell Jilly and Birdie and Rose what you told me."

Merry's face went blank as she stared back at the camera.

Birdie leaned forward, her heart aching as she watched intently. Here were the sure signs of Merry's brain damage.

"When I show your sisters this movie," Mr. Collins's voice continued with admirable calmness, "what do you want them to know?"

"They'll see me?"

"Yes."

Her face grew serious, pouty. Then she wagged her finger at the camera and said in all seriousness, "I want you to find Spring. I want you to go get her, okay? And tell her——" She paused to think, looking upward, then, with inexpressible sweetness, she smiled straight into the camera like a pro and said, "Tell her I love her. Please?"

"Who is Spring?" he asked.

Merry's face clouded and she shook her head. "I'm not supposed to talk about that."

"Who said you cannot?"

"Rose said not to talk about that."

"I see. Well, is there anything else you want to say?"

Merry grew distracted again and appeared to fatigue. She slumped her shoulders and shook her head no. "Will you give the picture to Rose and Birdie? And Jilly?" She brightened briefly. "We're the Four Seasons," she said with obvious pride, raising four fingers up to the camera. Her hand dropped to her mouth as she began coughing, mildly at first, then hard and gasping.

The camera was cast aside, the picture tilting wildly, settling on an angled shot of the carpet and Merry's slender legs, then a man's trousers hurrying toward her. All the while the hacking cough continued in the background, then the video went blank.

No one spoke. Rose moved to turn off the television. Jilly continued staring at the black screen. Birdie sniffed and rose to collect a box of tissues. She blew her nose, then dabbed at her eyes as she returned to her seat.

"What about the letter?" Rose asked after a moment.

"Oh, yes," Mr. Collins said. He held the letter in his hand. "It's sealed. Who would like to open it?"

"I would," Rose said, reaching out across the floor for it. Mr. Collins delivered it into her hand. She held the envelope reverently, smoothing one palm over it in a tender stroke. "I knew she had gone to Mr. Collins's house, of course, just as I knew what was troubling her, though I hadn't seen the video before." She smiled sadly. "Merry could be very secretive when she wanted to be. Thank you, Mr. Collins. It was very moving. We're not much of a family for taking videotapes and I believe this is the only record we have of Merry. It was so powerful to see her and hear her speak." She paused, collecting herself.

"But I know what is in this letter," she continued after a moment. "It's in her own handwriting. She worked quite hard at it." A faint smile crossed Rose's face. "She tossed out quite a few until she was satisfied."

"Why don't you read it?" Birdie said.

Rose opened the envelope with her finger and tugged out a piece of stationery of matching print. Smoothing out the paper, she glanced briefly at Jilly, then cleared her throat. "It's dated March 5, 1999."

"That was a month before she died," Birdie said.

"That's right," Rose replied, then raised the letter. "There isn't much...."

Dear Jilly, Birdie and Rose,
Under my bed is the time capsule. You gave it to me. Please give it to Spring. Please give all my money to her, too. She needs a nice house.

Your sister,
Merry

P.S. You have to find her first.

"That's it," she said, folding the letter back.

Jilly rubbed her temples, then leaned forward and said, "Excuse me, but am I the only one missing something here? There's that name again. She used to ask me about her. Who or what is Spring?"

"Isn't that the name of her doll?" asked Birdie. "The one that she's had forever. Oh, you know the one, the baby doll with the red hair? She used to carry it around with her wherever she went."

"Yes," replied Rose. "The doll's name is Spring. But that's not who she's referring to."

"Why keep us in suspense? Is she some friend? Real or imaginary or what?"

Rose looked to Mr. Collins for support.

He nodded, indicating she should continue.

Rose wiped her palms on her thighs. "Jilly," she began in earnest, then stopped.

Jilly sat still and frozen, as though posing for a photograph.

Birdie searched Rose's face, so intent and yet fearful. She looked finally at Mr. Collins, whose gaze was all-knowing.

"Well, surely it can't be all that serious," Jilly said in a glib manner. "Dolls and time capsules are hardly earth-shattering."

"Please believe that this is not meant to hurt you or invade your privacy in any way, shape or form," Rose said. "Merry loved you, in some ways I believe more than she loved any of us. You were always someone, well, exotic. Special. She talked about you all the time, and oh, she loved your movies. She didn't understand the Italian, but she watched them two or three times a week just to see you."

"That's very nice, but what does this have to do with Spring? Am I Spring? She wanted me to come home? Is that it?"

"Not exactly." Rose sighed, resigned. "This is so hard."

"Rose…" Birdie urged.

Rose nodded. "I'll just tell you everything straight out and then we can talk, okay? That's the trouble, actually," she said as an aside. "No one ever talks in our family. If we had… Well, never mind."

Rose looked directly at Jilly. "The fact is, even though no one ever talked about it openly, Jilly, we all knew where you went in 1973. We didn't know the details back then, of course. Mother made up all those stories and we were in a fog. But we knew you went somewhere to have a baby."

Jilly went ashen, her only movement the rising of her hand to her throat.

Birdie put her fingers to her lips, stunned, and furtively studied Jilly's reaction.

Rose took a breath, then pushed on. "Even Merry knew. I don't know how she figured it out, but she always did have a knack for ferreting out the truth. This is a big house, but not so big that whispers at night are not heard, or crying behind closed doors, or angry fights between you and Mom and Dad."

Jilly clutched at the arms of her chair, digging her nails into the soft, worn upholstery. Her voice was cold and demanding. "What do you know? Exactly."

Rose looked into her eyes with sympathy and spoke clearly. "Back then, not much. I was only eleven and Merry was six, so we weren't in on the details. Birdie wouldn't talk to us about it. Later we did, naturally, but not then. And, of course, Mom explained things to me, many years later."

She paused to give Jilly a chance to speak, but when she didn't Rose pushed on.

"The point is, Merry never truly understood what really happened. All she knew was that you went away to have a baby. She latched onto this, though none of us knew it at the time. If we did, I'm sure Mom would have tried to explain

things to her right away. So when you came home without
the baby, she was confused. Actually, she was really upset.
She cried night after night for that baby. Do you remember?"

Jilly said nothing.

"I remember vaguely," Birdie commented. "There was a
lot going on and everything was tense. I guess we all thought
Merry was crying in response to that."

"When Mom finally figured out that she knew about the
baby," Rose continued, "she was thoroughly flustered. She
gathered all of us for a family meeting and put the fear of
God into us, telling us never to talk about it. Not even to one
another. She told us that's how reputations are ruined and so
on."

"That's when Mom bought her that baby doll," Birdie
added. "I think she did it both to calm Merry down, and to
use it as an excuse if Merry started talking about your baby."

"But she never did," said Rose. "Except to me, and I
always told her never to discuss it with outsiders. You heard
her on the tape. Since the baby was born in spring, she called
the doll Spring. You know how Dad nicknamed us after the
season we were born in. I guess she wanted the doll to be
named like the rest of us. But I knew, and Mom knew, that
she had really called your baby Spring. The doll was just a
substitute."

Rose rubbed her arms and looked off into the distance.
"It's odd, but by giving the baby a name, I think we all
could settle it in our minds. I mean, the baby became real. It
wasn't just another one of our games. But while we moved
on with our lives, Merry clung to her belief that Spring was
out there somewhere—with you, Jilly. And when you came
home again without the baby, she was very upset. She
thought Spring was somehow lost and needed us."

Jilly's face was white, her back straight against the chair.
She stared at Rose for a moment, shell-shocked, as though
trying to comprehend all that she had just heard.

"But I don't understand," Birdie said, wrinkling her brow. "What does this have to do with the letter and the videotape? She wants us to find the real Spring? The baby Jilly gave up for adoption?"

"Yes," Rose replied.

"But...but why?"

"She wants us to give Spring the time capsule. And her money."

Jilly put her palms to her face. "Oh, God..."

It didn't take Birdie long to put things straight in her mind. "But that's ridiculous! Give more than half a million dollars to a stranger? That's our inheritance. To be divided three ways. I'm sorry, Jilly, but I have a child, too. Doesn't she figure into the equation?"

"She didn't mean the house money, just what's left of her trust fund. She didn't have a firm grasp of money but she knew she had some in the bank. Besides, she was mostly interested in our finding Spring," Rose explained.

"Mr. Collins," Birdie said, "legally speaking, Merry wasn't mentally competent, was she? That letter won't be viewed as a codicil or a will?"

"It could be, but I wouldn't worry about that." He put out a quieting hand to ward off any worries. "As I said at the onset, in my opinion, Merry was not legally competent. But if any one of you argue that she was—" he looked at Rose "—her letter would have to be contested as to its legal bearing. I doubt the courts would support it. I only presented her request to you because she wanted very much for me to do so. And now I have."

"Rose, I can't imagine why you encouraged her in this," Birdie huffed. "What were you thinking?"

"I didn't encourage her, but neither did I discourage her. Like it or not, Birdie, this search for Spring was Merry's wish."

"Well, it's not *mine*."

Everyone looked over at Jilly, startled by the cool, harsh tone of her voice. She'd been so quiet, almost forgotten in this discussion.

"I've had quite enough of this talk about searching for Spring as though it was Merry's baby," she said in measured tones. "She had a *doll*. Let's keep that firmly in mind. As concerns the, the...*other*," she spat out, grasping for a word that was impersonal, "that decision is mine and mine alone. And I won't do it. Do you hear me? I won't do it. And neither will anyone else. I forbid it. You have no right," she said to Rose. "Merry had no right to bring it up. It's my history and none of you have any idea what I went through. And I'll be damned if I dredge it all up again just to satisfy your perverse curiosity or to appease the nonsensical rambling of my sister. That part of my life is closed. Over. There is no Spring."

Jilly's eyes were flames in her thin, pale face as she sat regally and glared at them, daring them to challenge her. Rose put her hands to her trembling lips. Birdie folded her hands together.

Mr. Collins put his hands behind his back and said with admirable calm, "We quite understand."

Jilly lowered her shoulders, appearing older and inexpressibly weary, eager to be gone. She slowly rose with as much dignity as she could muster, then hurried from the room. A moment later they could hear her bedroom door slam.

"Well..." Birdie said, exhaling and unbuttoning her suit jacket.

"I was afraid that would happen," Rose said.

"What did you expect? How could you have done this to her? Do you have any idea what she went through back then? The decision to search for an adopted child has got to be one of the most painful, not to mention personal, decisions a woman can make. It's one thing for Merry to go on about her doll and her idea of a lost baby, but it's quite another to couch it in terms of a last request."

"But that's exactly what it was," Rose exclaimed, rising to her feet. "I knew this would cause a furor, but who was I to deny her? Birdie, you always saw Merry as someone broken who needed fixing. Something half and not whole. Just another responsibility. And as for Jilly... Who knows? I love her, but I haven't seen her but a few times in twenty years. She never made the effort to get to know Merry. Merry was a rare, beautiful individual. She was my dear friend. And when my sister, my friend, begs me to make a last request to her sisters, you better believe that I'm going to do it."

"Well, good for you," Birdie snapped back. "Except did you consider the consequences?"

"As a matter of fact, I did." Rose lifted her chin and squared off with Birdie. "I've spent a lifetime in this house. I was the one who left college to stay here and take care of Merry. I watched you and my friends get married and have children, have lives of your own while I watched the years go by. I don't need you to tell me about consequences, thank you very much." She paused to collect herself. "You forget that I was Mother's caretaker, too, and when she drank, she liked to talk. I know every dirty little secret that's been swept under the rug, and frankly I think it's time to clean house. We have to, or we'll let it fester and rot. Our parents are gone. Merry is gone. There's nothing left to hold us together, to force us to keep contact. It's time for us to talk, at last."

Birdie rubbed her eyes. "I'm not sure that's always for the best."

Mr. Collins stepped forward to stand between them. "I think it's time that I go. Whatever you decide, on this issue or concerning the house, is strictly up to you. However, my course as executor of the will is clear. The money and the property will be distributed equally among you as stipulated in your father's will. If I hear otherwise, then we'll have to have legal documents drawn up. Certainly, you don't have to make those decisions tonight. I suggest you sleep on it.

Goodbye, Birdie. Rose. Please extend my sympathy to Jilly and tell her that I regret any pain she has experienced.''

"I will," Birdie said, rising to take his hand. "Let me walk you to the door."

Rose brought him his briefcase. When she handed him the video, he shook his head.

"No, that's for you to keep. You may want to watch it again." He paused and his gaze swept the living room. He appeared lost in thought, as though seeing ghosts of a happier time long gone.

"It was a difficult decision for me to agree to Merry's request," he said. "Highly unusual, needless to say. I feel sure that if you look at the tape again you will see that Merry had only love in her heart for all of you when she made her request. Oh, that reminds me."

He bent to open his briefcase. His long hands, pale and gnarled with age, pulled out a child-size shoe box. It was brightly painted and wrapped with tape, over and over again, creating a tight seal.

Birdie recognized the box immediately and held out her hands. "The time capsule," she said on a breath.

"Quite right," he replied. Then, handing it to her, he said in utmost seriousness, "As co-executor of the will, I hand it over to your care. It is my client's wish that it be delivered intact to Spring, should you find her. I assume you know its contents."

Birdie shook her head, accepting the small box with reverence. "No. At least not all of it. You see, we gave it to Merry as a gift when she came home from the hospital after the accident." She paused as a million memories of her childhood flooded her thoughts. "My, I can't believe it's still here. It was so long ago, I'd forgotten all about it."

Rose stepped closer, wrapping an arm around Birdie's waist. "It was supposed to be very private so we each gave our gift to Mom to put into the time capsule. It was a very big deal, rather ceremonial. She's the one who put everything in the box and sealed it with all the tape.''

"You've never opened it?" Birdie asked Rose.

"Of course not," she replied. "It didn't belong to me. It belonged to Merry."

Birdie wondered if she would have been so noble. She suspected curiosity would have gotten the better of her over the years.

"This time capsule is a piece of our childhood," Birdie said, holding it with a trace of wonder in her voice. "And now it belongs to Spring."

Six

After Mr. Collins left, Dennis walked lethargically down the stairs. He'd removed his jacket and tie and in his hand he carried a pile of papers.

"Is the coast clear?" he asked.

Seeing him obviously so self-engrossed in his own world did nothing to improve Birdie's mood. She was tired and emotionally drained and she blamed him for not being there for her.

"Where were you?" Birdie asked sharply.

Dennis halted on the stairs and slapped the papers against his thigh. His face could look very cold when he tried. "Where do you think? I was upstairs grading term papers. I told you a hundred times that I had work to do."

Rose grabbed her coat from the front closet. "I'm going for a walk," she said, making a hasty exit.

"You always have work to do," Birdie countered.

"What do you mean?" he asked defensively. "You make that sound like a criticism, like I'm having a ball upstairs drinking beer and watching a football game. I was upstairs working. Where should I have been?"

"Maybe with me, in the dining room, during the reading of the will." She knew she sounded bitter but couldn't help it. Why did he even have to ask? Turning on her heel, she marched through the living room, picking up dishes en route to the kitchen.

Dennis followed her, tucking his hands in his back pocket. "That was Season family business," he said after the kitchen door closed. "Between the sisters."

"You're family," she said through tight lips, tying on an apron.

"If you wanted me there, all you had to do was ask," he said, reaching to pick up empty bottles from the kitchen table and carrying them to the sink.

"Why do I always have to ask?" She turned on the water faucets with brisk turns. "Can't you see for yourself when I need you? And you ducked out of the luncheon pretty quick, too."

"You know how I hate those affairs."

"Oh, and funerals are happy affairs for the rest of us?" She turned off the water and dried her hands. Behind her, he moved around the kitchen, putting the bottles and cans into a plastic bag for recycling. The clink of glass against glass sounded in the silence.

"Mr. Collins and Rose hit us with a bomb today," she said in a softer voice, "and it would have been nice to have had a little support."

Dennis nodded, acknowledging her change of tone as much as her words. He lowered his own tone. "What did they say?"

"You won't believe it." She turned to face him. "Merry wrote this letter to all of us, and made a video."

"A video? That's rather macabre."

"It was. But then in it, she tells us this…this last request. She wants us to search for— Are you ready for this? For Jilly's baby."

Dennis spun his head around to face her, shock registering on his face. "You're kidding?"

"I am not." She flattened her hands on the counter and leaned forward, pleased to see his reaction.

Dennis went to the fridge to pull out a beer. He was lost in his own thoughts. "What did Jilly say about all this?"

"It came as a shock. At first she just sat there with this stunned expression, like a bullet had zipped through her brain."

"Yeah, I'm not surprised."

"Then Rose went on and on about how Merry knew about the baby all along and had been wondering about it. I never knew that. It's hard to imagine her remembering, much less caring about it enough to make it a dying wish. Jilly never knew any of us even knew about it."

"God, what a shock." He looked away and said in a distant voice, "I'm sure she considered that part of her life closed."

"I'm sure, too. We all did. Except deep down, I know Rose was right. It was never really settled because we never openly talked about it. Jilly just sat there and listened. When she finally did speak she was furious. Not yelling or such, but controlled—and maybe scared. In any case, she won't have us conducting search for the child she put up for adoption." Birdie paused and put her hand to her cheek. "Listen to what I just said. *The child Jilly put up for adoption.* Do you have any idea how many years those words were whispered? And then only behind closed doors?"

Dennis tilted his head and squinted his eyes in thought. "She shouldn't search. She has her life and the child has hers. She shouldn't shake things up."

"I don't think that's a big issue these days. Oh," she exclaimed, "but that's not all. Apparently, Merry wanted us to give this Spring her money, too."

"The whole estate?"

"No, Rose seems to think she meant the twenty thousand she had left in her trust fund. Jilly was ticked off about that, too. I can't figure it out. She's got oodles of dough, so why is she so uptight? The one you'd think would care about money is Rose. She hasn't got a dime, but she's the one who wants to give the money away. There's no need to be greedy. We'll all have more than enough after the house is sold."

"How much do you think the house will fetch?"

"I don't know. Over five hundred. Maybe more."

He considered this as he took a long swallow from the bottle. "We could take that trip we've always talked about," he said, leaning back against the counter.

"To Italy?"

His eyes warmed. "Yeah. Just you and me. No agenda, no phone calls to make or chores to get done. The biggest decision we'll have to make is what to eat for dinner. In fact, we'll starve ourselves for weeks before we leave, then eat our way through the country." He moved closer, wrapping his arms around her waist. "We never got a honeymoon. We need time, Birdie. Just for us."

She nodded her head and leaned into him. "I know."

He hugged her and she thought she really did know. Especially at moments like this, that harkened back to a time when they were close and intimate. When they touched a lot and each touch set off a fire between them that had them having sex like rabbits. Back to when they'd thought of each other all day long and missed each other every moment they were apart. That all seemed so long ago. For years they'd promised themselves a trip. It was a dream that served as a lifeline during the rough years of juggling her medical residency and Hannah's early childhood. Then came the start of her medical practice and his acceptance to the faculty at the University of Wisconsin. As the years passed, the dream slipped farther and farther away. Now they were floundering.

Something was very wrong between them, something they couldn't put a name to. They were cohabiting space, more like roommates than husband and wife. She knew she snapped at him a lot. She couldn't help it; he irritated her so often, more than anyone else. It was almost as if he did it deliberately, to get her attention.

Or maybe it was just that after twenty years, they were both getting a little too familiar with each other's habits and flaws. He was pretty good at getting his digs in, too, and he excelled at tuning her out. But she never questioned that she loved him. He was her husband. The father of her only child. Her friend.

He nuzzled at her ear suggestively, and all she could think was how she didn't want to be touched.

"We're both tired," she said, pulling back, pretending not to notice the stark disappointment in his face. "Why don't I make us something to eat and we'll plop in front of the TV."

"Why do you always do that?"

"Do what?"

"Break away whenever we get close?"

She laughed nervously. "I don't!"

"Yes, you do." He was utmost serious.

Birdie's face grew somber. "I don't do it to hurt you, and I do want to be close to you, it's just... Lately, I don't want to make love and I know you do. I don't know why. Maybe it's hormonal."

"Maybe," he replied. Dennis picked up the bag of empty bottles in a swoop. "But it's not been just lately. It's been a long time, Birdie. Too long." He turned away, then headed to the back door.

Birdie felt the space lengthen between them as she looked over her shoulder to watch him leave. The empty bottles clanked against his leg as he walked out from the house. It was a hollow, lonely sound.

The snow had melted under the day's warm sun so Rose was able to walk easily along the sidewalks of her neighborhood. Hers was a block like many others in the country and she knew each house and yard almost as well as she knew her own. She noted where one neighbor had pruned the front hedge, or another was beginning an addition. Most of the houses were well cared for, even lovingly so. Passing by she could peek in the windows overflowing with light and see typical American family scenes being played out. These houses had a feeling of family and cheerfulness that was warm and inviting.

When she'd arrived back at her own home she remained on the sidewalk, her coat collar up close around her neck and her small hands tucked tightly under her armpits. She tried to look at the Victorian with the same dispassionate eye she'd looked at the neighboring ones. Mrs. Kasparov's list of flaws came to mind, and though it rankled, they were all too true. On the block, their house was the eyesore, the shabby one that prompted neighbors to say, "What a shame. If only they would fix it up." It was a shadowy, melancholy house that sat on a huge double lot on the corner, hidden by overgrown pines and a forest of shaggy shrubs. Light flowed through torn shades or missing blinds, adding to the somber sense of depression.

Looking at it now, she found it hard to remember when happiness flowed bright from these dreary windows, or when the family had lived and laughed and talked in those darkened rooms. Merry had been the last flicker of light in the old house and now that, too, had been snuffed out. The old Victorian appeared exactly as it was—a house of secrets. Suppressing a sigh, she walked up the front steps and slipped, unnoticed, into the house.

Hours later, the house was deathly quiet, save for the me lodic clanging of the five-note wind chimes outside her window. Rose sat alone in the blanketing solitude of her room while the computer whirred. She opened the side drawer to her desk and pulled out a file from far in the back where no idle eyes would find it. It was a plain manila file with only the initials D.B. on it. DannyBoy. Copies of his e-mails were inside. Not love letters—theirs wasn't that kind of relationship. She thought of them as letters from her dearest friend. By the time the computer had booted, the words were ready to spill out of her. Laying her hands on the keys, she took a deep breath and typed.

Dear DannyBoy,

Tonight I feel a despair that frightens me. I feel I am nothing of value. My sister Merry at least depended on me but now she is gone. My older sisters have their own lives that do not include me. Soon they will leave, too. Even this house, which had once been my haven, feels hostile and forbidding. But no matter, because I, too, must leave. The four Seasons have been cast to the wind.

I'm sitting here in the darkness, listening to the wind chimes outside my window and waiting for the dawn. I'm reminded of Emily Dickinson's "slant of light," and wonder to myself where nothing goes after death?

Rosebud

An e-mail came almost immediately.

Dear Rosebud,

Don't you dare despair. Turn on the lights!

I swore I wasn't going to do this. We've been chatting online for a long time, though we've only talked privately like this for a few weeks. I think of us as friends. I hope you do, too. So I hope you won't think I'm one of those Internet creeps when I say this, but I get the sense I better tell you now.

I drive a truck all day through town after town. The miles roll beneath me and I have to tell you, it gets pretty lonely. One day is pretty much like the next. The

roads are always crowded and some of the drivers are
nuts. It's not like the old days when the road stretched
out before me.

But lately, I know when the day is done and I park
my rig that it'll be okay because I'll find a letter from
you waiting for me. I don't know what you mean by
that "slant of light," but I can tell you that your letters
are the bright point of my day. I don't have any wind
chimes outside my cab, either, but your words are music
to a lonely man.

You think you are nothing? You are something! Real
special. I feel lucky just to know you. Like I said, I'm
no nutcase and I don't mean to get too personal, so don't
worry.

DannyBoy

Rose put her hands to her heated cheeks and laughed out
loud. She couldn't write much, afraid that she might get
maudlin and start getting really, really personal. So to ease
his mind, and because she sensed he was waiting for a reply
from her, she wrote again.

Good night DannyBoy.
I'll sleep well, now.

Your friend, Rosebud

Down the hall, Jilly lay in her twin bed staring at the
ceiling. So they'd known all along, she thought with chagrin.
Even Merry. For years her sisters had whispered about her
secret. *Guess what? Jilly had a baby!* Mother had explained
it to them. *Jilly always was the wild one, you know. You
don't want to end up like Jilly.* Did they know that in all
those years she never once allowed herself to think of it?
Never once so much as breathed the words in her sleep?

The nuns at Marian House had promised her redemption if she pretended that it had never happened, *it* being the scandalous, sinful cycle of conception, pregnancy and birth outside the sacrament of marriage. She'd lowered a veil over that episode of her life, a black fog of forgetfulness so impenetrable that, as the years passed, she actually fooled herself into believing none of it had ever happened.

Occasionally, over the years, something insignificant would trigger a memory: the sight of an infant in a carriage, the smell of cafeteria food, the sound of rain on the window in the early morning. Jilly would dismiss the memory with a quick shake of her head and a willful command of her mind to think of something else. She'd cast the memory into the deepest, darkest compartment of her heart, locked it tight and thrown away the key.

But Merry had managed to open it. Sneakily, when her guard was down, Merry had come forth with this request to search for the child. This Spring. It felt like her ghostly hand was stabbing into Jilly's chest, wrenching out her heart and rummaging through the myriad compartments, and in doing so, releasing the memories like demons taking flight.

How wrong Sister Benedict had been! Years of silence were obliterated in one fell swoop by the simple words of a child. *Find Spring.*

Now she had to face that it had happened. She had had a baby. And tonight, she knew the memories were waiting, a powerful, relentless army of them, just beyond the ridge of her resistance. Waiting for the moment she fell asleep.

Then the long-delayed onslaught would begin.

Seven

January 5, 1973

Jilly was seventeen and pregnant. She rode in the passenger seat of the black Cadillac Brougham, resting one hand on her gently rounded belly and looking out at the dull, monotonous scenery of Interstate 95 north to upper Wisconsin. The morning was bright and sunny, mocking the dark, brooding mood within the car.

"Do you need to stop?" Her father kept his eyes on the road. In the past four hours he'd offered little conversation besides brief inquiries as to whether she was hungry or had to use the rest facilities. He wasn't the talkative type on the best of occasions, and rarely carried on the usual father-daughter banter about such things as school grades, boyfriends or plans for college. The silence today, however, was punitive.

"No," she replied, glancing at his stern profile. She felt herself recoil and wanted to weep. "Thank you. I'm okay." She turned away again, tightening her bladder muscles against the straining urge. She would not ask to stop again so soon after his pithy comment on how this trip was taking forever due to pit stops. She could kick herself for having that soda.

Despite the long drive, her father maintained his usual crisp and immaculate appearance in his dark suit and pressed white shirt. Next to him she felt like a ragamuffin in a baggy dress and her mother's old coat. The blue wool wasn't warm enough for the January cold, but the voluminous A-line style was the only one they had that allowed for Jilly's expanding waistline. What did it matter what she looked like or how warm it was, she told herself. She didn't plan on going outside much in the next few months so she would make do with her mother's hand-me-down.

She sighed and looked again at the raw bleakness outside her window, feeling each of the miles that separated her from her home and the life she once knew in Illinois, from the carefree high school girl she once was.

Jilly knew she'd crossed the line from child to woman ever since that evening last November when she walked into her parents' bedroom, closed the door behind her and quietly told her parents that she was pregnant.

Her mother had accepted the news with her usual hysteria.

"Oh, my God! Pregnant? Oh, my God. You must have been drinking. You were, weren't you?" she accused, sitting up in bed and pointing. She'd been watching TV and her heavy lids, the slurred words and the telltale empty glass on her bedside table revealed she'd been drinking. "I told you she was drinking," she'd screeched to her husband, as if it was his fault.

"Mom, I wasn't drinking."

"How could you have done this to us? I knew you're irresponsible, you've always been. But I didn't know you were immoral, too! It's a mortal sin what you've done. A mortal sin! And the scandal! Your father is a judge in this city. Did you think about him? Did you think about anyone but yourself?"

Her mother cried then, not for Jilly, but for herself. "Oh, Bill, I can't take this. Two daughters ruined." Then turning back to Jilly she narrowed her eyes and cried, "Your sisters' reputations will be ruined, too. And so will mine!"

Her father compressed his lips and didn't say a word. His thick red brows, streaked with white, furrowed as he slowly closed his magazine and let it drop to the floor.

Jilly turned her eyes to the ground, embarrassed and ashamed for bringing such scandal to the family. Everyone knew that "good" girls didn't go all the way. "Good" girls did not get pregnant. Standing there at the foot of their bed, she looked in her parents' eyes and a part of her died seeing the judgment written there: Jillian Season was not a Good Girl.

After a short but noisy cry her mother sobered up and spent a while in the bathroom. Jilly glanced at her father to see him staring at her, an odd expression on his face, as though he couldn't quite believe what he was hearing. How many times had they argued about her curfew in the past? He'd always told her it wasn't that he didn't trust *her*, he didn't trust the boys she dated.

"Well, when is the baby due?" her mother asked when she emerged from the bathroom. She had washed her face, brushed her short red-gold hair, and she appeared to have collected her composure. Jilly took heart that they'd have a real conversation instead of histrionics, but her hope wobbled as her mother crossed the room and climbed back into the bed.

Jilly remained standing. "In early May sometime."

"Have you seen a doctor? Really, Jilly, how do you know you're pregnant?"

"I went to Planned Parenthood."

"Good God," her mother exclaimed. "That place?" As far as she was concerned, Planned Parenthood's clinic, located in a poor, dangerous part of town, was a bastion of fanatics—enemies of the Church who offered birth control and abortions to a new, immoral generation that preached free love. And now her daughter was one of them. "Bill..." she said, reaching over to clasp his hand in a dramatic gesture.

"We'll send her to Dr. Applebee," he said, the voice of reason. "Then we'll get the facts."

"I *am* pregnant. Three months pregnant. I had a blood test and there's no mistake."

The calm authority in her voice, the very fact that she had found her way to Planned Parenthood, had the test done and could report to them this finding, all without their help, took them both by surprise. She could see them look at her differently, more as an adult.

"Who is the father?" her own father asked.

"I don't want to say," she replied, looking away.

"Don't press her just yet," her mother intervened. "I'm sure she hasn't gotten used to the idea. I certainly couldn't believe it when I found out I was having you. I was married, of course," she said, letting Jilly know that this shift of attitude by no means forgave her. "But was I surprised. Stunned, in fact. I had to give up my dancing career."

Jilly knew the worst was over once Mother's dancing career was mentioned. Her mother cherished her years in the Chicago Ballet Company as the highlight of her life and she never let an opportunity go by when she couldn't remind them of all she'd given up for her family.

Once the idea of her pregnancy sunk in, the horror and shock subsided and the concept that they would be grandparents began to take root. Their voices grew solicitous. They painted rosier scenarios. Her parents assumed that she had a special beau, someone she was in love with and wanted to protect. She felt like dirt under their feet as she stood there listening while they calmed down and began talking about how they'd help her—and him—through this ordeal. Abortion was briefly mentioned in an academic sense, but they were Catholic. It wasn't really an option.

The kindness was killing her. It was easier when they were mad and yelling at her. At least then she could shut down emotionally. As it was, the guilt was paralyzing.

"Sit down," her mother said, patting the mattress. "It bothers me to see you swaying back there. There's no sense you wearing yourself out, not in your condition." She put her fingers to her breast. "I can't believe I just said that! To my own daughter. That's better. Now, Jilly dear, you'll have to marry the boy, of course."

"Marry him? Mother, I'm—"

"You're young, I know. But not *that* young. Lots of girls get married after high school. You could live here."

Jilly could see her mother's mind whirring with possibilities, not all unpleasant. Ann Season made no secret of her desire for weddings and grandchildren. She never saw much merit in sending a girl off to college, especially one as stunningly beautiful as her eldest.

"No, I don't think—"

"I could redo the third floor to make it into a little apartment for you."

"That's too—"

"Oh, it's no trouble. I've always meant to do something with that floor. When you were children it was your playroom, but now…" Her eyes lit up. "To think, babies again in the house."

"Mom, I didn't say I was getting married."

"But what else can you do? It's what a girl in your situation must do. Provided he's a decent enough fellow. Isn't that right, Bill?"

He sat very still for a while, pondering not his wife's question, but several of his own. The hour was late and his eyelids were beginning to droop. Jilly thought he looked very tired and very old. He had married late in life and was an "old" father, never the type interested in sports or goofing around with his kids. His was a reserved, quiet love that was proved in constancy and concern. All the girls felt loved, but knew the one true passion in his life was his wife, Ann. He was old-fashioned; he would take the question of marriage very seriously.

"Do you want to marry the fellow?" he asked in a sober tone.

She shook her head. "No, Daddy."

Her mother released a puff of frustrated air and sat back against the pillows.

"Who is the father of the child?" her father asked again. His voice was quiet but she heard the force of his will in the undertone.

"I can't say." She felt inexpressibly weary.

"Of course you can. What's his name?"

"Is it that Connor boy?" her mother interjected. "You went out with him awhile."

"No."

"Well who?"

Jilly looked at her hands. "I don't want to say."

"You *will* say," her father demanded.

"I won't." Her voice was equally soft and equally firm. There was total silence.

Bill Season studied his eldest daughter, his eyes narrowing in the same manner that she'd seen him scrutinize a witness on the stand in his courtroom. He took his time, letting everyone know he was weighing his decision.

When she was young, she used to close her eyes when she heard her father talking to a client on the phone. He was so thoughtful, so persuasive. She'd be lulled by the soothing tone of his professional voice. He used that tone now, trying to convince her to tell him the name of the baby's father.

"Jillian, you are my eldest daughter. My firstborn. I'll never forget the pride and joy I felt holding you in my arms the first time. I'm only interested in your welfare. As your father, it's my duty to protect you, and my grandchild. And remember, I am your father first, a judge second. So tell me now, who is the baby's father?"

It took all her determination, all her love for him, not to give in and tell the truth.

She didn't know who the father was.

She knew who the father could be, but she wasn't sure. There were two boys she had been with, one from her school, another a college man. Getting pregnant was bad enough, but how could she tell her parents that she'd been with more than one boy? They'd be devastated. Call her a tramp, a whore. They'd cast her out, disown her. But worst of all, she would hurt them more than she already had. She was more afraid to lose their love than she was of losing the baby.

"I can't tell you," she replied.

After Jilly's adamant refusal to name the boy, all talk between them came to an abrupt stop. Her father cut her off emotionally. Her mother abandoned all dreams of babies in the attic and stepped in to make the necessary decisions. She could be quite effective when she put her mind to a task instead of her drinking. The following morning she contacted Catholic Social Services and, with their help, selected Marian House.

And that was where she was headed this cold January morning. Jilly leaned her head against the cool glass of the car, recalling the chilling sensation that trickled through her blood when she heard the words—*Marian House: A Home for Unwed Mothers*. It had the same foreign sound, the same illicit and dangerous association as a home for juvenile delinquents. *Juvie Hall*. Those names were whispered as a threat to naughty children. "You'd better be good or you'll go to Juvie Hall." Or, "If you fool around, you'll end up in a Home for Unwed Mothers." There wasn't much difference between them, not in most minds. Whichever one you went to implied you'd broken some law, that you were unfit and had to be removed from society.

As she stared out at the barren trees and the vast, isolated, snow-covered fields of northern Wisconsin, she shivered in her thin coat and wondered what Marian House would be like. There were no brochures for her to browse through or interviews granted. No one asked her opinion. Jilly was being *sent*.

She imagined that the other girls would be older, tough, even vulgar with bleached, ratted hair and thick black eye-liner. Greaser girls with loads of experience and an attitude against middle-class girls like herself. Or dirt-poor country hicks who made love in the haystacks like barn cats or in the backs of pickup trucks with boys with dirty hands. Would they smack their gum and make snide remarks as she passed? She was sure she would have nothing in common with any of them and prayed she'd survive the next few months of hell. She rubbed her hand across her belly, feeling the baby kick within. Her poor little baby, her only friend. She didn't care what they did to her, but just let anyone try to hurt her baby.

The car rolled through the countryside without a word of counsel from her father, a man known to be generous with his advice to strangers. It hurt more than she could admit that he didn't offer her what she needed most right now: his love. Riding in the silent car, glancing at his unyielding profile, Jilly swore that if her father could never forgive her, then she would never forgive him, either. And she would never tell him—or anyone—the truth about the baby's father. Never. It was her secret alone.

The torturous journey at last ended when her father turned the long, sleek Cadillac through a heavy, ornate, black iron gate. Behind it was a hill covered with majestic trees. Jilly sat up in the car, scouting out the unexpected majesty of the entrance. They traveled up a steep, winding road. It was a vast property overlooking a large lake, secluded and absolutely gorgeous. She spied tall wire fences bordered by barbed wire and wondered if they were intended to keep the public out, or the girls in. After a final curve, they passed a large stone grotto carved into the hill that was dedicated to the Virgin. The irony wasn't lost on Jilly. Just beyond, the road flattened and they pulled into a large, well-plowed parking area.

A severe, redbrick building stood isolated on top of the snow-crusted hill. Though the woods were close, not a tree or shrub broke the slab of blacktop that stretched right up to the front door. Four unshuttered windows were lined across the top two floors and three more below them. A single white door was at the right, a single-bulb light fixture affixed over it. This was a no-nonsense, no-frills place. This was Marian House.

"Here we are," her father said, pulling into a parking space. Theirs was the only car in the lot. He heaved a sigh of relief, glanced her way, then said, "It seems a decent place."

It wasn't the derelict flophouse she'd expected, but neither was it welcoming. Nervous, with a feeling of dread, she opened the car door and stepped out, careful not to slip on an ice patch. She trembled as she obediently followed her father to the entrance, wanting to disappear inside her voluminous coat while he rang the bell.

"Hello and welcome," said the diminutive, elderly nun who opened the door. The woman only reached her father's chest and had to bend her head far back to smile into his face. Her own face had that paper-thin, pasty-white color unique to elderly nuns, but her eyes shone a brilliant blue from behind wireless glasses.

"I'm Sister Celestine. You must be Mr. Season. And you must be Jillian."

She appeared outwardly meek, all sweet smiles and welcomes, but from the moment she rested her laser-sharp gaze on her, Jilly knew that Sister Celestine was the force to be reckoned with at Marian House.

"We expected you at eleven," she said through a hard smile, her tone laced with reprimand. "Lunch is due to start in twenty minutes and Jillian and I are expected in the dining hall. We'll just have time for a brief tour."

Turning with a swish of her long black habit, she walked quickly into a large recreation room with forest-green-and-white linoleum flooring and modern 1960s-style wood-frame couches and armchairs upholstered in bright orange, brown and gold nubby fabric. They lined the walls and formed a semicircle before a large, old television. There weren't any magazines on the flat, wood coffee tables, only the *Catholic Observer* newspaper and a few Bibles.

"This is the rec room," she said with pride as she whisked them through.

Jilly thought it had the immaculate, cold aura of a hospital waiting room.

"You may watch television in the afternoons and in the evening until ten o'clock," she said, leading them across the highly polished floors. "The phone is located outside my office in the stairwell. It's a pay phone and you may use it until ten o'clock. We don't want the noise to disturb the girls who retire early."

They entered another large room with a small L-shaped kitchen and two metal-and-vinyl dinette tables. This was the snack room.

"Here the girls can make snacks when they're hungry. But no cooking is allowed," Sister Celestine warned. "You may heat up water for coffee or tea. There's a refrigerator for juice and milk and plenty of apples that you can help yourself to. Did you know there is an orchard on the grounds? In the fall, the girls help to pick the apples for applesauce."

Jilly smiled and thought how glad she was it was winter.

For the most part Sister Celestine directed her comments to her father, while casting little more than a few, quick assessing glances her way. He towered over the nun as they walked quickly through the rooms on the first floor, never removing his coat and holding his hat in his hand, as though looking for a quick getaway. He was polite and listened courteously but had no comments or questions. Jilly followed them, virtually unnoticed, carrying her coat over her belly, craning her neck from left to right as she passed through the rooms, each one more cold than the next. This would be her new home.

Men were not allowed upstairs in the private rooms of the girls, but Sister Celestine showed her father a small guest room on the first floor so that he could get an idea. She assured him that the austere room with two narrow beds covered in a dull green cotton coverlet with a crucifix overhead was typical.

"Lights are out at ten o'clock. We rise early for daily mass at six-thirty with the other nuns in the chapel. On Sundays, the girls can sleep in until eight o'clock since we celebrate high mass at nine." She seemed to think this an enormous treat.

Jilly bit her tongue and smiled again. She hated to rise before eleven on the weekends. Oh, God, how was she going to survive the next few months?

"The old high school is that small building across the parking lot. We are fortunate to have retired teaching sisters who can provide tutoring for our girls. We have Jillian's transcripts and curriculum and I feel sure we can keep her from falling behind. The younger girls are required to take advantage of this program. It's optional for the high school graduates. In addition, we feel it's necessary to instruct all the girls in religion and health." She fixed him with a commiserating look.

Her father's lips tightened and he turned to look at Jilly

for the first time since they'd begun their tour. She could see the shame in his eyes that he, a respected judge, an upstanding Catholic who sent his children to Catholic schools and went to mass every Sunday, had a pregnant daughter who had to be instructed in religion. And "health" was clearly a euphemism for a refresher course on pregnancy, childbirth and abstinence.

Sister Celestine then made her way back to the front door, ending the brief tour.

"The dining hall is shared with the novitiate across the way," she indicated with a brief wave of her hand. "I'm afraid I can't show you that, Mr. Season."

"There's a novitiate here?" Jilly asked. No one had told her she'd be living with nuns.

"Oh, yes, of course. This building is just a small part of a much larger complex of buildings here. This was once an old family estate," she explained. "The order purchased the property in 1960 to become the motherhouse. We've added on wings to the original mansion to house and educate the novices in training. Farther down the road is a conference center and the nursing-retirement home for the elderly nuns."

Jilly looked out the window but could see nothing but a glimpse of brick beyond the thick wall of pine and spruce. Apparently, they didn't want the sinners to mix with the saints.

"This was once a high school for girls who had aspirations of entering the sisterhood," Sister Celestine continued. "But sadly, the numbers were dropping so precipitously that, a few years ago, we had to close the school. Instead the order opened Marian House to meet another need of the community." Sister Celestine sighed and clasped her hands together. "It's a sign of the times, I'm afraid."

She cast a loaded glance at Jilly. She didn't have to say that the new residents of Marian House were a far cry from the sweet, naive virgins who used to inhabit these halls.

Her father looked out the window toward his car.

Jilly looked past her belly at her polished shoes. The tour had ended, and though brief, Sister Celestine had efficiently demolished the last shreds of Jilly's self-esteem and put her firmly in her place.

"I think it's best to say your goodbyes now," Sister Celestine said, tucking her hands into the sleeves of her habit. "Jillian and I have a few things to discuss before lunch and we've run out of time. Meals are served punctually."

She didn't leave the room but stepped back a few feet to allow them a small measure of privacy. As it was, privacy wasn't needed. Her father stepped closer, placed his hands on her shoulders in a fatherly gesture and looked into her eyes.

A tenderness passed between them that crossed the barriers of anger and recrimination. She saw in his eyes that he loved her, was sad that this had all happened, and also disappointed. Jilly held her breath, waiting for the words of love or advice that she so desperately needed to hear. She wanted to tell him that she was terrified of living here in this impersonal place with these strangers, of adapting to this nun's institutional lifestyle while her belly grew and grew. Most of all, she wanted him to know she didn't know anything about having a baby. Wasn't this the time when a girl needed her parents most of all? All this she tried to convey in her eyes. Her throat ached from holding back the torrent of words.

From outside she heard the tolling of a church bell. Twelve bongs, calling the nuns to lunch.

The moment ended. He was the dignified judge again. He bent to kiss her cheek with dry lips. "Goodbye, Jillian. We'll be back to pick you up after..." He stumbled with the words. "When you're ready to leave," he amended.

She stood in the doorway and watched him go. He walked quickly and didn't stop at the car door to wave. Jilly gripped the door's wood frame, fighting the urge to run crying after him. *Daddy, don't go! I'll be good. I'm sorry! Take me home.*

"Jillian? Won't you come this way, please? And bring your bag."

Jilly turned to face Sister Celestine, startled from her thoughts. The other woman was smiling, but her tone allowed for no disobedience. Jilly picked up her small suitcase and hurried to follow the rustling habit to a small office at the edge of the stairwell. Inside, there was barely room for the wooden desk and two chairs.

Sister Celestine took the seat behind the desk, briskly indicating for Jillian to take the seat opposite. Once settled, she offered a weak smile then looked at her watch, clearly aware of the ticking away of each moment.

"We hope you'll have as pleasant a stay as possible, under the circumstances," she began, getting right down to business. "Now then, I have all your paperwork here, but let me go over a few points." She picked up a fountain pen and unscrewed the top. "Your due date is..."

"May 1."

She checked this on her paper. "You've been under a doctor's care?"

"Yes. Dr. Applebee. In Evanston." She flushed, remembering how shocked and humiliated she'd been during her obstetric exam. She'd closed her eyes and choked back the tears as his ironlike fingers probed and poked her tender skin, hurting her, not offering any friendly words to try to calm her down. When he was done, he'd looked at her with thinly veiled disapproval. "Next time, use a condom," he'd said before he left the room.

"You will visit a doctor every Monday while you're here," Sister Celestine said. "And there is a staff of nurses at the sisters' nursing home should an emergency arise. St. Francis is the hospital where you'll deliver. It's close by and

they know our girls. We usually escort the girls by private
ambulance service.''

Ambulance? Jilly hadn't even thought that far into the future. She had horrid visions of spinning red lights and sirens.

"And you're still decided to release the baby, I assume?''

Jilly squeezed her hands together in her lap. This was the
moment. Her mother wasn't beside her like a guard. Now
was her chance to ask the question she'd most wanted to ask
when her mother filled out the adoption forms.

"Is there any way... I mean, what if I want to keep my
baby?'' She took a deep breath, waiting for the reply.

Sister Celestine was not pleased. Her lips compressed and
she glanced again at her watch before answering the question.

"Now, Jillian,'' she said in a tone that thinly disguised her
frustration. "I'm sure this has all been explained to you. It
would be very difficult, even impossible for you to offer this
baby the same respectable home and lifestyle that adoptive
parents could provide. We will make certain that your child
goes to a family of similar ethnic background and appearance. And the child will be raised Catholic, of course.
Why—'' she smiled perfunctorily, as though delivering a
well-rehearsed punch line "—we'll even try to find a parent
with green eyes and red hair like yours.''

When Jilly didn't smile, Sister Celestine frowned and
glanced at the papers on her desk. "Your parents have made
it clear that it is their wish that the child be put up for adoption.''

Jilly clenched her hands tighter. "I understand.''

Sister Celestine looked up now, solicitous. "Think of what
it would mean to the child to be raised as illegitimate. A
bastard. That is a crude term, but we both know the child
will hear it. The adoptive parents will want your child. He
or she will complete their family. They will provide a better
home than you could for this child. And we must keep in

mind that the child's needs should come first. Truly, if you love your baby you will give him up."

Jillian looked at the small, wizened nun. She saw in Sister Celestine's eyes the hardness and lack of sympathy of a seasoned veteran, one who had gone through this same routine with far too many girls for far too many years.

She lowered her head in defeat. Her hand rested on its usual spot over her belly. Would the adoptive mother know what she had given up to provide this perfect couple with a complete family? Would her child know that she'd tried to keep it? That she was doing the best thing by giving her baby up?

I'm sorry, she told her baby.

"I'm sure in time you will see that this is the best for you as well. You will be able to return to the life you just left, finish high school, maybe college. And some day, you will marry and have other children."

Sister Celestine gathered her papers, tapping the edge of the pile to even out the sheets. "We can continue this discussion another time," she said, not giving Jilly a chance to respond. "We really have to go, so you can meet the others. There are twelve girls here now and we expect two more in the next few days, bringing us to our capacity of fourteen. You'll find all the girls to be friendly, but remember, these are not easy times for any of them and you can expect more emotion and tears than you might under normal situations. I hope you will make friends while you are here, but—" She paused to fold her hands over the table and lean forward. Her voice was stern.

"Privacy is absolute at Marian House. All friendships begin and end here. It is very important that you remember that. When you leave, do not try to make contact with any of the girls. To that point, you must never divulge your last name or ask it of another. Everyone is on a first-name basis only. Nor may you tell anyone where you are from, what school you attend, or offer any other information that might reveal personal clues about yourself or your family.'' She speared Jilly with a look. ''We do not tolerate any infraction of this rule. Should you break it, you would be sent home immediately. Do you understand?''

Jilly nodded.

''There are a few other rules, but I can tell you them on the way to the dining hall,'' She was already rising from her seat. ''We'll have to hurry. I'm afraid lunch will have already begun.''

Again, Jilly hustled to follow the amazingly quick-paced nun out of the building and across a brick-paved walkway, a kind of shortcut through a tall hedge. Beyond was a gracious, redbrick mansion bordered by tall white pillars and a series of glorious arched Palladian windows. It took Jilly's breath away.

''I'll walk you through the front entrance, just this once,'' Sister Celestine said as they hustled up the circular drive. ''The novices are all in church now, so we can slip through unnoticed. They are not allowed to mingle with the outside world.''

Especially not with the worst kind of sinners, Jilly thought to herself as she followed along the path that linked the austere Marian House for unwed mothers to this lovely mansion for the young, virginal brides of Christ.

Inside, the house was even lovelier than the outside, but she wasn't allowed time to admire it. They rushed through a maze of doors, at one point leaving the high ceilings and elegant dark-paneled walls of the mansion to enter the pea-green-colored walls of the institution. In here she could smell the scent of food, nothing she could identify, just a general, pleasing aroma of meat, cooked vegetables and potatoes. As they drew near a pair of double doors, she heard the sound of chairs moving, dishes clanking and the animated, high hum of women's conversation.

Sister Celestine paused before opening the doors, smiling encouragingly, her eyes sparkling. Then she pushed open the doors to a large, bright, institutional cafeteria. Sun poured in through enormous plate-glass windows that dominated three walls. A dozen or more gray metal tables were set up in the middle, and there was a school-like cafeteria serving area to the right, complete with brown plastic trays and silver. Hanging on the back wall was the sole decoration: an enormous wooden crucifix.

The talking ceased when she entered the room. She felt paralyzed as Sister Celestine introduced her to the girls, using only her first name. In her ears she heard the rush of blood and she looked at the blur of faces staring up at her. Only one thought raced through her mind, over and over again, as she stared back at them.

These were not the toughened, wisecracking, gum-smacking bad girls she'd expected. They looked like the girls who went to her school.

They looked just like her.

The months passed quickly. By February, Jilly was already entrenched in the routine of Marian House. They lived by the bells. At six o'clock, the bells rang to roust them from their beds. The air was always chilly and the floors always icy to their feet. By seven o'clock, they had to have their beds made and be dressed and ready for mass. The sound of the young mothers' stomachs growling competed with the high chant of the nuns' morning prayers. After breakfast, they went to the school where retired nuns of the order tutored them. Lunch was at twelve sharp and was the main meal of the day.

Lunch time was also special because mail was delivered and spread out on a table in alphabetical order. The return addresses were all blacked out in magic marker to conceal any personal information. At home her mother collected the letters from Birdie and Rose, as well as from her friends, and put them into a large envelope to mail once a week. Jilly would then respond, carefully writing about the fascinating and *très amusant* experiences she was having at the French immersion school at the University of Wisconsin she was supposed to be attending. The nuns had agreed to the scam of mailing her letters from the extension in Green Bay on days when a few of the sisters went to the university to study.

Benediction at five signaled the end of their free period, followed by dinner at six. Then it was television time until the bells told them to go to bed at ten.

By March, she was really showing and her baby was somersaulting within her. When her baby stretched, she could just make out the round outline of a small rump, or feel the sharp pressure of a little kick. In April, Sister Benedict gathered Jilly, Simone and Sarah in a small, private room with comfortable chairs and a stereo. They were the next batch of girls due to deliver. She played ballads, mostly Joan Baez and Judy Collins, which Jilly thought was incredibly cool. She also served them hot chocolate and cookies. Jilly loved Sister Benedict, not only because she taught them the difference between an epidural and general anesthesia, but because she treated them like contemporaries, not naughty children without feelings or opinions that mattered. The girls were starved for information and asked hundreds of questions. "Were blindfolds really put over their eyes so they couldn't see the baby at birth? Were earmuffs placed over their ears so they could not hear their baby's cry? Did that really happen? Were the stories true?"

Sister Benedict's face grew somber and reflective, then she shook her head. "Years back, perhaps. But don't worry. It's definitely not true now."

But they never once discussed the developing baby or infant care. All the girls were encouraged—expected—to relinquish their babies after birth. During the last visit, Sister Benedict told them it was only recently that Marian House even allowed the girls the option of holding their babies after birth. Many homes still did not. "Don't look at—or hold—your baby," she advised them. "Endure the ordeal. Pray for strength, then later it will be as if none of this had ever happened."

May 1 came and went. Then, on May 9, Simone went into labor. She returned from the hospital two days later, flat-bellied, subdued and unwilling to talk to anyone. It was as if the baby that had ballooned in her body had held all her joy and energy. After the delivery, all that was Simone had deflated, leaving behind an empty shell. She kept to her room. It was an unspoken rule among the girls that no one was to be disturbed in their rooms after the return from the hospital if the door was closed. The following day Simone's parents came to pick her up and return her to wherever she came from. She was dressed in her "normal" clothes, and though they were obviously brand-new, she looked like a lost waif standing in the foyer, her suitcase by her side. When she turned to wave goodbye to Jilly, her usually dark and expressive eyes were dull and vacant. Jilly wept that night, feeling very alone and knowing she would never see her friend again.

That same night, Sarah went into labor. Jilly clutched her thin pillow tight as she heard Sister Celestine hurry past her door to Sarah's room. Sarah was groaning miserably, making a terrible racket and complaining of pains in her back. Jilly's breath came short, knowing she was next. She couldn't escape the inevitable. There was only one way for this baby to come out. Oh, God, she didn't want to do this, she prayed as she heard Sarah's moaning escalate to a keening wail as they escorted her down the hall. When the girls rose the following morning, Sister Celestine announced that Sarah had given birth to a son.

For the next several days, she lived in a state of heightened senses. Every thought, every movement was predicated on whether she would have the baby. She took long walks, avoided spicy foods and went to bed early. Finally, on May 17, two weeks overdue, Jilly felt her first contraction.

Dawn was just piercing the darkness. Jilly lay in bed, wide-eyed, listening to the birds chatter in the trees outside her window. In her hands she held a small alarm clock to time the pains that gripped her abdomen. No one had to tell her that labor had begun. She was filled with both bubbling excitement and overwhelming sadness. Before the sun set again, her child would be born. Most women would be jubilant. For her, these were the last few hours she'd ever be able to spend with her baby.

"Hush, little baby, don't say a word. Mama's gonna buy you a mockingbird." She sang to her baby in the gray light of early morning, cradling her belly in her arms as the tears flowed down her cheeks and contractions hit in an increasingly steady pattern. When the morning bell rang at six o'clock, her contractions were five minutes apart.

She rose with aching slowness and carefully made her way to the large communal bathroom on the floor. The other girls had been watching her closely all week and there were hushed whispers as she made her way into the shower. She didn't want to tell anyone what was happening, not yet. There was so little time left. The hot water felt glorious on her back where a dull ache was pressing hard and low. She placed her palms against the tile and leaned forward, allowing the precious hot water to hit and massage the small of her back, not caring if she was using up more than her allotted amount of hot water. Just this once…

"Jilly, hurry up in there! You'll be late for mass."

"Go on without me," she said, opening the door. She was wrapped in her terry robe. "I'm staying here."

"But you'll get in trouble." This came from Pat who,

along with Nancy and Julie, had been watching her suspiciously all morning.

"I think it's a bit late for that."

"Do you want me to get Sister Celestine?" asked Julie, a kindly girl of sixteen due to deliver twins the following month. Her room was next door to Julie's and they'd become friends.

"No! Please don't. Don't tell anyone!" she begged. "I'm not ready to go to the hospital. It's not time yet. I know. I learned all about this from Sister Benedict, really."

Julie, who was currently taking those classes, looked unconvinced. "Okay, but I'll stay with you, just in case. Oh, don't look at me like that. So Sister Celestine will get angry with both of us. What else is new? I'm not going to leave you here. You've got that look."

"What look is that?"

"The same look my dog had when she began sniffing closets and corners to drop her litter. How far apart are your contractions?"

"Oh, God," whispered Nancy with fear. "Contractions?"

"Oh, I don't know, not too close," Jilly lied. Then she doubled over, her eyes closed, and released a muffled wail as her first serious, wholloping contraction hit.

"Oh, God," Nancy whined again.

"Uh-huh," said Julie, nodding her head. "Nancy, you'd better get Sister Celestine. I'm sorry, Jilly, but you know we have to. You may not want to admit it, but you're having a baby."

So much happened so quickly in the next few hours Jilly could only remember it as a blur of quick movements and sounds. The rustle of Sister Celestine's billowing habit and the clicking of her long, wooden rosary beads, the wailing siren of the careening ambulance, the glaring brightness of the emergency room light, the harsh tone of the admitting nurse telling another, "She's one of those Marian House girls."

It was a busy night at the hospital and the labor rooms were full. The nurses were harassed and muttering something about a full moon. Jilly cringed and thought it must be true because all around her women were howling at it. She tried to relax, to smile and cooperate, but at every turn cold looks and even colder hands met her. Sister Benedict had told her that she'd be well taken care of at the hospital by a professional and courteous staff. Perhaps they were that to the married women who came in with their husbands, but at every phase she was treated as something expendable, the indigent case they didn't have to be nice to.

She lay alone in the labor room for uncounted hours, terrified. Only two people inhabited her world: herself and her baby. *Endure. Pray,* she repeated to herself. By late afternoon the pains that gripped her abdomen escalated quickly, coming hard and fast. Jilly tried not to cry out, digging her heels down and gritting her teeth. She swore she'd salvage some shred of dignity. Then a huge wave of pain swelled over her, then another one right behind, not giving her time to regroup. "Will somebody help me?" she cried out.

The staff moved quickly, wheeling her to a room where bright overhead lights and medical equipment of stainless steel surrounded her. The nurses strapped her arms and hoisted her useless legs high into the stirrups. Jilly was terrified, numb and shackled.

"The baby's crowning," the nurse called out.

Instantly, the room was charged. Perhaps the nurse at her side got swept up in the excitement, or perhaps she had a moment's sympathy, but she pointed to a small mirror behind the doctor's back and said close to Jilly's ear, "You can look in there if you want to watch."

Jilly startled, whipping her head around to follow the pointing finger. "What? See the baby?"

Euphoria and gratitude swirled within her, tumbling in her mind with the strict warnings of Sister Benedict—*Do not look at the baby!* Driven by the need to see her child, Jilly pushed herself up onto her elbows, straining her neck and squinting into a small circular mirror over the doctor's shoulder.

"One more push," the doctor said, guiding the baby's head with his gloved hands.

She took a deep breath, felt the cresting of a wave and pushed. Again and again. Dots swam before her eyes, her elbows shook against the table and she felt she could not keep herself up a second longer. Yet pure determination kept her focus on that six-inch span of reflected glass.

In Dr. Brewster's hands lay a slippery, purply-pink, pug-faced, bloody bundle that was the most beautiful thing she had ever seen. She flopped back onto the table, smiling, foolishly happy. *Her baby.* Eagerly, she watched every movement the doctor made, mentally devouring every detail of her child. He held her baby up and she saw itty-bitty toes, fingers, a nose, a chin and puffy eyes. She heard a gentle slap, then a lusty wail.

The nurses worked quickly, putting drops in the baby's eyes, washing and weighing it, then wrapping the baby in a thin cloth. Jilly flexed her fingers at her side. She desperately wanted to hold her baby, feel the soft, tender skin. It was a need that came from deep within. "Please," she murmured, struggling to reach out.

In a flash she realized that the nurse was taking the baby away. Her breath froze in her chest. That couldn't be happening. She strained against the leather straps. "No...no please...stop!" Her voice cracked. Her uterus contracted. Her throat burned with choked cries as she saw her baby disappear behind the closed door forever.

She had had a girl.

* * *

For years to come, Jilly would often hear stories of delivery room travails while sitting with other women. Whether they were young mothers or older grandmothers, if the topic of childbirth was broached the women would circle around in the upholstered chairs of living rooms or on the hard wood of barroom stools like old soldiers and share war stories. If she was noticed sitting silently, one of them would inevitably tilt her head, pat Jilly's hand and say some equivalent of "Don't worry, you'll know all about this someday." Jilly always smiled politely and shrugged indifferently.

She did know, though. She was a casualty of that war. For her, there was no ultimate triumph, only terror and unspeakable loss. Lying in the darkness of her small, cell-like hospital recovery room while the rain pattered outside her single window, Jilly sobbed relentlessly. A maelstrom of tears gushed until she felt shriveled and depleted, without a teardrop left in her. Then the drizzle of depression soaked straight through to her bones, bringing a real, physical ache.

By the time dawn broke, Jilly was lying flat and motionless on her back. She stared at the striated shadow lines across the ceiling, her hands resting on her empty belly, and came to the realization that she was alone. Without parents, sisters, friends or even the kindness of a stranger to comfort her. No one could take away the pain she felt in her heart or understand what it took for her to make the decision to give up her child. She'd had to do this alone. There was only herself to rely on, her own abilities, her own wits.

As she cleansed her tender skin with witch hazel and dressed for her return to Marian House, she felt a lifeless calm that the social worker interpreted as resignation. The truth was, the Jillian she once was had washed out with the tears. Having given birth to a child, she could never go back to being a child herself.

Walking from the hospital out to the sweet spring air of

rural Wisconsin, Jilly left a part of herself behind. The very best of herself remained with her daughter. And walking away from her daughter was the very best thing she could do for her.

What kind of a mother could she be to this child? What kind of example would she set for her? What could she offer her? Sister Celestine was right. If she loved this baby, she would give it a good and decent home with the right kind of parents. What her mother said about her was true: she was irresponsible, promiscuous, selfish.

But she had the chance now to make things right, at least for her daughter. She may have done a lot of things wrong, but the decision to give up her child would be the one responsible, unselfish act of her life. It was the best thing she'd ever done. But it felt like the worst.

Jilly stood outside the hospital and, drained but resolute, stared up at the nursery windows for the last time. She felt a tangible tie to Baby Girl Season sleeping there even though she'd never held her child in her arms, touched her skin or kissed her cheek.

"Be strong, my baby girl. Be happy. You *will* survive."

And so, she vowed, would she.

Eight

⮞⮞⮞◆⬥◆⬥◆◆◆⬥◆⬥◆⬥

The morning after the funeral Rose woke early. Her heart felt ready to receive the morning light and obliterate the darkness of the night before. How incredible that one letter from someone she'd never even met could make such a marked change in her life. With the sun on her cheeks, she felt the dawning of hope.

She slipped into a long black skirt and a gray sweater, worn and comfortable from years of use, then walked through the hall, descended the great wide staircase and made her way into the kitchen. She moved as a dancer would through a well-rehearsed routine, surefooted, smooth and moving to an inner music. She pulled out her largest ceramic bowls, bins of oat flakes, raisins, nuts and small jars of cinnamon and other spices from the pantry. There was nothing like a bowl of her own special, healthy granola to give the day a good start.

Mixing the ingredients, she thought how Jilly had looked shell-shocked when she went to bed the night before. And Birdie was definitely off-kilter, snapping at Hannah and Dennis. As though in retaliation, Hannah had seconds, even thirds, of the cakes at the funeral. Well, at least while they were here, she would see that they all ate good food.

She added extra cinnamon for Hannah, then stirred the cereal and poured it into big stoneware baking dishes. After fifteen minutes the whole kitchen smelled of cinnamon baking in the oven. Her eyes looked up toward the ceiling as she heard the thump of feet walking across the floor. She smiled, thinking today was fresh and new.

She couldn't wait for her sisters to come for breakfast.

Birdie awoke sick. She felt the world spinning as soon as she sat up and her stomach seemed to leap to her throat. Her groan brought a stir from Dennis beside her.

"Wha—" He blinked heavily, raising his head, half-awake. "Are you okay?"

"No. Ugh. I must have eaten something bad. Oh, God, what's that smell? What's Rose baking down there? I think I'm going to be sick...." She put her palm on her forehead and waited several minutes till the pumping in her stomach subsided.

"How're you doing?" Dennis asked, his eyes closed.

"I'm a little better," she replied. "I could use a cracker or something dry. How about you? Are you sick?" She didn't know why misery loved company, but there it was.

Dennis mopped his face and sat up on his elbows. After a minute he replied, "Nope."

"I hope it's not the flu. I don't have time to be sick."

"You never do. Where are you going? The funeral's over. Come back to bed and rest."

Birdie was already rising, slipping into her chenille robe. "I won't give in to it. I'll just dress and have some weak tea and toast and then we'll see how I feel. Besides, Rose is downstairs already, probably cooking up a five-course meal. She always knocks herself out."

"That's Rose. Always doing for others."

"She needs a rest or she'll crack."

"So will you. Stay with me, Birdie, come back to bed...."

She ignored his hand that reached out for her. "I'll bring you coffee...." Slipping her feet into slippers, she hurried out the door. Even after the spats of yesterday and with her stomach spinning this morning, she felt a tangible pull to hurry downstairs to the kitchen.

She wanted to be with her sisters.

Jilly woke up groggy. She'd lain in a stuperous state for hours, watching the light of dawn change on the blue wallpaper. The memories had left her feeling vulnerable, as though she'd just given birth all over again, except this time she was coming home and everyone knew she had delivered a baby. When she walked downstairs this morning, she realized with both horror and relief, everything would be different.

The secret was out.

After all these years, what did honesty feel like? she wondered, wiping the sleep from her eyes. Did Birdie and Rose have any idea how much she needed them right now? She felt the stirrings of the devotion she felt for her sisters as a child, when they were playmates and Birdie and Rose were her very best friends. It had been so long since she allowed herself this connection and she felt wary. She had changed over the years. And so, she knew, had they. But they were sisters. Bound by blood and history.

She sniffed, catching the scent of cinnamon and coffee in the air. Hunger for food, for coffee, for life, growled within her. Rising from the bed, she wrapped herself in her lavender silk robe, pulled her wild hair back with an elastic and went to the bathroom to splash cold water on her face. Despite the lack of sleep, she felt lighter, younger, and not the least bit tired. She followed the sound of clanking dishes and soft chatter down the stairs. She was a bit nervous about facing them, but pushed open the door and walked into the room.

She couldn't wait to see her sisters.

* * *

She found them in the kitchen, laying the table. Birdie and Rose each had hold of an end of a lovely robin's-egg-blue tablecloth and were spreading it out over the long wood table. The mood was chummy and they were chatting without a trace of the tension that had permeated the air the day before. Jilly stood at the door, hesitant.

Birdie spied her first. Her face revealed caution, followed by a searching glance. Then, seeing the openness of Jilly's expression, her face broke into a warm smile without restraint.

"I don't believe it. Look who's up."

Rose hurried to fetch coffee. "Good morning!"

Jilly felt a tremendous relief that no one was going to dive into angst while the sun was still rising. She also felt a bit sheepish and looked at her coffee, the table, anywhere but her sisters' eyes. "Yes, I'm up," she replied with bluster. "Me and the birds. If you can't lick 'em, join 'em."

And Jilly did join right in, fetching tableware from the cupboards. Rose went to bring out the freshly baked granola while Birdie set large earthenware bowls. They readily fell into the old, comforting habits of childhood. Then, while they ate, Birdie brought them up to speed on the estate.

"Mr. Collins wants us to inform him of what to do with the house and estate by Thursday. Let's just table those decisions for the day to give us a little more time to think. Agreed?"

The others nodded their heads, relieved.

"The big job now is to divvy up the household between us. The furniture, paintings, and all the china, crystal and silver. The house is jam-packed with stuff. Mother was a first-class pack rat. But before we do that, we have to catalog what's here. I shiver to think of the attic and basement."

"The attic is full of treasures," said Rose, quick to rise to the defense. "I don't want to throw any of it out."

"Rose, we all know Mother isn't the only one who's a pack rat," Birdie said teasingly.

"Let's just agree not to throw anything away unless we all agree."

"It will take forever that way."

"Then I'll do it myself."

"Hold on," Jilly said, holding up her palm. "Let's start with the top and work our way down. We can make decisions as we go. All together."

A short while later, Jilly stood in the dusty, dimly lit third floor with her mouth agape. It was worse than she could possibly have imagined. The place was imploding. The roof showed signs of sagging and waterstains on boxes, walls and floors revealed numerous leaks. The windowpanes were rotting, the glass was cracked in places and the whole place, smelled of dust, mold and mouse droppings.

This had once been their playground. These rooms were the glorious dominion of the Upper Kingdom where the royal Season sisters ruled. To see the untidy shambles coated with gloom and spiderwebs cast a harsh reality over what was once the realm of the imagination.

The third floor of the large Victorian house had originally been designed as the maids' quarters. There were two cramped bedrooms with pitched ceilings, another slightly larger room that was once presumably a sitting room, and a single, small bathroom with an ancient, yellow-stained tub and sink fit for midgets. The girls had loved these rooms when they were younger because they were somehow separate from the domain of their parents. Undecorated, unspoken for—theirs for the taking. And they took them, claiming rooms and creating make-believe villages. Until their mother chased them out, furious that they'd foraged through all her storage boxes searching for choice items they could use for their pretend "houses."

"It looks like a rabbit's warren," said Birdie, coming up from behind, her arms filled with supplies.

Jilly couldn't deny it. Narrow paths between boxes stacked from floor to ceiling were the only way one could maneuver through the low-ceilinged rooms. What was most daunting, however, was that it wasn't an organized mess. Everything appeared to have been tossed up there willy-nilly. It was a great, giant kitchen drawer full of junk.

"We'll never live long enough to get through it all," said Jilly, aghast. "It's like the deep Congo in here. They'll find our bodies someday, after a long, arduous search. We'll be in some stage of decay, our bones reaching into the boxes."

"I say we should just get one of those enormous Dumpsters, open up the windows and pump ship." Birdie's face was set.

"Don't you dare!" Rose called out, rushing up the stairs.

"Look at this mess!" Birdie opened a plastic bag filled with nothing but wire hangers. "This is what I'm talking about. What in God's name were you saving hundreds of wire hangers for? And old magazines? There must be hundreds of *Good Housekeeping*." She picked one up, leafed through it, then tossed it into the bag with a flip of the wrist. "Just what we need, another recipe for Velveeta."

"I meant to take them for recycling," said Rose.

Birdie rolled up her sleeves, a woman on a mission. "Yeah, well, I'll recycle them, all right." She pushed her way through the path to the other rooms. "It's not so bad here," she called out from a bedroom. "I think the worst of it is right by the door. Let's start back here where there's room to move."

"That's Rose's castle," Jilly called out.

"What?" Birdie poked her head around the corner.

"Rose's castle, remember? And that room over there was yours. Mine was the big room, of course. The Castle of Splendor, I recall."

Rose's face became dreamy. Jilly could feel the memories flutter back by watching the expressions on her face.

"See what I mean?" Rose said with heart, seeking an ally. "There are so many memories up here. I don't want Birdie to toss them all out as garbage. She has a one-track mind."

Jilly wanted to tell her that the garbage dump might be the appropriate place for them, but refrained. "Don't look so worried, Rose," she said reassuringly. "We don't need to make any big decisions today. Birdie's right, though. We'll keep what we can, but be prepared to dump stuff like hangers and magazines. I don't intend to spend weeks at this chore. We've got to clear it out and we simply can't keep everything."

They donned aprons, opened plastic garbage bags, set aside twine and scissors and set to work. They chatted companionably while they opened dozens of boxes, groaning when they found old bank records starting from twenty years back, two leather-bound sets of the Encyclopaedia Britannica, old books falling from their covers, framed pictures of the dime-store variety, dusty, plastic Christmas poinsettias and wreaths, and countless odd dishes, platters and bowls, none of them making a single matched set. In another room there was an old pram, miscellaneous tools none of them wanted, rusty silver toasters and other old appliances with frayed cords and missing parts, bags of rolled wire, and their old skis and ice skates.

Hours later, exhaustion got the best of their enthusiasm.

"Where is that Dumpster?" Birdie groaned.

"Look at me," Jilly complained, staring down at herself. "In filthy jeans and a sweatshirt. Me! And my mani-cure...ruined."

"I've never seen such a collection of worthless junk in all my life," grumbled Birdie.

Rose's head jerked up.

"No, Rose!" Jilly exclaimed, holding up her hand against

Rose's protest and taking sides with Birdie. "Don't even say it. We don't want to hear it. It's all junk!"

In the larger room, however, they found more personal items. Treasures, Rose called them. There were large boxes in which their artwork, papers and report cards from kindergarten onward were packed away. In others, old family photographs had been carelessly tossed, many of them dating back generations, their sepia-toned edges curling. They found boxes filled with their old baby clothes, and more with toddler dresses with frills and pinafores. They howled when they found Jilly's clarinet, Birdie's flute and Rose's ballet slippers.

They sipped iced tea and shared quips, comments and memories. As the afternoon sun waned, however, Jilly felt her old restlessness overtake her. History mingled with the dust and grime to thicken the atmosphere. The rooms were feeling too close and she was desperate for some fresh air. Glancing over her shoulder, she noticed Rose and Birdie sitting shoulder to shoulder, browsing through photo after photo with expressions of nostalgic pleasure on their faces. Fidgety, she rose to her feet, eager to be done and out of there.

"Okay, that's enough for me," she burst out when Birdie and Rose giggled over another photograph. "I'm exhausted, dirty, and I want a glass of wine and a hot bath. Let's just toss this junk and finish up."

"Rose was right," Birdie said with a lazy smile. "There are treasures in here. Look at this one," she said with a light laugh. She lifted a photograph of the three of them in their Easter dresses. "Your hair is in a flip with one of those little bows pinned in front. And Rose, you've lost your front teeth!"

Resting her chin on Birdie's shoulder, Rose chuckled and said, "Look who's talking. You're scowling again! In every picture!"

"What a motley crew we were," Birdie replied, but her

voice was filled with affection. "I'd like Hannah to see these. They're her heritage."

"Fine," Jilly snapped. "Then keep them. All of them. Toss them in the box and take them home. But can we just keep moving on? This is taking forever."

"Jilly, don't you want any pictures?" Rose asked.

"No. You keep them."

"Or your old school papers at least?"

She shook her head. "No. I don't want anything. There's no value in any of it."

Birdie's brows shot up.

"How can you say that?" Rose asked with unflagging patience. "These are records of our past."

Jilly took a deep breath and brought her fingertips to her temples. All these old family photographs, compounded by the memories of the previous night, had brought so much of her past whirling back to mind. And none of *those* incidents were included in this collection of their mother's selected memories.

"They're not the records of our past, that's the point. Look at the two of you, hovering over those photographs, laughing, as if there was something wonderful to remember. Treasures, you call them. It's all in your heads. There are no happy memories buried in that dust, only dear darling Mother's orchestrated memories."

"Oh, Jilly…" Birdie muttered with a wave of her hand, dismissing her.

"Don't do that," she snapped. Jilly was exhausted and Birdie had pushed the wrong emotional button. "Don't dismiss me. I'm the eldest, not you. I was there. And all I see when I look at those photographs are smiling faces because Dad told us to say cheese when he clicked the camera. It's all a facade. Mom loved to pretend downstairs every bit as much as we did up here. It was a game. A real and dangerous game of self-preservation and desperation. I covered for her drinking every day, pretending everything was normal. We all did, Dad included, and it makes me so goddamn angry to see all those photographs of the perfect American family. Here comes Judge Season and the four little Seasons!"

"Jilly, stop it!" said Rose.

"You dug up all the dirty little secrets yesterday, Rose. You can't go back now. Let's be honest. Where are the pictures that show what it was really like?"

Her sisters looked back at her, anxious and hesitant.

"Come on, don't shrink back now." She pointed to the box of photographs. "I'll bet you won't find a single snapshot in there of Mom toting a gin bottle around the house, or one of us sitting in front of the TV stuffing peanut butter sandwiches in our mouth after school because she didn't bother to pack us a lunch. Or one of Dad escaping out the back door to go to the office. Or of me sneaking out the bedroom window, or of Birdie swimming her heart out to win another prize for them, or of Rose knocking herself out around the house trying to please them. Aren't you angry?"

When they didn't respond she cried out, "Well, I am! I'm so damn angry, even after all these years. The hurt is still so fresh. What kind of a mother was she? She neglected her duties. She wasn't present, Birdie. She abandoned us. She—"

Jilly stopped abruptly, her own words sinking in with bruising intensity. *Not present...abandoned...* God help me, she thought as her face drained of color. I'm just like my mother. Looking at Birdie and Rose, she saw in their eyes that they understood she was thinking of her own child.

"I can't go into this," she said in a choked voice. "I just can't."

Rose's face crumpled. "It wasn't all like that and you know it."

"How do you know? Rose, look at the pictures!" Jilly went to grab a handful of photos from the box. She held them out to her. "You were so little. In this one you look about four years old, and in this one, what—two? Do you know why you think these photographs are your heritage? Because you don't remember what really happened. These pictures *are* your memories! And you know what? They're not real!"

Rose looked up, her hazel eyes full of hurt and reproach.

Jilly dropped the photographs into the box and walked to the corner of the room to lean against a tall box. "I'm sorry," she said, more calmly than she felt. What she felt was that the ceiling was falling down on her. "I didn't want to dredge all this muck back up. I've deliberately avoided thinking about any of this stuff for years, and believe me, it's the last thing I'd intended to get into when I came home. But you forced open Pandora's box, Rose. With Merry's letter. Now all the demons are released and I can't keep them from pouring out. I don't mean to hurt you, or you, Birdie. I don't want to hurt anyone. But it's obviously not settled in my mind because, it still hurts me."

"I didn't mean to hurt you, either," Rose said, her eyes filling.

Birdie opened her mouth, but shut it again. Her face looked older, tired. In the resulting thick silence, she picked up a handful of photographs and idly flipped through them. Then, intrigued, she grabbed another handful, and more quickly sorted through these. "Wait a minute," she said with a ring in her voice. Rising to her knees she began digging into the box. She scanned a dozen photographs, then went to the clothes boxes and sorted through them while her sisters watched. "I think there's a pattern here."

Jilly and Rose didn't reply, lost in their own thoughts.

"Yes, there's no question about it," Birdie continued. "Take a look, Rose. Jilly's right. All the photographs are of us when we were very young. All these things that Mom collected were from the early years back when Merry was still a baby."

"So what?" Jilly raked her hair from her face. She was dying for a cigarette.

"Jilly, don't you see?" Birdie straightened to face her. "Mom wasn't drinking then."

Jilly took a deep breath and put her hands on her hips. She didn't want to go where Birdie was leading.

"Look," Birdie urged, and held some photographs out. "These pictures...they *were* happy times."

Jilly didn't take them. "You're saying that she stopped saving and collecting all this stuff after she started drinking."

"Right." Birdie paused, letting the photos in her hand slip back into the box. "And she started drinking *after* Merry's accident."

There was a moment's pause as the words sunk in.

"I don't remember when exactly she started drinking," said Rose. "I just remember there was a happy period of time when I was little, then there's this blank when I don't remember hardly anything, and then I remember being older and her being drunk a lot. But it makes sense that she'd start drinking after Merry's accident."

"Makes sense that it's a blank period in your memory, too."

"That's so sad. Poor Mom. That explains it."

Jilly turned to look at Rose carefully. There was something in the way she moved, or maybe it was the dim light, but with her tiny frame and pale strawberry-blond hair, she looked so much like their mother just then. "Rose, we don't need to make excuses for her. Mom was an alcoholic."

"No she wasn't."

"Oh, no, here we go...."

"Jilly," said Birdie, her voice demanding, halting Jilly from walking off.

Jilly stopped and turned her head. Her face was impassive.

"I really don't want to go into another of one of our 'mom was an alcoholic' debates. We all know she drank like a fish and if some of you can't bear to give it a name—" she looked at Rose "—well, we each have to deal with it in our own way."

"Can we just drop it?" asked Birdie with urgency. "That's not the point, anyway. What I'm trying to show you is that you're wrong about *us*. We had a wonderful childhood. The best. Mom was there, fully present for us every day while we were young. You and I were the lucky ones, Jilly. We were in junior high when it happened. Rose was only six. I'm old enough to remember, and while I'm not denying it was hell when Mom started drinking, when I think of my childhood, I think of the early days. Come on, Jilly, when we came up here you remembered the make-believe we use to play here. You can't deny those weren't some of the best days of our lives."

"And you're wrong, Jilly. I *do* remember," Rose declared, her eyes flashing. "Like they happened yesterday. I remember all the games."

"Like this one?" Birdie held out a photograph for them to see. In it, smiling, tanned Jilly, Birdie and Rose were shoulder-deep in the pool, all wearing dime-store tiaras and bright red lipstick. They were posing dramatically, clinging to the metal ladder, their legs held out like fins. Above them on the terrace stood two-year-old Merry, also wearing a tiara in her soft red ringlets. She was arching on tiptoe, her chubby fingers grasping either side of the pool's ladder and smiling with red lips as bright as the summer sun overhead.

Jilly stared at the photograph. "Mermaids," she murmured, immediately sucked in.

"That was my favorite game," said Rose with a bittersweet smile, reaching up to take the picture. She studied the photograph as though imprinting it into her brain.

"It was everyone's favorite," replied Birdie.

"Merry sure was cute," Jilly said, lowering herself to her haunches to look over Rose's shoulder. She gave a short laugh. "A real show-stealer. When was this taken?" she asked, but in her heart, she knew.

"She's got to be two years old," Birdie replied. "So it would be the summer of the accident."

Before the accident. The thought floated in the air.

Jilly rose to stand and walked to the window, wrapping her arms tight around her. The glass was grimy and cracked, fitting for this view of the outline of the swimming pool. In her mind she saw a macabre collage: floating white limbs, streaming red hair, wavy blue water. In her ears she heard birdcalls that changed to a high, young girl's voice calling her name. *Jilly! Jilly! Help!*

"Look at her eyes," Birdie said with a thick voice. "You can just tell she's excited to be playing with us."

"Her greatest thrill was being one of the Four Seasons," Rose said. "She always referred to us as that. I think it made her feel connected to us." She shrugged her shoulders. "You heard her say it on the video."

"Do you think Mom packed away the tiaras?" Jilly turned from the window to face them again. "*That* I'd like to have." Her eyes rolled upward and she spread out her arms and said with a slight, dramatic bow, "A final tribute to my youth."

"Most likely she buried them when she had the pool filled in with dirt," said Birdie.

Jilly felt a quick stab in her gut at the image of the big truck dumping load after load of soil into the pit of the pool, burying the memory of the accident. After a few breaths the pain subsided. Rubbing her stomach, she joined them again on the floor. She reached for the photograph of the mermaids with a sigh of resignation and looked at it again, long and intently.

"This was the end, you know," she said after a while.

"The end of what?"

"The end of our childhood. The last game." She looked at Birdie, then at Rose, her eyes narrowed under one raised brow. They didn't reply but she could tell that they understood her meaning.

"I never think of it," Rose said in a soft voice.

After a short silence Birdie said, "Me, neither, but maybe we should. Maybe we should talk about it. Don't you think it's time?"

"No," Jilly replied curtly. "There's nothing to be gained. The past is past. Let it lie."

"But it isn't past," Rose argued. "That's the problem."

"A minute ago you told us that we were afraid to look at the way things really were, and now you're telling us to let the past lie. So which is it?" asked Birdie.

Jilly shook her head and raised her hands. "I don't know. I don't know and I don't care! I mean, shit! How much guilt do you expect me to deal with in one weekend?" She dropped her hands in a machete-like sweep. "I'm out of here." She tossed the photograph at Rose, swooped to her feet and almost ran out of the small room.

"Jilly!" Rose scrambled to her feet. "Wait! It's not just *your* guilt," she called after her. "Do you think you're the only one who feels responsible for what happened to Merry?" She stood at the top of the stairs, calling after Jilly who was pounding down them. "This happened to all of us. Look at the photograph. We were all in the pool. All four of us!"

Jilly didn't slow down, disappearing around the corner. Rose turned to Birdie, her face pinched, and asked plaintively, "Why does she always do that?"

"Do what?" Birdie felt weary and coated with grime and memories.

"Run away."

Birdie shrugged sadly, then lugged herself up from the floor. "Let's go find her."

They looked in Jilly's room, but she wasn't there. Nor was she in the living room, the dining room or the kitchen. But Hannah, who was snacking on leftover cake, told them she saw her aunt Jilly head for the basement.

"Of course," Birdie said as they made their way there. "She went to the Lower Kingdom."

"My God, I haven't heard that expression in forever."

When they were children, they'd created worlds of the attic and the basement. With a child's simple clarity, they saw the world divided into two classes: the rich and the poor. So they'd created the Upper Kingdom in the attic where the royalty reigned in light and splendor. And in the basement, the Lower Kingdom, where the poor and desolate survived.

"I always liked the Lower Kingdom better," Rose said.

"Me, too. It was much more fun starving and begging for food than being royalty. Remember the chamois rag I used for my shawl?"

"Remember it? I coveted that chamois. And it wasn't yours," she said, her eyes teasing. "It was Jilly's." Before they opened the door to the basement, Rose paused to ask, "Do you think we should bother her? She's been hit with a lot. Maybe she needs time alone."

"It's time to hit her with a lot," Birdie said with a look of fierce determination on her face that Rose was accustomed to. "You're right that Jilly always runs away. But as long as she does, she'll never deal with the issues and they'll just continue to haunt her. Why do you think she's been married three times? It's not unusual for women who've given up a child to have rocky relationships. We can't solve her problems, but we can at least try to force her to ask the questions. She needs help, professional help. She went through that whole experience without a single word of counseling. That's what haunts me. And God only knows what she went through as a young girl alone in France." She shook her head. "I don't know if I'd have been that strong."

"But let's be gentle," Rose cautioned.

"You forget, I love her, too."

"No, of course I haven't forgotten." Then, turning to open the door, she added, "But you can be pretty forceful, Birdie. I just don't want to see Jilly hit with a Mack truck."

Chastened, Birdie said, "I'll be good."

They found Jilly leaning against one of the steel poles in the basement, an unlit cigarette in her mouth. The cavernous, damp basement was depressingly dim. A Ping-Pong table was covered with boxes, and old tools and appliances lined the cement walls. They approached slowly, Rose tugging at her hair, Birdie tucking her hands in the rear pockets of her jeans.

Jilly saw them coming and slid down the pole in defeat.

"Mom, what are you guys doing down there?" Hannah called down from the top of the basement stairs.

"Just talking," Birdie called back.

Hannah took a few steps down the stairs.

"Go on back up," Birdie called. It was an order. "We're talking privately."

Jilly saw the tips of Hannah's clunky black shoes and frayed jeans on the stair stop hesitatingly. The shoes turned around and she heard a heavy, angry pound as Hannah stomped away, slamming the basement door behind her.

"She could have come down," Jilly said gently.

"No. We need to talk without kids around."

Jilly felt hounded and looked longingly at the stairs. "I'm about talked out."

"I know, but we didn't like the way that ended upstairs," Rose said, stepping closer, then plopping down on the floor beside Jilly.

"No big deal." Jilly's face was closed.

Birdie came to join them on the floor.

It seemed there was nowhere for Jilly to hide. They were

determined to have this out and her butt was getting cold on the hard, damp cement. She fingered her cigarette.

"Go ahead and light up," Rose said with a flip of her palm. "I only said 'no smoking' when Merry was alive because of her lungs and all. It doesn't matter now."

"Are you sure?" Jilly asked, but she was already pulling out her matches.

"They'll kill you someday," Birdie warned.

"Yeah, so?" She lit up and inhaled deeply, feeling better the moment she felt the burn of smoke snake down her throat. She exhaled lustily, not missing the disgusted expressions on their faces. She could not begin to explain to them why it didn't matter to her in the least what happened to her lungs, her body, her life. She was old and washed up, anyway, filled with a darkness that was more insidious than any cancer could ever be.

"Well," Jilly said, looking around. "Since we're here in the Lower Kingdom, I believe it's time for suffering and angst."

"Why does it all seem so sad now?" Rose asked. "Playing here was so happy. I lost myself in the game. The little villages we made seemed so real, I never wanted to leave. I remember I used to cry when Mom called us upstairs."

"Maybe it feels sad because we know those days are over," Birdie replied. "Do you know what I remember the most? The confidence. And the optimism. I really believed I could do anything I wanted." She took from her pocket the photograph of the four of them as mermaids by the pool. She looked at it for a while then said, "What happened to us? We were so full of dreams and imagination. We're not the same girls we were then."

Jilly laughed and shook her head. "I'm definitely not."

"We *are* the same people," Rose said. "We've just lost the girls somewhere deep inside of us. We're remembering things none of us have even thought of in thirty years. This

is exactly what I wanted to happen while we were all together. Jilly, Birdie, don't you see? This is what Merry
wanted, too. For us to remember. To bring us back to our
childhood. It's ironic, isn't it, that she never left hers and she
was so happy. I think that's what this search for Spring is
really all about.''

Jilly stretched out her long legs, crossing them at the ankle.
Birdie's face sagged at the jowls. Rose neatly sat on her
knees, attentive, rather like a Japanese geisha.

"We should do it," Rose said.

"Do what?" Jilly asked, looking up sharply.

"Find Spring."

"Oh, come on…" Jilly moved to snuff out her cigarette
with jabbing strokes.

"We've gone over this," said Birdie wearily.

Rose took the photograph of the mermaids from Birdie and
held it out to them. "It was her last request."

"No." Jilly's voice was cold.

"Rose, let it go."

"We *owe* her."

Jilly and Birdie both silenced.

"We owe it to her to do this one thing," Rose continued,
stronger now. "Each of us, for our own reason. Merry never
blamed us for what happened, never did anything but love
us all her life and she never, ever asked anything of us before.''

Jilly suddenly felt a little breathless. Her heart was beating
like a rabbit's.

"You didn't know Merry like I did," Rose continued in
a gentler voice. "That's too bad, really. I don't mean that as
a criticism, but as a point of fact. Jilly, you left at eighteen
and really never came back. You only knew her as some
perpetual little girl that you loved from a distance. Birdie,
you managed the finances and fielded the medical questions,
but you never came just to chat with her, to get to know who

Merry was as a person. You saw her as a responsibility. Maybe you both were afraid to find out who she was. You only saw her as the woman she never became.

"I know everyone talks about how much I've given up to take care of her, but it wasn't like that. Not at all. She was gentle and sweet and a real hoot sometimes. Did you know she was a natural in the garden? She could make anything grow. And she loved to put out food for the birds and listed over two dozen different species she'd spotted right here in the yard. Merry was so curious about so many things. Most of all, she loved with all her heart. Merry would just sit and listen to me talk about anything, no matter how I went on and on. She'd know when I was sad and be cheery for me. And she loved to play games, all kinds of games. Oh, I can go on and on. There's so much I can tell you about her.... I'd like to tell you. When you know her better, maybe you'll understand her request."

"Maybe you're right, Rose. Maybe I *do* need to do this," Birdie said quietly. "I've been unhappy for a long time and I don't even know why. When I think about all the dreams I had growing up, how excited I was to wake up every morning... I miss that girl, you know? I want to be her again. I need to find her again. And I think maybe you were right, too, Jilly." She took the photograph and looked at it again. Four young girls were beaming with joy and confidence. "Maybe this *was* the end of our childhood. But maybe by doing this for Merry, we can rediscover it." She shook her head and squeezed her eyes shut in a pained expression. "God knows, I've got to try something."

"I need to do it because it was Merry's last request," explained Rose.

"I can't," Jilly whispered, feeling cornered.

Birdie opened her eyes. "You don't have to. No one wants you to be unhappy. We'll find Spring and deliver the time capsule."

"No." Her fear made her voice firm. "I don't want you or anyone else searching for this child. Is that clear? Spring isn't some idealistic concept. She's not even a baby anymore. Spring, or whatever her name is, is a real person. An adult with a life of her own. We can't just go track her down and barge into her life. Maybe she doesn't want to be found. Have you thought of that?"

"We won't force it. We could just gather some information and make a decision later. We don't even have to meet her."

"It could take years to track her down."

"Then we'll search for years."

"I haven't the first clue where to begin," Jilly said, hunted. "I don't remember any names."

"That's the easy part," Birdie countered. "Those are just details, Jilly. The hard part is saying yes."

"Please say yes, Jilly," pleaded Rose. "We'll search together. The three of us. We'll be there for you, won't we, Birdie?"

"Every step of the way."

If she'd known what they were going to do, she never would have come back.

And yet, in her heart came the whispering that that wasn't totally true. She'd always harbored in the most secret pocket of her mind the hope that someday she'd see her daughter again. Not meet her, that would be expecting too much. But just to see her child again, grown up. Yes, she was curious. Beyond that she wouldn't even dream.

She opened her mouth, "yes" poised on her lips, then shook her head and climbed to her feet. "No. Please don't ask me. I can't do it. It's over."

Late that evening, Jilly sat on her bed, knees to her chest, a blanket wrapped around her, looking out the window at the yard. The room was dark. The moon, round and bright, cast its spell on the garden below. Bits of leftover snow looked like islands in the sea of dark mud and grass. Beyond lay the rectangle of sidewalk that surrounded the filled-in pool. When she heard the soft knock on her door, she rested her chin on her knees and called out, "It's open."

She heard the door squeak and Rose's voice, soft and tentative. "Can I come in?"

"Sure." She didn't turn her head. She heard Rose's footfall across the floor, then felt her weight on the mattress as she sat on the bed and moved closer.

"You didn't come down for dinner. I was worried about you."

"I wasn't very hungry."

They sat together for a while, not speaking, just staring out into the yard. Eventually, when the mood was right, Rose spoke.

"I'm sorry, Jilly. We shouldn't have pushed you that way. We didn't mean to upset you. We'll do whatever you decide. You matter more than anything else to us."

Jilly rested her forehead on her knees and fought back the tears, undone by kindness. She felt Rose's hand on her knee, a silent comfort that abolished the enormous loneliness she'd been feeling. "I'm not blaming anyone," Jilly began. "Except maybe myself. You don't know what you're asking me to do. How could you? Maybe if we'd talked about it years ago, when I came home from Marion House, everything would've been different. There wouldn't have been all those secrets and maybe I wouldn't have gone away." She shrugged. "But that's not the way it was. You have no idea how hurt I was. I felt that everyone wanted me out of their lives."

"No, Jilly! We didn't want you to go. We didn't know what was going on."

"I know, I know. I knew it then, but it didn't stop the hurt." Jilly turned her head to look out at the garden in the moonlight. "You know what I was doing when you knocked on the door? I was looking out there remembering what it was like when I was about thirteen." She rested her chin back on her knees. "One of my favorite things in the summer was to lie up here in front of the window and just feel the breeze against my skin and watch the bats swoop down to skim the water in the pool. It was so peaceful. Used to make me sleepy. Birdie was right. Those were great days. Whenever I think of them I feel a longing that aches right here." She pointed to her chest. "I was so…" She searched for the word. "Content. That's the last time I can remember feeling that way. After that summer I went a little wild, you know?" She turned to face her sister. Rose was listening without speaking. Jilly liked that about her. She knew when to be quiet.

"Maybe not a little. A lot wild." She turned away again. "I ruined it, you know? I ruined it for everyone."

"That's a lot of blame to take on your own shoulders."

"Yep."

"You just told me that you don't blame us. Jilly, you have to stop blaming yourself. It was a long time ago. You were so young. Let it go."

"How can I when you want me to go on this search and dig it all up again? I've been thinking and thinking about it and I don't think I should find her. I'll only mess up her life like I've messed up my own. Besides, she's lucky I gave her up. I'm not the mother type. I'm not responsible. I'm not dependable. I'm not—"

"Stop beating yourself up! Yes, you put your child up for adoption but you did it for all the right reasons. You say yourself you didn't have the support you needed. What choice did you have? You were a child making an adult's decision. You did the best that you could. But now you deserve to forgive yourself."

"Maybe she hasn't forgiven me."

"Maybe she doesn't think there's anything to forgive."

To Jilly's surprise, her eyes filled with tears that overflowed and trickled down her cheeks. Alone with Rose, in the dark, she allowed them to fall unchecked. Her sister sat beside her, silent. "I'm afraid, Rose," she confessed. "When I think of having to contact this child—this woman—I feel a huge, gaping gulf of fear that I just can't get past. I'm terrified of going back there."

"If you don't go back and clean up the issues you left unresolved, you'll be stuck dealing with the past forever."

Jilly took a shuddering breath. "What should I do, Rose?"

Rose took her hand and offered a reassuring smile. "What do you want to do?"

"I want to come home." The words slipped out without thought.

"Oh, Jilly." Rose leaned forward then and put her arms around her.

Jilly hadn't realized how much she needed to feel that just now. She felt safe. She wanted to feel again the blissful, innocent peace of that sweet summer when she was content with the world and who she was in it. To feel that way again would be worth all it took, and it was going to take a lot.

Jilly saw that gulf of fear and denial spread out before her and knew she had to go through her past to get over it. She grabbed Rose's hand, closed her eyes, took a breath and, feeling like she was jumping off the cliff, exhaled her answer.

"Yes."

Nine

Dear DannyBoy,

So much has happened in the past twenty-four hours. I don't know where to begin. I suppose what's most important is that my sisters and I are beginning to talk, really talk. It's like the Walls of Jericho are tumbling down! After one pretty tough session, we all agreed to search for my sister's child that was given up for adoption. It was my late sister Merry's last request. We're beginning the search as soon as we get organized and pack up.

The other decision we have to make concerns the sale of this house. I know my sisters are being cautious so as not to hurt my feelings. I appreciate that more than I can say.

I'm so torn about the house. I've lived in it all my life. I hate leaving it. You see, I stayed home from college to take care of my mother who was ill and my sister who suffered brain damage as a child. Someone had to—and I wanted to. Anyway, I never asked for the house, but to be totally honest, I wanted it. I deserved it. After all, my staying home freed my older sisters to go off and forge lives of their own. Jilly, my oldest sister, was a high-fashion model in Europe. She was even in a spaghetti western with Clint Eastwood. (Not one of his famous ones, but still pretty exciting.) Birdie went to medical school, got married and started a family of her own.

No one asked me to stay home, but who else was there? I couldn't put my sister in an institution. I couldn't live with myself if I did.

I don't know why, but I can admit the truth to you. In retrospect I see that another reason I stayed was because I slipped into the decision. It wasn't something I weighed or considered, or even really wanted. But now I have the choice to change my life. I can decide what to do next. And oddly enough, I don't want the house. It's too big, too old, too expensive, too laden with memories, both good and bad. I feel the need to start fresh.

But I'm afraid. I don't really have anywhere to go to. I don't have any particular skills. I suppose I could hire myself out as a companion. I certainly have a lot of experience with *that!* Honestly? I don't know what I want to do yet. That's what's so scary.

Anyway, it feels better just writing all this to you. Thanks for being there,

Rosebud

Dear Rosebud,

Sure sounds like a lot's going on all right. Be careful to take things slow. My mama always used to tell me that haste makes waste. Or something like that. But I do believe this is true. I see what you mean about how the house should rightfully go to you. But life isn't always about what's right or wrong. Sometimes it's just what it is and it's best to go along with it as best we can. Let me tell you about my Grandma Sue's ring.

She didn't have much to leave behind when she died. She rented her apartment, there were bits of furniture that got passed around, a few dishes, but like I said, nothing much. Except for her diamond ring. It was a fancy thing, a spray of itty-bitty diamonds swirling around a bigger one. I think it's called a cocktail ring. Truth is, I don't think it was worth all that much money, but Grandpa Hank gave it to her and she wore it as proud as could be to every wedding, funeral and party in between. So when she died, everyone wanted it. She had three daughters and two sons, my mama being one of them. Well, let me tell you, there was squabbling for that ring. Grandma Sue should have left it to someone, but I guess she couldn't bear to part with it even in her mind.

One day, the ring just disappeared. Nobody could find it. Of course, the finger-pointing started, everyone was blaming everyone. That was almost ten years ago and my mama still hasn't talked to her one sister yet.

We'll never know what happened to Grandma Sue's ring, but my guess is Grandpa Hank pawned it. He did love to bet the trifecta at the races. But we'll never know for sure. I only hope the race came in for him, God rest his soul. We often talk about Grandma Sue's ring, usually after a few beers when we get to feeling loose in the tongue. Most everyone agrees the sisters should have just sold the ring, even if they each only got ten dollars apiece for it. Fact is, no one really wanted the ring. It was an ugly thing, big and gaudy. Everyone only wanted it because it was something Grandma Sue loved, and after she was gone, they needed something to know that she loved them back. I know my mama misses her mama. But she misses her sister that she doesn't talk to even more. So go on and sell that house! Share the money with your sisters and start that new life you're dreaming of. You don't want to be a companion again—though if you're serious, this truck gets pretty lonely. Come on and join me on the road for a while!

Remember what my Grandma Sue said. "I'm taking the ring with me." Ha, ha. No, what she really said, and I think she even stitched it on some pillow, was A House Is Not A Home. Corny, but true.

Let me know what you decide.

> Your friend,
> DannyBoy

The following morning, Birdie telephoned Mr. Collins to let him know Jilly's decision.

"This is wonderful news," he said, his usually hushed voice effusive. "Mrs. Collins and I both hoped she would reach this decision. Let me assure you once again that, though the letter would hardly be held legally binding if any one of you chose to contest it, I feel certain she's making the right decision."

"Thank you, Mr. Collins, for all your help, and for your kindness to Merry. It took a bit of talking and rehashing, but I believe you're right. Merry's request deserves to be honored."

"Jillian is quite brave."

"Yes, she is. But she won't be alone. Rose and I've decided to go with her."

"Is that so? That's wonderful. She'll need all your support. Have Jillian give me a call," he advised before signing off. "I may be able to help."

Jilly dressed in a smart navy pantsuit, pulled her hair back into a severe chignon, then walked down the block to see Mr. Collins. She was greeted warmly by Mrs. Collins, a pretty, blue-eyed elderly woman dressed in expensive yet understated clothes. She knew why Jilly had come and didn't delay her. After a few moments of polite chitchat, Jilly was ushered into Mr. Collins's office.

He rose when she entered, extending his hand. Even in his home, he wore a suit and tie. Taking her hand, he led her into his large, dark-paneled office. There were heavy velvet drapes on the windows and an impressive desk. Definitely the room of the successful lawyer that he was, Jillian thought as she took the comfortable leather seat beside the desk.

Sensing her tension, he smiled and began to chat about everyday pleasantries. Gradually, however, they moved on to the subject utmost in their minds.

"A search such as this is not only complex, but emotional. You will likely encounter any number of people who will complicate your search by lying or by sending you off on a fool's errand. Or there are those who may tell you outright that you have no right to search at all. They'll offer all sorts of reasons. 'You'll ruin the child's life' is probably the most common. Don't you listen to them or let them interfere. In no state, county or province has searching for one's adopted child been made illegal. However, there are obstacles and dead ends. As the lawyer who represented you and your parents in the adoption, I hope to eliminate a number of these obstacles."

"Mr. Collins, I don't have any idea where to begin. I thought I'd start with trying to get the adoption records."

"Unfortunately, it's most likely that the adoption file is sealed. If you were to petition for it, it could be denied outright and you would receive nothing. Or the judge could appoint an intermediary." He smiled kindly at her distress. "But not to worry. Here is where I hope to help. I can call a friend of mine who's a judge up in Wisconsin to petition for a direct release. However, I am not licensed in Wisconsin where the adoption took place. The adoptive parents will likely have hired their own lawyer as well. So it's best for you to travel north and do a little investigating on your own. Go first to Marian House and see what files they still have, then the hospital where you gave birth.''

"Go to Marian House?" Her stomach tightened and she felt another sharp pain.

"The convent is still there, I believe, but I don't know if the home for unwed mothers still exists."

"I hate that name. It always made me feel like a criminal."

Mr. Collins looked at his hands. "I'm sorry you felt that."

"I'll go. If I must." She paused. "Aren't there agencies I can contact who will do all this searching for me?"

"Yes, there are paid searchers, but the key again is to find someone reputable. You'll need to check references thoroughly. And it can be costly."

"My financial situation is, shall we say, desperate."

"Ah." He paused. She saw a deep sympathy in his eyes. "Searching by yourself may be more difficult, but you might discover many personal rewards along the way. You may even find it therapeutic. And remember, Jillian, you won't be alone. You'll have your sisters with you. And I'll work here on my end to do what I can to open doors. As a matter of fact, I've already been in contact with someone I know at the Adoption Information Exchange. She has her own resources, rather underground, and though I'm not at liberty to discuss her means of operation, I'm sure she can get me a list of names and at least narrow the field."

When she looked at him, confused, he added, "One of those names will be your daughter's."

Jilly sat back in her chair, stunned. *Her name.*

"It will take time, of course. And you'll have to narrow that list down. Once we obtain the adoption files, however, things will move along more quickly. Also, I advise that you file a waiver of confidentiality at the adoption agency as soon as possible. That way, if and when your daughter contacts the agency or court seeking information about you, identifying information will be immediately released to her so that she can contact you directly. Do you have a cell phone?''

''I'm sure Birdie has one.''

''Make certain it connects across state lines.'' He folded his hands on his desk. ''We'll need to keep in close touch. I suggest you leave my number with the agency and allow me to act as intermediary.''

''How long do you think it will take?''

''It's hard to say. Each search is unique. For some it may take only a few days. For others, as long as a year or more. So much depends on what information is available, and if your daughter has initiated a search herself.''

Jilly sat back in her chair. ''My God, I hadn't considered that.''

''There are many reasons why a child seeks her birth mother. Let's see, your daughter would be how old now?''

''Almost twenty-six.''

His brows rose. ''So old? It's hard to believe. Well then, I'd say the likelihood is good. At eighteen, she could legally make contact without her parents' approval. Then there are medical reasons she might search for you. If she has children of her own, she'd want medical histories. Or she might just want to make contact. Who knows?''

''What do I do first?''

''First, you should begin a journal. Write down all you remember, then all you learn as you go along. Include every detail, no matter how trivial it might seem. It's like a puzzle. You never know which piece is pivotal.'' He smiled benevolently. ''The search is made up of many steps. Just take the first and the rest will follow.''

She took her cue and unclasped her hands. She didn't realize she had been holding them so tightly. ''I don't think I ever thanked you for your help back then.''

''There was no need.''

She laughed. ''To be honest, I wasn't really grateful. I was angry. I think I hated you because you helped sign my baby away.''

He seemed pained. "I'm sorry you felt that way."

"I was young. I never wanted to give the baby away. Did you know that?"

His brows furrowed and he shook his head.

"Well, it doesn't matter anymore, does it?" Her smile was quick and perfunctory. Then more soberly she said, "I only pray my child went to kind parents and she had a wonderful childhood and—'' Jilly's throat constricted and she pressed her fingers against her trembling lips lest she cry. "Why did they make me give up the baby?" she blurted out with a strained voice that hurt her throat. "Would it have been so horrible for me to raise the baby on my own? Mom and Dad wouldn't even consider that choice."

"Those were different times," he reminded her gently. "There were fewer choices."

Another pat answer, she thought, dismissing it. Jillian sniffed into the handkerchief he offered, dabbed her eyes and returned it as she rose to leave. "Well, thank you now, Mr. Collins," she said politely. "Twenty-six years late."

He rose to take her hand, but didn't release her immediately. "If you don't mind me sounding a bit like a father... I think Bill might want me to."

The mention of her father's name, in this setting, sealed her determination to find her child. She no longer blamed him, but there was still alive in her the will to *show* him she would find her baby.

"A search can be very emotional. It may dredge up old insecurities and fears. But you might also experience things unexpected and fulfilling. Open your mind and your heart. Rely on your sisters and me for support. This time, Jillian, you are not alone."

He paused and she thought she saw his eyes moisten.

"I realize that everything we did was shrouded in secrecy.

And you suffered because of it. I'm an old man and I've seen a lot of change. I like to think that if your father and mother were alive today, they'd rejoice in your search.''

She released her breath slowly, taking in his sincere words. She wanted to believe that what he said was true, but the message was too ripe with history and it was too soon. She would take his words with her on the trip, she decided, to mull over as she searched for Spring.

As the family gathered for dinner around the long, oval dining room table, Jilly told them all she had learned from Mr. Collins.

"We might know where Spring is by the end of next week!" Rose exclaimed. "But that's incredible. More than I could have hoped for."

"Her name will only be one of many on the list," Jilly cautioned. "Let's not get our hopes too high. We'll still have to go to Marian House to get more information. And I won't go back there alone, I promise you."

"You won't have to. We promised to go with you each step of the way," Birdie assured her.

Dennis swung his head around to stare at her with surprise. "*You're* going along?"

Birdie's face colored and she hesitated. "Yes," she said firmly.

Dennis's silverware clattered on the table. "When were you going to tell me?"

"Can I come, too, Mom?" Hannah was leaning forward in her chair.

"If it's a problem for you, Rose and I can go alone," Jilly interjected.

"No. I said I would go, and I will. Dennis, can we talk about this privately?"

"It seems," Dennis said, "that your mind is already made

up. As usual." He tossed his napkin on the table. "If you'll excuse me."

His departure left a thick atmosphere of tension in the room.

"Really, Birdie…" Rose began.

"I've made up my mind. I'm going." She paused and said more gently, "I need to go."

"Can I go with you?" Hannah begged again. "I really want to go. School's out next week for Easter break, anyway, and I've nothing to do at home."

"Oh, Hannah…" She didn't need any more stress right now. It was on the tip of her tongue to say no. The last thing she needed to do was look after her daughter during all of this.

"Please, Mom?"

Looking into Hannah's face, upturned, eager, eyes shining with hope, Birdie couldn't do it. She wanted to find her lost youth on this trip, but here before her was her own daughter, caught in the quandaries of losing that same confidence and joy.

"Okay," she replied, feeling a sudden pleasure at the surprise and excitement that flushed Hannah's face. "I'll just go tell your father."

Birdie walked to the guest room to find Dennis tossing his clothes into their black suitcase. She stood with her hand on the doorknob and her heart in her throat.

"Where are you going?" Her voice rang with an authority she used to mask her fear.

"What do you care?" In contrast, his was void of emotion.

"Dennis, you're behaving like a child."

He tossed a pair of dark socks into the suitcase. "Thank you."

She watched him walk into the closet and come out again

with three shirts and a few ties in his hand. He didn't bother to fold them, just threw them into the suitcase.

"You're doing it again," she said. "You're withdrawing." When he didn't reply, she came into the room and closed the door behind her. She hated this guest room, with its prissy white lace everywhere. She didn't feel comfortable in here.

"Stop packing for a minute, Dennis," she said, sounding more like his mother than his wife. She softened her tone, wanting him to listen. "We have things to talk about."

He stopped, thought a moment and then lifted his head. When he spoke again it was with a controlled and deliberate voice, but his dark eyes flashed behind his glasses.

"I don't see that there's much to talk about. You've decided to go off on this wild-goose chase without talking to me, so I've decided to go on one of my own."

"Go? Go where?"

"I don't know. Somewhere. A trip. I need a vacation. A break." His laugh was short. "Maybe on a motorcycle." He went into the small, pink-and-green-tiled bathroom and began tossing toiletries into his leather bag.

"A trip?" she asked, trailing after him. "Where did this come from? What are you talking about?"

"Talk, talk, talk, talk." He walked past her back into the bedroom and put the toiletry bag into his suitcase. When he looked up again, his expression was inscrutable. "We don't engage in that particular sport. Talk, conversation, discussion. That's a pleasant exercise that uses words to communicate. We don't do that. You use words to order me around. You use words to tell me what I'm doing wrong, or to tell Hannah what she's doing wrong. You find things to complain about, things to shout about. But talk?" He shook his head. "No, Birdie, we don't do that."

"You don't talk, either!" she cried, retaliating. "You never discuss anything with me. You clam up."

"It's hard to discuss something when the other person is dictating."

Her face pulled tight, like a wall. "That's not fair. I'll be at the table and I'll bring up topic after topic after topic and you just sit there and don't respond. It's true, I know. I've tested you. I've sat through a whole meal, deliberately not talking, just to see if you'd pick up the slack. You don't. Neither does Hannah. There's utter silence till I think I'll go mad with the sound of metal hitting china."

"Some people might call that peace."

"I give up," she said, throwing up her hands. "Really, I've had it. You and Hannah both. You—"

"And that's another thing!" he roared, spinning on his heel to face her, surprising her with his vehemence. "You attack Hannah. You're on her case all the time. Don't you see what you're doing to her? She sulks and stuffs her face—"

"Don't you dare blame me for that! Don't you dare!"

He skipped a beat and she could feel her own heart thumping wildly in her chest.

"You can come after me all you want, but you leave her out of it." His voice was low again, but trembling with rage, and she caught an unmistakable flicker of cold hatred across his face.

She was undone. Her breath whooshed out. "I don't—"

"Yes," he snapped, cutting her off. "You do. Nothing she does is right. You order her around like a drill sergeant. You're on top of her all the time. You're on me, too. It's abuse. And I want it to stop."

She shuddered with revulsion at the thought she was verbally abusing her own daughter. She loved no one in the whole world more than Hannah. He was wrong.

And yet, some voice in her mind shouted out that what Dennis said was true. She'd recognized the anger in herself. It spiraled higher and higher lately, out of her control. She'd been trying to stop the cycle, attempting to find ways to get close to Hannah again, but she'd failed.

"Dennis, don't you see what's going on with her? She's so depressed and remote. And look at her eating. It's out of control. And the more weight she gains, the more depressed she gets. It's a vicious, dangerous cycle for a teenage girl. Of course I'm watching her like a hawk. Depression runs rampant at this age."

"She's not depressed. She's just going through a phase."

"That's too easy. If you want to turn the other way, that's your business. I love her too much to just throw her out in the world to fend for herself. My parents did that with Jilly. No child of mine is going to slip through the cracks."

"For God's sake, Birdie. She's not slipping through the cracks! She's a good kid. Ease up."

"Of course she's a good kid! That's why I'm grabbing tight."

"You're overreacting!"

Her back went straight. "You're *under*reacting!"

He released a short, bitter laugh and shook his head with remorse. "See what I mean? We don't talk…." His voice trailed off.

"I'm trying…I'm trying so hard to be a good mother." Her voice caught and she whipped her hands to cover her eyes. Damn, she hated herself for this emotion. He'd only use it to throw back at her.

But, surprisingly, her tears calmed him. He lowered his shoulders, raking both hands through his hair as he exhaled a long breath. "I know you are."

He sounded more like himself again, except sad. Very sad. And that frightened her even more. She dropped her hand to search his face for clues.

"I know you're a good mother. And I know your heart's in the right place. But you take on too much, Birdie. You think you can do everything. You want to prove something to the world, but you end up so overburdened everything is a battle. You want everything to be perfect—but life isn't.''

He lowered his voice. "You may be right. I'm withdrawing. The more you nag, the more I pull in.'' He looked her in the eyes and said without anger, "You're turning into a nag, Birdie.'' He put his hands on his hips, warring with himself, then said quietly, definitively, "And I can't take it anymore.''

A long, deadly silence filled the room. Birdie's face drained with shock and hurt. He was looking at her critically, dispassionately, in such a way that made her self-consciously aware of the dumpiness of her figure, the old sweatshirt she had on, her flat, uncombed hair. Time dragged on while she studied Dennis, too, as though for the last time. She saw details as though they were blown up on a screen: his dark piercing eyes were edged with deep lines, his light brown hair was thinner and streaked with more gray than she'd remembered, his full lips were pale from anger or exhaustion— or both.

They'd grown old together, she realized with a start. And they'd grown apart.

He rested his hands on the suitcase, then closed it with a flip of his wrists and zipped it. "You may have been trying with Hannah, I recognize that.'' He jabbed his index finger to his chest. "But you haven't been trying with *me*. I'm tired of getting the short end of the stick every time. I need more. I need a connection. I need some fun. Goddammit, I need some sex. I'm not getting any younger. And you know what really makes me burn?''

She shook her head and wrapped her arms around herself protectively. She knew this one would hurt.

"I wanted to go on a trip with you. For years I've practically begged you to come away with me, anywhere. I've brought brochures home from travel agents. I've even gone so far as to book flights. But you've always been too busy, or you wouldn't go without Hannah. Not even for a weekend! And now you tell me you're going off on a trip with your sisters? At the last minute? Somehow you can manage to arrange coverage for them but not for me. How the hell do you think that makes me feel?''

He turned his head downward, but not before she caught the flash of tears that she knew embarrassed him. ''Try to understand, Dennis,'' she said in a voice made husky with emotion. ''It's hard to explain. I *need* to take this trip. I know it in my gut. I don't know why, but I think it's all tied in somehow with why I've been so unhappy lately. It has to do with *me,* not you. Can you understand that?''

He nodded.

She took a long breath, relieved.

''I know there's something wrong with you,'' he said, but his voice wasn't sympathetic. It was flat. Unforgiving. ''And you're half of this marriage. So I want out.''

He said it with such coldness of feeling it burned like dry ice. She stood with her mouth open and her arms hanging at her sides as he grabbed hold of his suitcase and walked out the door.

Ten

```
⋙⟶⬗⟵⋘
```

Dennis stormed into the kitchen. "Come on, Hannah," he ordered. "We're leaving."

Jilly and Hannah both sat bolt upright in their chairs. Jilly had seen the worry and indecision cloud Hannah's face when the shouting began upstairs so she'd brought her into the kitchen, closed the door and, to distract her, begun making a list of things they'd need to bring for the car trip. Now Hannah was sitting with her eyes wide with shock at seeing her father in such uncharacteristic fury.

"What's going on?" Jilly asked.

He didn't look at her but kept his gaze on Hannah. "We're going home. Get your stuff."

"No, I'm not," Hannah countered, her face rebellious. She glanced at Jilly, her eyes pleading for help.

"Birdie said she could come along with us," Jilly replied in an easy tone. "Why not let her? She'll have a good time."

"I said no. Go on," he ordered Hannah.

"No!" Hannah bolted from the chair. "I won't go home. And you can't make me." She pushed away from the table and ran out the back door, leaving the screen door banging open, caught in a gust of wind.

Dennis was hot on her trail. Jilly leaped to her feet and

hurried after him. "Let her go," she called out, catching up to him on the back porch and grabbing hold of his arm. She saw Hannah dart across the yard and out through the tall hedge "Give her a minute. She'll be back. Where's she going to go?"

She felt the tension in his arm tighten, then subside. She released her grip, feeling a bit embarrassed at having grabbed him. Dennis raked his hand through his hair as he stared out at the empty yard, then he turned toward her with critical eyes.

"Why are you doing this?"

"Doing what?"

"Getting everyone to go on this quest of yours."

"*Me* getting everyone to go?"

"You always get people to do what you want. You always have."

"I don't know which makes me angrier," she replied, stepping back. "That you call this search a quest, or that you think I was the one who started it. You're wrong on both counts. If anyone's a victim here, it's me."

"Then stop this madness."

She drew herself up, warring inside with a thousand things she could tell him. Her head was swirling with what felt like a swarm of angry bees—all stinging. "Just what is it that bothers you the most about this?" She was acting on instinct, letting one of her bees out to sting him and test his reaction.

"Okay. Okay, I'll tell you. I wanted a little time with my wife but she never has the time to give. Then suddenly, out of the blue, bam! She has time for you."

"She's not doing this for me. She's doing this for herself. And more power to her. If you'd think of someone other than yourself, you'd see how unhappy she is."

His face mottled. "I see. So this search is all altruistic on your part, is it? Did you every stop to think how the child— this Spring—might feel about being found? Maybe she doesn't want to be located. Maybe she doesn't want to face her long lost mother. You could be ruining her life.''

After a short laugh Jilly said, "Mr. Collins warned me I'd hear stuff like that, but I didn't expect it so soon. And certainly not from you."

"If you hear it it's because it's true. And you're not only ruining *her* life. Look what you're doing to *ours*."

Jilly's head snapped up and she eyed him narrowly. "Just what am I doing to your life?"

"You don't know what this trip will unearth." His eyes were questioning. Challenging.

She squinted. "Go on."

He looked down as the cold air billowed around them. She held her breath.

"I've got to know, Jilly," he said in a confidential whisper. "Am I the father?"

She knew it was coming, but hearing the words still came as a shock.

"Well!" She exhaled, stepping back again. "It's a little late to be asking *that* question."

"Am I?"

She looked down at her bare feet, her head spinning. She wasn't sure what to tell him—a hell of a predicament after twenty-six years. She studied her fuchsia-pink toenails as she wondered whether to say no. It would be the easiest reply to give. Just like when her mother had asked, *Is it that Connor boy?* That one word, "no," made everyone happy and got them all off her case. She could do it again.

Except that she was done pretending. She'd vowed when she decided to face her ghosts that there would be no more lies in her life. She wouldn't sacrifice herself again for the sake of peace or another's well-being.

She looked into Dennis's brown eyes and said, "I don't know." There, it was said. She felt years younger.

Dennis looked years older. "What…what do you mean? I *could* be the father?"

"Yes."

He swore under his breath and the look he gave her was tinged with accusation.

"I didn't sleep around," she fired off. "And you know it. There was only that one time with you. And one other boy."

She saw in his glazed look that they were both remembering that emotional summer week.

She and Dennis had dated for most of the summer of 1972. Dennis was popular enough but a loner. Kind of weird smart, the editor of the school paper and yearbook. He was cute enough to attract the girls and good enough in basketball to pass muster with the guys. It was his eleventh-hour heroism on the television show *It's Academic,* when he answered a remote literature question for the win that first attracted Jilly to him. He was different, sensitive, intriguing…adorable with that cleft in his chin.

So she set her sights for Dennis Connor, and it didn't take long. Terribly flattered to be wooed by someone as popular as Jillian Season, Dennis promptly fell under her spell.

It was a lovely summer. They lived at the beach, hanging out with Jilly's most popular group. Dennis soaked in the envy of the other guys as he spread suntan oil on her luscious bikini-clad body. The nights were balmy. They drove in packs to McDonald's to hang out, then headed back to the beach to sprawl out on blankets and make out, draped by the dark night and the roar of the surf.

She was his first time. It was a mistake, she knew instantly, not only because she didn't feel a spark with him, but also because after they made love he became slavishly devoted. Jillian was wise enough to know it was just the sex, but Dennis didn't. He tagged around like a hungry puppy, always touching, always eager, so she had to break it off with him.

The following week she met an adorable college boy at a party and after too many beers, she let him in the back of his car. Dennis heard about it, as he was supposed to, and stopped calling.

"You broke my heart with that college man, you know." He was only half-serious, and his smile was sheepish.

"We both know that neither one of us was in love. We were in high school, for God's sake."

"When I found out years later that you'd had a baby, I was stunned and couldn't help but wonder if it was mine. I did the math. Then I figured you would have told me and let it go. It was easier. And Jesus, I was married to your sister. The last thing I wanted to think about was the possibility of having had a child with you."

"You may not have."

"Just the possibility..."

"Did you love Birdie when you married her?"

He seemed surprised by the question. "Madly, desperately. Truly."

"Thank God," she murmured. "I'd always wondered."

His face pinched and he looked up toward the bedroom. "She's always been anxious that the two of us dated. Even for such a short time. I told her it was ridiculous, that it was long before I ever dated her. But if she hears this, she'll be devastated."

"*I'm* not going to tell her."

"You may not have to. What if the baby looks like me?"

Jilly's breath caught. "I hadn't thought about that."

"If Birdie finds out she'll be crushed. She'll think—" His face hardened with resolution. "I don't want her to ever doubt that I loved her."

"Loved?" Her ears perked. "Past tense?"

Dennis only shrugged in reply. "One thing is certain, I sure as hell don't want Hannah dragged into this."

"You're worrying too much. First of all, Hannah doesn't even suspect the connection so she won't be looking. Secondly, there is no baby. Spring, or whatever her name is, is twenty-six years old. Third, whatever the truth is, we'll have to deal with it."

"It's not always wise to expose all truths, Jilly. In families, sometimes it's best to keep a few secrets."

"What you don't know won't hurt you, right?"

"Something like that."

"Wrong." She absently tapped her pockets for a cigarette and mentally cursed when she found nothing. She lifted her head, then saw with a wry smile a pack of Parliament cigarettes offered. Dennis smoked? She pulled out a cigarette, put it in her mouth, then bent a bit forward, allowing him to light it. She had to touch his hand to steady it, just a laying of the fingertips on his knuckles, but she felt the heat. Just the time it took for two drags, but it seemed to last forever. She pulled back, drawing in, then releasing a long plume. Oh, boy, she thought to herself. She *would* feel the spark now. Looking up, she knew from the uncertain expression on his face that he felt it, too.

"Like old times," he said.

She was relieved to hear him chuckle. With his hands in his pockets, leaning against the porch beam with a shy smile on his face, she could see the high school boy in the man. "I didn't know you still smoked."

"I sneak one once in a while."

It was a pitiful statement for a grown man to make. "Birdie?" she said with affection.

"Yeah, Birdie." His voice was pained.

He loved his wife, it was written all over his face. "Listen, Dennis, I don't want to hurt you or Birdie, or Rose, and least of all sweet Hannah. I won't tell anyone anything. Unless they ask me. And then—" she lifted her hands "—I'll tell the truth. We may think we're lying for the family's good, but the bottom line is we're just perpetuating the lie." She looked up at the old, deteriorating Victorian. "We're cleaning house," she continued. "Inside and out. And when we're done, we're all going to have to pack up our baggage, no matter how tattered, and move on."

Dennis looked at her for a long time. His seriousness was one of the things she liked best about him.

"I'm asking you not to take Birdie and Hannah along."

"You're asking the wrong person. That's not up to me. But I won't urge them to go. I can do this without them."

He considered this and she saw his face harden in decision. "I'm leaving now. Tell Birdie I've taken the train. I'll leave the car for her."

Jilly did a double take. "You're leaving Evanston?"

He cleared his throat. "I'm leaving Birdie."

"I don't believe it."

"It's been a long time coming."

"If it's about this trip, I'll talk to her. I know she's headstrong, but nothing is worth..."

"No. It's more than that. I'd rather she didn't go." He sent her a pulsing look. "You know why. But she's determined and I know her too well to argue with her when her mind's made up. And frankly, I'm tired of arguing. Tired of asking. Don't, Jilly," he said as she opened her mouth to speak. "Please. Just tell her that I've gone."

He turned, then stopped. When he turned back toward her she saw the emotions at war in his eyes. He placed his hands on her shoulders, kissed her forehead and said softly near her ear, "I wish I could have been there for you years ago, at least as a friend. I won't stand in your way now." He pulled back and his eyes dimmed. Suddenly he appeared older once again. "Goodbye, then, and good luck."

Her eyes moistened so she only saw a blur of motion when he walked down the stairs and away from the house.

Dear DannyBoy,

I can't believe it! We're actually going. Tomorrow morning.

I'm nervous. I'm scared. And it's all absolutely delicious. Imagine me, going on a trip! I've gone over the route a hundred times. I got the best maps from the Internet. Plus, I'm making lots of tapes of my favorite music to listen to in the car, packing nutritious snacks so we won't have to eat junk, and don't laugh, but I'm even bringing lots of bubble bath. Jilly says it's her best remedy for being keyed up. I could keep a journal, but I have you. I love knowing I'll be able to write to you on the road. I remember what you wrote about looking forward to my letters at the end of the day. It's true for me as well. It makes me feel more connected to you.

Bye-bye!
Rosebud

Dear Rosebud,

Welcome to my world. You will love the open road. Sometimes the traffic can be tough around the cities, but in the country, especially up in northern Wisconsin where you're headed, the hills are mild and the roads are winding. You'll see big dairy farms with black and whites grazing, silos waiting to be filled with grain, and pretty soon, you might catch the first faint spring green haze that seems to float around the gray tree branches.

I'm still heading west toward Wichita. The roads here are flat and I can see for miles. Easy driving.

Times like these, I wish you were sitting here beside me chatting, instead of only talking on this e-mail. As I ride along I think of you. I wonder what you look like. What color is your hair? Your eyes? What's your smile like?

Curious,
DannyBoy

Eleven

─❦─

Jilly, Birdie, Rose and Hannah drove north toward Wisconsin. They'd packed lightly, stashing their luggage in the back of the Land Rover along with Rose's laptop computer, bottles of water and juice, audiotapes, books, and several bags of groceries that Rose had insisted that they'd need.

Birdie had volunteered to take the first turn at the wheel. Dressed for comfort in khakis, a long-sleeved flannel shirt and a down vest, she drove with her eyes on the road, not much in the mood for conversation. Jilly took her turn next. She enjoyed the feel of the road and the scenery; it had been a long time since she'd traveled across America. Likewise, Rose's eyes, vivid behind her pale lashes, were limpid with worry as she turned to gaze out the window. She was dressed simply in a long denim skirt and a white cotton sweater. Her tiny feet were tucked into scuffed black penny loafers and were propped up over bags of snacks she had packed for the journey. Her long red hair was tied back in its usual braid and hung over her shoulder.

Jilly's heart ached for her. Even though she'd been excited to go, the act of leaving the house that morning had been a trial. She had to count the bags in the back of the car over and over, then she went over the route with a simmering

Birdie for the tenth time, and before she'd leave, she had to check that she had locked every door. Jilly had traveled so much in her life, she'd felt jaded in comparison.

"I suppose we should start thinking about a place to spend the night," she suggested.

"I've marked the page of the area we'll be staying in," said Rose, opening up the tour guide from the AAA. "It's slim pickings, I'm afraid."

"I'm starved," Hannah moaned.

"Let's settle into the motel first and then find a place to eat," Birdie replied.

"Or we can bring food in," Rose said.

"I don't care where we stay as long as it has a nice bathroom," Jilly chimed in. "I'm dying for a hot bath."

"We should probably get two rooms. One for Hannah and me, and one for you and Rose," added Birdie. "I'll cover the cost of ours and you two can split the other."

"I want to stay with Aunt Jilly," Hannah said.

Birdie felt the pang of rebuff and replied, "Do what you want. Makes no difference to me. Oh, look, there's a sign for a Marriott. They're usually quite nice."

"That's not one of the ones I circled." Rose flipped through the pages until she found the listing. "It's pretty expensive."

"How much?"

"Let's see… One hundred forty-five for a double." She frowned and skipped a beat. "How many nights will we be there?"

"I can't afford it," Jilly said bluntly, keeping her eyes fixed on the road.

"What?" Birdie said with surprise.

Jilly's hands tightened on the wheel. The day had brought them closer together, and the feeling of camaraderie was high. It was now or never. "I guess this is as good a time as any." She cleared her throat. "I'm broke." She glanced

in the rearview mirror to see all eyes on her. "I'm not kidding. I don't know how long this search will take or how
much cash I'll have to lay out for information. I figure I've
got enough to last a few weeks if we stay at modest motels
and away from four-star restaurants. I'm talking real modest
motels, Birdie. As in, clean would be nice, if you get my
meaning."

There was a stunned silence.

Jilly flushed, but was relieved to have told them.

"What happened to all your money?" Rose asked when
she could find her voice. "You had gobs of dough. And what
about your fur coat and jewelry?"

"Your husband was a Rothschild!" Birdie exclaimed.

"The jewelry's been sold. This ring?" Jilly lifted her hand
and wiggled her finger, upon which sat a chunk of diamond.
"Fake. You never get anything for a fur so I kept it, and as
for my last husband, he was as fake as the ring. A handsome
but poor relation to the main branch of the family. He swin-
dled my money to pay off his gambling debts. I woke up one
morning with a hangover and an empty bank account."

"The creep!" Hannah exclaimed, but it was clear from
her dazzled expression that she was eating this drama up.

"You're lucky to be rid of him," Birdie said.

Jilly was pleased to see fury shoot from her sister's eyes.
"Well, yeah, I know that now. Unfortunately it was a very
expensive mistake made at a bad time in my life. In four
short years my charming husband managed to squander what
it took me twenty years to save. The cushion I'd planned on
is gone and I can't readily make my fortune again. I'm too
old."

"You're not old," Rose countered.

"Look at Hannah's fresh skin, then look at mine. The camera never lies." She peeked in the rearview mirror and her
eyes crinkled to see Hannah sit up, alert and glowing to have

been singled out for the compliment. "So the bottom line is, until I get my hands on my share from the sale of the house, I'm living on a shoestring." She paused. "I'm sorry I was such a stinker about the money when we read the will, but now you know why. Being broke scares me."

"I understand." Rose's lips turned upward in a teasing smile. "Especially if you're as broke as me."

"Oh, I get it," Birdie chimed in. "I guess you think I'm Miss Flushpockets on this joyride."

"Relatively speaking," Jilly said with a laugh that spread to the others.

"I'm glad you're all laughing. Here's the punch line. Ready? I'm spread so thin with mortgage payments, I'm in the same boat as you. It's all on paper. All the cash is tied up. I'm what's known as house poor."

"So we're all in the same boat? Well whaddaya know?" Jilly tooted the horn as they started laughing in earnest.

"I hate to say it," Birdie said to Jilly when the laughing subsided, "but I'm rather glad you're broke." She smirked. "It levels the playing field a bit."

"You lived such a glamorous life," Hannah said with an awestruck expression. "Compared to us."

"It wasn't so glamorous," Jilly replied thoughtfully. "Actually, it got very tedious. Everyone trying to compete with one another, no one ever really listening, or caring. There wasn't anyone you could really trust. Ambition can get quite ugly. It was all about being seen. Very empty, actually. Very lonely."

Rose leaned forward in the seat, resting her arm on the headrest. "But won't you miss living in Paris?"

"Me? No, not at all. My career is over." She paused, then added with a hint of sentiment, "It was time to come home."

Home. Rose had always thought of Evanston, Illinois, as home. She'd never lived anywhere else. What would it be like, she wondered, to explore a new place, to create a new home, all on one's own? How would she go about trying to find a new grocery store, or get a new library card? How would she feel not knowing where to go for the best flowers or bread, or to walk down the street and have no one know her name? She turned her head and stared out the window at the strange landscape they whisked by.

Home. Birdie shivered under her down vest, wondering what was to become of her home. How could Dennis just leave on the afternoon train to Milwaukee without saying a word to her? They were tense, that was all, she told herself. The funeral, Jilly's arrival, the will, and now this search for Spring—it was all too much. She'd call him later tonight, just to make sure he was all right. He was cruel to call her a nag. She *had* to keep on top of things or else everything at home would fall apart. That was her job, as the mom. She was only trying to help him—and Hannah. She glanced at her daughter on the seat beside her. Try as she might, she couldn't shake the worry that her home had fallen apart already.

Home. Jilly drove for a while in a comfortable silence, rolling the word over in her mind. It held such meaning, even for a homeless wretch like herself. She'd lived in houses and flats, one more grand than the next, all over Europe. But she'd never really considered anywhere else home but the old Victorian on Michigan Avenue. With its overgrown hydrangeas, wraparound porch and marvelous filigree, it was the place where she stored all her memories.

Yet, driving north in this large car with her sisters and niece, it occurred to her that this small space was home, too. And whatever two-star motel they could afford to stay in tonight would also be home. Whenever, wherever the Seasons were together, that was home. Because home wasn't a place but a state of mind.

* * *

"Are we there yet?"

The sisters smirked at the classic kid's remark from Hannah.

"Did you know that the polka is Wisconsin's state dance?" volunteered Rose, trying to make things interesting.

"It's getting late," said Birdie with a groan. She was driving the last leg of the trip. "I think we should just take the next motel we can find."

"Please do," Jilly said, gently massaging her neck, "before Rose tells us the state flower."

"It's the wood violet."

Everyone groaned.

They had long passed through Green Bay, a bustling town dominated by paper mills and bordered by hardwood forests. They'd also passed plenty of Holiday Inns, Comfort Suites and Super 8 Motels. They'd all agreed to move on closer to Marian House. Now they were back in the country, snaking around wooded hills and muddy fields still littered with patches of snow and ice. It was a harsh landscape this time of year. Spring had not yet taken hold this far north.

Birdie was getting worried. The temperature was dropping by the minute as the late afternoon cast a gray pall on the horizon. She hoped it wouldn't snow. She boosted the heater a bit, deciding that she didn't care how much the next place cost. She'd pay for everyone, go into debt, whatever, if she could just get out of the car. She rubbed the small of her back; it was killing her. They should be in the town of Hodges soon, she told herself, pushing on the gas pedal and risking the ticket.

A half hour later they came to the small dairy town. Hodges was a quaint place, though rather depressed. Charming redbrick buildings tilting with age and disrepair were graced with elaborate but timeworn architectural details. They lined both sides of Main Street and housed the town's newspaper, a small drugstore, a diner, a bank, a bookstore,

Meeske's grocery and a number of antique shops. Birdie slowed to the speed limit of twenty-five, and as they drove along the narrow street, they all peered out the windows with heightened curiosity.

"This would have been a thriving town back when dairy farming was booming," Birdie commented.

"It's like something out of a Stephen King novel," Hannah said.

"Oh, I don't know. I think it's charming," Rose said. "Did you know that milk and cheese products are still the chief exports of Wisconsin?"

"I could go for a little wine and cheese about now," said Jilly.

"Let's just hope they have a motel."

Jilly was about to say "Don't worry, we'll find a place" when she saw a small sign: River's End Motel. Clean Rooms, Friendly Service, Reasonable Prices.

"Sounds like our place," Birdie exclaimed, noting the address. "What a nice name, River's End."

They all agreed and had visions of comfortable beds, a television and a prettyish little river meandering outside their window. As Birdie crossed a charming bridge over a narrow river of clear water, her hopes soared. They passed a lovely white house with black shutters that was a bed-and-breakfast. Unfortunately, it had an Occupied sign in the window. The road dipped lower. They crossed a railroad track and there, wedged on a narrow strip of land between the track and a shallow tributary of the river, was the River's End Motel.

Her heart sank, and from the silence in the car, she knew the feeling was mutual. There was no graceful entry or even a driveway to the motel. A dozen small rooms fanned to the left, each with an identical picture window and a cheap brown wood door. A dozen identical rooms spread to the right, joined by a small A-framed office.

"Oh, great," said Jilly, giving voice to what they were all

thinking. "Just what we wanted. A cheap imitation of an early Howard Johnson. Man, oh man, if the girls in Paris could see me now."

"Paris? Heck, if the girls in Milwaukee could see me now," Hannah joined in.

Birdie pulled to a stop in front of the office and rolled down the window. "It's worse than I thought. The building is made of cement blocks. Look, you can see the square outlines under that lovely shade of poo-brown paint."

"Now, don't be harsh," Jilly teased. "At least the poo-brown paint is fairly fresh. And don't you think that vat of red geraniums at the front door lends it a certain je ne sais quoi? Even if they are fake."

"Speaking of pooped, I am. It's this or keep going," Birdie announced. "I'm for giving it a try."

"Well, it looks cheap," Rose said.

"It'd better be," quipped Jilly.

They tumbled out from the Land Rover into the moist, frigid northern air, yawning and stretching, each looking at the sorry motel with resignation.

Birdie went into the office while the others began unpacking the car. Inside the small office was no better. The brown-and-white decor was from the fifties and showed its age. A high motel counter of wood separated the back of the room from the front. It sagged in the middle from too many years of elbows leaning upon it. A stand beside the door was filled with brochures showing people riding Jet Skis and boats in lakes, touring caves and buying clothing at countless outlets for tourist shopping—all of them miles from Hodges in Door County.

"Hello!" she called out, and waited. No one came out. "Hello!" she called again, louder. Again, not a sound. Great, she thought to herself. There wasn't a car in the parking lot and he or she probably didn't get any customers this time of year. Her stomach rumbled and she thought they should prob-

ably go look for something to eat and then return. She walked
to the window and peered out the yellowed venetian blinds.
She groaned, seeing their luggage sitting in the parking lot
already.

"Hello. May I help you?"

It was the richness of the voice that startled her. And the
accent. She put her hand to her breast and spun around on
her heel.

Standing behind the counter was a tall, bronze-skinned
man whom she guessed to be East Indian. He wasn't so much
handsome as he was exotic, with prominent cheekbones and
a full, sensual mouth. His hair was dark and worn combed
back to lightly graze the top of his starched white collar. It
was his eyes that arrested her; they were dark and shone with
tremendous magnetism.

"You startled me," she said, suddenly uneasy.

"I'm sorry. I was out back and didn't hear you come in.
Were you waiting long?" He spoke with a unique, clipped
British accent.

"No," she replied, regaining her equilibrium. "We've
only just arrived. Do you have rooms available?"

His lips turned upward just enough to hint at amusement.
Behind him the wall was covered with keys. "I do," he
replied. "How many rooms will you be requiring?"

"Two. With double beds. There will be two of us staying
in each room."

He turned to remove two keys from the wall. "Rooms 101
and 102. They have double beds and a small patio out back
facing the river. Though with this weather…" He lifted a
brow. "How long will you be staying?"

Birdie didn't want to commit without seeing the rooms.
The bed-and-breakfast down the block was inviting. "Tonight. Maybe tomorrow, too. We have appointments and are
not yet certain."

"Very good," he repeated. Then, as though he'd read her

mind, "If you find you'll need to stay longer, that will be no problem."

"I assume there are phones and televisions and..." She left the rest hanging.

"Of course."

They completed their business quickly. She took the keys and, thanking him, hurried from the office. Something about him made her feel nervous. It might have been his foreignness, or his swarthy, masculine good looks, but in that small, warm space, she became very aware that she was a woman and he was a man.

"Okay, girls," she called out, shivering when she met a blast of cold air. "Let's move in."

They lugged their bags to the two rooms at the farthermost end of the motel. Birdie opened the door to her room, snaked her hand in to flick on the light, then felt her heart hit her toes.

"We're staying *here?*" Hannah's voice rang with dismay. "What a dump!"

Birdie moved farther into the cramped square room, closing the door against the chill air. The air inside wasn't much better. The first thing she did was to lift the cheap metal heater and push it to High.

The room was tiny and cramped. Two double beds were squeezed into the room only inches apart from each other. They were permanently affixed to the wood-paneled walls by headboards, which were, in fact, mere extensions of the wall. Beside them, on either side, were two nightstands, each holding a futuristic lamp that was only missing the lava. However, the room smelled of clean soap, and though the furniture was dated and chipped in spots, at least it was real wood.

Birdie stood for a moment, suitcase still in hand, trying to decide if she should call the others to load the car back up, or toss her stuff on the floor and rough it for one night. Her bladder decided for her.

"It's not that bad," she lied, hurrying between the retro built-in dresser and the edges of the beds. The space was so narrow she had to turn sideways to pass without bumping her knees. She passed the avocado-green Formica vanity-sink combo so popular in motels and opened a chipped wood-grain door.

The bathroom was even worse. It was the size of a small closet. A small toilet was squeezed in beside a narrow shower stall with a natural-cotton cloth curtain hanging on metal hooks. She hadn't seen one of those since summer camp, and that was for the outside shower. Sitting down, she peeked behind the curtain, holding her breath.

Oh, Lord, she thought, wondering what Hannah would say to this. And Jilly? She put her palm to her head and shook it. The stall was rusting at every joint. The faucet was sticking out from the wall by the metal pipe and the drain on the floor was a hole in the cement slab floor covered by a metal grate. She thought of her home in Wisconsin with its big, tiled bathroom and Jacuzzi tub. The thought of those jets massaging her aching back made her groan again. Dennis used to love to rub her back....

When she returned to the room a few minutes later, Jilly and Rose were already there commiserating.

"Welcome to Punjab Palace," Jilly said with a smirk. "Get a load of the artwork."

Birdie looked to see prints of various Hindu gods she couldn't name.

"Did you see the bathroom?" Jilly asked, her face aghast. "I use the term loosely, considering there isn't even a bath."

Birdie nodded. "My shower has a grate that goes into the floor."

"You've got a grate? Ours is an open hole." She waved her hand in a dismissive gesture. "Look, I know I said I wanted something cheap, but this is beyond the pale. We simply cannot stay here."

"It's late," Birdie replied, trying not to yawn. "Unless you know of somewhere else we can go… At least this place is clean and there's a bed."

"I don't care!" Jilly exclaimed, her eyes wildly scanning the room. "There isn't a bath. No iron, no fridge." She took a breath. "There's no room service!"

"Jilly," Birdie snapped. "You said you couldn't afford the three-star hotel we passed down the road. This place we can afford."

"This place has *no* stars. It's minus stars."

"It's not so bad," Rose interrupted. "It's…"

Suddenly, the air was rent with the sound of grating plumbing as the ancient system tried to deal with the novelty of a flushing toilet. Birdie ran back to the bathroom in time to discover the water in the toilet bowl rising fast to the top.

"It's gonna blow!" Birdie ran back. "Quick, call the office!"

"Where's the phone?"

Birdie jumped on one bed then to the other, the quickest route in the crowded room, but the phone wasn't on either of the nightstands.

"Here it is, by the TV," Hannah called. She picked up the receiver and dialed 0. While she reported the flooding toilet, Birdie watched a trickle of water escape from the bathroom.

"Here it comes!" she screamed, jumping from foot to foot. Then a laugh exploded from her mouth. She didn't know where it came from, but suddenly the whole scenario seemed hilarious.

Jilly caught the absurdity immediately and burst out laughing, collapsing on the other bed. Hannah joined her, kicking her legs in the air while she howled. Only Rose stood somewhat uncertain, staring with horror at the flow of water seeping from the bathroom.

Thwack. Someone hit Rose with a pillow. She looked up, stunned, her neatly braided hair smooshed by the blow.

"Why, you little…" Rose kicked off her shoes and leaped to the bed. Instantly, they were all diving for the pillows, fighting for them, the victor getting off a good whap while another pillow found a new victim. They were squealing and jumping like wild women, laughing till the tears and the miles flowed from their eyes.

No one noticed the door open.

"Excuse me!" The voice was loud and unmistakably male.

The hilarity came to a sudden stop. They presented a tableau of twisted shapes, their bodies a blend of bent and grasping legs, pillows, shoulders, their mouths agape with choked laughter, their eyes wide with surprise.

The man stood at the door, a pillow in hand, his hair disheveled. His thick, dark brows gathered like thunderclouds over his proud, straight nose. His eyes flashed. In his other hand, he held a bucket filled with tools and sponges.

"I'm Mr. Patel, the manager. I knocked several times…." He was trying to maintain his dignity.

Birdie, Hannah and Rose responded instantly, smoothing their slacks and hair, then stepping from the bed in whatever ladylike manner they could muster.

"We're terribly sorry for making you wait," Birdie said.

"And for hitting you with a pillow," added Rose, smoothing her loosened braid from her scarlet face.

"We…we didn't know you were there." Hannah giggled.

"Excuse me," he said again, all politeness, but no one could miss his disdain. He looked past them toward the bathroom. As though he'd spoken, Hannah and Rose hurried from the narrow path of walking space to let him pass. He cast a quick, assessing glance at Jilly from under thick lashes, then disappeared into the bathroom.

Birdie, Rose and Hannah each slapped palms across their mouths to keep from laughing.

Jilly still stood on the bed, a pillow hanging from her left hand. She had not moved from the moment that she lay eyes on the man at the threshold. His dress and appearance were proper and immaculate. He wore black trousers and a long-sleeved white shirt buttoned high. Nonetheless she saw in him an animal ferocity, like that of a tiger tethered by a slim leash. As quickly as a blink of an eye, however, he had reined himself in, leaving her to wonder if what she had seen in his eyes was really there or a trick of the light. She dropped the pillow, tumbled from the bed, then, grabbing her purse, went out into the cold twilight for a smoke.

By the time the toilet was repaired and they'd showered, they were too tired to go out in search of food. They were commiserating about what to do when Mr. Patel returned to Birdie's room carrying a chilled bottle of white wine and four sparkling glasses.

"I apologize for the inconvenience," he said. He didn't smile but the hard lines of his face had softened.

Birdie took the wine, handed it to Rose, then accepted the glasses with profuse thanks, assuring him it wasn't necessary, but very nice. She closed the door, then turned and leaned her back against it, her eyes wide. When she looked into her sisters' eyes, she knew instantly that they had all gone weak at the sight of the ruthlessly handsome Mr. Patel. Again, they burst out laughing, making a show of fanning themselves. Hannah pretended to be shocked at their lascivious behavior but everyone knew she loved seeing her mom in this new light. For the first time, Hannah was being accepted as a woman.

They poured the wine. When Jilly raised her eyebrows at Birdie, she splashed some into Hannah's glass. For dinner they ate runny Brie cheese and French bread left over from the funeral, carrot and celery strips, along with oranges and grapes from Rose's glorious picnic. It was like a big slumber party. They got into their pajamas, turned on a movie from the cable television—a luxury Hannah was ecstatic to discover the cheesy motel actually had—pulled out their private stashes of chocolate, and just relaxed for a few hours. But the day had proved too long. One by one the eyelids drooped. Yawning, Jilly and Hannah returned to their room.

When Birdie fell into a fitful sleep, Rose quietly set up her computer to write to DannyBoy.

He'd asked her for a description, something she was loath to do. She composed and deleted a dozen e-mails that gave a vague description of her appearance. How could she make herself sound attractive without sounding like she was trite or boasting? In the end, she went to the newspaper and studied the personal ads, trying to choose wording that was the least offensive. At last she managed to write a kind of newspaper ad/e-mail combo that she figured was as good as it was going to get.

> Dear DannyBoy,
> Okay, here goes. I'm not very good at describing myself. It makes me feel very uncomfortable, even immodest. But because you asked…
> I'm single, white and thirty-six years old. I'm medium height, have red hair that goes to my waist. Most people describe me as thin. You know I love to collect stamps. I also like to read (a lot), cook, surf the Net, and I've recently found I've taken a liking to road trips.
> Well, that's me. I'm quiet but hopefully not dull. I have lots of interests and I'm looking for someone to share them with.
>
> Rosebud

It was the most horrid e-mail she'd ever written. She couldn't believe she was actually writing that about herself.

Her hand hovered over the delete button as she read and reread the letter. Beside her, Birdie shifted again in her sleep, muttering fitfully. Birdie had confided about her fight with Dennis. Rose had never known Birdie to be so confused or scared, but when she'd spoken of Dennis, she had wrung her hands, something totally out of character for her. Rose cast a worried look at her and knew she should turn off the light soon.

She shifted her hand, then pushed Send. As soon as she sent it, her stomach fell and she wished she could take it back.

He must have been waiting for her letter, though, for he wrote back almost instantly.

Dear Rosebud,
You're late tonight. I hoped it was because you were on the road and not because I asked you what you looked like. Maybe I shouldn't have. You seem a bit put off. Please don't be. Now I can imagine a face behind the words. A real nice face. But you didn't tell me the most important thing. What color are your eyes?
DannyBoy

She took a deep sigh of relief that he'd written back. A short laugh escaped her as she wrote her reply.

Uh-uh, DannyBoy. You have to describe yourself first.
Rosebud

Before she could receive his reply, she turned off the computer, and a moment later, the overhead light as well.

Twelve

Jilly woke up the following morning to what sounded like a tornado roaring through her room. She sat bolt upright, clutching her blanket close to her chest.

Hannah scrambled from the bed and pulled open the dusty paisley curtains to the sight of a rumbling, clanking, grinding freight train just on the far side of the parking lot. The water in the glasses shook from the vibrations that Jilly felt clear to her marrow. On the grassy hill alongside the tracks, a scruffy white dog with a patch of black over its eye was barking ferociously at the train, his whole body lifting from the ground with the effort. Jilly let out a hearty laugh, lifting her knees and hugging them close.

Hannah slumped against the window, rubbed her eyes and yawned. "Good morning." She had to shout to be heard over the rattle.

"I haven't seen a good ol' American freight train like this in more than twenty-five years," Jilly called back, staring out the window with a child's excitement. "We used to count the cars."

Hannah turned to look at her face. Her aunt Jilly looked older, less luminous in the morning sun. Without any makeup her skin revealed faint vertical lines at the tips of her full lips, crow's-feet at the eyes and deeply etched, interconnecting lines evident even when her face was passive. Still, she had the look of a model, Hannah thought, with that elegance of line that she saw in magazines. She wished she could look like that rather than big and stocky, like her mother. She wished her aunt Jilly were her mother. She looked out again at the rumbling train. "Here comes the caboose. And it's red!"

Sure enough, an old, rather dilapidated red caboose chugged past their window. From the room next door they heard Birdie's and Rose's voices sing out, "Woooo-woooo!"

Hannah and Jilly shared a look, then in unison called back, "Wooo-wooo!"

This, and an arm motion imitating an old train whistle being pulled, was de rigueur for the sisters growing up. Jilly was glad to see that Birdie had passed on the tradition to her daughter.

A moment later, their phone rang.

"How did you like the wake-up call?" It was Birdie and she was in high spirits.

"Innovative," Jilly replied. "Nothing but first class all the way for the Seasons."

"I'm hungry. Mr. Patel said there was a nice restaurant in town that we could walk to."

"Talking to Mr. Patel already, are we?"

She heard Birdie tsk. "Want to go eat in about twenty minutes?"

Jilly looked at her watch. It was already eight-fifteen. She wanted to get an early start for Marian House. "Be there or be square," she replied.

"God, Jilly, I haven't heard that in ages."

"I haven't said that in ages. I think we're regressing."

"You think? Nah... Well, see you later, alligator."

"After a while, crocodile." Jilly hung up, chuckling at how they were all beginning to dip into the well of their childhood expressions and behaviors. After all these years, it felt good.

It was a cool, sunny morning that promised to warm up by noon. They left the motel together in good spirits, walking in pairs across the parking lot and the train tracks to Main Street. Jilly was chic as usual, all in black, from her tailored slacks to her soft, knee-length Italian leather coat. She looked too European for this tiny town in remote northern Wisconsin and drew the attention of the locals. They turned their heads as she passed but Jilly was oblivious. Hannah walked beside her, showing her youth in flared jeans and a white puffy parka. Birdie wore a long khaki skirt and her navy pea coat. She kept her arm linked with Rose, who was again wearing her calf-length denim skirt and a camel-hair jacket that had once been their mother's and was a bit frayed at the cuffs.

People were already moving about the sleepy town of Hodges. An old man swept the pavement before his barber-shop with metronomic strokes. The florist was setting out buckets filled with daffodils, daisies and long branches of pussy willow that Rose claimed she must have.

The Country Diner was a cheery, airy place with blue-and-white gingham at the windows, round oak tables and rabbit-eared chairs, and little framed plaques with homespun sayings like Home Is Where The Heart Is scattered on the wall. The front of the restaurant had an old-fashioned soda fountain complete with Hamilton blenders and stainless steel milk-shake mixers. Behind the counter were shelves filled with gleaming glasses and dishes for sundaes, and best of all, a glorious old cash register that was a collector's item. The wood and chrome-trimmed counter was a thing of beauty, lined with twirly stools topped with red leather seats, most of them torn in places and carefully taped.

"This place hasn't changed a whit in all these years," Jilly muttered.

"You've been here before?" Rose asked.

She didn't want to start dredging up memories before a cup of coffee. She only nodded, her lips pressed tightly together.

Even the waitress looked like an original from way back when. She was a jovial woman in her seventies, as tall as Jilly but broader in the chest and hips and without any of Jilly's reserve. She greeted them with a robust voice and led them toward a table near the window.

As Jilly passed the fountain, empty now, in her mind's eye she saw five teenage girls sitting on the stools, twisting left to right, their ankles hooked around the stool, sipping on straws like teenage girls all across the country. Except that each of these girls was dressed in baggy clothes to disguise the bulge of her belly. Not that they fooled anyone. Whenever the girls were allowed to town for their once-a-month outing, they traveled in a pack, closing ranks as a defense against the pointed fingers and behind-the-palm whispers.

"I'm Maude," the waitress said, pulling out her pad. "You girls aren't from around here, are you?"

They shook their heads, smiling cautiously.

"Where you from?"

Rose, Birdie and Hannah looked at Jilly, unsure.

Did they think this was a secret spy mission, for heaven's sake, Jilly wondered? "Chicago," she replied with her reserved smile.

Maude smiled broadly. "Chicago, huh? We don't get too many Chicago visitors this time of year. In the summer they like to pass through on their way to Door County. Nice antique shops in town. That's a draw."

In a casual voice, Jilly said, "We're looking for the convent that's not too far from here. Do you know the one I mean?"

"That'll be Holy Hill."

The name rang a bell in Jilly's mind. *Holy Hell.* "So, it's still there?"

"Oh, sure. But it's pretty lonely up there now. Not too many nuns anymore. Just the old ones who go there to retire and die. It was different years ago. Lots of folks used to stop here on their way to and from Holy Hill. The girls from up there still come for a visit from time to time, too, just to see it again. You one of them?"

Jillian startled. She closed her menu and folded her hands. Her smile was brittle. "The girls?"

"Well, women really," Maude corrected, misunderstanding Jilly's response. She twiddled the pencil between two fingers. "You know, the gals who were in the novitiate." Seeing their empty stares, she added, "The young ones in training to be nuns. As the years went by most of them dropped out, then they just stopped entering. Young folks want different things these days, I guess. A couple of ex-nuns come by, too, from time to time. I just thought you might be one of them. But—" she laughed and shook her head "—mercy, no. You don't look the type." She turned to Birdie and Rose with her brows raised in question, but her eyes were on Birdie.

Birdie bristled and reached up to tug at her short haircut. "I'm afraid not."

"Oh, well, I'm gabbing here." She pushed back her black-framed eyeglasses and put her pencil to her pad. "And you all want your breakfast."

"I'm not very hungry," Jilly said. The burning pain in her stomach was starting up again at the prospect of returning to Marian House. "Just coffee and orange juice for me."

"Me, too," said Birdie.

"Oh, no you don't," Rose admonished. "We all need a little sustenance for the day's work. Are those bakery goods on the shelf homemade?"

"We bake them ourselves every morning," Maude replied with pride.

"Perfect. We'll have a basket of blueberry and corn muffins, jams, and orange juice and coffee for everyone." She pursed her lips. "Better add a double order of bacon, too."

Her sisters stared at her.

"I'm hungry," she said, closing the menu and handing it back to Maude with a smile.

When the order was delivered, Jilly ignored the pain in her stomach and asked as casually as she could, "Maude, can you tell us how to get to the convent?"

As they approached the black iron gates of Holy Hill, she felt she was again a seventeen-year-old pregnant girl, unsure and scared. Like then, she wanted nothing more than to turn around and go home. She shrank into the corner of the car and looked over at Birdie, who was driving. Her sister looked so much like their father, with the same angled nose, the same broad build and the same serious set of the mouth. She was about to tell her to stop, that she'd changed her mind and couldn't go through with it. To say what she wished she had cried out the first trip through these gates.

But Birdie turned at that moment to look at Jilly, and seeing the terror in her eyes, her own blazed with the fervent message: *Buck up, sis! You're not alone.*

So Jilly persevered, but she felt very small as they wound up and around the wooded hills of the impressive estate. They passed the lake, quiet and still, surrounded by cypress, then the grotto where the Blessed Virgin still reigned in splendor. The engine hummed as they rounded the highest hill—and there it was.

Marian House. The plain-front, three-story redbrick building that she had lived in for four life-changing months in 1973 loomed before her. She sucked in her breath. When they pulled into the parking lot, she shrank back in her seat, her hand hard against the dashboard as though to ward off a blow.

"Jilly, are you okay?" Rose's hand was on her shoulder.

She'd leaned forward from the back seat to press her face close.

"I don't want to be here," she said in a tight voice. "I don't want to come back here."

Rose looked at Birdie, alarmed.

"Just stay in the car," Birdie said with decision. "I'll go knock on the door. The place looks pretty deserted, anyway."

Birdie opened the car door and stepped out, breathing deeply. She had looked a little green around the gills earlier, but the crisp spring air seemed to revive her. Jilly watched from hooded eyes as Birdie approached the front door. It was crazy, she knew, but she expected Sister Celestine to open the door with her razor-sharp smile. Birdie rang the bell, waited a moment, then knocked loudly.

Jilly rolled down her window and breathed in the morning air. Above, the birds cried and circled in the treetops. Jilly closed her eyes and heard again the calls of the girls as they cut across the lawn of the convent on their way from chapel to Marian House. *Jilly, wait up!* Everything was so quiet now. Ghostly.

"No one seems to be here," Birdie said, leaning in the car window, startling Jilly from her reverie. "Is there another building we can go to for information?"

They drove over a small rise past the tall, shaggy border of pines and trees. Suddenly the mansion appeared in the distance, eliciting the same sighs of surprise from Jilly's sisters as it had from her the first time she saw it.

"You lived *there?*" Hannah asked.

"Fat chance," Jilly replied, halting any ideas they might be forming in their minds of a sweet life she had led here at Holy Hill. "That house was only for the young brides of Christ. Strictly off-limits to the Mary Magdalenes. We were pretty much confined to Marian House. Not that we could waddle that far, anyway." She smirked, disguising the burn of shame she still felt. "You could say we lived on the other side of the tracks."

She saw Rose frown before she looked out the window.

"Who's Mary Magdalen?" Hannah wanted to know.

Another time, another place, Jilly would have enjoyed niggling Birdie over that one, but now her mind was overflowing with voices and faces from her past. As they drove away from Marian House, she looked out toward the bedroom windows and thought of Simone, Sarah, Julie and the others. What were they doing now, she wondered? Had they searched for their babies? She longed to see them again and talk to them. They'd understand what she was feeling now, as only they could.

They drove on past the apple orchard and vineyards, overgrown now from years of neglect. Seeing the lovely green open spaces Jilly felt a vague sadness, knowing it was only a matter of time till they were gone. It was clear the old nuns were dying off and young women were not entering the convent. The estate was prime land, likely to be soon sold and parceled into development plots.

The road ended at a long, yellow-brick building, more modern and updated than the others on the compound but equally bland. This was the conference center where the main offices of the motherhouse were located; the likely place any files would be stored. Jilly stared at the municipal-looking entrance and wondered if she'd run into Sister Celestine here, or Sister Benedict, or any of the nuns she once knew.

Well, if it isn't Jillian Season. What's become of you?

Well, Sister, I'm a thrice-married and divorced ex-model, ex-spaghetti-western queen a bit down on her luck.

Hardly a success story. During her time here she used to dream that she'd come back one day, a huge success, just to show them she was somebody. Her return only seemed to magnify her failures. She'd crumple if they gave her that superior look again, the one that designated her as her parents' shame, the unrepentant sinner, the lost soul.

"You don't have to come in if you don't want to," Rose said, always the perceptive one. "Just give us the journal with all the information. We can handle it."

"You have nothing to be afraid of, you know," Hannah told her.

Jilly felt a quick pulse of anger at her niece. What did she know? She was fifteen years old!

"I mean," Hannah continued, inching forward on her seat with youthful earnestness. "Think about it. You're, like, so successful. You're famous! You made something of your life. In another country, no less. And no one helped you. You did it all on your own. That's so cool. You can look anyone in the eye and not be afraid. I'm really proud you're my aunt."

Jillian's heart soared. This was so unexpected. So sincere. And so perfectly timed. This young woman viewed her life not as something pitiful, but as something to be proud of. The words flowed over her bruised self-esteem like a soothing balm. She never knew anyone to be proud of her.

"Thank you, *chérie*," she said, reaching out to cup Hannah's face. "All my life, people have only complimented my beauty. I wondered if that was all they saw when they looked at me. Without question, this is the best compliment I've ever received. I love you, baby." Jilly took a deep breath, then grabbed her journal. "Let's go."

Inside, the large institutional building was also seemingly deserted.

"Looks like no one is here, either," said Birdie.

"Someone must be. Or little elves come at night to clean the place," Hannah joked. "The place is spotless."

It was true. Endless halls of cream-and-green linoleum, smelling of pine soap and glistening in the filtered light of the venetian blinds, seemed to go on forever. Jilly stood mute, assaulted by the scents and sights from her past. She knew the nuns slaved over these halls to keep them pristine. When she looked down the halls she saw shadowy images of them, their long habits billowing and their wooden rosary beads clicking as they hurried from one task to another.

Even after all these years, she felt she'd get in trouble if she was caught in the conference center. It was off-limits to the girls of Marian House. She had stepped foot in the conference center only a few times—for Sister Benedict's sessions and to formally sign away her baby before leaving. She looked down the hall, then, on a hunch, walked to the third oak door on her left. The echo of her heels seemed to click thunderously on the floors. The door swished silently open and her breath seized. This was the room. There was the same round oak table upon which she had signed the adoption papers. Even the picture on the wall was the same—a large framed print of Rubens's *Blessed Mother and Child.* She could not bring herself to go in.

The memory of that afternoon flashed in her mind. She saw the social worker sitting in the chair, staring at her through Coke-bottle eyeglasses. She could smell again her cloying perfume in the cramped quarters. Sister Celestine stood beside her, erect and tidy, her hands tucked into her voluminous black sleeves. Why couldn't she remember the social worker's name? She could remember her voice, though. It was husky, like a man's.

"Sign this one," she'd said, placing a paper in front of her.

Jillian, exhausted from childbirth only forty-eight hours earlier, had just returned to Marian House from the hospital and was taken directly to the conference center. Jilly weaved in her chair as she stared down at the papers with a vague, numb appreciation of what she was doing.

"Go on, Jillian, we don't have all day," Sister Celestine said tightly.

Jillian did as she was told.

"Then this one. And this. Very good," the social worker said, satisfied. She quickly collected the signed legal papers and tucked them into her briefcase. "You've made the right decision, Miss Season."

The deed was done. Her parents were in the foyer at Marian House, waiting for her. Exhausted and emotionally drained, Jilly felt a deadening relief that it was over. At last, she could go home.

"Jilly?"

Startled, she turned to find her sisters standing beside her, worry etched on their faces.

"I'm okay," she hastened to assure them, quickly wiping a tear from her cheek and closing the door. "I was just looking around. That's the main office over there," she said, pointing in the opposite direction. She walked briskly away, leading them to a closed, unmarked door to the right of the entrance. "This used to be the receptionist's office. Let's see if anyone's here."

The pale mint-green office was also deserted. Behind a shiny Formica counter there was a large old-fashioned switchboard, the kind high schools around the country used to have, complete with an enormous handheld microphone for the PA system.

Birdie walked up to the counter and called out, "Hello? Is anybody here?"

There was a scurrying from the back, the sound of a chair scraping against linoleum, and then the unforgettable swish of long skirt and rosary. Jilly automatically stood straighter. From around the switchboard appeared a short, stout elderly nun, remarkable both for the fact that she still wore a habit and had a single, bushy black brow hanging over her eyeglasses like a wooly caterpillar.

"Good morning," Birdie greeted her with an imposing cheer that demanded response.

The nun smiled, but her eyes were filled with confusion. "Good morning."

"Apparently she isn't having a good morning," Hannah whispered to Jilly behind her palm.

Jilly gave her a silencing look, then stepped forward. "Hello, Sister," she said in her parochial school voice that showed respect. "My name is Jillian Season. I'm hoping you can help me. I'm looking for some records. Can you tell me where they'd be stored?"

The nun scrunched up her face and peered at her. "Records? What kind of records?"

Jilly felt as if she were walking on quicksand. Mr. Collins had warned against telling anyone that she was a birth mother seeking information. But she'd vowed she would not lie again. To lie would mean she was doing something wrong, illegal or even immoral.

"Adoption records," she replied smoothly.

"Adoption?" The old nun seemed momentarily confused. She stared vacantly for a moment, then realization dawned. She cast a dark glance at Jilly. "Are you one of those Marian House girls?"

Birdie and Rose closed ranks.

"Yes, I am. I was, rather. I'm searching for the adoption records of my child," she repeated, looking her straight in the eyes. Inside, however, she was quivering. "Can you tell me where I can find them?"

"They aren't here anymore. They're gone."

"Gone? Gone where?"

"I don't know. All the files of that place were moved when Marian House closed down. Back in 1981 or '82. I don't remember." Then, in a voice laden with accusation, she asked, "What do you want to go searching for those records for?"

"I'm hoping to find—" Jilly paused, then said the words

that she'd never allowed herself to use before. "I'm hoping to find my daughter."

The old woman shook her head. "Leave the child be. What's done is done. You don't want to go in and disrupt that child's life, and the life of the whole family. To do so would only be selfish, if you ask my opinion."

Birdie drew back her formidable shoulders. "I don't believe we asked your opinion."

"Birdie..." Jilly put her hand on Birdie's arm.

The nun's face flushed red against the white wimple. "That's all I know. You should go now. I'm sorry, but we can't help you."

"One more question, please," Jilly said, hating the pleading tone in her voice. She remembered Mr. Collins's advice not to leave any stone unturned. "Is Sister Celestine still here?"

The nun seemed surprised by the question and softened with sadness. "No, Sister Celestine died. More than ten years ago now, God rest her soul."

"I'm sorry to hear that. What about Sister Benedict?"

"Which one is she?"

"She was in charge of Health Services in 1973."

"Oh, I remember her." The nun shook her head. "A troublemaker. She left the order, not too long after."

They're all gone, Jilly thought to herself. Marian House— the whole estate—was a ghost town.

Jilly felt a tug on her coat sleeve. It was Birdie, indicating with a nod of her head that it was time to go.

Birdie, Rose and Hannah dropped Jilly off at the motel on the excuse that she would wait for word from Mr. Collins. They all knew, however, that she needed a little time alone after Marian House. They walked back to the Country Diner for lunch, the familiarity and the friendly face of Maude exactly what they needed after the cold reception at the convent.

"Did that give you a hint of what Jilly must've gone through living there?" asked Birdie, feeling a renewed loyalty to her sister. "I thought the place was positively morbid."

Rose nodded in agreement. "Everything was deserted. Melancholy was so thick I could hardly breathe." After a moment she added, "It's no wonder she never thought about it."

The three fell silent. Birdie picked up her bacon sandwich and looked at it with resignation. "Go figure. They bake their own muffins but they make the sandwiches with Wonder bread! No tomato. And greasy potato chips." She wrinkled her nose. "They must have gotten ahold of Mom's cookbook."

Rose nibbled her grilled cheese. "I still can't believe how unfeeling that nun was."

Birdie agreed, dabbing at her lips. "But can you blame her? She's old and she lives up there in that morgue where everyone is just waiting to die. It's no different than a lot of nursing homes."

"I wonder if it was like that when Aunt Jilly was there?" Hannah asked.

Hannah had been very quiet on the road home. She now sat quietly just stirring her vegetable soup around in the bowl.

"Are you okay, honey?" Birdie asked.

Hannah nodded. "I just feel so sorry for Aunt Jilly," she replied. "She was just a little older than me when she went there." She looked at her mother to reinforce her point.

Birdie set down her half-eaten sandwich and stared. Could that be true? She'd never thought of it in that light. Hannah looked so young. She was a child! She still needed her mother's guidance and advice, curfews and limits. Love and understanding. Could Jilly really have been *that* young when she was cast out of the family? When she had had a baby?

To think of Hannah being alone at such a time, without her—
it was unthinkable.

"My poor Jilly."

"She never talked about her experiences at Marian
House," said Rose. "Remember, she left for Europe soon
after she returned. And we certainly didn't talk about it, not
even among ourselves. The subject was taboo. I can't imagine her days at Marian House were pleasant. I can't imagine
them at all, frankly. Except it would have been more lively.
There would've been many more nuns living there back in
the early seventies. And then there was the novitiate, not to
mention the other girls at the home."

"Do you think they're searching for their children?" Hannah asked.

Birdie lifted her shoulders to indicate she didn't know. She
looked into her daughter's brown eyes, so like Dennis's, and
wondered what it would be like if she were searching for her
own daughter. She felt a flutter in her heart as she realized
how empty her life would have been had she not shared it
with Hannah.

"I'm afraid we're back to ground zero. The adoption file
has been archived somewhere and the nuns aren't saying
where. The nuns Jilly knew are gone, and she can't remember
the name of the social worker that handled the adoption. Marian House was a total dead end. No pun intended."

"Merely a detour," Rose replied, not to be thwarted.
"We've only just begun."

"So what do we do now?" Hannah asked.

"We'll check for messages at the motel," Birdie replied.
"Mr. Collins might have tried to reach us. At the moment,
he's our best bet." She looked to Rose for confirmation.

"There have to be other places to contact we haven't
thought of." Rose tapped her lips in thought. "There's got
to be information on the Internet. I'll go online as soon as
we get back."

"There *are* places to look, but we don't have much to go on," Birdie said. "We have to be realistic. A search can take months. Years."

"Who else would have records of the birth? The county seat? The library?"

"Yes, but right now we're stuck with little to go on. It's like a jigsaw puzzle. Everything links." She held up her hand and began counting off her fingers. "We know the mother's name. We know the date of birth, but not the time. We know the area she delivered in." Birdie sat upright; her face lit up. "Of course! What a dolt I've been not to think of this sooner. The hospital! Jilly delivered at a local hospital, not at Marian House. That's a lucky break. Obstetrics units keep an OB log that lists the babies born each day. They'd have to have some record of a live birth."

"Well, let's go," Rose said eagerly, grabbing for her purse. Hannah was already pushing back her chair.

"Hold your horses," Birdie said, waving them back. "We need the name of the hospital first."

"How many can there be? We just need a phone book." As Rose tapped the table with her fingers, she said more slowly, "I suppose we'll have to have Jilly with us, anyway, to ask for the files."

Birdie swallowed the last bit of her sandwich, then cast them a shifty glance. "You forget," she said, dabbing her lips, "I'm a doctor."

Back at the motel, Jilly sat on the mattress poring over the telephone book. She'd found the listing for Catholic Social Services and duly noted the number, but she couldn't remember the name of the social worker that had worked on her case. She tried scanning the hospitals. Her mind may have been playing tricks on her, but none of the three hospitals listed rang a bell. She could have sworn it was a Saint Something Hospital, but there wasn't anything remotely Catholic listed. She'd never forget that frightening ride in the ambulance, but she had no bearings as to what town the hospital was in. On the way home, she had been a zombie, too exhausted and shell-shocked to recall something as relatively mundane as an address.

Tossing aside the phone book, she scratched her head vigorously. Closing her eyes, she saw faces of the girls she'd lived with at Marian House. So many faces...why couldn't she remember any names? She'd spent a lifetime deliberately forgetting them, and now she was worried that she'd never scrape up even one essential detail. Feeling the urge for a smoke, she rose, stuck a pack of cigarettes and matches in the pocket of her leather coat and went out the back door.

Mr. Patel had referred to the four-foot square of cement crisscrossed with cracks as their *patio*. She snorted. Well, if he could call this dump a motel... Four nondescript, white resin chairs circled a similar table, and a stone planter, crumbling at the edge, was filled with cigarette butts and litter. "You've really scraped the bottom now, Season," she muttered.

The woodland just across the river, however, was beautiful in its wild, unkempt naturalness. Over it, the sky was a brilliant blue and the fresh breeze was pleasing on her face. Jilly pulled a tissue out from her pocket and wiped away the dirt and leaves, then sat and looked out.

In this area, the river was more a brook that ambled prettily across rocks and pebbles along the ridge of the hill behind it. It made a soft, swishing sound that was soothing. She breathed deeply and exhaled, releasing her troubled thoughts to the woods beyond. A dog's bark sounded to her left, followed by a man's shout. Curious, she leaned forward toward the sound.

It was Mr. Patel. He was farther down the river, standing on the banks below a small wooden bridge and appeared to be clearing branches and debris. The little white dog she'd noticed earlier that morning was at his side, testing the water with one paw, barking an opinion, then retreating back to sniff the small pile of debris already collected. He ignored the dog, working at a steady pace. The afternoon sun had turned warm, as promised, and he had removed his jacket. She spied a khaki oilskin hanging on a nearby tree branch. He was dressed for labor, wearing high rubber boots and heavy work gloves.

Jilly stretched her long legs out before her and idly watched him work. There was a mesmerizing quality to his movements as he bent to pick up branches and twigs then hurl them to the embankment with seemingly little effort. His body was long and lean and he worked steadily, smoothly, sure of what had to be done. She leaned far back in her chair and smoked, studying him more closely, remembering the sudden, strong attraction she'd felt for him at first sight.

He was handsome, yes, and very exotic. He also appeared a very proper sort of man—even while doing hard labor. She chuckled softly, noting that his work shirt was a worn and frayed business shirt, rolled up at the sleeves and exposing beautiful brown forearms that contrasted with the white cotton. Most likely the result of the British influence on East Indian culture, she thought to herself, much like his clipped accent.

It was the dog that betrayed her. When she coughed lightly, the dog's head sprang up, and he barked once in warning. Mr. Patel straightened then, too, his eyes searching. She held still, the cigarette trailing smoke in her outstretched hand. He didn't speak when he first saw her, or wave his hand in greeting. He studied her for a moment, and she thought again how much he resembled a great dangerous cat in his caution and stillness. At length, he acknowledged her with a nod of his head.

She did likewise.

The dog was not so reserved. He bounded up the slope to

investigate, his legs springing out from beneath his short, stocky body. When he reached her side, he raised himself up to paw eagerly.

"You naughty pup! Such muddy feet. Aren't you the rude one?" she said with a light laugh. He really was an adorable beast. Small, white and compact with floppy ears, he was some kind of terrier mix. It was his eyes that hooked her, however. Almond-shaped and dark, they had an uncanny intelligence that made them appear almost human. His head was long and narrow and pure white with a chocolate-colored patch that covered his left eye. "You're a rogue, I can tell," she said, reaching over to scratch behind his ear. "And I'm a sucker for a rogue. You know that, too, don't you?"

She heard the footfall of Mr. Patel approaching but did not look up, keeping her eyes on the little dog. Her body tensed in the chair and the dog jumped down to turn and bark. Slowly, she moved her gaze to meet his face.

His expression when he looked into her eyes was confusing. It was both serene and guarded, an unusual combination that implied a man comfortable with himself yet intolerant of disturbance.

"I hope the dog didn't annoy you," he said.

"No, not at all. He's really quite adorable."

"He's rather a pest."

"I can believe that," she replied, smiling down at the dog who was now sniffing at something under a rock on the far side of the patio. Looking back up she asked casually, "Would you care for a cigarette?"

"No, thank you. I don't smoke."

"Oh." She paused, then said with seductive tilt of her head, "Smoking isn't allowed in this room, is it?"

"No," he replied. Then, his eyes glittering with faint amusement, "But I don't think you'll disturb the neighbors, considering there aren't any."

She smiled, too, and something between them shifted. A

lightening in the air, a nanosecond of connection that confirmed a mutual attraction.

"Do you have everything you need, then?" he asked.

It was more of a dismissal, but she wasn't quite ready to be dismissed. She put out her hand. "My name is Jillian Season. Jilly."

He hesitated, then quickly removed his glove and took her hand. She felt the stirring contact as his hand enclosed hers.

"I am Rajiv Patel."

"You're the manager?"

"Yes. And the owner."

She registered this.

"I hope you don't think I'm being too curious," he said by way of polite apology, "but you're all related, aren't you? There is a strong resemblance." He lifted his hand toward his head. "The red hair."

"Two of the women are my sisters, the other my niece. The red hair is a Season family trademark."

"Are you visiting family?"

Jilly shook her head. "No, at least, I don't think so. Actually, we're trying to find a family member. Someone I haven't seen in a very long time."

A shadow of sadness flickered over his face. "Family is everything. You are fortunate to have your sisters close."

A sensitive man, she thought to herself. She liked that. "Would you like a soda? Some water?"

"No, thank you," he said, shifting his weight. "I'll be going back to it."

He turned to leave, then stopped to look once more in her face. His eyes searched hers and though she recognized the searing gaze that signaled attraction, she also sensed a reining in. "Good luck with your search," he said with sincerity. Then he walked off. The little dog trotted to the edge of the patio, watching Mr. Patel's departure with his ears cocked, but stayed back.

"Mr. Patel!" she called after him. "Your dog!"

He slowed to look over his shoulder. "He's not my dog," he called back. "He's just a beggar. I warn you. Feed him once and he'll be at your door forever." He turned back to his path.

"You're a poor little beggar, are you?" she asked the dog. He sat at her feet and cocked his head to the side. Her heart swelled. "You're a pro," she said, bending over to pat his head. "You remind me of my former husbands."

She reached into her pocket and pulled out one of Rose's cookies, thinking the dog might be hungry. Her mother used to scold her whenever she put out a cup of milk or a bit of hot dog for some dog or cat, but Jilly had always liked strays and mutts. She chuckled again at the too obvious and painful parallels to her choice of husbands.

As she started to unwrap the cookie, the wily dog sneaked up and, with a quick jump, snatched the cookie, saran wrapper and all. Startled, she looked up in time to see the little thief scuttle back down to the riverbank and settle in the tall grass beside Mr. Patel. She stood for a moment watching the dog as he relished his stolen lunch and Mr. Patel as he squatted on his haunches tying twine around a bundle of twigs. Both appeared unaware of her presence.

It was no wonder, she thought, tossing her cigarette to the cement and grinding it with her shoe. They couldn't see her for she wasn't really here. She was traveling at the speed of light on a journey through time.

Thirteen

Agnes Muirfield.

Jilly sat up in bed, eyes wide from her nap. She'd remembered the name of the social worker. Maybe the fresh air had loosened her memory, or the rest, but whichever, she had the name.

She climbed from the bed to splash cold water on her face, tie back her unruly hair and, for good measure, brush her teeth. She felt more like her old self after her nap. Being back in Marian House had made her feel like an outcast once again. But her memories succeeded in making her angry. Rose was right. She'd made the best decisions she could have at the time, without the help of her parents, the nuns or social workers like Agnes Muirfield. She'd paid her dues with guilt and suffering. Now she wanted some answers.

She picked up the telephone and punched the number for Catholic Social Services in Green Bay.

"Hello? I'd like to speak to Agnes Muirfield, please." She liked the strong tone of her voice.

"I'm sorry, but she retired years ago."

"Oh." Damn. She was afraid of that. "Could you connect me with the social worker assigned to her cases?"

The secretary connected her to a woman named Donna

Strobel who had an authoritative voice, rather like Birdie's. For a moment, Jilly froze, wondering if she should be truthful and just ask for the adoption records, or come up with a story. Mustering her resolve, she stuck with the truth.

When she told Mrs. Strobel why she'd called, to her surprise the social worker's tone grew more friendly. She told Jilly that she would search for the file and call her back, probably in half an hour.

Jilly set the receiver down and stared at it for a moment. She'd get the file! Jilly couldn't believe it; it had been too easy. What luck! Thirty minutes seemed like hours. She hunted for a cigarette but remembered she was fresh out, so she grabbed her purse and hurried down the narrow strip sidewalk toward the motel office. The sun was setting and the northern chill cut straight through her silk sweater and black slacks. Wrapping her arms around herself, she hustled with her head tucked to her chest.

She entered the motel office cautiously, glancing at the dated brochures and decor. Surprisingly, a small wooden table in the corner had been draped with white linen. On it sat a pot of fragrant tea on a hot plate, white china cups and saucers, and silver spoons. A few cookies were spread out on a plate. The scent of the heady tea filled the room and she looked at it longingly. From behind she heard a door open, then a man's footsteps.

"Jilly, may I pour you a cup? It's all there for my guests."

From the corner of her eye she saw Rajiv step from around the counter, moving into her line of vision. He had changed back into dark slacks and a white shirt and his hair was still damp from his shower. He stood waiting at the table with his seemingly infinite patience.

"Please," she replied, feeling the tension in the room thicken. Once again, the attraction she felt was immediate. She had experienced this too many times in her life to miss it now. She watched him conduct the simple everyday tasks—lifting the teapot, pouring the amber liquid into a cup, placing the cup on the saucer—her experienced eye catching every detail. In the world of fashion, where there were so many fabulous fabrics and creative designs and where beauty was commonplace, she'd learned to seek out the small details for clues to a person's character and taste. How many times had she seen a designer-original dress worn over an un-washed body, or a button missing on a two-hundred-dollar shirt?

Rajiv's clothes were not expensive, but they were spotless and well pressed. His nails were neatly trimmed. His black lace-up shoes were of good quality leather that, though quite worn, was polished.

He seemed aware of her perusal but she couldn't be certain. She liked his diffidence. It implied good manners. And self-control. He took his time, offering her cream with a raised brow. She shook her head no. Sugar? No. He handed over the cup and saucer with quiet aplomb. It struck her as all rather bizarre. His Old World elegance was as out of place in this shabby motel office in northern Wisconsin as was the custom of British teatime.

The tea was lovely, but her mind snapped back to the phone call that was due. "Do you have cigarettes for sale?"

"I do, but not much of a selection."

"I'm rather desperate."

He smiled. "In that case, I've made a sale. One moment, please."

She swallowed the tea in short, quick gulps. The Darjeeling was fragrant and she welcomed the warmth to ward off the chill of the late afternoon. She glanced at her watch, impatient to be back in her room, worried that Mrs. Strobel might not find the file before the end of her workday. When he offered three brand choices, she chose one and paid quickly.

"Oh, damn," she exclaimed, setting down her cup and searching frantically in her purse. "I've forgotten my key."

"I can open the door for you with the master."

"Thank you. Could you hurry, please? I'm expecting an important phone call."

The phone was ringing when they came to the door. He opened the door quickly and she ran inside, but the line was dead when she picked it up. She felt her heart drop to her shoes and sat on the bed with a heavy sigh, cursing herself for even leaving the room in the first place. She couldn't have been gone more than ten or fifteen minutes!

"Was it very important?" he asked.

"Yes, very," she replied, raking her hands in her hair.

"Then whoever it was will call again." He stepped outside the door. "I should be going. I'll bring you a cup of tea while you wait."

"Thank you." The phone rang. He opened the door a bit to catch her eye and deliver a grin that said, *See, I told you.* Smiling, she answered the phone.

"Hello, Miss Season?"

"Yes! I'm so glad you returned the call. I doubt I would have endured the night waiting."

"I'm sure after twenty-six years, you've waited long enough."

Her voice was kindly and Jillian knew by the comment that she had already read the file.

"I have the file before me," Mrs. Strobel began. "But you realize that by law I cannot disclose identifying information."

Jilly wanted to ask why not? This was her daughter, after all. Why could Mrs. Strobel know where her daughter was and not herself? But she knew her complaints would be useless and that Mrs. Strobel was only doing her job.

"First of all, I'm sure you want to know that your daughter was born healthy and normal in every respect. The adoption was final in 1974 and there are several notations indicating that the adoptive family was overjoyed with their new daughter. In their words, they thought themselves blessed.''

Jilly tried to be happy for them, yet she couldn't help begrudge them the blessing that should have been her own. She looked out the window and swallowed hard. "Please go on," she said. "What was the family like?"

"Well-educated. Catholic. Father is a professional. Mother stayed home with her daughter. Follow-ups reported that your child was well-adjusted, bright, social. She excelled at school."

"What does she look like?"

"Let's see." Jilly heard the papers rustle and was in agony wishing she could see them. "She has blue eyes and red hair. It's noted that she is quite beautiful." She could hear the smile in Mrs. Strobel's voice.

Her daughter had the Season red hair. Her heart skipped a beat. "What did they name her?"

There was a pause, and Mrs. Strobel said with remorse, "I'm sorry. I cannot divulge names or addresses."

"Not even her first name?"

"I'm sorry. I wish I could."

She thanked her and hung up the phone. For a while, she stood still and stared at the little motel room. The paisley-covered beds, the futuristic lamps, opened suitcases on the floor—all looked as they had minutes before. Yet her whole world had shifted.

It was real. She had a daughter. A redheaded, blue-eyed girl. The urge to find her came suddenly and overwhelmingly.

There was a knock on the door. Jilly reluctantly went to answer it, knowing it was Rajiv, but wanting to be alone with her news. She opened the door to find him standing there with a small pot of tea and a single cup.

"Here is your tea." He handed her the cup and moved to

place the pot on the bureau. Then he paused and studied her face, compassion written on his own. "Are you all right? You've been crying."

Jilly's lifted her fingertips to her cheeks. She hadn't even realized that tears were flowing down her cheeks. "I'm okay," she replied, smiling wide and quickly wiping them away. She felt a sudden elation, like a balloon had just filled her chest. "I've had some news. Wonderful news, actually. About my daughter." The word *daughter* still hung on her lips and floated in the air, unfamiliar, but very, very welcome.

He smiled, pleased. "She must be beautiful, like her mother."

Jilly laughed then, she couldn't help herself. "She is," she replied, amazed that she knew this. "I only just found out." When he looked perplexed she went on, "I'm searching for my daughter and I only just learned the first bit of information about her. That was the phone call. You see, I gave her up for adoption after her birth. That's why we're here. We're searching for her. Me and my sisters."

"I see."

She heard no judgment in his comment. "I had her when I was quite young, not far from here. At Holy Hill."

"The home of the Catholic sisters?"

She smiled at his phrasing. "Yes. A long time ago."

"I see," he repeated. "And did you locate your daughter?"

"No, not yet. But I will."

He turned to pour out a cup of tea and handed it to her. "It's not champagne, but it is a good-quality tea. Congratulations!"

The fragrance of the tea floated between them. She thanked him and took a sip. It was heavenly. She closed her eyes, thinking the heady tea much more perfect for a quiet celebration than champagne.

"Such wonderful tea. Where do you get it?"

"My family sends it to me from India."

"Have you been here long?"

"Not very. I arrived a year ago this May. My father and uncle came to America twenty years ago. They started with one motel, and now they own several, mostly in the south. Georgia, the Carolinas, Tennessee. I suppose you can call them examples of the American Success Story. They only recently started branching out in the Midwest. I have brothers and cousins managing other motels. My father offered me a start with this motel." He smiled briefly as his gaze scanned the room. "A rather rough start," he added without rancor. "I don't know that he was convinced of my sincerity at this profession. But I'm grateful for the opportunity. I needed a change. My life in India became—" He paused. "Untenable."

"You mentioned your family in India. Your wife?"

His face clouded. "My wife died three years ago."

She saw again a glimpse of the fire raging in his eyes and had a hint now of its source. How hard it had been for her to give up her daughter to live with another family. How much harder it must be to give up a loved one to death. "I'm sorry," she replied, knowing it was inadequate, but enough.

He accepted her sympathy with a polite nod. His stillness gave nothing away.

More knocks sounded at the door. "Open up, Aunt Jilly. It's me!"

There was a second's discomfort between them, as though his being there in her room implied something illicit. Refusing to acknowledge it, she opened the door and smiled with exaggerated enthusiasm. "Wonderful news!" she exclaimed.

"No, we have wonderf—" Hannah's sentence ended as she caught sight of Rajiv. Her gaze darted from him to Jilly, her expression changing from surprise to suspicion en route.

"I had better leave you to your good news. Don't worry about the teapot," Rajiv said, outwardly resuming his formality. "I'll have the maid bring it back when she cleans your room. Good day."

When their eyes met, she shared with him a private communication that dissolved the formality between them.

Birdie and Rose came from their room in time to see Rajiv leaving. Their eyes were as round as the teacups.

"He came to bring me tea," she explained, indicating the teapot. "Now, what is your good news?"

Accepting her explanation at face value, they hurried inside to sit on the bed, excitement brimming in their eyes.

"We found your hospital records!" Rose exclaimed.

"What?" Jilly's breath caught in her throat. She stared dumbfoundedly at her sisters. "But how did you know which hospital?"

"We didn't," Birdie explained. "But we figured it had to be one of the three in the area so we started off at the closest one, and bingo! We got lucky. Does the name University Hospital ring a bell?"

"No."

Birdie laughed. "That's because the university bought the hospital seven years ago. How about St. Francis?"

Jilly's mind clicked as another piece fell into place. "That's it! That's it!"

"We could have been stymied with that for days...weeks. Like I said, we just lucked out."

Jilly couldn't believe their good fortune. "And they just gave the file to you?"

"Well...no. I told them a plausible story about research I'm doing on live female births in the region in 1973. I gave them my identification and because I'm licensed in the state of Wisconsin, they granted access."

"Hannah and I stayed out of the way to avoid suspicion," Rose added.

"I had the date of birth and the mother's name to go on.

But guess what? Your memory's off. You had the birth date wrong by one day."

"No!" Jilly said in a hushed whisper, sitting down on the bed. Her knees felt weak. "No. I can't believe that. How can that be true? I'm the mother. I was there."

Birdie shrugged. "Sometime the memory gets a little hazy. You didn't write it down anywhere or have a birth certificate, and it's been a long time. Where's the journal?"

Rose reached into the shoulder bag, pulled out the green leather journal and handed it to her. Birdie opened it and sat down on the mattress beside Jilly to share the notations. Rose and Hannah clustered near.

She cleared her throat. "Your daughter was born at 4:14 p.m. on May 17, 1973, at St. Francis Hospital. The attending physician was Dr. Joseph Brewster. The anesthesiologist was Dr. Robert Clayton. Baby Girl Season weighed 7.2 pounds, was twenty-one inches long and in excellent health. She was discharged to Catholic Social Services on May 20." She looked up and smiled triumphantly at Jilly. "Your daughter's name is Anne."

That evening they went to the Country Diner to celebrate all they had learned. They brought wine with them and shared it with Maude and the older, timid gentleman behind the soda fountain, who turned out to be Larry, Maude's husband of forty-seven years. Together they owned and worked the restaurant.

"Were you working here back in 1973?" Jilly asked them.

"I sure did," Larry answered a bit shyly. His bushy white brows wagged. Under them, his pale eyes shone warmly. "Not the missus, though. She was at home with the children. And if you're wondering if I served you a soda, I probably did. I made sodas and milk shakes for a lot of them Marian House girls. Always added an extra scoop for them, too."

"For all the girls, I thank you," she said, raising her glass in a toast.

More toasts followed. They felt triumphant. Anne had really been born! Another Ann Season with blue eyes and red hair was out there somewhere.

By the time they arrived back at the motel, everyone was exhausted and a bit tipsy. Hannah and Jilly went directly to their room for sleep. Birdie and Rose did the same.

"I think I'll brave it and face the shower," Birdie said, rubbing the small of her back.

"Go ahead," said Rose. "I'm going to go online."

Birdie's back was aching and she felt mild cramping. She was overdue for her period again and had the wishful thought that perhaps she might be pregnant. It was mere reflex after years of trying for another baby and she shook the notion away with irritation at the reminder of all the disappointment. At her age, it was much more likely signs of approaching menopause.

She stepped into the hot downpour and relished the feel of the water pounding against her back and stiff neck. Laying her palms against the tile, she thought of Dennis and wondered what he was doing at that moment. Was he alone or with friends? Was he thinking of her, too? Over the past several days she'd tried not to think of him at all, or the words he'd flung at her before he left Evanston so abruptly. She could not believe he really meant them. He wouldn't toss away twenty years because of an argument.

But he hadn't returned any of her phone calls. A part of her wanted to punish him for ignoring her, for saying such cruel things and for making her cry, but she missed him. Just the possibility of him leaving her made her ball her fists and start crying. Hating the tears, she put shampoo in her hair and began to scrub her scalp vigorously, all the while sobbing, her tears mingling with the hot water, her cries blending with the loud hiss of the shower.

When her hair was washed, her tears seemed to be finished as well. Reaching for a towel, she felt a bit foolish but immeasurably better. She began drying her rounded body, noting with dismay how her breasts sagged pendulously and how her once curved waistline flared out in the classic pear shape teens made fun of. Leaning closer to the mirror she plucked at her hair with a frown. When did all that gray come in? she wondered, stunned at seeing the crop creeping in like weeds. How had she been so busy that she didn't pay attention to such things as her hair, her weight and her nails? Living with Jillian the past week had made her painfully aware of how she'd let herself go over the years. She felt like an elephant next to a gazelle. No one would guess now that Jilly was the elder sister. It was no wonder Dennis left, she thought with utter dejection.

Stepping out into the chilly room, she was glad Rose wouldn't be able to tell if she had been crying or just had soap in her eyes. She saw her sister wrapped up in her old baby-blue terry robe, her feet covered in thick wool socks, hunched over the computer busily pounding the keys. Her long strawberry-blond hair was roped up in a disheveled mess on her head that managed to look fetching. Did Rose know how pretty she was? Hers was not a glamorous beauty, like Jilly's, but a soft, natural one that was easy on the eyes. Birdie felt an old twinge of regret bubble up that, when compared to her sisters, she was not much of a looker.

Rose looked up briefly to smile, then dove back to whatever it was that had captured her interest. Birdie began to dry her hair. Rose was a funny one, she thought to herself. She remembered how she could sit for hours as a child and sort through her stamps. The family joke was that a bomb could go off and Rose wouldn't notice if she were concentrating on something.

"Hey, Rose, what are you doing?"

Rose looked up again, her eyes sparkling with an excitement rarely seen in her. "I'm researching adoption on the Net. Some of these stories by the birth mothers are incredible. I swear they'll break your heart when you think of our Jilly. Do you want a look?"

"Yes," she replied wearily. "But not now. I'm pooped and I want to call Dennis first."

Rose's smile slipped and Birdie saw the worry crease her brow. "Do you want to talk about it first?"

Birdie didn't want to talk about it with Rose—or anyone else. Her problems with Dennis were her own business. "There's nothing more to tell," she responded breezily. "I'm just checking in with him. Really, we'll get over our little tiff."

"You'll want to use the phone. I'll get off the line."

"Don't be silly. I'll use my cell phone."

"Are you sure?" Rose didn't look convinced. "Don't you want privacy? I can go to Jilly's room."

"Rose! You don't have to stop what you're doing for me. It wouldn't be fair to you. I love you and I'm grateful, but you really shouldn't put yourself out so much."

Rose sighed and looked deeply into her eyes. Birdie knew a sudden feeling that, here again, as with the night of Merry's death, Rose had a depth that she had never appreciated.

"I don't mind putting myself out," she replied by way of explanation rather than defense. "I rather enjoy it. Especially for those I love."

Birdie rubbed her hair vigorously with a towel, deeply affected by Rose's words. "Go on back to your Internet and I'll use my cell phone. Besides, it's clear you're on to something."

"I am. But if you change your mind about the privacy thing, just let me know. I'll go offline and leave the room.

It's no trouble.'' She turned back to the monitor and in a moment was lost in her world again.

Birdie quickly slipped into her long nightgown, boosted the heat a bit, then came to her bed and tucked herself under the covers. Picking up her phone, she dialed her home number. While the phone rang she told herself several times that this wasn't a major call. She was just calling to let him know where she was.

After the fifth ring, the answering machine picked up.

''Hello, you've reached the Connor residence. This is Dennis. Please leave a brief message after the beep.''

She opened her mouth to speak but found she couldn't. Why had he changed the message? Why didn't he mention her name? After a moment's hesitation, she disconnected the phone, then stared at it for a moment. Her gaze flicked over to the alarm clock. It was 10:50 p.m. Where could Dennis be? It wasn't like him to be out late on a weeknight. With a shaky hand she slowly set down the small cell phone on the bedside table. She inched her way under the blankets and brought her legs up, cuddling her pillow. Birdie fell asleep with a whimper.

Later that night, Rose was hot on the adoption search trail and had struck gold. She wanted to wake up Birdie, to call Jilly and tell her right away. Glancing at her watch, she frowned, cursing the lateness of the hour. Birdie was out like a light and Jilly had said she was exhausted and was going right to sleep too. Tucking away her disappointment, she bookmarked the location of the Soundex Reunion Registry, telling herself it could wait until morning.

Then, with a deep breath, she switched to the e-mail. When she saw one from DannyBoy waiting for her, she grinned from ear to ear. She knew at that moment just how much he had come to mean to her.

Dear Rosebud,

I thought about you a lot today. I thought about what to write to you about myself. It would be easier just to send a picture, but I know you don't want to do that. So, here goes.

I'm 38 years old. I'm 5'10'' and weigh 170 pounds. My hair is brown and my eyes are blue. I don't have a mustache now, but the jury is still out on that. I'm a simple man. I like to camp and hunt. I guess I'm in the truck so much that when I'm not, I like to stretch my legs and get away from the road. I like to cook and I'm pretty good at it. I prefer to mix things myself and not follow recipes. I guess you could say I'm more of a loner. My job and my hobbies point that out. But I like people, too, especially family.

I'm divorced. I have a ten-year-old son. He lives with his mom. She's a good mother. My son means the world to me and I see him whenever I'm home. Which is in Nebraska.

I know you're not too far from Green Bay right now and I'm wondering if you know how long you'll be in Hodges? My haul will be finished in a few days and I can try to make it to Wisconsin in about a week. If it works out, would you like to meet?

                                             DannyBoy

Rose felt the blood drain from her face. Meet? My God, he wanted to meet?

She slumped back in her chair and exhaled the breath she'd been holding. All along she'd supposed in the back of her mind that he'd want to meet her. But she'd managed to keep that possibility pushed far, far back in the nether regions of her brain. She'd read stories of how couples who had communicated by e-mail finally met and either got married and lived happily ever after or figured out pretty quickly that they weren't meant for each other.

She didn't want that to happen to her and DannyBoy. She liked things just the way they were. Dropping her gaze she closed the e-mail and shut down the computer. She suddenly felt very cold and very tired. She climbed into her bed as silent as a mouse so as not to wake Birdie, who was once again sleeping fitfully. She lay staring out into the dark, listening to the clank and whir of the ancient heater while her mind cranked out different solutions to his simple question: "Would you like to meet?"

She was only able to fall asleep much later when, exhausted, she told herself that it would be okay if she just didn't reply to his e-mail, at least not for a while.

Fourteen

◦─◦◦◦─◦

Jilly sat with her nose close to the screen, one hand clutching the mouse and the other a cup of coffee. Her blood raced with the first real ray of hope since being told by Catholic Social Services that they could not release information about her own child.

"What is this place?" she asked, bubbling with excitement.

Rose sat beside her on the bed grinning with delight that she'd been able to contribute to the search at last. "It's the Soundex Reunion Registry. I just found it on the Internet last night."

"I can't believe it. This can put me in direct contact with my daughter?"

"Only if she registers, too. Think of it as a match service."

"So, how can I sign up? What do I have to do?"

"It's not an e-mail registry," Rose explained patiently. "But we can write to request a registration form by mail or phone."

"Hang the mail. Let's call."

"Okay, we will, but hold on. There's something else I want to show you first." She moved to the keyboard to type in an address and took Jilly to a site where birth mothers contributed information and stories about their search. Jilly set her coffee cup down, settled into a comfortable position and began to read.

An hour later tears flowed down Jilly's cheeks. The stories of other mothers who had gone through similar birth experiences had shaken her belief that she was alone. She wasn't. There were so many who felt like her. Their pain was hers. Their loss was hers. Like her, many of them had had no real choice but to give up the baby for adoption. Like her, they'd been made to feel like a criminal deserving of some punishment. Some women had denied that the experience had happened. Others were haunted by worries for their child. Some women had gone on to have other children while others never had any more. All of them, however, shared a profound grief at having been separated from their child.

Afterward, Jilly felt energized with hope and was eager to chase down every trail. On the Internet she'd collected the names and addresses of many groups and agencies that offered help and support. She dressed quickly in jeans and a sweater, heaved her soft leather handbag over her shoulder and went to Rajiv to buy stationery and stamps.

"What brings you here this afternoon?" Rajiv asked, looking up from a stack of papers on his desk. "Looking for tea?" His smile transformed his serious, almost severe expression into a warm one Jilly couldn't help but return.

"I'm not quite the beggar that little dog is." Then looking around, "But if you have some handy…"

"I could make a fresh pot."

"Don't bother. I'm starving and should go get something to eat. I've been so busy I sort of forgot." She stepped closer to the counter and leaned against it, slightly flirty. "I discovered the Internet this morning."

He leaned back in his chair and raised his brows. "Your search has expanded, I see. Gone high-tech."

"Don't tease. I knew what the Net was all about, barely,

but I never really got involved with it. I didn't need it in my line of work. I had no idea what I'd been missing. Thank goodness for Rose.''

''What line of work were you in?''

''Oh…modeling,'' she replied somewhat defensively. ''In Europe.'' She struggled to keep her hand from straightening her hair. She knew she must look a fright with her hair a wild mess pulled back with a plastic clip and her sleepy face void of makeup. At least she'd brushed her teeth this morning, thank God. ''Do you sell stamps?''

''No. But I can give you one.''

''Thanks, but no thanks. I need lots. In fact, I think I'll express-mail this application. Where is the nearest post office?''

''I'll take you there. I have some things to mail myself.''

Her brows lifted. ''Thank you,'' she replied, glad to spend some time with him. After all, she imagined talking to him was infinitely better than just thinking about him.

The following day when she returned from her walk she was met at her room door by Rose waving a large envelope. Birdie and Hannah hovered close, their eyes shining.

''This came for you while you were gone,'' she said, handing over a FedEx.

Jilly accepted the package reverently. ''It's from Mr. Collins.''

''We were dying here waiting for you to get back.''

She cradled the envelope like a newborn baby. It was neither thick nor heavy. What could be in it? she wondered. One name? Many? Maybe an address? She felt the supportive presence of her sisters as she pulled the string and opened the envelope. She pulled out a few sheets of paper topped with a letter from Mr. Collins. Sitting down on the bed, she licked her lips and began to read.

''He says that this is the list of names that his contact had provided for him. He reminds us that the contact could not reveal her sources, blah, blah, blah, but he feels confident that one of the names on the list is…'' She looked up, her eyes round. ''Is my daughter.''

''Thank God,'' Rose said. ''Go on!''

''He also writes that there will be a delay in the release of the adoption records.'' She looked up. ''Damn.''

''Go on!''

''The judge felt it necessary to appoint an intermediary,'' she read. ''Mr. Collins is surprised by this development and suspects it's because the adoptive family might be wary of any contact with the dreaded birth mother.''

''They didn't say that!'' Hannah was indignant.

''I may have embellished a bit, but that's my take on it.'' She looked back at the letter. ''He also warns us not to lose hope, that this is merely a delay. Yours sincerely, et cetera.''

Jillian lay the papers in her lap. ''I'm afraid to look.''

''I'm not,'' Birdie said, nudging her shoulder. ''Aren't you dying of curiosity? We already know what the baby was named.''

''It's getting so real. With each step we take, we're that much closer to contact with her. After years of denial, this is all happening pretty fast.''

''I understand how you feel,'' Rose said, moving closer. ''Sometimes we're not ready to face things. We need a little more time. If you want to go slow, we'll understand. We told you we'd support you.''

Part of her wanted to wait. But hadn't she waited too long already? Unlike Rose, it was her nature to be impulsive. Taking a deep breath, she moved Mr. Collins's letter and looked at the list.

There were eight names, three of them were variations of Anne. Two of them had foreign-sounding last names, which she doubted could be her daughter's. The Seasons were English and Irish with red hair and blue-green eyes. Sister Celestine had assured her that they'd make every effort to match ethnicity and coloring.

"I thought we knew her name was Anne," Hannah said, looking over her mother's shoulder as they crowded around the list.

"I thought so, too," Birdie replied. "But they may have changed it again.

Jilly shook her head. "I don't think so. It would be different if I'd named the baby Ann." She rolled her eyes. "Fat chance of that. But for the sake of argument, if I had, then I could understand the adopted family wanting to choose a name of their own for their child. But I *didn't* name the baby. I was told not to, since it might make me more attached. So, if the adopted family named her Anne, why would they change it again? It wouldn't make sense." Looking at Birdie she asked, "Would you have changed Hannah's name after you arrived home?"

Birdie shook her head. "No, I see your point."

"Then why the other names?"

There was a silence as they thought about this.

"I think we should eliminate all the names except the variations of Anne," Birdie said. "That way we'll narrow our search focus. We were lucky to get the tip from the hospital records. Let's go with it."

"I agree," said Jilly. She took out a pen from the drawer, spread the paper out on the desk and she put an X beside three names.

Ann Josephine Neville.

Anne Rutledge.

Anne Marie Parker.

They stared at the list, each of them wondering which of these names was the one.

"Who would have thought in a million years that the baby would have been given the same name as our mother?" said Birdie with a touch of awe. "What kind of irony is that?"

"I think it's poetic justice," Rose said.

"I call it sweet revenge," Jilly scoffed. "Mother is probably rolling over in her grave."

"My God, are you bitter!" Rose exclaimed.

"You bet I am," Jilly replied, feeling the same pulse of fury she did every time she thought of her mother. "I never would have named my daughter after her."

"Get over it, Jilly," Birdie retorted. "She wasn't in the labor room with me, either. I wouldn't have wanted her to be. She wasn't that kind of mother."

"Oh, come on, Birdie," Jilly snapped. "Let's not pretend to compare our situations. I'm not referring to Mother being in the delivery room with me. She pretended that this delivery didn't even take place."

"She was a flake, yes. She probably never should have had four children, but she loved us. I never doubted that."

"Sometimes loving a child isn't enough," Jilly countered.

"Yeah," Hannah muttered, crossing her arms.

Birdie swung her head around to search her daughter's face. It was mutinous and full of accusation.

Jilly saw the stark pain etched on Birdie's face, and a second later, saw it start to crumple. That was something she never thought she'd see. They'd called her The Iron Bird in high school because no one or nothing could make Beatrice Season cry.

"Let's not argue. This is our first real lead. Let's get to work instead," she said, rising to a standing position. She met Rose's gaze and was relieved to see her nod in agreement.

"Okay then!" Rose said, eager to begin. "We've got names. What do we do next?"

"I'll get the journal," said Jilly. Her lithe, catlike body stretched across the bed as she grabbed the journal from inside her leather bag. "Okay, junior birdmen. Do you have your decoder rings on?" She looked up to see Birdie's lips twist into a reluctant smile. Glancing at Hannah, she saw that the teenager had missed the reference completely. "We're lucky Mr. Collins got us last names. From what I read on the Net this morning, it can take months for some women to get this far. According to the journal," she said, scanning the page, "we should start at the county library and check out the city directories for the year of the birth."

"We know that the baby was born in Green Bay County. If we get a map, we can begin with a radius of fifty miles and start spreading out. Then we'll hit the local phone books."

"It could take hours," Hannah whined. "Days."

"Hey," Jilly said sharply. Hannah's head snapped up. "What are we here for? If you prefer—" she cut her niece a withering glance "—you can stay in the room and watch TV."

Hannah appeared a bit shaken by her favorite aunt's sharp tone. "No, no, I want to come and help."

"Good," Jilly said with a quick nod. She didn't want to play the "good" aunt if it was causing trouble between Birdie and her daughter. Plus, she was getting increasingly concerned about the deliberate snubbing Hannah was giving her mother. Little digs like not sharing a room with her, not choosing a seat beside her in the restaurant, ignoring her mother's comments or paying extraordinary attention to anything Jilly said.

They all stood and grabbed their coats. Hannah left the room first, followed by Rose. As Jilly dug the key out of her purse to lock up, Birdie touched her sleeve.

"Thanks," she said.

"It's nothing," she replied breezily, then paused to meet her eye. "But between you and me, try not to see Hannah just as a child. Try to see her as a woman. You might find out she's pretty mature." She winked and started walking out of the room. "Hey, listen to me. I'm starting to get a handle on this mother-daughter thing."

The task of searching for an address match was not as easy as they'd thought it would be. Even dividing the labor between the four of them, two more days of searching had not uncovered a single match. The tension began to mount. Each afternoon, Jilly raced home to see if there was anything in the mail from Mr. Collins. Each evening Birdie called Dennis only to reach his answering machine. Each night Rose looked longingly at the computer, but did not turn it on to check her e-mail. It sat closed and cold, like her heart felt.

They filled their spare time prowling through Hodges' shops. Rose bought an old hooked rug, lamps, doilies and a coverlet at the antique shop. Jilly bought glasses and teacups to cozy up their rooms. But nothing could lift their spirits as the search stalled. After three days of searching addresses, their morale was slipping. Jilly looked at her sagging troops and decided they needed reinforcements.

"Girls," Jilly said, popping a Hershey kiss into her mouth the way Caesar would a grape, "I think I've hit a new low."

Spread out over the two double beds in her room was a greasy cardboard carton with one cold slice of cheese-tomato-olive pizza left in the center. A bag of Hershey Kisses, a bag of chocolate chip cookies, an empty bag of Doritos and a bag of gummy bears lay opened beside it.

"Let me guess," Birdie said, pummeling her pillows to prop up behind her aching back. "In elegant France, the ladies never binge."

"*Chérie,*" Jilly said with a pout, "perhaps on fine Swiss chocolate and champagne. But on pizza and beer? *Mais non!*"

"They don't know what they're missing. This is what I

like to call the All-American-All-Girls Slumber Party. It's better than Prozac.''

"I don't think I've ever had so much junk food in one sitting," said Rose, rolling over onto her stomach beside Jilly. "I think I'm going to be sick."

"No, you aren't. You're just too full of lentil and soy. A little decadence is good for the soul," Birdie said, popping another cookie.

"But bad for the waistline," Jilly countered. Then, tossing a candy at Birdie, she added, "I can't believe you're a physician."

"You know what they say," Birdie replied, catching it readily. "Physician heal thyself."

"We'll pay tomorrow," Jilly predicted, pushing the bags of candy farther away from her on the bed. "All except Hannah. Look at our budding beauty over there." She pointed to Hannah who was sitting on the floor doing her nails. "Am I the only one who noticed she only had one piece of pizza and not a single bite of chocolate?"

Birdie hadn't noticed. She swung her head around to study her daughter.

Hannah shrugged coyly and went back to filing her nails. "I'm just not hungry."

Birdie thought back to Hannah's eating pattern of the past several days and recalled that she'd been very choosy about her food, avoiding the sweet and fatty foods she usually preferred. She ate salads with vinegar dressing, lots of fruit, and no desserts. When she did order a dinner plate, she ate small portions. She was also taking greater pains with her clothes and putting on makeup with a lighter hand.

"Are you on a diet?" she asked, amazed. Hannah had never agreed to any of the diets she'd suggested in the past.

"Not really," Hannah replied in a lofty tone. "It's more a life pattern."

Birdie's brows rose on that one. A life pattern? That didn't sound like Hannah. She turned to look at Jilly and saw from the expression of pride on her face where the source of this new attitude in her daughter came from. She could imagine long, cozy chats with the light out about diets and beauty and boys and maybe even sex. All the things that Birdie should have been the one to talk to her daughter about. She felt an unexpected surge of jealousy. "Just what kind of life pattern are we talking about?"

Hannah tsked loudly. "What do you think? That I'm taking drugs or something? Or that I'm anorexic? I'm eating healthy foods!" she exclaimed. "Cutting out snacks and sweets. Jeez, Mom, it's the kind of thing you've been preaching at me for years. Except you don't do it yourself."

The dig was intentional and meant to hurt. It succeeded. Birdie tried to rise above it, hating the telltale blush she could feel burning her cheeks. "I don't think you're on drugs. I was just asking."

Hannah didn't reply but began to file her nail with vigor.

"She's exercising, too," Jilly added. "Every night. I've got her doing a nice little weight routine and every morning we're taking a long jog. These hills can be a good workout."

"I'm going to be buff by the time I get back from spring break."

They were walking together, too? Birdie felt terribly left out. Why didn't they invite her? She knew that Jilly was just trying to be helpful, but she was only making matters worse. Didn't Jilly understand that Hannah saw everything she did as so much better than her mother? Jilly was slim and beautiful and Birdie felt like an old bat next to her.

Jilly groaned and lay on her back, rubbing her fingers against her disgustingly flat stomach. "My stomach hurts. Get this stuff away from me. Throw it away. I never want to see chocolate again."

Birdie grabbed the bag and despondently unwrapped another chocolate and popped it in her mouth with a toss of the wrist.

"Until tomorrow," Rose said with a chuckle.

"Oh, listen to you," Birdie teased. "I didn't see you dive into the candy."

"I had some," she replied defensively. "I just don't like candy that much."

"I hate it when skinny people say things like that."

"Well, maybe that's why they're skinny and others are not," Hannah muttered.

"Hannah…" Jilly's tone was a warning. Hannah gave her a pointed look, then shrugged and went back to her nails.

Birdie ate another chocolate.

"What should I do with my hair?" Jilly asked as a change of subject, pulling herself from the mattress to walk over and stand in front of the sink mirror. "Look, do you see? Gray hair! Right at the temples. It's starting."

"Join the crowd," Birdie said sullenly.

"Not as long as I've got a breath in my body and a dollar in my wallet!" Jilly leaned close to the mirror searching for gray hairs.

Birdie could see from Hannah's worshipful expression that she found it utterly charming. Birdie pinched her lips and thought she wouldn't be surprised if Hannah switched languages from Spanish to French in school the next year.

"I'll have to find a salon," Jilly said. "No, I shudder to think of what could happen to me up here. I can do it myself. I don't want my daughter to meet me for the first time with gray hair. Do they still sell hair products in the supermarkets here?"

"Sure. All sorts of choices," Birdie replied. "But to be honest, Jilly, I can hardly see the gray."

"Me, neither," Rose piped in, raising herself up on her elbows.

"Hardly? That means you see some?" She swung around to the mirror again. "I hate my hair."

"It's funny that you say that," Birdie said, twisting a candy wrapper in her hand. "I've always loved your hair."

Jilly caught her pensive gaze in the mirror and dropped her hands from her hair.

"And yours, too, Rose," Birdie admitted. "With that gold-red softness."

"It's orange. Like a pumpkin," Rose said in her self-demeaning manner.

"It's beautiful and sunny," Birdie countered. "Like Mom's and Merry's. I was so happy when Hannah was born with that same color. Red hair is the Season family trademark and everyone has it. Except me." She gave off a short laugh, trying to diffuse the sympathy she could feel pouring out from her sisters. "When we were little and Dad would call out that awful 'Here come the Four Seasons' whenever we walked into a room, I used to cringe thinking that everyone was looking at me and wondering who the big, gawky kid was. I felt I didn't belong. Me and my plain old brown hair. Do you want to know what my first reaction was when I read in the hospital report that your child had red hair, Jilly? I felt cheated. Another Season with red hair. Why was I left out? I swear, if I didn't look so much like Dad, I'd think I was adopted."

"But you have lovely hair, Birdie," said Jilly, the sympathy rich in her voice. She was suddenly sorry for all the years she'd chided and teased her sister about her appearance, never guessing she'd hit the mark. Birdie had always shrugged and said with an air of superiority that she'd rather have brains than beauty. "You have lovely red highlights."

"I *used* to have red highlights. Now they've turned gray."

Jilly tapped her lips and said dramatically, "That can be changed."

"No, no, no. Dye and all that is not for me."

"Why not?"

"This is me, for better or for worse. I prefer to be natural. I hardly wear anything other than a little lipstick and mascara." She heard the uppity tone in her voice and instantly regretted it. She didn't feel uppity in the least. She actually felt quite sorry for herself but had to salvage some smidgen of pride after all she'd just gushed out. Embarrassed, she wished she could just wipe her whole confession up like a glass of spilled water.

But Jilly wasn't giving up. "There are many products that are all natural." Coming to sit beside Birdie she said in a gentler tone, "Mother Nature isn't very kind to us women as we get older. I think it's up to us to do what we can to best her." Her face lit up and she looked at each of them with mischief in her eyes. "Let's do makeovers!"

"No," Birdie replied stubbornly.

"Come on, it'll be fun and you'll look fabulous when I'm through."

"No."

"Go ahead, Birdie," Rose argued, her lips holding back a laugh.

"Look who's talking! You've had the same hairstyle since high school. I'll do it if you'll do it."

"Oh, no," Rose said, backing off. "I'll never change my hair. It's me. I couldn't imagine ever…"

Birdie guffawed and threw up her hands.

"Why not?" Hannah asked, lazily stretching across the bed. "It's just hair. It'll grow back. Do you think you could cut mine, Aunt Jilly? I'd love something radical. Maybe really short, like Winona Ryder's."

"I think you'd look adorable in something like that," Jilly agreed, appraising Hannah's youthful, flawless skin and dark arched brows. She tapped her lips, taking her role as beauty consultant seriously. Hannah sat up straight under the professional scrutiny. "You have wonderful bone structure.

Maybe a little longer than Winona's. A little more Meg Ryan's. It would show off your doelike eyes. And some gold highlights to bring out the pinkness of your skin. And lighter makeup. Soft and feminine. Yes,'' she said, nodding. ''Absolutely. You, too, Rose. A new haircut might be fun for you.''

Rose clutched her long hair in her hands and shook her head. ''Stay away from me, you madwoman.''

''Whatever,'' Jilly replied, turning back to her main target. ''Frankly, Birdie, you should shoot your hairdresser. That haircut does nothing for you. And neither does the gray. It makes you look—forgive me, but I'm your sister and if I don't tell you who will?—it makes you look older. You want to be a redhead? I think you'd look fabulous as a redhead. If Mother Nature made a mistake, so what?'' She smiled smugly. ''We can correct it.''

''Forget it.''

''Well, you two sticks-in-the-mud,'' Jilly said, totally exasperated with her sisters.

''Why not, Mom?'' Hannah asked, jumping into the fray. ''I think you'd look great as a redhead. Won't Dad be surprised when we come home?''

That was the one argument that caught Birdie's attention. She didn't miss the knowing glance between Jilly and Rose, or the silent look of expectation in Hannah's face.

''I don't think he'd notice one way or another,'' she replied. Or care, she thought to herself.

''Yes he *would*,'' Hannah replied with a poignant urgency. ''You should do something special for yourself, Mom. You never do. And it will be fun. I'll do your nails. It will be beauty night. We used to do that when I was little, remember?''

She did remember and it brought a pinprick of bittersweet pain to recall how much fun they used to have, just the two of them. Birdie looked into Hannah's eyes and wondered

what it was she was trying to tell her in the intensity that
lurked there.

"You really think I'd look good as a redhead?" she asked
flippantly, fooling no one.

Hannah's eyes widened with excitement that transferred to
Birdie. "I do," she replied, playing lightly with her mother's
hair. "You'd look hot."

"Hot?" Jilly repeated. "That does it for me. Come on,
Birdie, how can you resist looking hot?"

Birdie saw Hannah's face lit up like when she was three,
gazing up at the Christmas tree. She felt a spontaneous wave
of elation and laughed in resignation. "I can't resist. Let's
do it."

Hours later, Jilly stood at the sink, rinsing out the plastic
containers that came in the box of hair color, and listened to
the sound of laughter fill the walls of the little motel room
that had been their home for the past five days. A rollicking,
uncontrolled kind of laughter that had them holding their
sides and howling till tears flowed from their cheeks.

Jilly never thought she'd hear that kind of laughter again
or feel the same flush of tenderness and devotion that burned
in her heart right now. She paused to lean against the sink
and watch her sisters lying on their bellies with their toes
and fingers spread apart as their manicures dried. Beauty
night was a huge success.

Birdie looked ten years younger as a sexy redhead. She'd
chosen a color very much like Hannah's, only a tad redder
and a smidgen more daring. Jilly had softened the lines of
her harsh haircut, accentuating her cheekbones. Her new
color made her blue eyes shine like brilliant stars and the
makeup Jilly had masterfully applied made them appear even
larger and more luminous. Throughout the evening, Birdie
kept reaching up to touch the short hairs along her neck, or

peeking into the mirror. Jilly smiled with satisfaction when she saw the disbelief written all over her face.

Hannah looked pretty good, too, if Jilly did say so herself. She'd cut Hannah's drab, shoulder-length style into wisps of different lengths that bounced around her chin and played with the dramatic blond highlights she'd added. The heavy black eyeliner was gone and in her soft colors she positively glowed.

Even Rose got into the act at the last minute. After begging and cajoling, Rose had finally agreed to let Jilly give her long hair its first real trim. Rose closed her eyes when Jilly put the scissors to her hair. Never before had Jilly been so nervous to cut. This was positively virginal. Birdie and Hannah clustered near, mouths agape. Jilly only lopped off the uneven, frazzled ends, but just that was six inches. Rose's hair now swung around her breasts with an even, blunt fullness that made her hair look healthier and thicker. When Rose opened her eyes, she didn't even notice that her hair was shorter. Instead she laughed the same joyful laugh she did when she was six. Rose didn't laugh often but when she did it burst from her throat so full of life it sounded like a peal of bells.

Jilly listened to the music of their laughter and was carried back to the days when they used to laugh together all the time. Back to that golden time when they believed that they were princesses waiting to grow into queens and rule the world.

Fifteen

A soft knocking on her door woke Jilly up from a deep sleep. She pried open an eye to the surrounding darkness. A line of gray light was outlining the dusty olive-green paisley curtains.

"Wha—" Jilly raised her head. "Who's there?" she called out groggily.

"It's me. Birdie. Open up."

Jilly stumbled from her bed to open the door. She was surprised to see a glorious pink dawn rising up beyond Birdie's shoulder over the hill. Birdie walked in, rubbing her hands.

"Don't you dare say the early bird catches the worm," she warned. Then, taking in the dark room and the obviously sleeping guests, she scrunched up her face in disappointment. "I thought you two went jogging every morning," she said. "I wanted to join you."

Jilly scratched her head and yawned. Birdie seemed to bring a bit of the dawn inside with her. Surrounded by the rosy color of her hair her face glowed with light. She was wearing jeans and a burgundy sweatshirt with University of Wisconsin emblazoned across her chest. She kept jogging in place.

"Forget the bird analogy. You're like a rabbit. Stop hopping around," Jilly said, a bit grouchy.

"I'm warming up."

"That's not a warm-up, Mom." Hannah had awakened and was sitting up in bed, yawning. "You need to stretch."

Birdie stopped hopping. She peered into the dim room and hoped her eagerness wasn't too obvious. "Will you show me how?"

Hannah scratched her belly then smiled angelically. "Sure."

"You two go ahead," Jilly said in a sleepy stupor. "My stomach is rebelling after last night. I'll follow at a slower pace." Her stomach really wasn't upset, but she wanted to be sure that the two of them had some time alone.

"You're getting old," Birdie teased, but she didn't push her.

Twenty minutes later, Jilly stepped outside in her sweatpants and jacket and began stretching her long legs against the cement wall. The morning was soft; it would be a lovely spring day. Drops of earlier rain still hung heavy on the leaves and the grass. From somewhere she caught the sweet scent of a blossom. Could it be lilac so soon?

She took off on an easy jog back along the river. The earth was soft under her feet. She found she enjoyed the early morning run here much more than in the city, even more than Paris. She loved feeling the coolness of a country morning on her cheeks and catching the smell of the woods, the damp grass and the earth as she passed. Running for her was a kind of communion both with nature and her body, a centering of her mind and spirit when everything else in her world was spinning off axis. She ran along the river, picking up her speed until sweat pooled and her heart rate accelerated, then turned around and headed back. As she drew closer to the motel she spied another figure just across the river coming her way. In the early morning fog, she couldn't be sure who it was. A few steps farther, she squinted to see a little white dog running along beside him. So, it was Rajiv Patel. She felt a shiver of anticipation.

A few yards ahead was the small wooden bridge that she'd seen him working under before. She slowed to a walk and wiped her brow with her sleeve. Before she could wonder if he'd cross to say hello, the little dog made the decision for them, darting over the bridge and running to her, barking. Jilly bent to pat its head as he jumped up and made muddy pawprints on her pants.

"Are you quite sure this isn't your dog? she asked when Rajiv approached.

He laughed. "I'm sure, but I don't think he's convinced."

"Does he have a name?"

"If he does, he's never told me."

"Then what do you call him?"

"I don't. I usually ignore him but he doesn't seem to care. For whatever reason, he likes to hang around."

"You could give him a name."

"He's not mine to name. He's an independent sort. He knows every inch of the area and where every handout lies. I think he's quite popular with the ladies, too. I've seen a few mutts around town with a patch over the eye."

She laughed then, admiring the dog's lean but wiry body and his bright eyes. There was no doubt the rascal had a way about him. "But he needs a name. Everyone needs one."

"Perhaps. But not given by me. Then I should become attached to him."

She wondered at that remark and what pain caused him not to want to be attached to a stray, even to the point of not giving the dog a temporary name of reference. Looking back at the dog, she thought, too, of her daughter. She'd never named her, either.

"I'll name him, then," she decided, moving once more to rectify the past. She considered for a moment, studying the black patch over his eye, his jaunty stance. "How does Pete sound to you?"

Rajiv studied the dog. "Rather a human name, don't you think?"

Then she remembered his profession as a thief. "I know. Pirate Pete."

Rajiv smiled and nodded. "It suits him."

She was inordinately pleased that he thought so.

"Are you going anywhere in particular?" he asked.

"I'm just walking. Nowhere in particular. And you?"

"The same," he replied. "Care if I join you to nowhere?"

They walked past the motel and on to where the river widened and rushed, overflowing with the spring melt. As they walked they talked in generalities, seeking clues to each other's interests, intelligence, experiences. He was fascinating; he knew so much about so many things. Yet Jilly was stymied by his seeming reluctance to speak. She had to work to pry each word, like a pearl from an oyster.

He was very good, however, at asking her questions, mostly about her search. He grew very interested in her story, eager that she meet with success. As they walked, Pirate Pete ran to the woods and back, hunting. Or as Jilly said, looking for his next heist.

"How long has it been since you had your daughter?"

"Twenty-six years. Hard to believe."

"And the father? Did you ever marry?"

She shook head. "No. I married three times, but never the father."

"Three times?" He didn't remark further, only looked off at a hawk circling overhead.

"It's a long story," she said with her nonchalant laugh.

"It's a long walk back."

She considered an old rule of hers: never talk about money and love with strangers—at least not *her* money and love. He seemed so unconventional, however, with his mysterious aura and his polite reticence. She looked up at his handsome profile and thought, what fun was a rule unless it could be broken?

So she started telling her story, hesitatingly at first, omitting details. She began with her arrival in France, an ill-prepared, tall, thin young girl totally unsuited for au pair work. She talked on about her quick success in modeling, her flirtation with film as a bombshell in Italian westerns while married to an Italian filmmaker, and how along the way to fame she married three very handsome, very wrong men. Jilly enjoyed speaking to Rajiv of things she hadn't told anyone else about. Certainly not any of her husbands. They were not the type of men she could confide in. Not in any language.

It wasn't simply because Rajiv was a stranger and she knew she could walk away from him without a look over her shoulder that gave her such freedom. Though this was true, Rajiv was an excellent listener. His face was serious and attentive and his eyes reflected what she told him with compassion.

"So now I've come home, seeking my fortune," she concluded, walking slowly. "And who would have thought that the fortune I sought would be my daughter? And the treasures I've found are my sisters?"

They stopped at a small, charming, redbrick house tucked on a ledge at a high point of the hill. A black wrought-iron fence bordered it and seemed to keep the tenants from falling over the cliff. Beyond the fence lay a panoramic view of the meandering river and the small town of Hodges below.

"What a delightful place," Jilly said.

"Thank you. I live here," Rajiv replied.

"Really? I didn't expect that you'd live in such a quaint house. I envisioned you in a dull, rather severe tract house. Made of cement blocks, perhaps?" She leaned into him, teasing.

He reluctantly gave up a smile. "It's hard enough to work in such a place. God forbid I'd have to live in one, too."

"How did you end up in such a, well…"

"Let's be kind to my father. Shall we say, such an architecturally uninspired motel?"

She laughed.

"He won it in a card game. I'm absolutely serious! I never was interested in the family business. I stayed in India, pursuing my own career. Did I tell you I was in software engineering?" He turned his head to smile at her, his eyes sparkling with mirth. "I know a little bit about the Internet."

"I see," she replied, enjoying their first joke. "So, what brought you to the illustrious River's End Motel?"

His smile fell and he looked off into the valley at some point far beyond. "My father called and told me about this little place in Wisconsin that he had won. He talked to me about karma." He released a short, bitter laugh. "Perhaps it's best not to get into a discussion about that. I could end up leaping over that flimsy little fence."

"I'd only have to jump over and try to save you." She shrugged. "Karma."

He looked at her askance. "I don't think you understand about karma."

She shrugged and said with a suggestive hint, "Perhaps you should teach me?"

A frown flickered across his face. "I'm afraid you won't find me a very good teacher." He looked at his watch, his face set. "I'm sorry, Jillian, but it's getting late. I really must get to work. I enjoyed our walk."

"I did, too." Then, because she wanted to see him again, she said boldly, "Another time, perhaps?"

"Yes. I'd like that."

"I'll be walking tomorrow morning." Could she be pushier, she thought to herself?

Their eyes met and she felt again the singe of attraction between them. Yes, she could, she decided.

"I'll look for you," she added.

"Until tomorrow then." With a perfunctory nod of his head, he turned and walked through the wrought-iron gate into the redbrick house.

Jilly watched him leave feeling a shudder of frustration. "Nice dodge," she muttered. She'd exposed her own past so freely but he clammed up pretty fast. At her feet, Pirate Pete sat staring at her adoringly, waiting for some cue.

"Well, at least you're not afraid of me," she said to the dog. "Come on, boy, let's get something to eat." She took off down the road back to the motel with Pirate Pete trotting at her heels. Jilly looked over her shoulder at the house, cursing herself for breaking her own rule. But she was intrigued, and definitely attracted to him. The more he pushed her away, the more curious she became. Curiouser and curiouser.

Later that morning, two events got their search moving again. First, the mailman delivered the application for the Soundex Reunion Registry. Jilly completed the forms quickly, giving pertinent information and leaving Mr. Collins's number as a contact. She returned the form by overnight mail, along with a donation. The second event was a name-address match.

They were in the library again, poring over the address books, when Rose leaped up from her chair in the library with a hoot of triumph. "I found it!" she cried, waving the paper over her head. "I found it!" She came rushing toward them with a squeal that had the librarian frowning.

"What did you find?" Birdie asked, already on her feet.

"A match! I found an address for Ann Josephine Neville. There's a Neville in Lake St. George in 1973. Father David, Mother Susan." She looked up. "About seventy miles from here."

"Neville?" Jilly searched the journal. She ran her finger down the pages until she came to the list of names. She looked up, surprised. "It's the first name on the list."

"Who knows if the Nevilles are still there?"

"They're still listed at the same address"

She looked up and met their eyes. "It's a start."

Jilly sat by the phone, her hands clenched in her lap. She picked up the phone, then set it down again, amazed that her hands were trembling. She reached out again for the phone, but midway diverted her reach to her purse. Digging into the black bag, she pulled out a pack of cigarettes, lit up, then exhaled slowly.

What was she so nervous about? She didn't even know that this person was her child. It was simply a match. Even if it was, what was the worst that could happen?

Maybe that the woman would not be her daughter. Or she'd find out the Nevilles didn't live there anymore. Or Ann—or her parents—could be angry that she'd tried to make contact. Yes, that would be the worst. If her daughter found out that she'd called and didn't want to meet her.

She took another long puff. No, that was unlikely. Ann was already twenty-six years old and probably wasn't still living with her parents. Jilly's best hope was they'd tell her where Ann was living, if she was married and what her new last name was. That wouldn't be so hard.

She got up and paced the narrow strip in the room. In any case, she told herself, obsessing about it wouldn't change the outcome. She might as well get on with it. Besides, she knew her sisters were hanging outside the door waiting for word. She took another drag from her cigarette then set it down in a plastic cup. She sat on the bed, picked up the phone and punched out the number before she could chicken out.

"Hello?" It was a woman's voice.

"Hello, Mrs. Neville?"

"Yes?"

Jilly's heart was pounding and her mouth was dry. "Is Ann there?"

There was a long pause. "Who is this?" The voice was suddenly guarded.

"You don't know me. I don't mean to intrude, but my name is Jillian Season and I believe I may be Ann's mother. Her birth mother, that is."

There was pause, longer this time. "That can't be right," Mrs. Neville replied shakily. "No, that can't be right."

"Is Ann Josephine Neville your daughter?"

"Yes. She was."

Was? Jilly felt a shiver run down her back. "I'm afraid I don't understand."

"My Ann died four years ago."

Jilly's mind went blank.

"In a car accident. The Lord took her from us." Her voice shook.

Jilly couldn't believe what she was hearing. She was prepared for them to hang up when she called, or to say they didn't want contact. She was ready to engage them in a long conversation to learn about birth dates and birth places, details that would help determine if *this* Ann was *her* Ann. But she didn't have a response planned for this answer.

"I—I'm sorry." Her hands trembled at her lips. Could her search for her daughter end like this? "I'm at a loss for words."

"I don't think you have the right family," Mrs. Neville said after she'd collected herself.

"It doesn't matter. I'm sorry if I intruded. You have my sympathy."

"I said," the woman replied more urgently, " I don't think you have the right family. We've already met Ann's real mother. Six or seven years ago. Ann wanted to find her when she found out she was carrying Ben. She tracked her down and they met, though nothing much came of it. I never felt that I mattered any less to Ann for her wanting the meeting. I know I was Ann's true mother. I'm the one who took care of her and loved her for twenty-three years.''

"Of course," Jilly responded. "I'm sure there was never any doubt."

"I just wanted you to know that Ann was happy to have met the woman who gave her life. It meant a lot to her. And I'm happy knowing that she had that much before she died." There was a deep sigh. "So...good luck to you. I hope you find your daughter."

Her last words were choked in a sob. Jilly mumbled a heartfelt goodbye and hung up, then wept for Ann Josephine Neville and both her mothers.

"I need a drink," she told her sisters when she staggered into their room.

When she told them what had happened, they were unified in their horror and grief.

"The scariest part is that it never occurred to me that something bad might have happened to my daughter," Jilly said, clutching her throat. "I mean, in all these years, almost anything could have. She could have been in an accident. She might be paralyzed. Or missing a limb. Or what if she's sick and dying?" She covered her eyes with her palm. "Or dead. She could be dead like poor Ann Josephine Neville."

"Yes, she could be all of those things," Birdie said calmly, coming closer to put her arm around her shoulder. "That's part of life."

"I don't know, Birdie," Jilly said, leaning her weight against her hip. "I'm not sure I could stand to go through that again. What if my Anne was the Ann the woman was talking about?"

"We've come this far in our search. We can't stop now. What is, is."

* * *

Birdie took her turn at the phone. She went outdoors and sat in her car, running the engine for warmth and listening to the radio. The sun was setting on another day and the evening chill was making itself felt in the blue-gray skies. The others were getting dressed for their evening walk to the diner. Maude had promised them her world famous beef stew tonight.

The easy listening station was playing "Unchained Melody" and Birdie took it as a positive omen. That was her and Dennis's favorite song while they were dating in college. She thought back to the very evening when she knew this would be "their" song. They were at a party at her sorority house celebrating Northwestern's swim team's state championship. Birdie had won a new record for the team and was exhilarated not only for the win, but because Dennis Connor had been cheering her on. They'd met again at college and had been dating for a few months. On that particular night, Dennis was walking toward her carrying their drinks while this song was playing. They were margaritas. She watched him carry the drinks with the seriousness that had always endeared him to her. Looking down, one lock of his long blond hair fell from behind his ear into his face. Just then, another guy drunkenly bumped into his shoulder causing him to spill most of a drink down his shirt and pants. Birdie gasped. The guy apologized profusely, succeeding only in spilling more margarita down Dennis's shirt in his slobbering attempt to help. Dennis looked up and, instead of cussing the guy, he met her gaze, smiled a crooked, self-mocking smile and shrugged. Birdie, who had lived in a household of ill humor and tight lips, knew in that moment that this man was right for her.

Oh, my love, my darling…

She'd worried about getting too attached to Dennis Connor, knowing that Jilly had dated him. But she couldn't help

herself; she'd always been in love with him. She had looked
into his brown eyes later that night, eyes so dark and fath-
omless that she felt she was looking into his soul, and believed him when he'd told her that Jilly was a summer's high
school fling, nothing to compare with what he felt for her.

"And what is that?" she'd asked him, only half-teasingly.
"What do you feel for me?"

"Love," he'd answered with devastatingly sincerity. And
then he'd kissed her slowly, tenderly, as though he had all
the time in the world. She closed her eyes and she was swimming again, stroking her arms and moving through wave after
wave of lust and limbs. She heard his intake of breath as he
plunged into her. She gulped for air, drowning.

I've hungered for your touch....

They made love for the first time that night to this song,
and they danced to it at their wedding a year later. It occurred
to Birdie, sitting alone in the car staring at the cell phone in
her hand, that they had not listened to the song together in a
very long time.

She lifted the phone and quickly dialed her home phone
number in Milwaukee. The phone rang five times. She exhaled each time. Then the dreadful machine answered and
she heard his voice, so cold, talking to strangers. Beep.

"Dennis, it's me. Birdie. Call me on my cell phone.
Please."

She hung up without saying more. Tears flowed down her
cheek as the song reached a crescendo, filling the car.

Are you still mine?

Rose took advantage of being alone in the room to quickly
turn on the computer and check her e-mail, something she'd
not done in the past several days. She told herself that she
just needed a day to think about it, then one day turned to
two, then three, four, until she'd built up a wall of fear

against replying to DannyBoy at all. What she didn't know wouldn't hurt her, right?

But when she saw Jilly confront her fears and place the call to the Nevilles, Rose knew she was just being a chicken-heart. Only a coward would leave a man like DannyBoy hanging after he'd asked to meet her.

There were four e-mails waiting for her from DannyBoy. She couldn't *not* read them. She clicked the first letter and it flashed on the screen.

Dear Rosebud,

There was some bad weather in the southwest today. Tornadoes were flying around a dime a dozen. Trucks were pulled off the road and we had to find what shelter we could. I was lucky to get off the road and into a room and not have to wait it out under an overpass like I've heard some other poor fellows did. But it was a tense night of waiting. When that Texas sky turns a murky green that stretches for miles and the humidity is so thick you can cut it with a knife, all eyes are turned toward the heavens. Have you ever been in a tornado? I have. It's not an experience you ever forget.

I see the weather has been pretty good up in Wisconsin. You're getting a little bit of spring. I'm glad. There's nothing more beautiful that the hills of the Midwest when they start turning green and the air smells so fresh your lungs hurt. I can hardly wait to go home. I'd like to take you to some of my favorite hiking places, that is, if you'd like to. There's one spot where there are so many wildflowers you won't believe it.

This tornado delayed my trip. I won't be back for a week.

Gotta go. The surge protector is flicking. It must be those storms.

DannyBoy

Dear Rosebud,

I'm wondering if there was a problem with the e-mail on account of the storms. I haven't heard from you. Maybe you're having trouble with your connection on the road? If you receive this, write back so I know all is okay.

The weather here is clear again. A town twenty miles away got clobbered by a twister, poor folks. Houses were torn up and three dead. Makes you realize every day how lucky we are just to be alive.

DannyBoy

Dear Rosebud,

Not finding your letter waiting for me at the end of the day is a real disappointment. It makes me realize how important your letters...you...have become in my life. I'd hate to lose your friendship.

I know you said right off that you were the shy type. I like that about you. I've tried not to do or say anything that might make you uncomfortable. I went over my old mail and I see where in my last e-mail to you before you stopped writing I asked you if we could meet. Now I'm wondering if that is why you stopped writing me back.

Please don't think I'm trying to rush you. If you don't want to meet, that's okay. I won't deny that I'd like to. I've heard that some people are afraid that the other person won't like what they see and that's why they never want to meet. I don't feel that way. I'll be glad to send a picture and I know I'd love to receive one from you. We can do that if it makes you feel better.

Or if you'd rather not meet at all, I won't say I'll like it, but I'd rather have your friendship on e-mail than

lose your friendship altogether. So please, write back
and tell me what you're thinking.

Your *friend,*
DannyBoy

Dear Rosebud,
Well, I guess I can take a hint. I keep hoping that you're
on this trip and something's happened to your computer
and you can't reach me. Maybe you're as upset as I am
about missing our letters. (I hope so.)

But if that's not it, I'll stop pestering you. If you want
to write me, I'd love to hear from you. I hate to think
we'd just stop without saying goodbye.

DannyBoy

Rose read and reread the letters three times. Each time she
cried a little harder. When the knock sounded on the door,
she was too upset to worry about being seen crying and just
rose from her chair to answer it. Hannah was at the door and
when she saw Rose crying, her smile fell flat.

"Are you okay?" she asked, stepping into the room to
give Rose a hug.

"I'm fine," Rose said, slipping away and walking across
the room to grab a tissue from the vanity.

Jilly walked into the room and closed the door behind her.
"I'm really worried about Birdie," she said to them, tossing
her purse down on the floor. "I saw her sitting alone in the
car. Crying."

Hannah nudged Jilly in the ribs.

"What?" She turned her head, blinking. When she looked
to where Hannah was pointing, she saw Rose standing at the
sink. In the reflection of the mirror, she could see that Rose
was crying.

"Honey, what's going on here?" Jilly asked, coming immediately to her side. "You and Birdie have a fight or something?"

Rose tried to laugh but it came out more of a hiccup. She was cringing inwardly at having been caught teary-eyed. "No, no," she said, not looking at her. "It's nothing like that."

"Then what is it?"

She shredded her tissue, wondering how she could tell Jilly what was happening. She hadn't told *anybody* about DannyBoy. They might snicker, or perhaps warn her against it. DannyBoy meant too much to her to have people laugh at their friendship. "It's nothing, I told you."

Jilly placed her hands on her shoulders and turned her around to face her. The look in her eyes was both entreating and determined. "Tell me what's going on, Rose," she said, giving her a gentle shake. When she turned her head away, Jilly said, "Come on, play fair. We all agreed no more secrets."

"You promise you won't laugh? I'll die if you laugh."

"I promise." Jilly raised her fingers into the Girl Scout sign.

"Do you want me to leave?" Hannah asked, already turned toward the door.

Rose shook her head. "No. We've all gone through enough. You should stay."

"You've earned your badge," Jilly said to Hannah.

After they each stretched out on the beds, Rose tucked her legs under her in her geisha pose and rested her hands on her thighs.

"What would you say if I told you I had a particular friend?"

Jilly scrunched up her face. "What the hell is a particular friend?"

"Don't tease. And don't tell Birdie. I don't want to hear her proclamations on the subject." She eased off her thighs to stretch out on her belly. "I have a friend that I met on the Internet."

"That guy you were telling us about before?" Hannah asked.

"Yes. We met in a chat room for stamp collectors."

Rose saw a vague expression of disbelief spark in Jilly's green eyes. Rose held her gaze, challenging her to say anything teasing. When she didn't, she looked over to check Hannah's reaction, then continued. "We started e-mailing each other privately and we've become good friends. I like the way he thinks at so many levels and we share so many interests. We've never met. We've not even exchanged photographs. But we can tell each other anything and… I think I'm in love with him."

"Aunt Rose! You're having an Internet love affair?" Hannah was getting a kick out of this, which annoyed Rose to no end. "I've read about things like that but you're the first person I've ever known who's actually done it."

"What do you know about this man?" Jilly asked. "His background, his job. Rose, he could be a some lecherous guy who—"

"No! He's not like that. I'd know if he was a creep. I may not have been around as much as you, Jilly, but I'm not so ignorant that I couldn't figure that much out."

"Hey, I've been fooled. Plenty."

"I read about people getting tricked all the time, Aunt Rose. There are a lot of losers out there on the Net."

Rose bridled. "Thank you very much."

Hannah blanched. "I don't mean you."

"Hannah," Rose said a tad sharply, "I'm a lot older than you and my idea of a good time is not hanging around in bars. I'm not the least interested in getting 'the look' from some strange guy. I don't have a lot of friends to introduce me to someone and I'm not a joiner so I'm not involved in church groups or clubs. Face it. There aren't a lot of ways for women my age, in my situation, to meet nice men. And vice versa. That doesn't make us losers. That makes us lonely."

"I'm sorry, Aunt Rose. I didn't mean it that way."

"You're young, Hannah. Kids your age hang out together and go out and do things all the time. At my age, things are different. For one thing, a lot of folks are married. Besides, meeting someone on the Internet is innovative, if you want my opinion. We're certainly not unique. Tons of people are doing it. My friend is a truck driver. He's on the road a lot and doesn't have a chance to meet many people."

"A truck driver?" Jilly's voice rose.

"Yes," Rose said defensively. "Don't you dare get snobby on me, Jilly."

"Okay, okay," Jilly said. "So, what's his name?"

Rose faltered. "We don't actually know each other's names yet. Exactly. Just our screen names. I'm Rosebud. And he's DannyBoy."

Jilly's lips twitched. "Let's just call him Danny for now. I think that's a safe bet."

"I like Rosebud," Hannah said, trying to make up.

"So you've got a *particular* friend on the Internet," Jilly said in way of summary. "His name is Danny, he's a nice fellow and he drives a truck. I'm assuming he's not married." She delivered a pointed look. "You do know that, don't you?"

"Of course. He's divorced."

"Some guys just say they're divorced but they're not," Hannah interjected.

"No," Rose replied emphatically. "Not him."

"Uh-huh." Jilly narrowed her eyes. "I hope so. Assuming all that's true, are we missing something here, Rose? Why are you crying?"

"He wants to meet me."

Jilly's brows rose. "So?" She glanced at Hannah, who merely shrugged.

Rose pursed her lips, miserable, wanting to tell Jilly everything and nothing. "I'm afraid to meet him, okay? So I've not written to him for the past four days and now he's just written to me that he doesn't want to be a pest and he's stopped writing. Oh, here, see for yourself," she said, seeing two pairs of puzzled eyes staring back at her. Standing with a swoop of frustration she waved at them to follow.

Rose led them back to the computer and, connecting to the e-mail, showed them the files of DannyBoy's letters. Jilly sat in the chair and Hannah read over her shoulder, muttering, "Slow down," when Jilly scrolled too fast.

After they read the letters, Jilly looked at Rose and said with a look of wonder on her face, "Oh, Rose, you're right. He sounds absolutely wonderful."

Rose's worried frown melted into a smile of relief. "He does, doesn't he?"

"What's holding you up? You should meet him."

Rose paced the room and took several deep breaths. "Jilly, I'm not like you. Meeting people has always been hard for me and it's been getting harder as I get older. Birdie thinks it's because I've been cooped up in the house with Merry for so many years, and that might be partly true." She shrugged. "But meeting Danny is another thing altogether. He's not just anyone. He's *someone*. It matters that he likes me."

"Why don't you exchange pictures?" Hannah asked, awkwardly tugging her hair, trying not to ask another stupid question. "Everyone does these days."

"I know," Rose replied. "I guess I didn't want to get to that level. I don't know why. It seems pretty silly now that I talk about it."

"Not really," Jilly said kindly. "The stakes are high."

Rose exchanged a grateful glance. "I've read on the Net about people who really liked each other in their e-mails and even liked the photographs, but when they met face-to-face something was missing. They just didn't click. What if it doesn't click with DannyBoy and me? Would we just stop writing to each other? I'd hate for that to happen. I'd really miss him.''

"You just have to take that chance. He asked you to say goodbye and at the very least, you should do that. But frankly, you're a fool if you do. I always ask myself what's the worst that can happen if I do something. So, what's the worst that can happen to you if you meet him?''

Rose thought for a moment and replied, "He wouldn't like me.''

"Okay. Then what would happen?''

"He'd stop writing to me.''

"Right. And isn't that what's happening already?''

Rose looked down and nodded.

"So what have you got to lose by meeting him? Fear is your greatest enemy. And did you ever stop to think that *you* might not like *him?* Or you might adore him and he might adore you and you'll live happily ever after.''

"Now who's being silly?''

"Sillier things happen every day.''

"I've heard about a lot of people who get together and even marry after meeting on the Internet,'' added Hannah with encouragement. "There are stories about them in the magazines all the time.''

"I know. I know. I just don't believe those kinds of happy endings happen to people like me.''

Jilly rose in a graceful swoop, then reached over to cup her hands around Rose's cheeks like blinders. Her own eyes were blazing as she looked at her with convincing tenderness. "Rose, Rose, what am I going to do with you? Do you remember our dreams as children? Do you remember who the man of your dreams was? Who you wanted to marry when you grew up? Think back.''

Rose was surprised by this question from nowhere, but Jilly's gaze was relentless. Rose's eyes glazed over as her mind traveled far back to recollect that tidbit, buried deep within. She remembered hot, summer nights when it was too humid for sleep. She remembered following her older sisters out of their rooms, dragging blankets and pillows behind them to lie out on lawn chairs by the pool. They'd chat for hours, swatting the mosquitoes, till sleep overcame them or Mother came out to fetch them back to their beds.

"I remember. I wanted to marry an explorer. Someone who traveled around the world."

"Exactly." Jilly's eyes were shining. "And he's waiting for your answer. No one can do this for you, Rose Season. It's up to you to make your dreams come true."

Sixteen

❧❧❧

Jilly was standing behind Rose as they worked to compose a reply to DannyBoy's e-mail when she heard the door swish open behind her. Then Hannah's voice, high and broken.

"Mom, what's wrong?"

She swung her head around to see Birdie walking stiffly into the room, her face white and drawn, her eyes filled with alarm and her hands holding her belly. "Birdie?" She pushed away from the table to get to Birdie's side.

"Don't worry," Birdie said in her serious doctor's voice. "It's just my period. It started quite suddenly. Help me to the bathroom. Please."

Jilly took her arm and helped her through the narrow path to the bathroom. Looking over her shoulder she squelched a surge of panic seeing drops of fresh red blood trailing Birdie on the floor. "Hannah, stand back. There's no room in that bathroom for one much less three. Rose, do you have any pads?"

"I just bought some," Birdie called out as she entered the bathroom. "Look in the bags by my bed."

With the other two busy with the task, Jilly turned and said in a low voice to Birdie, "Are you okay?"

Birdie sat down and grimaced, then, waving Jilly away,

she pushed the door closed. Jilly heard the sound of gushing fluid and brought her fingers to her throat. She wasn't sure what was happening, which frightened her all the more. Hannah approached with the pads in her hand. Rose was right behind her. They stared at her as though she knew what was going on.

"Birdie, we have your pads. Are you okay in there?"

There was no answer.

"Mom?"

"I'm okay." Birdie's voice was strained. "Leave me alone a minute."

"Why don't we sit down," Rose said, firmly herding them away from the door.

Jilly paced back and forth from the bathroom door to the room door, like a caged animal. Hannah and Rose got out of her way, choosing to sit on the side of the bed. Rose clenched her hands in her lap. Hannah chewed her nails.

After a while the bathroom door opened a crack. They all jumped up and hurried to the door in a rush. Birdie's hand shot out.

"Could someone hand me some towels, please? And the pads."

They scrambled to comply, passing things into her hand and trying not to look inside the privacy of the bathroom. When Hannah handed her a pad, Birdie called out with impatience, "The whole bag. Please."

"She's being so damn polite," Jilly hissed to Rose. "That's too much blood for a period. What's going on?"

"Are you sure you're all right in there?" Rose called through the door.

"Yes!"

"Do you want one of us to come in?"

"No! I'll be out in a minute. Goddammit, don't rush me!"

Rose stepped back from the door. Jilly moved closer and whispered, "That's better. Sounds more like Birdie, at least."

Then, moving to the door, she called, "Take all the time you need. We're out here if you need anything."

A few minutes later, Birdie called out in a calmer, lower voice, "It appears to be a miscarriage."

Jilly and Rose exchanged shocked glances.

"Is that okay?" Hannah asked, frightened now. "I mean, does she need to go to the hospital?"

Rose went to put her arms around her niece. "Believe me, Hannah, if anyone knows what to do in this situation, it's your mother. She'll let us know if she needs anything." Inwardly, however, she didn't feel so confident. She knew Birdie well enough to know that she didn't know when to ask for help. "I'll just check," she said to Hannah.

She knocked on the door. "Birdie? It's Rose. We could drive you to the hospital, just to be sure."

There was a moment's silence. "No. No, that won't be necessary. I know what I'm doing. A miscarriage this early on is not a hospital event."

Rose crossed her arms in worry. Birdie was using her clinical doctor's voice, the one she'd used whenever Merry had been sick and she had come to Evanston to personally give her a checkup. Merry had always been a little afraid of Birdie the Doctor. *That* Birdie was unemotional and methodical. Not the same Birdie who liked to bring candy and tickle her little sister just to hear her laugh. Rose always felt it masked whatever Birdie was truly feeling.

"I could use another towel," Birdie called out shakily. "I'm just going to take a short shower. I don't want you to worry about the sound of water, okay? And Rose? If you could grab me some Motrin, that would be great."

"Listen to her," Jilly said, her voice filled with frustration. "She sounds like she's having a beauty night in there, not a miscarriage. What kind of bullshit is that?"

"It's just how Birdie handles medical crises."

"Birdie," Jilly called at the door, her worry making her

voice harsh. "Unlock the door. What if something happens to you? Stop being so—" She bit off the words, not wanting to criticize. She knew it was just her worry causing her temper to rise. "Let us help you for a change." She jiggled the handle.

"I don't want anyone's help. Just go do something, would you?" Her voice hitched. "I want to be alone for a minute."

The clunk and hiss of the pipes abruptly ended all conversation.

"I've got to get some air. I'll be right outside." Jilly grabbed her coat and a pack of cigarettes and left in a hurry.

There she goes again, Rose thought to herself. Running away. "How are you doing over there?" she asked Hannah.

Hannah was sitting on the bed with her hands pressed together between her knees, looking a little pale. She shrugged.

"Do you think you could order us a pizza?"

"I'm not hungry," she replied, staring morosely at the closed bathroom door.

"Maybe *you're* not, but your mother might be later on. And I am."

Shame flushed Hannah cheeks. Rose was glad to see it. The girl was growing up quickly. "Oh, yeah, sorry. I wasn't thinking. I'll do it right away."

"Thanks, honey," she said soothingly. "We've got to be strong for your mom now. Go on, order your mom's favorite. There's money in my wallet."

"No, I've got some," she replied, surprising Rose with her generosity.

Fifteen minutes later, Birdie was lying on her back in bed, raised slightly by pillows. Her hair was damp and brushed back from her face, which looked sallow and grainy. But the fear was gone from her features, replaced with heartbreaking sadness and a new quality of defeat.

Everyone was fatigued. The miscarriage was unexpected and therefore all the more frightening. Birdie had lost a lot of blood but she assured them in a clinical manner that everything was normal.

"They say it's nature's way of getting rid of a defective baby."

"Are you sure you don't need to go to a hospital?" Rose asked, handing her two Motrin and a glass of water.

"All I need is some rest." Her voice sounded flat and unemotional. She swallowed the tablets and noisily drank the water.

"Is there anything we can get you?" Hannah was being solicitous. She sat by her mother's side with an expression of devotion. "Pizza's coming. I ordered cheese and fresh tomato slices. Your favorite."

Birdie weakly patted her hand. "Thanks, but I'm just tired. I'd like to sleep now." When Hannah squeezed her hand tightly and looked at her like a frightened child, Birdie squeezed back and mustered reassurance. "Okay, honey?"

Hannah nodded, then bent to kiss her mother's cheek. She held her lips to her cheek an extra moment.

Rose took the glass from Birdie, turned off the light by her bed, and then helped Birdie settle comfortably under the blankets. She was good at nursing. She always felt it was a quiet way of showing how much she loved someone.

"Why don't you go to your room now," she whispered to Hannah. "I'll be here for her if she needs anything."

"I'd like to stay with her. Not just for tonight, but to move in here, you know?"

Rose registered this. "I think that's a good idea. But why not start tomorrow. It's too much to move things around tonight, and if she needs anyone, I've got the most experience. Is that okay with you?"

Hannah nodded. "Yeah, okay. You'll call me if there's a problem?"

"There won't be a problem," Birdie called out from under the blankets. "I'm just fine."

Rose looked at Hannah and shrugged.

Hannah left for her room. Closing the door, Rose looked at Birdie, a big hulk huddled on her side with the blankets up to her ears. Her new, vibrant red hair stood out in damp spikes against the white pillow. Rose's heart broke for her sister. She was trying to be Birdie the strong one. Birdie, the one who could handle everything. Except that before she looked away, Rose saw the flash of tears in her eyes.

Jilly stood on the little wooden bridge away from the motel. The collar of her thin leather coat was stiff and cold against her neck and she was shivering in the blast of frigid northern air. She leaned on the railing, smoking cigarette after cigarette, enjoying each one less than the last. It was the repetition of movement she enjoyed more than the taste. The sight of the little red tip burning in the darkness was soothing.

She'd felt so useless in the room with Birdie and the others that she'd had to leave or go mad. Birdie's face and mannerisms were so cool and efficient it didn't seem natural. All they saw was a hand that stretched out through a crack in the open door. All they heard was a crisp and polite "Thank you. No, I don't need any help, thank you."

Jilly's arms had hung uselessly at her side as she stared at that closed bathroom door knowing that Birdie was losing much more than blood in there. She was losing a baby. No amount of competence would tidy up *that* realization so easily. She took a long drag, exhaling a plume that hung in the chilly air.

From far in the darkness she heard a familiar high bark. Looking out toward the sound, she saw the dim reflection of a man's silhouette in the moonlight and a blur of white at his feet.

"Hello," she called out.

Pirate Pete took off after the sound of her voice, barking joyously. She reached into her pocket for the dog cookie she always kept there now. Behind him, Rajiv approached hesitantly.

"Are we interrupting?"

"No, not at all. I suppose I should say something like we've got to stop meeting like this."

He laughed. "Now, this is karma. Are you sure we're not interrupting?"

"I'd like some company, actually. It's been quite a night."

He crossed the bridge, meeting her in the middle. He was wearing a navy wool pea coat and his hands were tucked into the pockets. The dark made his eyes even more mysterious.

"More news about your daughter?" he inquired.

"No. Actually, it was rather traumatic. Birdie had a miscarriage."

He startled at the news. "Is she all right?" he asked quickly. "Does she need a doctor?"

"She *is* a doctor. And she's fine—or so she tells us. The miscarriage was early in the pregnancy. In fact, she didn't even know she was pregnant. Imagine. Not knowing." She took another puff from her cigarette and leaned again over the railing, staring straight ahead into the darkness. "I've read that ten percent of all pregnancies end in miscarriage, usually in the first twelve weeks. Probably more, since so many go unreported." She looked up. "Do you know what I thought when I heard Birdie was having a miscarriage? I thought, why didn't that happen to me? If I had been in that ten percent, I wouldn't have messed up my life. Or the lives of my sisters. Or my parents. Do you think other mothers ever wonder about that? What their lives would have been like had they not had a child? Maybe? I wonder if my mother thought that about me." She laughed derisively. "Probably.

"But then I thought, how could I wish that my baby had not been born? My beautiful daughter? I know that, despite everything I went through, I would have chosen to have her." She turned her head to look him in the eyes and spoke from the heart. "If I could have changed anything in my life, anything at all, I would have kept my baby." She saw sympathy in his eyes. Turning toward the water again she tossed the cigarette into the river. "You don't understand. That's really big for me to say. Really big. I've never told anyone this before, but when I gave up my baby, deep down I was relieved. Isn't that awful? You must think I'm horrible. But that's how I felt. I was only seventeen and scared out of my mind. What did I know about being a mother? And everyone was telling me that giving the baby up was the right thing to do. So I did." She ran her hand through her hair and sighed heavily. "But later on...then it hits you.

"So I'm standing here tonight wondering what Birdie is feeling now. My poor, darling, strong, fragile sister. Is she sad about losing the baby she didn't even know was inside of her? Or is she relieved? Either way, she's going to feel so sad." Her voice cracked and she tightened her lips against the cry.

Suddenly she felt his hands on her shoulders, long and firm, pulling her up from the railing to his chest. She felt like a small pebble in the river, caught in the upstream. It felt so natural to step closer, to wrap her arms around his back, to rest her cheek upon the scratchy wool of his coat as his long arms wrapped tight around her, comforting her. He held her close against the cold night. She could smell the exotic scent of his aftershave and some delicious spice that she didn't recognize. His fingers brushed the hair away from her face. From somewhere in the night she heard the river rush.

He dipped his head. She raised hers. His lips met hers as easily, as readily, as though they had kissed many times before. She felt the kiss spark at the lips, then flow smoothly throughout her body, transported through her bloodstream, liquid and hot, up and down and swirling in her center. His arms tightened around her and his tongue coaxed her mouth open, testing, tasting. When he drew back she clung to him, grasping her fingers around his neck and pulling him close. His mouth crushed hers, this time urgent and demanding. She opened, coaxing, pleading with her tongue as her body pressed against his for the release she so desperately needed. It had been so long since she'd felt like this.

When he pulled back the second time, he reached up to gently disentangle her fingers from his neck. She opened her eyes, so close to his, and was stunned by the animal-like ferocity she saw in them once again.

"Is there somewhere we can go?" she asked.

She saw in his face his struggle to tug back on that mental leash he held in such rigid control. He still held her hands and brought them up to his lips to kiss each one before letting them go.

"I don't think that's a good idea."

She struggled with the rejection, stepping back. She raked her hand through her hair, grateful that the night cloaked her blush. "Maybe not," she replied flippantly. From off in the parking lot she heard a grinding of tires. Looking out, she caught sight of a pizza delivery sign over an old sedan.

"Well then, see you." She tucked her hands, icy now, in her pockets and began to walk past him. His arm shot out to hold her back.

"I know you're vulnerable now," he said, his eyes piercing in the moonlight. "I don't want to take advantage."

She looked into his eyes and this time resented the sympathy she saw there. She jerked his hand away, tucked her hand back into her pocket and forced a confident smile that was well-practiced and expertly delivered.

"Rajiv, if you knew me better, you'd know that no one takes advantage of Jillian Season."

Seventeen

❧ ❧ ❧

The following day was bleak and rainy, as though nature were trying to match the weather with their moods. The motel seemed even uglier in bad weather, if such a thing was possible. Birdie lay in bed under the covers in a comatose state. She'd awakened with the dawn, such as it was, and had lain motionless, going over and over in her mind how she could possibly not have known she was pregnant.

Yes, she knew she was late with her period, but that was not uncommon for her. At forty-one, she wrote off the early signs of pregnancy as symptoms of early menopause. If only she'd taken a simple test. If only she'd stayed home and rested.

She sniffed and swiped the tears from her cheek, scolding herself for being so emotional. She was acting immature and irrational. As a physician she knew a miscarriage was no one's fault. Even if she'd gone straight to bed and kept her feet up, there was no guarantee that she'd have kept the baby. It was nature's way.

Then why did she feel such loss?

She wanted her husband. It felt wrong to be going through this ordeal without him. This was his loss as much as hers.

He should know. But this wasn't the kind of message one left on an answering machine.

Where was he? Why didn't he call her back? Was he just angry or was it possible that she'd lost him as well as her child? She pressed her hands together and brought them to her lips. That thought was crushing. As she lay prone, staring out at the bleak dawn, Birdie came to the realization that her life was falling apart.

She'd tried pretending for so many days that Dennis hadn't meant what he'd said in Evanston. That he hadn't really left her. But each day that he wasn't home, that he didn't call, was a battering ram breaking down her wall of pretense. Pounding, pounding, until all the pressures and responsibilities that she held so tightly inside of her burst and bled out in huge, fist-size clots.

"I can't do it anymore," she whimpered, pressing her fist against her lips, trying hard to hold back the cry. She felt something crack deep inside of her. *I'm not perfect. I can't solve all the problems. I can't save anyone. Not even myself.*

Years later she'd still remember what felt like a splitting open, similar to an earthquake when the pressure builds and the earth shifts and there is a terrible roaring, renting sound as the land tears apart. After the release she began to sob— hard, shoulder-shaking heaves that she couldn't control. She cried loudly, openly, letting the anguish pour out as the blood had flowed the night before. She became aware of Rose rising up beside her, hurrying to her bed, not saying a word, just wrapping her arms around her and rocking her, back and forth like a child as she wept unashamedly. Her sister's delicate fingers smoothed the hair from her face as she crooned in her beautiful voice, "Good, Birdie. Good. Let it all out. That's right. You're not alone. I love you."

Jilly came into the room hours later carrying a beautiful tray covered with a blue-and-white-checked linen tablecloth.

Under her arm, she was carrying a huge bouquet of spring flowers.

"Surprise! Wake up, sleepyhead. Time for breakfast!"

Birdie's body ached and she wasn't the least bit ready for breakfast or a happy face. She didn't know how long she'd wept, or how long she'd slept afterward, but she did know it wasn't nearly long enough. But Jilly was determinedly cheerful, so she offered a tremulous smile and begrudgingly dragged herself up to her elbows. Moving, she felt a gush of blood flow from her body.

"Damn. Wait a minute," she said, hurrying as fast as she could with the diaperlike pad between her legs. When she came back into the room, she saw that Jilly had arranged the flowers in a vase near her bed, tidied up the room and cracked open the window. The scent of rain-fresh air cut through the staleness of the room.

"Come have breakfast," Jilly said, folding back the covers.

Birdie saw that she'd also changed the linen. The crisp sheets smelled of bleach and were heavenly against her skin. Small kindnesses such as these were blessings.

"Thank you," she said, climbing into the glorious sheets.

"Oh, it's nothing," Jilly replied with a too eager smile. "I am at your service."

Birdie rested back against the pillows and studied Jilly more closely. With her hair freshly washed and tucked neatly behind her ears and wearing a fresh white cropped shirt over slender slacks, Jilly had the air of the perfect hostess. Her bright cheerfulness seemed more like armor, however, one Birdie had seen her use when she put on a front for strangers. Was she making her sister nervous now, she wondered?

"I'm okay, you know," she said, meeting Jilly's eye. "I'm not falling apart or about to throw myself into the river or anything."

Jilly's smile faltered but she rallied. She came to sit on the bed beside Birdie and busied herself with smoothing the blankets around Birdie's waist, then moved the laden breakfast tray up on her lap.

"I know you're not," she answered perfunctorily. Then switching the subject, "I hope you like a hale-and-hearty breakfast. Eggs, bacon, hash browns and toast. Courtesy of Maude and Larry."

"Rose told you that I cried, didn't she?"

Jilly poured out coffee from a thermos into the china cup, then added cream to it and handed it to Birdie.

"Buckets," she replied. She poured a cup for herself. When she looked up, she met Birdie's relentless gaze. Her face softened. "I'm glad you cried. You don't do it enough. It's not fair to you to always be so strong. You need to let us be strong for you once in a while. We can handle it, you know." She placed her hand over Birdie's. "Goodbye, Iron Bird."

Birdie felt as though another wave of tears was going to hit and turned her head away. "Stop," she said with a curt laugh. "I can't seem to turn off the spigot."

"You've got years of stored tears to let go. Let 'em flow."

"It's so embarrassing. I hate to cry. It makes me feel so vulnerable."

"Maybe because you are right now. You've just had a miscarriage, honey. You'd have to be rocky now. No one is that strong. How are you doing?"

"It's not like I haven't had one before."

"How many have you had?"

"Four. Five, something like that. You're not always sure. I'm not even sure this time. It's possible that it's just a bout of unexplained uterine bleeding. It happens at our age."

"Does that make it easier to deal with?"

Birdie shrugged. "Not really. I'm dealing with the same issue whether it's a miscarriage or menopause. I'm not going to have any more babies."

Jilly's eyes were dark green pools of sympathy. "Neither of us are."

They sipped their coffee in unison, then lowered their cups.

"I cried like that once," Jilly said in an offhand manner.

"At the hospital?"

She nodded. "After I had my baby I cried all night long. And when I woke up, I didn't have any tears left. Or so I thought." She shook her head and smiled ruefully. "I just kept them bottled up for all those years. We're talking gallons and gallons of tears stored up in there, like a camel. But once they're released, whew. It's pitiful. I've been crying since I got home. The memories keep coming and I keep crying. I feel like I'm washing my brain out with tears."

"Maybe that's not a bad thing. A cleansing, the way a doctor washes out a wound."

"Sometimes it feels like an eruption. I was reading about how these scientists believe there's all this water building pressure under the ocean floor. It got trapped there millions of years ago when the earth's plates were shifting. They're worried that all this pressure is just building up in there and that one of these days, it's going to blow. If it leaks out slowly, then the water tables might rise, but we can deal with it. But if the ocean floor cracks, it will cause these humongous waves to hit the shore. Can you imagine? Some poor guy on the Jersey shore reading *Jaws* will sense a shadow and look up to see this enormous tsunami heading his way!"

Birdie chuckled but inside she knew what Jilly was trying to tell her. It must have been obvious to everyone how the pressure had been building up in her. She'd felt the rent and tearing of the eruption that morning and she was still feeling the aftershocks. "Are you saying Dennis is going to be hit by a tsunami of my emotion?"

"Better him than me," Jilly replied with a teasing smile. "No," she added seriously. "I'm just glad to hear you acknowledge that you need to let the pressure out. Me, too.

God knows we've both been storing it up for what feels like millions of years.''

"I think talking like this helps ease out some of that pressure.''

"We haven't talked like this in so long. Not since we were roomies. I didn't think we ever would again. I've missed you, Birdie.''

Birdie felt the impact of the statement seep slowly into her mind. "I'll probably cry about that one, too. Give me a few minutes to store up some fluid.''

Jilly picked up her coffee cup and lifted it as if in a toast. "Good!"

"You're remarkable, do you know that?"

Jilly looked surprised. "Me? Heavens, why?"

"I've marveled at your resilience on this whole trip. You come home with problems of your own, and then bam! We hit you with this search for Spring. All your history is hitting you at once, yet you are still able to bring me fresh flowers and a cheery face. I wish I had your optimism.''

"Optimism is what you cling to when you've nothing else,'' she replied. "Besides, remember those tears we talked about?'' Birdie nodded. "Still happening.''

Birdie poked at the food with her fork then set it down, unable to eat a bite. "Jilly, what should I do? I think Dennis has really left me.''

Jilly took a deep breath and exhaled a plume of air. "You know, you haven't asked me for my advice since you were fifteen. This is quite a moment for me.'' After a pause, she looked at her aslant and asked, "Do you want him back?"

Birdie nodded. "Yes. I do.''

"Then you'll have to work to get him back. Men's egos are like spun glass. Beautiful, but oh so fragile. I think women are stronger, really. More resilient. But when a woman is as outwardly strong as you, it's hard for a man to compete.''

"I'm not so strong."

"Oh, yes you are. You might be feeling fragile now, but you'll rally again. You'll set a new goal in front of you like a carrot, then strap yourself to the harness and plow, plow, plow. You've always been like that. It's one of your strengths, you shouldn't change that. But you might let Dennis be strong with you. Flatter him. Flirt with him. He's a man, not another child. And he loves you, Birdie. Anyone can see that."

She plucked at her robe's sleeve and whispered her greatest fear. "I don't know that he does."

"He told me so. Before he left."

She looked up sharply. "He told you that? What did he say, exactly?"

"God, Birdie, I don't remember verbatim!"

"Just give me the general idea. I mean, what were you talking about that he'd suddenly tell you that he loved me?"

"Well," Jilly puffed out air, recollecting. "He was chasing Hannah to get her to go home with him and I was trying to stop him. There was some talk about him leaving you and I asked him if he loved you, or something like that."

"And he said he did?"

Jilly looked at Birdie steadily and nodded. "He sure did."

Birdie swallowed the words whole for breakfast and she felt filled with happiness. Dennis had said he loved her.... Hope swelled in her chest. "I don't know what's going on," she said plaintively. "I've been calling and calling but I keep getting the answering machine. Where could he be all night? I never suspected anything before but now I'm afraid there might be someone else."

"Dennis fooling around?" Jilly thought for a minute then shook her head. "Nah. I doubt it. At least, not yet. I wouldn't have too long of a separation, though. Not now when things are so iffy between the two of you." She stretched out on the mattress, resting her head on her palm. "I meant to talk to you about this. I know Hannah has to go back to school next week. Maybe you should go back home. Rose and I will carry on. And we'll call you if anything turns up. You can always meet us wherever. I don't want you to risk your marriage on account of this.''

"I don't know what it is, Jilly, but I have a strong sense that I need to be here. With you and Rose, and Hannah, too, to see it through. It's like I'm recharging my batteries on this trip. I'm feeling like my old self. Sometimes when I'm out jogging or sitting out back just looking at the river roll by, the old me emerges. I recognize her and smile and think, Well, hello again. You're back.'' She looked up. "But she doesn't stay. I slip back into my old ways.''

"Keep calling her back.''

"I will. I am. That's why I'm not quite ready to go home yet. Plus… I really think we'll find Spring.''

Jilly's eyes lit up. "I hope so.''

Birdie moved the untouched tray off of her lap. "I'm not very hungry,'' she said, smoothing out the blanket. "I hope you don't mind. Thank you for thinking of me.''

"No matter,'' she said, standing up and picking up the tray. "I'll take the tray back to the restaurant.''

"Wait,'' Birdie said, holding out her hand. "Don't go just yet. It's nice to chat.''

Jilly smiled and put the tray down on the bureau, then, stretching out on the mattress, she said, "It is, isn't it? Like old times.''

"We used to talk a lot.''

"Incessantly. You knew my every secret.''

"Well, almost every secret. You left out one particularly big one.''

Jilly shrugged and plucked at the lint on the paisley comforter. "Quite.''

"I'll let you in on a little secret of mine,'' Birdie said. She looked up almost coyly. "Did you know I was insanely jealous of you dating Dennis?"

Jilly's head jerked up, shock in her eyes. "Oh?" she said hesitantly.

"I was. I had a crush on him even back then. I used to brush my hair and put on lipstick whenever he came by on his motorcycle to pick you up. Remember how you used to make me run out and meet him at the corner because Dad wouldn't let you go on a motorcycle? God, Jilly, didn't you ever wonder why I was so eager? I thought he was such a dream in his leather jacket, with his long blond hair. We used to talk at the curb while we waited for you to come out. Once he even took me for a ride. Oh my, I was in heaven. My arms around him and his leather jacket. I still get goose bumps every time I smell motor oil and leather."

"You never told me," she said breathlessly, staring at the swirling paisley pattern.

"I was embarrassed because I would've stolen him from you in a heartbeat without a moment's remorse. I was awful. The way I batted my eyes." She laughed. "He probably thought I had something in my eye. He was a junior and I was just going into freshman year. That was a world of difference back then. Besides," she said, feeling a twinge of the age-old jealousy she used to feel for Jilly. "He only had eyes for you."

"That was such a long time ago." Jilly's voice was soft. Birdie did not notice that her hands were trembling. "We were just kids."

"Oh, I know. Don't think I've got hang-ups about that," she said blithely, but inside her heart she knew she was lying. "When I saw him years later at Northwestern, it hit me all over again, only harder. I couldn't believe it when he pursued me that time. *Me*. Beatrice Season." Birdie looked long and hard at Jilly. Even though the bloom of youth had faded, she was still a natural beauty and would be at eighty. Birdie knew she never had and never would have that kind of beauty. "I guess I've loved Dennis Connor since the first moment I laid eyes on him."

"You know there was nothing between us. Not really," Jilly said emphatically.

Birdie looked up and saw that Jilly's face was pale and drawn. Instinct reared as she read doubt and something else—fear?—in her bright green eyes. She felt a dredging up of powerful feelings that she'd thought she'd outgrown long ago.

"No, I don't know that," Birdie replied slowly, voicing a long-held fear at last. She tore her gaze from Jilly's and looked at her hands, at the gold-and-diamond wedding ring on her finger. "I've always wondered, far in the back of my mind, just how involved you two were. I remember how he used to idolize you. But then, so did all the boys. I guess I always was a little jealous that he dated you first. I thought I was past it, but over the years I started putting the dates together and I couldn't help but wonder—" she paused to gather her courage "—if the baby was Dennis's."

She twisted the wedding band back and forth on her finger in the strained silence that fell between them. "Is he?" She looked up, her pale eyes searching. "Is Dennis the father?"

Jilly's face was as white as the sheets. She sat paralyzed. Her pale, full lips had opened to a gasp and her green eyes stared back at Birdie with a hunted expression. The seconds ticked by, each one adding to the suspense, each making her more fearful of the reply.

"No!" Jilly replied on a breath. She shook her head, then rose quickly and raked her hands through her hair, holding it in a ponytail at her nape. "God, Birdie, no."

Birdie wanted to believe her, so badly. Her fear seemed to suck the breath right out of her lungs. She searched Jilly's face, then slumped back on the pillows with relief.

"I don't know why but I always had this feeling," she said, rolling her eyes. "Crazy, I know. I just had to ask."

"I wish you hadn't."

"Hey, you're the one who keeps saying no more secrets."

Jilly turned her head away sharply. "Yeah, well, maybe it's not such a good idea to keep digging around. The spade can hit some tender spots."

"You're right. I'm sorry."

"Forget it." She began to busy herself, turning toward the untouched tray. The bacon sat in congealed fat beside the cold toast. "I've got to go. Are you sure you won't try to eat something? Maybe a little fruit?"

"Hey, it's not often I'm not hungry," Birdie said, striving to get the happier mood back. She watched Jilly toss her hair, a sure sign of agitation, then pick up the tray. Her face was smiling, but her mascara betrayed her with smudges under her eyes.

"I'll take a piece of that bacon for a friend of mine. I'm going off to find the little beggar." She seemed eager to leave.

"Okay. Thanks. I am really tired. I think I'll just go back to sleep for a little while."

"Sleep tight. Don't let the bedbugs bite."

Birdie slunk down and settled on her side, tucking her hands together under her cheek. She could feel her mouth move into a smile. "If you do, hit 'em with a shoe."

"Love you, Birdie." Her voice was a soft whisper at the door.

She yawned noisily and burrowed under the covers. "Love you, too."

Birdie heard the door swish closed then the click of the lock. Quiet settled heavily in the empty room. She thought again of her long, strange conversation with Jilly. They'd covered a lot of ground. She brought the green thermal blanket up around her ears and yawned once more. As painful as it was, she was glad she'd asked her about Dennis.

She closed her eyes and chuckled to herself, thinking of all that water under the ocean floor. She supposed she and Jilly just shot out a little bit of steam.

Eighteen

Her feet pounded the earth with thundering anger as Jilly put more and more space between herself and her sisters. Her speed accelerated, fueled by the whirlwind of accusations in her mind. She'd broken the one sacred promise she had made to herself: she wouldn't lie for anyone's sake ever again.

But Birdie had been sick and weak, already devastated by one loss, her heart argued back. How could she hurt her sister with a truth that could be equally devastating? She'd come to Birdie's room with breakfast and flowers and good cheer, trying to follow Rose's good example. She hadn't expected *that* question, damn her luck.

Because she loved Birdie, she had lied, and given her the best gift she could—a piece of her soul. A noble-enough motive for dishonesty.

Then why did it feel so wrong?

The rainy, gray cold only deepened her depression. She felt her old restlessness rise up within her and jogged for miles, pushing herself beyond the comfort level. At a high rocky ridge, Jilly stopped, panting while sweat pooled, and looked out over the valley. Its vastness seemed to go on forever. Like a lie, she thought to herself, then slumped her shoulders and wept.

On her return path, tired and resigned, she passed Rajiv at the bridge. He was back at his project of clearing the river for the spring thaw.

"Jillian, wait!" he called.

She ignored him, picking up her pace.

This time he ran after her, catching her arm and pulling her to a stop. Her breath was heaving and her eyes shot daggers at him as she yanked free.

"Jillian, let me explain."

She pushed a lock of red hair from her face. "Explain? There's nothing to explain. I understood everything." She started to walk again but he kept pace by her side.

"You think I rejected you."

"You don't know what I think." She kept her eyes on the road lest her flush reveal the truth.

"I didn't mean to offend you. I was trying to do just the opposite. Jillian, stop, please. Listen to me for a moment." He stopped in the path, slamming his hands on his hips.

She walked a few steps farther, then stopped, hands on her hips and head bent, catching her breath. She swung her head to look over her shoulder. Rajiv stood straight in his oilskin jacket, jeans and high boots. Mud streaked dashingly down his left cheek like a scar. Their eyes met and the seriousness she found there drew her back to him.

"Is Birdie all right?"

"Much better. Thanks."

"I'm glad."

Jilly tucked her hands under her arms and looked off.

Rajiv stooped to pick up a fallen branch and toss it off the path. "It's been a long time since I've kissed anyone," he said, surprising her with his sudden honesty.

"Actually, me too," she replied, glancing sideways at him.

"I was thinking of you when I pulled away. But I was also thinking of myself. I'm not sure I want to get involved with anyone. I like my privacy. I like living alone. I don't want attachments."

"Rajiv, I wanted to make love with you, not marry you."

He seemed flustered and looked off, squinting his eyes as though trying to make sense of what he'd heard.

"Look, this doesn't need to be so hard," she said. "I accept your apology, okay? Let's leave it at that."

"That's the problem. I don't want to leave it. I've made a mess of things between us, I know. I don't want to get involved but the truth is, I already am. I think about you all the time. You invade my thoughts. It's most annoying, really."

She looked up to see the humor in his eyes and couldn't resist smiling back.

They were standing very near each other, deliberately not touching but feeling the attraction crackle between them.

"I'd like to start over again, if it's all right with you," he said. "I'd like to spend some time with you. To be your friend. And then, perhaps…"

"Perhaps," she replied, her eyes crinkling. She saw the tension flow from his face and his eyes spark. Then she lifted one shoulder and said, "And perhaps not," before trotting off.

She ran back to her room just long enough to change into jeans and an old sweater, then ran back to the river with Pirate Pete at her side. Rajiv's head darted up when he spotted her. Beaming, he waved her close.

"I've come to be your friend and help," she announced.

His eyes kindled at her words, then his gaze dropped to the little dog standing loyally by her side. "Friend, are you?" he teased. "It looks as though my friend has stolen my dog. Seems rather cheeky."

"Ah, now, he's your dog, is he? What happened to no attachments?"

He bent to pat Pirate Pete. "A man can change."

She felt her heart flutter and tucked her hands deep into her jeans pockets. "I cheated," she said, feeling rather like a flirting schoolgirl. "I gave him a slice of bacon today and won him completely over."

Rajiv straightened to look at her. His gaze flickered across her face and softened as he reached out to pull a fallen lock behind her ear. Jilly knew at that moment that she was completely won over, too.

They began working together, tossing fallen branches, old soda cans and trash from the river and gathering it in bundles to cart away. The sun came out late morning to shine warmly on their cheeks as they raked out leaves that were thick and heavy, freeing the river water to race over the bed of rocks and pebbles. As she worked she wondered at the unpredictability of fate. She wasn't looking for someone right now, didn't really want anyone complicating her life. And neither, apparently, did he. But they'd met and she couldn't deny that he was different from any man she'd ever known. She saw him only briefly every day, but she felt a kinship with him unlike any other. As they mucked out the river side by side, she felt as comfortable as though they were a couple of old married folks.

Who would have thought serious, silent Rajiv Patel could be such a court jester?

Over the next few days, Rajiv came several times a day to Birdie's room carrying a pot of steaming, fragrant cardamom tea and special Indian treats—wonderful squares that they couldn't name that tasted of pistachios and cashews and perfume. When she wasn't at the library with Rose, or making calls, Jilly enjoyed the visits as much as Birdie.

He always stood near the door, his tall and lean frame relaxed, his long arms crossed, and paid court as though Birdie were a queen on a throne. His eyes sparkled devilishly as he told marvelous stories about his homeland. But with his dark good looks, Jilly thought he could just as well have stood mute. He was pure pleasure to look at. She couldn't look at his lips without remembering his kiss. Couldn't see his hands move as he told his stories without remembering the feel of them on her face. Seeing him so close, and yet so distant, was an exquisite kind of torture. She felt it viscerally. She had never wanted a man as much as she wanted Rajiv.

It was late when Jilly came back from the laundromat and saw a FedEx truck parked in front of the motel's office. With her heart thumping wildly in her chest she hurried to park the Land Rover, then leaped out and rushed to the office. Rajiv was just directing the deliveryman to her room when she entered. Rajiv's eyes were flashing with excitement and anticipation crackled in the air.

"I'll take that," she said, stepping in. She signed quickly and the driver left, chirping out a "Thank you!" She stared at the envelope, weighing its heaviness. It was from Mr. Collins—at last—and it was thick with information.

"I hope it's good news," Rajiv said.

She kissed his lips for an answer, then bolted to find her sisters.

"It's here!" she shouted as she entered Birdie's motel room. Bags of snacks littered the bed, the paisley curtains were drawn and the three women were lounging, watching still another movie. Jilly felt the news from Mr. Collins had come just in time to save them all from apathy.

She flicked off the television as she passed and plopped down on the bed with an energetic bounce. "We're back on the road, my friends," she said, rubbing her palms together.

"It's about time. I thought we were going to stay in this place forever," Hannah said with a groan of relief.

"I'm getting quite fond of this crazy place," Birdie surprised everyone by saying.

"Or maybe it's just the company."

Rose reached out to her.

"Mr. Collins is as good as his word," Jilly said, focusing only on the envelope in her hand. "He must have sent this on the day it arrived." She exhaled a long breath, then met Birdie's gaze. "Okay, here goes." She pulled the string, opened it and retrieved a file full of papers. She hadn't expected more than the birth certificate and leafed through the thick pile of papers in a daze.

"What is all that?" Rose asked, moving in.

Jilly flipped through the papers, then, taking a deep breath, decided to just start from the top and work her way down. "This looks like the original birth certificate," she said, lifting it closer. "Let's see," she said as she scanned. "Yep. Look here, it refers to my daughter as Baby Girl Season. Mother, Jillian Season, and—" She stopped herself. She read where the birth father was listed as unknown. "The hospital is St. Francis." She winked at Birdie. "Score one for our side. The date of birth, May 17, 1973." Scanned the form. "This one doesn't say much else," she said, moving on. "Here's another birth certificate." Her eyes feasted on the information. "They call it the Amended Birth Certificate," she said, mimicking an official tone. As she read further, however, her face grew still. She looked up at Birdie, Rose and Hannah with an ear-to-ear grin stretching across her glowing face.

"Her name is Anne Marie."

They squealed in delight, like little girls at a party, rushing forward for a group hug and kisses. It felt to all of them as though Anne Marie had just been born and they were celebrating her birth for the very first time. Anne Marie's name had been on the list! Bit by bit, their search was making progress and they all felt the momentum in their veins.

"Read the rest," Rose said, clapping her hands. "We want to know everything about her!"

"Yes, hurry up," added Birdie, color blooming in her cheeks. "We've waited long enough."

Jilly looked up at their eager faces and captured them in her heart as a photographer might, imprinting this moment forever. Then, wiping her eyes, she focused on the papers.

"Okay. Well," she said with a mighty exhale. What she read next deflated her enthusiasm a bit. "My name isn't on this birth certificate at all." She shouldn't have been surprised, but it still hurt. "It's weird seeing all the same information as the original birth certificate, but under *mother* the name is Susan Parker."

"Go on," Birdie urged. "This is important. Now you've got the adoptive mother's name."

"Under *father* is Robert Parker. My God, it gives their address in Sturgeon Bay. That's so close. He's a shipbuilder."

"That's cool," Hannah said.

Jilly thought so, too. "And the mom... It lists her as a homemaker." She paused and felt a bittersweet twinge. "I guess Anne Marie got a full-time mom after all."

"That's great. What else? This is so exciting." Rose moved closer till she was pressing against Jilly's shoulder.

"Father was thirty at the time of adoption. Mother was twenty-nine." She leafed through the other papers; there were so many just about the adoptive parents alone. The Petition to Adopt, the parents' home study, reports from the agency about them and their medical history. "Just picking up a few tidbits I see that Robert is a college graduate. His hobbies include woodwork and sailing."

"Well, yeah," Hannah interjected with a roll of the eyes. "He's a shipbuilder."

"What about the mother?"

"She graduated from high school. Some college. Loves to sew and garden. Very active in her church."

"She sounds wonderful," Birdie said.

Jilly frowned, feeling unexpected jealousy. "Yeah, she does, doesn't she? Everything I need to know about them is right here." She could feel the excitement bubbling in her veins as she looked up from the papers at her sisters. "All the information we need to find Spring."

"Anne Marie," Birdie corrected her.

"Yes," she said wistfully. "My baby has a name, a lovely name."

"Can we see some of those papers you're hoarding?" Birdie asked, putting out her palm.

Jilly handed her the papers, save the last one she hadn't yet read. Folding her long legs beneath her, she read this last sheet. It was a copy of the Adoption Decree, the final order of adoption. As she read through this form, the giddy joy turned icy cold in her veins. The legal language of the decree was brutal. Words that stabbed quick yet deep like daggers, shredding her fragile self-esteem. She sat motionless with the paper limp in her fingers, stunned and so ashamed.

The decree proclaimed to the world that Jillian Season had abandoned her daughter. It declared in black and white that Baby Girl Season was born illegitimate.

"What's wrong?" Birdie asked.

Jilly held her hand up for her to wait, unable to speak. Through tears, she read till the end of the document. The decree judged that Anne Marie, by virtue of her adoption, obtained all rights, privileges and immunities of children born in *lawful* wedlock.

"I hope to God no one ever showed her this," Jilly said, letting her hand fall in her lap.

Birdie picked up the paper and read it, followed by Rose. They exchanged worried glances as Jilly sat quietly, staring off into space.

"You realize of course this is all ignorance on their part. Absolute stupidity," said Birdie in a huff.

"You can't take this to heart," said Rose.

"Oh, can't I? What did it state that wasn't true?"

"That's the letter of the law," Birdie countered. "Not the spirit."

"That's all just formality. What matters is that you've got her name now," Rose said, trying to drum up enthusiasm again. "And her parents' names. We have a real hope of finding her."

"And then what?" Jilly asked. "What if she doesn't want to meet with me after we make contact? Me, the terrible, sinful mother who gave birth out of wedlock. They make me out to be some derelict who had a child outside of the law. Why should she want to meet *me* when she already has a good, solid, happy life with the perfect mother, the one who saved her from the stigma of illegitimacy?"

"Anne Marie wouldn't be like that," Hannah said in defense of the cousin she'd never met. "She'll want to meet you. If it was me, I'd want to meet my real mother."

"That's birth mother," Jilly said, silencing her. "What a god-awful term. It sounds like someone who just dropped the baby at the hospital, then strolled off. But I suppose it's better than *real* mother versus *fake* mother."

"Don't do this," Birdie said.

"Do what? I'm just being honest. Look at this. I'm not even named on the adoption form. It's as though I don't exist."

"But you do exist," Birdie said, using her authoritative voice for the first time since the miscarriage. "And you are her mother. And Rose and I are her aunts and Hannah is her cousin. By blood. This child is a Season. No one is discounting that the woman who adopted Anne Marie is her mother in every nuance of the word. Her real mother, as you put it. We should all pray that it's true, for Anne Marie's sake. This isn't some kind of contest. Susan Parker is Anne Marie's mother and we have to face that clearly and accept it—or stop the search now."

"I do accept that."

"Good. The fact remains, Jilly, that you are her biological mother. Half her DNA comes from you. We know too much about heredity and genes these days not to realize how critical that transference is. Anne Marie must know it, too. Believe me, Jilly, she'll want to meet you."

But Jilly had already stopped listening. She felt the walls of the small room closing in on her. She slowly stood and began walking toward the door.

"Where are you going?" Rose asked.

"For a smoke. I just need some time alone."

"Stay with us," Birdie said. "It's nasty out there."

Jilly gave off a short laugh as she opened the door. "Great. I'll fit right in."

When she left the motel room, she would have sworn on a stack of Bibles that she didn't know where she was headed. Jilly only knew she had to leave. It was unseasonably cold out, a result of the gray clouds that hovered over them, low and threatening, for days. She sniffed and tasted snow in the air. She found that incredibly depressing. "Snow in April," she muttered. "That's perfect." It was an omen. They'd never reach spring.

As she walked along the river road, she heard in the misty twilight the taunts and jeers that she had quieted for the glorious days with her sisters. In this strange little town that held no ties to the life she'd created for herself these past twenty-six years, she had allowed herself the luxury of thinking herself as one of the four Seasons again. In her mind she was still young and unscathed. She was Jilly the creative one, the ringleader, the fun sister. The search had been like an elaborate game that bound them together again. Just another Season make-believe with elaborate rules to follow.

The Adoption Decree, however, held enough brutal truth

to strip her of any pretense. *Abandoned. Illegitimate. Out of Wedlock.* No more pretending, Jilly, she told herself.

She walked till her Italian leather shoes were soaked and she found herself standing in front of a small redbrick house surrounded by a black wrought-iron fence, high on the hill overlooking the town of Hodges. A light was on upstairs. It appeared warm and inviting behind the drawn shades. She stood for a while at the gate, looking up at the light, wondering if he was lying in bed reading a book. She didn't see the telltale flashing of a television. As she stood in the garden, the night was so quiet she could hear herself breathe.

The gate squeaked loudly in the darkness. Pirate Pete sprang up from where he was lying and trotted up to the gate to investigate, growling deep in his throat. When she stepped inside the property, he began barking his high, shrill alarm.

"Hush, shh," she said to the dog. "Pete, hush."

The dog came closer, sniffing with his ears back. When he caught her scent, his growling stopped immediately and he began wagging his tail excitedly. But it was too late. The back porch light flicked on. She heard a click of a lock, then the door swung open.

Jilly stood with her hand on the gate and looked at the tall, dark silhouette standing on the porch. He was wearing a robe. His hand was on the doorknob and he held his body tense and attentive. With the light at his back, she couldn't see his face, but she could feel the intensity of his stare.

Another Jillian Season would have fixed a sultry smile on her face and walked with the forward, pelvic rolling gait of a runway model. But this Jillian Season was not so sure-footed. Her face was tearstained and puffy. Her clothes were wrinkled and worn. Her hair was pulled back in an elastic, unbrushed and wild. And she was cold, so very cold. This Jillian stepped forward, open and unsure. One foot in front of another along the crooked little garden path with wobbly stones that wound around old trees with thick, split trunks, and up the six cracked cement stairs to him.

"I need a friend," she said softly.

He held out his hand to her and she took it. She knew from the way his dark eyes quivered that he read everything in her gaze. She felt it in the electricity of his touch. She knew it in the way he stepped aside and ushered her wordlessly into his house.

The kitchen was a small, unremarkable room dimly lit by fluorescent task lights under the cabinets. Beyond, in the other room, she caught sight of bookshelves and a leather sofa, very modern and spare. Her wandering eyes fixed on a patch of bare skin in the V of his pure white terry robe. It was so marvelously smooth that she couldn't resist reaching out to touch it. Her fingers were icy. She heard his breath intake, but he didn't move away. Moving slowly, she slid one hand then the other under the terry cloth, gliding her fingers across the warmth. She relished the feel of his hard muscles and the sensation of his nipples tightening under her palms. When he reached up to tug her elbows and draw her away, she resisted.

"Please," she pleaded, bringing her lips to his bare chest. She rested her cheek against his skin and stood still, waiting. She could hear his heart pounding in his chest.

He reached up to touch her chin and lifted it enough so that she was staring into his eyes. His hair was soft and flowed down in thick black waves, framing his jawline. His dark eyes seemed to glow from the shadows as he pressed his fingertip to his lips to indicate silence. Then, with a finely arched brow raised, he took her hand and led her across the tile floor to his bedroom. In the small, neat room he held up his hand, gesturing for her to wait. Then he turned and went into the bathroom. She heard the creaking sound of faucets turning followed by the gush of water flowing into a tub.

Looking around she noticed that there were books everywhere—in shelves along the wall, on the floor beside the bed and stacked on the bedside table. Many of them were written in Hindi, but there were many others in English, mostly of classic literature and computers. And she was surprised to discover many in French as well. She picked up a well-worn leather book: Sartre. Opening it, she found several passages marked.

When he entered the room, she set down the book quickly, embarrassed for prying. He didn't seem to mind. He was smiling and holding out his hand to her, heightening the suspense with mystery sparkling in his eyes. His was an elegant body, not an athletic one. Slim at the hips but very firm. She remembered seeing him work in the river.

Taking her hand, he led her into the small bathroom. She stepped into a cloud of fragrant, warm steam and flickering, perfumed candles. There were candles everywhere—along the rim of the tub, atop the toilet, on the floor. He helped her undress, then guided her into the tub, balancing her as she eased herself into the sweet scented water. He left her there to soak, closing the door behind him.

How did he know she needed this solitude? she wondered. A soft moan escaped from her lips as she closed her eyes, sunk to her neck in the hot water and just let go. She didn't think of anything save for the feel of the hot water lapping against her breasts and the faint, rhythmic dripping of the faucet. She didn't know how long she soaked there, but when he came for her the water had begun to cool and she was ready to take his hand and be guided into the enormous, thirsty towel he held out for her. He was intent on pampering her. She was not permitted to do so much as lift her own foot. She'd never been treated with such tenderness, such reverence, and she found it both exhilarating and humbling.

He began toweling her dry, gently stroking her outstretched arms, her neck, her breasts, placing a kiss here and there gently. She luxuriated in his attention. His valetlike restraint was tremendously erotic.

He led her once again to his room. He'd put clean linen on his bed. Water glasses on the bedside table dripped with condensation. While she sipped, Rajiv moved the candles until once again she was surrounded with the flickering flames. Then he pulled back the blankets and laid her in the center of the bed. Sitting beside her, he began to smooth a small amount of sweet scented oil over her body. It had the echo of sesame and something heavenly in it, and her moist, warm body soaked it in thirstily. He looked into her eyes as he massaged her arms and breasts, then smiled wickedly as he spread the oil along her inner thighs, tracing small, sensuous circles with his nail. She rolled her hips in pleasure, longing for his hand to linger where the need was beginning to build.

But he was not to be hurried. Rolling her on her belly, he spread the oil along her back in strong kneading motions that eased away knots of tension from her shoulders. She groaned and slipped to another, deeper level of relaxation. The music was a soft background in the room; an Indian woman sang what could only be songs of love. His hands continued to massage, more gently, her lower back, then her bottom, her thighs, running his hand in between them, just flirting with her inner softness. When he rolled her again onto her back he gently spread her hair out on the pillow, then her arms and legs out to the side upon the crisp white sheets so that she was fully open to him.

Her breath came heavily now. From under half-lowered lids, she watched as he reached up to take the red rose from the vase and crush the blossom with his hand. He then sprinkled the sweet red petals over her naked body. As each delicate petal floated to her body, landing on tender, pliant skin with an inexpressible softness, she felt overcome. The petals, the candles, the oil, the chanting music, all combined to make her feel as though he were a high priest and she a virgin on an altar. What was the sacrifice? she wondered. What was the prayer?

He moved to straddle her. Looking at him through sex-drugged eyes she saw his dark-skinned thighs against her pale ones, as she had imagined so many times in her fantasies. His hands moved once again to touch her face, her lips and her breasts, then glided over her belly to begin new caresses. When she whimpered, cheating and voicing his name, he spread her thighs wider, moving to kneel between them. She raised her eyes and saw his, gleaming and dark with desire. There was a moment's communication, then he was within her.

She arched against him, feeling as though he was splitting her in two. She clung to him, kissing his ear, his neck and his mouth as he slowly, rhythmically, drummed the pace of their passion. She closed her eyes and from a distance heard the high, nasal chant of unfamiliar lands. A strange, heady incense permeated the air. She was in a hot, humid jungle where stars flickered overhead like candles and the man she loved was Rajiv and tiger all in one. They were human, they were not. They were two lovers joined for one perfect night. They rolled and pressed, kissed and caressed. She felt her climax rising, felt his body drum with increased urgency into her own. She flashed open her eyes and saw the eyes of a tiger before he lowered his dark head and put his teeth to her shoulder. He plunged one last time and they both cried out to the stars.

Afterward, when they could talk, they talked for hours.

Nineteen

"Where have you been!" Rose was wrapped in her fleece robe, her long red hair framing a face pink with fury.

Jilly sheepishly slunk into the room and closed the door behind her. She couldn't meet her sister's eyes, convinced that the past hours of lovemaking were imprinted on her face. She looked at the mirror, the sink, the bed, anywhere but Rose's face.

"I'm sorry, I know I should have called. I lost track of time."

"That's not good enough! I was worried sick. I was about ready to call the police."

Jilly spun around and stared in disbelief. Rose was yelling at her! She was hopping mad, pacing like a bantam and shouting at the top of her lungs.

"You can be pretty insensitive, do you know that, Jilly? When you want something, you just go get it and damn what happens to anyone else. Did you even stop to think how worried I'd be? Or Birdie?"

Jilly was so shocked by the sight of Rose losing her temper that she didn't answer the questions.

"Did you?"

"Did I what?"

"Oh, Jilly..." Rose threw up her hands.

Jilly let out a long, hard sigh. "What's the big explosion for? I was out. No big deal."

Rose was slightly calmer now, relieved just to see Jilly alive. She tried to speak evenly but the tremor was still in her voice. "You don't go walking out alone late at night, upset, and come back four hours later without word."

Jilly almost laughed. "I'm forty-three years old. I don't need to be told I have a curfew. This is how I've always lived my life. I go out when I want and come back when I want. Frankly, I only came back at all so you wouldn't worry, and I promise you—" she pointed her finger at Rose "—it was the ultimate sacrifice. I'm sorry if you were worried, but I didn't ask you to be my nursemaid."

Rose drew herself up, closed her robe around her neck and delivered a long, hard look.

"I'm sorry, Rose," Jilly said right away. "I didn't mean it like that." Jilly rubbed her forehead. In her heart she knew Rose had reason for worry and decided a little groveling was in order. "I'm not used to having people care where I am," she said in a gentler voice. "I'll try to be more thoughtful in the future. Okay?"

Rose's shoulders lowered and she tucked her hands in her pockets. "I guess I'm not used to living with independent people. I shouldn't have jumped down your throat."

The door opened and Birdie came in, her robe billowing, her short red hair flat on one side where she'd been lying down. But her eyes were blazing. "You took ten years off my life!" she shouted. "And frankly, I don't have ten years I care to give." Then she wrapped her arms around Jilly and squeezed her tight. "We thought you'd been eaten by bears. Or worse." Pulling away she added, "I could kill you myself."

She stepped back and looked into Jilly's face. Her blue eyes narrowed as she studied with a mother's eyes Jilly's damp hair, her chapped lips, the faint glow to her skin. Birdie's lips pursed with speculation. "Jogging, I suppose?"

Jilly knew that Birdie had figured out what she'd been up to. She took off her coat, feeling a flush just recalling Rajiv's tan, slender fingers doing each button of her blouse. "Yep. Nothing like it."

"Mmm-hmm. In those shoes?"

Jilly looked down at her bare feet in the light leather shoes. Her socks were in her coat pocket. "Well, power walking."

"I've never known anyone to smell quite so fresh and sweet after a four-hour jog."

Jilly tossed her coat over the chair, then faced Birdie, her lips twitching. "It's that sweet mountain air."

Birdie laughed and shook her head. "You're being careful, aren't you?" she said in all seriousness, then blushed when Jilly snorted a laugh. "Okay, I'm sounding like the mother again. I'm just worried."

"It's not that. I just got the third degree from my roommate." She looked over at Rose and smirked. "You should've heard her. What a temper! Who knew?"

Birdie swung her head around to look at Rose, who was standing with her shoulders back. "That was Rose doing all that hollering?"

"Felt pretty good, too," Rose replied with a jaunty lift of her chin. "Better get used to it."

Jilly burst out laughing, leaning against Birdie for support.

"We've created a monster," Birdie said between laughs.

"In your own image," Jilly retorted, jabbing Birdie in the ribs.

"Very funny."

"Whoa, back up a minute," Rose said. Then her features changed as understanding dawned. "Jilly...you and Rajiv Patel?"

Jilly renewed her laughter against Birdie's shoulder. Birdie only rolled her eyes. Rose shook her head incredulously. "I thought we were only kidding when we teased you about the attraction."

"Be happy for me," Jilly said, turning her head, revealing the grin of happiness that she felt down to her toes.

"It's nice to see at least one of the Season sisters having a little fun," Birdie said, sitting down on the mattress with a flop.

"You and Rajiv..." Rose sat beside Birdie, still trying to digest the information.

"No offense girls, but let's not get too comfortable," Jilly said with a yawn. "I'm exhausted. I just want to crawl under the covers and sleep. Tomorrow I intend to start bright and early searching those addresses."

"Well, well, well, you're in a better mood than when you left," Birdie said, slowly rising. "Eager to start the search again, are we?" Her face lit up with relief. "Whatever it is that he's offering, can I have some?"

"Not on your life," Jilly replied as she unbuttoned her blouse. "This one is strictly hands off." She started to sing in time to popping her buttons, "God bless the mister that comes between me and my sister. God bless the sister that comes between me and my man."

"That good, is he?" Birdie said with a smirk.

"Better."

"Don't tell me," Birdie said with a sorry shake of her head. "Given my situation, it would be too cruel."

"Well, you can tell me," Rose said, sidling closer. "I'm not too shy to admit I could use some coaching."

"Why?" Jilly stopped her fingers and cast her a suspicious look. "Any news from the front?"

Rose's face lit up. "He wrote back. And he said he'd wait to meet me. That I'm worth the wait."

Birdie let out a whoop.

"Oh, I'm so glad," Jilly said, wrapping her arms around

Rose in a hug. Then close to her ear she whispered, "Just don't wait too long. Trust me on this one."

Birdie joined the circle. "For every season, there is a turn, or something like that. Go for it, Rose. It's your turn."

The following morning, Rajiv reluctantly agreed to join them for breakfast at The Country Diner. He seemed very stiff and uncomfortable as he took his seat beside Jilly and politely smiled at the other patrons of the restaurant, who stared at him as though they'd seen a ghost.

"You don't get out much, do you?" Jilly asked under her breath.

He didn't reply. Rather, he fixed his attention on the menu.

"Well, look who's finally shown up," Maude said in her usual bellicose manner. "We'd begun to wonder if anyone really lived up there at the motel at all."

He seemed intent on the menu. "I've been busy," he said with a quick, tense smile.

"Larry's my name." The old man came forward to shake his hand. "Welcome."

"Rajiv Patel," he replied, taking his hand.

"We nicknamed you Heathcliff," Larry said with a quick laugh. When Rajiv raised his brows, he added, "Seeing as how you didn't socialize much."

"Heathcliff is far too romantic for my nature, I'm afraid."

"Oh, I don't know," Jilly said with a laugh. "I guess that makes me Cathy."

Rajiv turned her way and she could tell by his amused expression that he liked the analogy. They all relaxed and ordered a hearty breakfast, eager to get started on the day's search.

"It's back to the grindstone, I'm afraid," said Rose. She made no secret that she couldn't stand being cooped up in the cramped building the county called a public library. "At least we only have one name to search this time."

"What information do you have now?" asked Rajiv.

"We have the adoptive parents' names and address at the time of the adoption. But that address is twenty-six years old. We'll have to go to the library to search the directories."

"Their name is Parker. There'll be a gazillion Parkers in the directories. Why couldn't it have been one of those long, strange names with multiple consonants?"

"But why go to the library?" Rajiv asked.

His question was met with blank stares.

"Where else do you suggest?" asked Jilly, unsure of where he was headed.

"I have a software program that is a national phone directory. It matches names and addresses. We could start with Wisconsin, then go through the states one by one geographically or alphabetically, whichever you prefer. And we could work out of my office. It would be much easier that way."

Jilly leaned across her chair to wrap her arms around him, delivering a sound kiss. "What a guy," she said with a broad smile, enjoying every second of the stunned look of surprise on proper Rajiv's face—and on the faces of her sisters.

Rose wasn't blind to the bloom in Jilly's cheeks or the spring in her step. Watching her with Rajiv made Rose aware of the emptiness in her own life. The little, discreet signs of affection affected her the most: Rajiv resting his hand on Jilly's shoulder as he leaned over to look at the computer monitor while she searched, tucking a tendril behind her ear, Jilly absently leaning against him. Rose caught Jilly's sighs and Rajiv's fierce glance of possession when he wasn't aware anyone was looking.

Rose desperately wanted a man to feel that way about her, to look at her with such desire. Oh, she wanted romance in her life. She wanted the hearts and flowers, the whispered words of love, the hand-holding, the gazing at a moon to-

gether, and ultimately, the commitment. She wanted a child
of her own.

She hadn't known this about herself until this search for
Spring. She'd been so preoccupied for so many years caring
for Merry that she never contemplated wanting another child
to care for. But now, watching Jilly getting in touch with her
own maternal instincts, she knew she wanted to experience
that for herself.

No one can do this for you, Jilly had said.

It's your turn, said Birdie.

Emboldened by new goals, she laid her fingers on the keyboard and began to type.

Dear DannyBoy,

It's another chilly night in northern Wisconsin. But writing to you makes me feel warm. Have I told you lately
how much your letters mean to me? I've been tracking
your route on the map, imagining what you must be
seeing. The wide-open spaces of Texas, the beautiful
farmland in Kansas and Missouri. I'd love to see all
those places some day.

We've had some interesting news. Mrs. Kasparov has
found a buyer for the house! Apparently there is a couple who is absolutely nuts for our house. I can understand that. It's a wonderful house. Mrs. Kasparov reported back to us this morning that this couple does not
want the house to go on the market. Apparently, there
are bidding wars going on for houses in our area. So
they've made an offer considerably over our asking
price. As is! That means we won't have to do all the
repairs that I had thought we would, like the roof and
the painting and the floors. In fact, this couple is clear
they do not want us to do a thing. They have plans of
their own. One of the things they like best about our
house is its virginal quality. The woodwork hasn't been

painted over. As if we'd ever.

So, we've decided to sell them the house.

Whew. I had to take a breath after writing that sentence. Honestly? I thought I'd be really upset when this decision was made. Birdie and Jilly have been tiptoeing around me, convinced that I'm hiding my real feelings for their sakes. I used to do that a lot, you know. Hide what I felt or thought to make everything easier or more pleasant for everyone else. But I don't do that so much anymore. I can't explain it, but spending time with my sisters again, remembering our past, it's making me feel better about myself. I feel like I'm getting in touch again with the girl that I used to be. Does that make sense to you? I wasn't always so shy. I never wanted to stay in one place, much less one house. I used to want to travel around the world.

Remembering that makes it easier to sell the house. I really don't want to live there anymore, as much as I love it, and I'll be sad to see it sold. It's part of my past. But I'm so ready for new experiences. So ready to see new places. I'm ready to begin my future.

                                            Rosebud

She'd meant to write and tell him that she'd meet him. She knew that's what he wanted to read more than anything. Three times she'd written the sentence and each time deleted it. Maybe in tomorrow's e-mail, she told herself as she shut down the computer. Or the day after. But soon.

"Mom, what's going on between Aunt Jilly and Rajiv?"

Birdie leaned back against the pillows, thinking to herself she was glad that the question had finally come up. She'd been expecting it. Hannah was lying on the bed beside her, propped against the pillows. Since they'd begun sharing the room together, they'd skirted any serious discussions, almost as if they'd silently agreed not to tread on any ground that could start them off fighting. This was the first question that would require her to be "Mom."

"Are you referring to the fact that Jilly's spending the night at his house?"

"Obviously."

Birdie pursed her lips, trying to think of a good answer. "She's involved with him."

"Duh. Okay."

There was a silence that was painful for Birdie.

"You're old enough to know that a couple can be involved, emotionally and physically, without being married."

"So what you're saying is they're having sex."

She caught herself before launching into a mother-daughter sex discussion where she did all the talking and Hannah did all the listening. She'd been there before and knew it was a losing battle.

"I suppose it's a little late for the birds and the bees," she said with a wry smile.

Hannah rolled her eyes, but her face brightened when she realized her mother wasn't going to preach. "Mom, kids learn about these things in fifth grade. In school."

"Learning about sex is different than a discussion of moral values. I don't want to see you end up in the same situation that Jilly did at your age."

"Seriously, I have pretty good moral values, Mom. I'm the last person you need to worry about."

She smiled, thinking how much her daughter sounded like herself at fifteen. After Jilly's pregnancy her parents really went overboard on sex education and curfews. It reached the point where going over to a friend's house was tantamount to a prison escape. There were so many similarities between herself and her daughter that she'd begun to notice on this trip. Her stubbornness, the way she pursed her lips in thought, the lift of her chin when delivering an opinion, her love of romantic old movies, even the inflection in her voice.

"You're the first person I worry about." She said this with a smile.

Hannah smiled back, playing with the short curls along her neck. "But if I ever did, you know, get into trouble, would you send me away?"

"No." The answer was quick and sure. "I couldn't even imagine you going to a place like that. I like to think we'd work it out." She took a breath then went on, hesitatingly. "But you do know about contraception? Condoms?"

"Yeah, yeah. Who doesn't?"

"We're not just talking about moral values anymore. We're talking about life and death."

"If you only knew how good I was."

Birdie wasn't reassured by the look of dejection rather than pride at this statement. She knew how much Hannah adored her aunt Jilly—and emulated her.

"Hannah, I don't want you to get the wrong impression of your aunt Jillian. She wasn't this wild kid who slept around. She was a good girl. Beautiful and talented and bright." She paused, thinking back. "But troubled. I don't think she ever got over what happened to your aunt Merry, and afterward, it's like she didn't care anymore. She wasn't wild as much as irresponsible. She didn't think of the repercussions of anything she said or did. It gave her an edge that made her very popular. That and her beauty, of course."

"Yeah, well, I'm not exactly popular or beautiful, so…"

Birdie's heart lurched that she'd dare reveal this. "You *are* beautiful. And I love your new haircut, by the way." She refrained from mentioning a word about her dieting and exercise. As a pediatrician who'd dealt with patients with anorexia and bulimia, she knew better than to focus attention on weight. "And your Dad and I love you very much."

Hannah presented the classic "who cares about that?" expression. Then her face grew more serious. "What's going on with you and Dad?"

This was a question Birdie wasn't prepared for. She should have known it was coming, but her mind shied away. "I don't know."

Hannah frowned and crossed her arms. She clearly didn't believe her.

"I'm being honest. If I was trying to placate you, Hannah, I'd tell you everything was just fine." She took a breath then forged ahead. "I know that he's angry with me."

"For what?" Hannah was indignant. "For going on this trip?"

"Yes. And for other things that have been building over the years. It's hard to explain, even to myself, what went wrong."

"What do you mean?" she said, panic tingeing her voice. "You sound like you're getting a divorce."

"No," Birdie quickly interjected. "At least, I don't want one. I only hope your father doesn't. We love each other, I'm sure of that. Sometimes, however, a couple can grow apart, even with love. It takes work to keep the romance alive and your daddy and I didn't work hard enough. It wasn't deliberate. It just crept up on me. The hours at work, struggling to keep up the house, the appearances, trying to be a good mother. I wanted to succeed at everything and worked so hard at it that I ended up enjoying nothing. I was tired all the time. And cranky. That led to me feeling unappreciated. It's a vicious cycle." She turned to face her daughter and saw her as a young woman. "I know I've been hard on you. I've been hard on your father as well. He's told me he's had enough. So…that's how it is."

Hannah didn't say anything. Her face, gaminlike now with her short strawberry hair wisping around her face, her brown doelike eyes moist with tears and the cleft in her chin that was so much like her father's made Birdie's heart swell with love for her.

"Do you think if you had had the baby it would have made a difference?"

"Would it have made a difference to *you?*"

She nodded tentatively. "I've always wanted a sister."

"Oh, Hannah…" Birdie felt a swell of sorrow. How could she tell her daughter how crushed she was to have lost this baby? She'd tried for more than ten years to have another child, suffering each time her period began. She knew this was her last chance. There would be no more babies for her. But how could she tell all this to her daughter? And worse, how could she tell this to Dennis…again?

"Don't cry, Mom." Hannah tried to turn her choked sob into a laugh. "You know, it's weird. I used to try and make you cry and I never could. And now when I don't want you to…"

"Oh, you made me cry," Birdie confessed with a sniff. "Plenty. I just never let you see."

Hannah's eyes widened with surprise. "I got so mad at you for getting on my case so much."

"I didn't."

"Yeah, Mom. You did. It was like you wanted me to do everything like you. To be like you. And when I wasn't you'd get angry and call me lazy or stupid."

"I never called you stupid!"

"Not in so many words, but that's how I felt. Nothing I did was ever good enough. So I just stopped trying."

Birdie felt the tears stinging her eyes. "I was only trying to help you. I want so much for you."

"Let go a little, Mom! You're holding on too tight. I'm going to be gone in two years. If I don't do things for myself now, when I get to college I'll flip out because I won't be able to handle the freedom." She sneaked a look at her mother to gauge her reaction. "And I won't want to come back home."

Birdie stared at her, pursing her lips, trying to grasp all that Hannah was telling her. "I'd miss you. I sure hope you'll come home."

"It's been really different on this trip. *You've* been different. You've included me, instead of always making me feel like a kid."

Thank you, Jilly, she thought to herself. "You've been acting like a woman."

Hannah registered this, nodding. "I'd like to be friends with you. So we can talk about things, you know? It'd be nice."

Birdie felt a flush of pleasure so deep it flowed through her like a gush of springwater that began to slowly fill the empty space in her heart.

She held her hands clasped tight lest she get too mushy and hug her daughter and smack big kisses on her cheek. "Yeah," she replied. "It'd be nice."

Twenty

~~~~~⟶∞∞⟵~~~~~

Jilly sat on the small cement porch outside her room and watched the river gurgle on its journey to wherever. The water reflected the gray sky overhead that was roiling with fast-moving clouds. The birds were quiet this morning. There was a stillness in the air, a hush before a storm. She'd been sitting there since she'd woken in Rajiv's arms, then hurried back to the motel before anyone else woke up. She didn't feel like returning to sleep so she'd come out to sit, hoping the cool morning air could quiet her restlessness. There was electricity in the air.

So when the phone rang, she straightened in her chair, took a long drag from her cigarette and snuffed it out in anticipation. She turned toward the screen door with her chin up, waiting. When she heard Rose call her name, she was ready.

"Out here!"

Rose opened the screen door, pushed back her thick hair from her sleep-worn face and looked at her groggily. But her eyes were dancing with excitement. "There you are. Jilly, the phone's for you. It's the Soundex Reunion Registry!"

Jilly felt as though someone had just dumped a bucket of cold water on her. She bolted up then stood frozen on the spot.

"Go on. What are you waiting for?" Rose gave her a gentle push.

Jilly's heart rate took off again as she walked across the room to the telephone.

"Hello?"

"Hello. This is the Soundex Reunion Registry. Is this Jillian Season?" It was the voice of an elderly man, very warm and friendly.

"It is."

There was a brief pause. "I have some good news."

Jilly had felt each moment of the day pass. Since her phone call with the Soundex Reunion Registry early that morning, she'd felt she was walking in a fog. Up till now, the search for her daughter had been a collaborative effort of the Season sisters. And yet, they'd still be laboring through addresses and hunting through directories for who knew how long if Anne Marie hadn't begun a search of her own. Anne Marie was looking for her! The thought took Jilly's breath away. In the end, they'd found each other.

The Soundex Reunion Registry served as an intermediary between Jilly and Anne Marie to set up the first contact. Through the intermediary, Jilly received the current address and phone number of her daughter and an appointment to call Anne Marie at eight o'clock that same night. It all seemed so organized and matter-of-fact when inside all her emotions were in a whirlwind.

The one place she felt most secure was, oddly enough, the small, four-square slab of cement behind her room. They'd had a hard, heavy rain on and off all afternoon with a backup band of thunder and spectacular lightning. The storm had moved on and the earth smelled dank and very green. The swollen river gushed soothingly in the dark distance and the breeze was cool and moist on her face. Jilly crouched into her chair, brought her knees up and listened to the river and her own raging thoughts.

In a short while she'd be talking on the telephone with her daughter. Rather than fill her with joy and excitement, all she felt was blind terror and guilt. What was she going to say to her? I'm sorry? For she was. She was sorry about *everything*. Her whole damned life. In her mind she composed a litany of apologies. I'm sorry that I was a reckless teenager. I'm sorry I wasn't stronger under pressure and kept you. I'm sorry I never tried to find you before.

Maybe if she *had* kept her baby her life would have turned out differently. If she had, she would have forced the family to acknowledge Anne Marie's birth. There wouldn't have been decades of deceit and she wouldn't have become the family outcast. If she had, she might not have made such a mess of her life.

But how could she have kept her? Jilly shivered, remembering how she'd sobbed when she found out she was pregnant, convinced she would end up hurting this baby like she'd hurt Merry. And she couldn't bear that. So her life became what it was, a series of selfish, irresponsible acts. She'd never had another child.

She lowered her legs and straightened in her chair, breathing deep. Who did she think she was fooling? Anne Marie's life was better this way. She could be disrupting her life, making her unhappy. Was she only being selfish once again, as the sister at Holy Hill had told her?

She didn't hear anyone step out onto the patio so she startled when she felt a hand rest on her shoulder.

"Rajiv! My God, you scared me. My heart's pounding."

"You were a million miles away. And you looked so sad. Isn't this supposed to be a happy moment for you?"

"I'm miserable," she moaned, resting her head against his hand. "Am I doing the right thing making this call? Maybe I shouldn't meet her. What if she doesn't want to meet me?"

"Where is all this coming from? Of course she'll want to meet you," he replied, pulling out a chair and sitting knee-to-knee with her. "Why else would she have begun the search for her birth mother?"

"There are so many reasons she might have searched. Perhaps she was just curious about her genetics. She's of child-bearing age, it would be a natural concern. Or her medical history. She'd want to know who her parents were, her grandparents. What diseases they had, what they died of. Or maybe she was just curious if she had any brothers or sisters. Oh, Rajiv, I don't know why she tried to find me. But it doesn't mean she wants to actually meet me face-to-face, much less include me in her life."

"You're her family. And family provides one with a great sense of identity."

She heard the sorrow in his voice whenever he mentioned the word *family,* but didn't want to pry. Nor, she suspected, would he tell her. His face was shuttered.

"I'm not family. She has her own family now."

"True, but she must have hundreds of questions about herself, Jillian. She'll want to know if she looks like you." He turned his head and his smile warmed her. "She'll be lucky if she does. But she'll be luckier if she has your character and strength. Call her."

He always knew exactly what to say to make her crumbled self-image whole again.

"I'll call," she said, resigned, resting her head against his shoulder.

"We shouldn't crowd her," Rose said to the others. They were standing outside Jilly's room. Inside she was making the contact call.

"I'm afraid she'll bolt," said Birdie. "She had the look of a racehorse at the gate. You know, rolling eyes and skittish."

"Let her take it at her own pace," Rose argued back. "If she decides not to call tonight, all we can do is support her. We promised we'd back off. But don't worry, I don't think she'll bolt. She might throw up," she said, releasing a smile, "but she'll make the call."

"I'm so nervous," Hannah cried, stomping her feet in the cool air.

"We all are, honey."

"I guess this means our search is over." Hannah lifted her head and looked into her mother's eyes.

Birdie was surprised to see that they almost looked eye to eye. When did she grow so tall? "Guess so."

"I don't think I want it to be over." Hannah laughed nervously. "I mean, sure I want Jilly to find her daughter. But I'm having a good time."

Birdie hugged her and whispered, "Me too."

Hannah pulled back and looked at her sheepishly. "I kinda miss Dad, though. Don't you?"

"You don't have to be shy about saying that. This isn't a him-against-me scenario. I miss him, too. Very much."

"Then why don't you call him?"

Birdie balked. "I...I did call him. Lots of times. But he hasn't called me back."

"Then call him again. Just because he's being a jerk doesn't mean you should. You said you were going to do everything you could!"

"There comes a point..."

"Come on, Mom. Aunt Jilly is in there calling her kid that she hasn't seen in twenty-six years. You can call Dad after two weeks."

"She's got a point," Rose added.

"Call now," Hannah said, taking the advantage.

"Oh, Hannah..."

"Why wait? Go on, Mom."

"I'll take Hannah out for some ice cream and give you some space. Okay?" asked Rose.

Birdie gave Rose a long, level stare, ready to bean her. But in the back of her mind she was thinking, what the heck? Hannah was right. What was she waiting for? It was only false pride that was keeping her from calling Dennis again, pride that he wasn't pursuing her the way she wanted him to. She looked over at the motel room door and imagined Jilly in there sweating bullets, just trying to lift the telephone receiver. She and Rose were the ones who pushed her into this search. How could she expect less from herself?

She reluctantly gave up a grin of resignation and nodded, which sent Hannah back into her arms with a grateful hug.

"Oh, go on, get your ice cream," she said, gently pushing them on their way. "And take your time. Just don't forget to bring me back a turtle sundae. I don't care how many calories are in it!"

Shortly before eight o'clock, Jilly sat alone before the telephone in her room, dredging up all the words of support that she'd received throughout the day. She used them as the stone and mortar of the wall of protection she'd constructed around herself as she readied for the call.

On the table she had carefully set out a glass of chilled white wine, a pack of cigarettes and matches. She hadn't had a sip of wine yet. The last thing she wanted to do was slur her first words to her daughter. The wine was there in case she needed to drown her sorrows afterward. On the bed, neatly lined up in a row, was the adoption file, documentation from Mr. Collins, a pen and a Wisconsin map for directions. In her lap was her journal. Everything was ready.

She picked up the phone, then set it down again. Sighing, she got up and paced the narrow strip in the room, feeling as though her clothes weighed a hundred pounds. After a few passes she glanced at the clock, then stopped before the phone, frustration bubbling in her veins. Right or wrong, she had to stop obsessing about it. It was eight o'clock—too late to back out now. Somewhere in the Green Bay area Anne Marie was sitting by the phone. She couldn't just leave her stranded. Without allowing herself another thought, she sat down and picked up the phone, dialing the number that the Soundex Reunion Registry had given her that morning. "God help me," she prayed.

The phone rang twice.

"Hello?" A woman answered the phone. Her voice was soft.

Jilly's mind went blank. She opened her mouth but nothing came out.

"Hello?" the voice asked again.

"Hello," she forced out. "Is this Anne Marie?" Jilly was amazed to hear her own, well-trained voice squeak and tremble.

"Yes. Is this—" There was an awkward pause as Anne Marie grasped for a word. "Mrs. Season?"

Mrs. Season? The name wounded her. She knew she didn't deserve to be called *Mother*, not yet, maybe never. But she'd felt for a moment that *mother* was the word about to slip from Anne Marie's tongue.

"Yes, it is. Well, no. Actually, it's Miss Season. Jillian Season." Why wouldn't her tongue move?

"Oh."

"Please, just call me Jilly."

There was a pause that seemed to Jilly to stretch as wide as the Grand Canyon and she had no idea how to cross it. Jilly put her head in her palm and sighed.

"I'm glad you called." Anne Marie's voice was tentative.

Jilly's mind went blank again. In a panic she opened her journal, looked at her notes and asked one of the questions she'd been advised to ask.

"Is this a good time to talk?"

"Yes. Of course. I've been waiting all day."

She'd been waiting? Jilly released her breath. That had to mean that she did want to talk to her after all. Jilly felt a flood of relief and sat up; she didn't realize she'd been hunched over the phone as though expecting a kick in the stomach.

"Good. Good," she replied. "I'm glad."

"Is it a good time for you? To talk?"

"Oh, yes, sure. It's fine." She was grasping for things to say, overwhelmed by the magnitude of this moment. This was her daughter's voice. Her child! She'd only once before heard her lusty cry at birth.

"Are you…" They both started talking at the same time, then both stopped abruptly.

"Go ahead," Jilly said, twisting the phone cord.

"No, you go." Anne Marie sounded as though she were in equal agony.

"Well," Jilly began again, flummoxed because she couldn't remember what she was going to ask. "I was just wondering, um, what you thought when you learned there was a match."

"Oh, God! Well!" She laughed nervously again. "I thought, wow. I guess I couldn't believe this was really happening."

Jilly smiled, taking her first easy breath. "Me, too. I was told when I started looking for you that it might go quickly, but I didn't know how quickly."

"I have a thousand questions but I can't think of one of them."

"Now I know why they advised me to write them down. All I can think right now is how wonderful it is just to hear your voice." She paused, giving Anne Marie a chance to speak. When she didn't, she tried filling in the long silence. "I could begin by telling you that you have your grandmother's name. Ann."

"Really?" She sounded very surprised. "Did you give me that name?"

"No. I..." She didn't want to tell Anne Marie that she wasn't given a name at birth, rather like Pirate Pete had not been named for lack of attachment. "Your adoptive mother chose your name."

"You mean my mother."

Jilly cringed, squeezing her eyes tight. Darn, she hadn't meant to get into that. "Yes!" she replied quickly. "I was just trying to be clear about who I was talking about."

"I think I should be clear about this, too. Right away," Anne Marie said with more firmness in her voice than Jilly had heard yet. "I have a mother. I don't need another. That's not what this is about."

"Of course not." Jilly reached frantically for her pack of cigarettes on the bed. Her hands were shaking so violently that she had to shake out a couple of cigarettes to grab hold of one. While she lit up, she listened as Anne Marie's words riddled her like bullets.

"When I started looking for my birth mother, it wasn't to replace my mother. She's been wonderful. Is wonderful. I love her very much. I just wanted to know more about myself. And my roots, you know? My biological family." She paused. "And I wondered about you. I didn't know anything about you." Her tone revealed a hint of hurt and anger that Jilly hadn't tried to contact her sooner.

There was a roaring in Jilly's ears and all she could reply was a stuttered, "No, no, how could you know anything about me? Everything was so locked up, like state secrets."

Jilly berated herself for being a fool. Everything Anne Marie wanted to know could have been mailed to her in an envelope and they both could have been spared this painful conversation.

Anne Marie had the grace to laugh, even if it was a bit forced. "It *was* like state secrets, wasn't it? It took me two

years just to find out that I got my red hair from you.'' She
laughed again, and this time it sounded a bit more real. ''That
was nice to know.''

''I'm sorry, '' Jilly said haltingly into the telephone. The
black receiver felt as heavy as lead. ''I didn't mean to im-
ply... That is, please believe I'm not trying to interfere in
your life. I'd never try to wedge myself between you and
your...'' God, she almost said *adoptive mother* again. What
the hell did she call her? ''Your mother,'' she forced out.
She dragged hard on her cigarette all the while praying,
Please, God, don't let me cry. ''It's just that I'm having such
a hard time trying to figure out what to call people. Adoptive
mother, birth mother, real mother...it's all rather confusing.''

''Tell me about it.''

At last! A sliver of commiseration. Jilly put down her cigarette.

''Anne is my grandmother's name on my father's side,''
Anne Marie began again. Her voice was conciliatory. ''My
mother's mother's name is Marie.''

''You have an aunt Meredith, but we called her Merry.''
Oh, no, the tears were beginning to well up again. She
couldn't even *begin* to explain Merry's connection to this
odyssey.

''Do I have other aunts or uncles?''

''Two aunts. Beatrice and Rose. Meredith passed away
recently.''

''Oh, I'm sorry.''

''We all are. You would have liked her.''

''Any uncles?''

''No. Just the four girls. You also have a cousin. Hannah.
She's fifteen and another redhead. When you're ready, they'd
all love to meet you.''

''I don't have any brothers or sisters, but I have lots of
cousins. Seven. And a husband. I'm married.''

''Wonderful. Though I shouldn't be surprised. You're

twenty-six, after all." Jilly laughed lightly. "Still, it's hard to believe."

"Did you wonder why I started this search for you?"

Jilly picked up her cigarette and leaned back in her chair, wondering where this was headed. "No," she said hesitatingly. Was Anne Marie ill? She thought of Ann Josephine Neville and felt a wave of prickles travel along her spine. "Then again, I haven't had time to wonder. I only just found out about the match this morning, like you. All day long I couldn't get past the idea that I'd be hearing your voice."

"I started the search three years ago. I wanted to know my medical history. Because I was pregnant."

Jilly clutched the phone tighter as the news hit her. She reeled with it, slumping back in her chair, her cigarette dangling from limp fingers. This couldn't be true. Suddenly she was a mother *and* a grandmother?

"Hello?"

"I'm here. I'm just…overwhelmed," she replied haltingly, trying to find her voice as tears of emotion flooded her eyes. She reached up to wipe her face and clumsily dropped her cigarette. "Oh, no, wait," she blurted into the phone, leaping up to sweep the cigarette from her lap. She bent over to pick it up, dropping the receiver from her trembling hands. She grabbed for it, calling into the receiver, "I'm still here! I just dropped a cigarette. Hello?" She jabbed the cigarette into the ashtray while clutching the phone with her other hand.

"I'm here. I…I didn't mean to shock you," Anne Marie said with a tone of self-defense. "I thought you'd be pleased."

"Oh, I am, I am!" Jilly blurted out, placing her palm on her forehead. She took a deep breath. "It's just that, well, it is a bit of a shock. I still think of *you* as a baby. I'm trying to imagine my baby having a baby now." She laughed brokenly and was relieved beyond words to hear Anne Marie join in.

"Her name is Lauren and she's two and a half now. She's gorgeous and bright and the best little girl. We feel blessed."

"I'm sure she's wonderful," Jilly replied, sitting back in her chair and regaining her composure.

"Are you sitting down?" Anne Marie asked with a lilt in her voice.

Jilly grabbed for her wineglass. "I am now."

"Another is on the way. The baby's due next month."

"Two! Why, I'm delighted!" Two grandchildren? How could the years have flown by so quickly? She was pained by the flashing realization that she'd never seen her own little girl's first steps, or walked her to the classroom on her first day of school, or witnessed her walk down the aisle on her wedding day. All this and so much more was lost to her.

And yet, she thought, maybe having grandchildren was like getting a second chance.

"Your parents must be so delighted," she said, wonder still in her voice. "Speaking of which, do your parents know about our contact?"

"Oh, yes. At least, my mother does. My father died years ago, but he would've been happy for me. Mom's very supportive and completely understands why I wanted to meet you."

"Thank her for me," Jilly said honestly.

"I will. Thanks. Well, it's getting late and I have to go. Lauren won't fall asleep tonight. I think she senses something is up. Would you like me to send pictures of her? And me, of course."

Jilly's breath caught in her throat. Was this it? Information exchanged via mail? A few pictures? Wouldn't there be a meeting?

"You know we're in Hodges, don't you?" she asked with hesitation. "That's quite close to Green Bay. Not much more than an hour."

There was a short but strained pause. "Yes, I know. They

told me. Actually, it's less than an hour." Her nervous laugh again. "Talk about another act of fate."

Jilly thought that she could dance around this question for a while or just jump right in. "Why don't we go along with fate? Would you like to arrange a meeting? I know I would love to meet you. And my grandchild, of course."

"Uh, yes. Sure."

Her hesitancy pained Jilly. She held her breath.

Anne Marie exhaled hers. "Look, I have to admit this is all a little sudden. When I got the call this morning, I didn't know what to think. I wanted—prayed—that we'd find each other. But now I'm so pregnant and…" Her voice trailed off.

Jilly twisted the phone cord tight around her fingers. "I understand. We could wait." She squeezed her eyes tight.

"No. Let's meet."

Jilly leaned back, sighing in relief. "I have to admit it would have been hard for me to wait. Waiting is not my strong suit. We're just in a motel here, so why don't we come down to De Pere? We can meet at a neutral place if you like. Perhaps I could take you to lunch?"

"I'd like that." But her voice was hesitant again.

"You can pick anyplace you like. Someplace you love."

"Well, there is a nice French restaurant in Green Bay. The Left Bank."

"Perfect. I can leave here tomorrow morning. Shall we meet at The Left Bank at, say, one o'clock? Or am I rushing things too much? Can you go out to lunch so far in your pregnancy?"

"Oh, sure. I'm fine. But I waddle and I'll eat like a horse. I think maybe it's better that we meet right away. That way I won't chew my nails worrying. And pretty soon I'll just be thinking about the baby and all. I'll still be nervous, but at least not for as long."

She laughed again, and Jilly realized with a burst of happiness that she now could recognize her daughter's laugh.

"You won't be able to miss me," Anne Marie said with ease. "I'll be the elephant in the red dress."

Jilly liked her sense of humor, so much like her own. She even sounded like a Season, with the same breathy voice. "I can't tell you how much this means to me. I've waited a very long time just for this much." Jilly stopped herself. She hadn't meant to get emotional. It just slipped out.

"Me, too," Anne Marie responded with appropriate seriousness.

"Well then. Until tomorrow."

"Goodbye."

Jilly was reluctant to put down the phone, afraid to lose the slender line of connection between herself and her daughter. She held the receiver to her breast and just sat quiet and still for a long time.

Twenty-One

~∽∾⊙∾∽~

Birdie looked around the little motel room that was as drab today as when they'd arrived. She hadn't purchased odds and ends at the antique shops or added color, as Rose had. Hannah didn't care what the room looked like and this was not the trip for Birdie to clean and decorate. She'd done plenty of that in her home and look where it had gotten her. On this trip she was cleaning the inside of herself. Now that the trip was coming to an end, she felt she'd done a pretty good job rearranging the mental furniture. Just being able to admit that her marriage was failing was proof enough.

She sat by the telephone but didn't reach for it. She'd decided to take Jilly's advice and work to get Dennis back. She *wanted* him back. She was accustomed to his body next to hers in their bed, to him making the coffee in the morning while she buttered the toast. She liked that they shared the chores around the house. He was good with his hands and handled the painting, caulking and repairs. She was better at electrical problems, fixing appliances and changing light-bulbs. She paid the bills. He played the stock market. They were so comfortable together.

She wanted to make love again, too. Maybe her hormones were back in line, or maybe she just realized how much she loved him. But did he still love her? she wondered.

Dennis had called her a nag. It was a horrible word that rhymed with hag and drew the same images. When he'd left Evanston, she'd thought he was entirely to blame for their argument. She'd called him a withdrawer, which was really just another expression for coward. That argument was one in a long, continuous game that they'd been playing for years, she realized now. The Blaming Game. She couldn't remember who started it and it didn't really matter. They both played it. They both were getting good at it. All that she wanted now was for the cruel game to end so that they could try to change and get back to the place they were before.

She'd given this a lot of thought. She realized at last that she was powerless to change Dennis. And when she thought about it honestly, she didn't want to try anymore. But she could begin to change herself.

She wouldn't nag. She wouldn't tell him what to do. And she'd swallow her pride and not be angry with him for not returning her calls. If Jilly could find the courage to call Anne Marie, then she could damn well call her husband.

She picked up the phone and called her home number. It rang and rang, without the answering machine picking up. Where could he be? There was school tomorrow. The longer it rang, the more her disappointment grew. But she was determined, and she let it ring on. She was slipping her shoe off from her foot when she heard his voice.

"Hello?"

She froze, trying to make certain it wasn't the answering machine. "Dennis?"

"Yes."

"It's me. Birdie."

There was a pause. "I know."

So his anger was still white-hot. "I'm surprised you still recognize my voice. But then again, I've left enough messages for you to remember it." She spoke in an airy manner, but she doubted he was fooled.

"I got the messages."

She took a deep breath, telling herself to hear the hurt in his anger, not the meanness.

"Where are you? Hannah was due back in school last Monday." His voice was level.

"I know. That's why I'm calling. We're still in Hodges and were planning on coming back today."

"Were?"

"Our plans changed. We can't leave just yet. Dennis, Jilly just made contact with Spring! Or, rather, Anne Marie. That's her daughter's name."

There was a long silence.

"Dennis?"

"I'm here. So," he said, exhaling. "She found her."

He didn't sound very happy about it. Even if he didn't like Jilly, he could be happy for her. For all of them. She tried to tap down the spark of anger.

"Just today. In fact, she's on the phone with her now."

"I'm surprised she found her. I didn't think she would."

"We were lucky. Everything just clicked." She felt a sticky tension between them that distance only thickened. She tried again.

"And Dennis, you'd be so proud of Hannah. It's like she's grown up overnight. She's been so mature and so giving—she's giving one hundred and ten percent."

"That ought to make you happy."

Birdie heard his sarcasm and had to take a breath. "It has," she replied evenly. "But only because it's making her happy. She feels good about herself for a change. We're *both* feeling good about ourselves, actually. We're not fighting all the time anymore. Sometimes we still do, but it's different. Not so nasty. She's told me how she feels and believe it or not, I've told her how I feel. Remember how I used to say I couldn't be her mother and her friend? Well, I was wrong. It's very sweet to listen to her tell me her thoughts and not feel like I'm her judge and jury. We're really talking."

"Must be nice."

Again the sarcasm. She squeezed her eyes tight, wondering if it was too late after all. "Maybe we can try talking when I come home," she said tentatively.

There was a pause. "When would that be?"

"Soon. Hannah and I want to see this thing to the end." She spoke rapidly, twisting the phone cord. "Anne Marie lives only an hour from here, in the Green Bay area. So we'd like to spend another night, maybe two. Just to meet her. I mean, after all this we'd like to see her. Then we'll come home."

"No. You know as well as I that Hannah's grades haven't been good. It's been a struggle with her all year just to keep on track. This will screw things up good. She's had her vacation. I want her home. Now."

His voice was harsh and it stung that he specifically said he wanted Hannah home. He didn't mention whether he gave a damn if Birdie came with her. "She'll learn a lot more about life in the next few days than she will in school. This is important to her. She can miss a couple more days. Come on, Dennis, we don't need to be so inflexible all the time. We need to loosen up." She couldn't believe these words were coming out of her mouth, or that she meant them. Nor, she imagined, could Dennis.

"I'm tired of always being the flexible one," he replied with anger. "I've asked you to come home and you won't. One of us has to budge. And it ain't going to be me."

Ah, so this was the stand he'd decided to take. But it was true. He was usually the one who changed his plans. Birdie's schedule always took precedence since she was the main breadwinner in the family. One of the things she'd always loved most about him was his reasonable nature. Had she driven him to fight back? A wave of guilt made her want to tell him yes, she would come home immediately. But a stronger voice told her that she couldn't, not yet.

"Dennis, you have no idea what's been going on here. What I've been going through."

"You have no idea what I've been going through, either."

Birdie thought of Jilly's advice to remember that he was a man and not a child, but it was hard when they were playing tit for tat.

"Okay, you're right, I don't know what you've been going through," she said, making a last effort. "I tried to talk to you but you didn't return my calls. So tell me, what have you been up to?"

"I've been on a motorcycle trip."

She almost laughed. "What?"

"A bike trip. I told you I might. I've always wanted to go on one and I thought what the hell?"

Birdie conjured the image of Dennis back in leather and on a motorbike. It took her far back to when she'd first set eyes on him and fallen head over heels.

"I'd love to have seen that," she said, hearing her smile in her voice. "I always liked seeing you on a bike. It's been a long time. Must've been fun," she added lamely.

There was a pause and she imagined he was regrouping, having expected a pithy comment.

"Nah," he replied. "It was cold as hell." His anger seemed to have deflated but he was still testy. "I headed south a bit along the Mississippi, then just came back home. It's not really biking weather yet." He skipped a beat. "But I bought the bike."

She could hear the challenge in his voice. "What's this?" she asked teasingly. "A male menopause thing?"

"I dunno. Maybe."

"Okay. That's fair. Maybe we're both going through a few changes."

"We could use a few."

There wasn't any sarcasm in that. If anything, she thought she caught a hint of hope. "You're right. We could." She took a chance. "When I come home, will you give me a ride?" Those were the words she'd used as a kid that summer when she hung around him as he waited for Jilly. She knew by the length of the pause that he'd remembered.

"Come home now, Birdie," he said. His voice was strained. Even pleading.

"I'm almost done. I have to finish this with Jilly."

"Let Jilly finish her own problems. You can't always be there to save everyone."

"I know! Really I do. That's what's happening here that you don't understand. I'm not saving Jilly. She's saving me. And Hannah. And Rose. We're all saving one another. We're close again, like we used to be, and it's changing us. I wish I could explain it better, but I'm not sure I understand it myself. I'm beginning to feel like my old self. Energized. Hopeful." She reached up to touch her red hair along her neck. "I meant what I said about wanting to try and talk again. You were right about that. We didn't talk. And I have so many things I need to talk to you about."

She waited, but he didn't respond. The silence stretched and she clutched the phone tightly in her hand. "Please say you'll be there for us when we get home. Hannah needs you. But I need you more. Be there—for *me*."

Closing her eyes tight, she silently mouthed the word, *please*....

She heard his sigh rumble over the wire, then his voice came, soft but firm in decision. "I'll be here."

Dear DannyBoy,

We've made enormous progress in our search today. I hope you're sitting down. Jilly found her daughter! Her name is Anne Marie and she lives just outside Green Bay. They found each other from that reunion registry I told you about. I guess that makes another couple united by the power of the Internet! So we'll be heading down to Green Bay tomorrow and we'll probably stay there for a few days.

Okay, I'm taking a deep breath. Still sitting down? I'd like to meet you. I don't want to wait any longer.

We've waited long enough already. I'm sorry I delayed to the last minute. I've always wanted to meet you but I was afraid that if we met, we might not like each other and I didn't want to risk what we had. But I realized, watching Jilly set up an appointment to meet her daughter for the first time, that I could only find happiness if I took risks. So if you're still coming to Green Bay and you're still willing to meet, then so am I. If you can't make it while I'm in town, Evanston isn't at the other end of the world and we can try again. All we can do is try.

We'll be staying at the Embassy Suites, if you know where that is.

I've got to start packing. It's hard to believe we're leaving our little oasis. We've made some good friends here. Larry and Maude, and especially Rajiv, have been great. I'm sure I'll come up to see them again. I also can't believe how much stuff we've accumulated in just two weeks. I think I'll have to donate the stuff to Rajiv, except that I'm rather sentimental now about the Chinese lamps I found in a small antique store in town. They'll always remind me of the great Season Odyssey, as Jilly calls it. It's funny, but in a way, I feel like I've finally dug my way to China after all. It's a long childhood story that I'll tell you about sometime.

Let me know if you can meet in Green Bay!

Love,
Rosebud

Dear Rosebud,

Yes, I'll meet you in Green Bay!

I have to make a delivery on Saturday, but if you can just stay there till Monday, I don't care what I have to do to get there, but I'll be there. Screeching tires, but I'll be there.

Love,
DannyBoy

* * *

Late that night Jilly lay in the crook of Rajiv's shoulder. His long fingers stroked her spine, luxuriously moving up and down in a soothing pattern while their bodies cooled. She'd told him that she was leaving in the morning and he'd reacted as she expected he would, without so many words as with a grasping, frenzied passion in his lovemaking that spoke eloquently of his true feelings for her.

Rajiv still kept his soul barred from her, locked behind his unfailing civility and intelligence. As her fingers flexed against his chest, she had to hold herself back from forming fists and pounding him with them, crying tears and begging him to tell her that he loved her.

"You're so quiet," she said to him, moving her head on his chest to look at his face. "Are you meditating?"

She heard his chuckle in his chest. "Every time an Indian thinks silently does not mean he's meditating."

She pinched him lightly.

"Jilly, what am I going to do with you?"

Hold me, she thought to herself. Keep me here with you.

"I'm leaving tomorrow and I realize I know very little about you. That makes me sad."

"What do you want to know?"

"Everything."

He chuckled softly. "You'll not be able to leave tomorrow if you want to know everything."

"Ask me to stay, then." She held her breath as his chest moved up and down in a steady rhythm.

"I can't do that," he replied at length.

"Why not? Don't you care enough to ask me to stay?"

"Yes."

She felt a moment's exhilaration. "Then ask me."

"No. I can't."

Her heart twisted and she pulled herself up to her elbows to look down into his face. His gaze was open but she saw the tiger lurking within.

"You can't or you won't?"

"Both."

"If you don't care enough to ask me to stay, then why should I? What are you offering me?"

"I'm offering you nothing, Jillian. This is your decision to make."

"No, it's not! It's not just my decision. It's yours, too. Just tell me what you want me to do."

"Jillian, my love. I won't tell you what to do."

"You're hiding again in your silence," she fired off. "You're wallowing in the mire."

"Do you think so? I feel like I'm standing on a precipice, very, very high up."

She lay down on her back again and stared up at the ceiling. Tears smarted in her eyes and she felt a sudden chill emanating from her heart. "I thought we had something very special between us. But you can't feel anything for me at all if you'll just let me go."

After a moment he asked quietly, "Would you stay if I asked you to?"

She stumbled. "I'd have to go to Green Bay to meet my daughter, of course. But afterward…"

He rose up over her to put his fingertip over her lips and silence her. "Don't make any promises you can't keep. You don't have to. Not to me. Not to anyone. I'm not asking for anything more than you've given me already. And believe me, Jillian, I care about you a great deal to be able to say that to you. You know you have to go. Let's be honest with each other. We've always been so."

He lay on his back and pulled her up so that her head rested once again in the crook of his shoulder. No man had ever been so direct and honest with her before. There was always flattery and false promises with the others; she'd grown accustomed to hearing the indulgent compliments. The white lies simply covered up the painful truth, a facade Rajiv would not indulge in, nor allow her to. She felt the tears pool in her eyes and flow hot down her cheeks to his shoulder. "This hurts so much."

"I believe we have to suffer in life to progress to the next level." He spoke in his beautiful voice against the soft hairs of her head. "But life is not all suffering. In order to attain the highest level, the soul must strive for bliss. For years I was a fool. I was wallowing only in despair."

He moved onto his side, resting his head on his outstretched arm to look into her eyes. "Then you came to this place, Jillian Season, and saved me from myself. You were relentless. You wouldn't allow me to shut you out. You showed me the courage to face the past and to continue undaunted." He stroked a stray lock of hair behind her ear, then smiled his old-soul smile. "And you certainly showed me bliss."

He moved his beautiful fingers to cup her face. "You *are* courageous. You'll make the right choice, if you simply trust yourself." They stared at each other for a long time, their eyes pained, each probing, seeking, asking. Then he moved his hand to the back of her neck, pulled close and kissed her. It was not the desperate kiss it had been earlier. It was slow and tender, searching her mouth for answers in the same manner his eyes had done seconds earlier.

He was seeking his bliss, she thought to herself, feeling her blood stir in response to him again. He was searching for bliss within her body, even within her soul. As her long limbs wrapped around him and their kisses deepened, Jilly wondered why bliss felt to her like suffering.

Twenty-Two

❧❦❧

It was time to hit the road.

The decision, once made, sent them packing, making reservations, checking the route and saying their farewells. Their goal was in sight.

Birdie and Rose had agreed to stay close to Jilly. The fire usually found in her bright green eyes was banked. She'd discreetly returned to her room at the crack of dawn and silently tossed her clothes and belongings into her bag. The air around her crackled with turmoil but she wasn't talking and they weren't asking.

Outside it was a surprisingly sunny day. Spring decided it was time to stop dallying and arrived in full force. Birds sang, tulips bloomed and a soft spring green haze of new foliage exploded almost overnight on the trees. They packed the Land Rover quickly. When they had emptied their rooms and finished picking up their trash, they stood at the doors and looked into the small spaces they'd called home for the past weeks.

"I'll never forget this place, but it looks like we've never been here," Hannah said regretfully.

"Oh, I don't know," Rose said with a lilt in her voice. "I think that rag rug does wonders for the god Shiva."

"Let's go," Jilly said, interrupting their burst of laughter. Her mouth set in a tight line as she walked to the car and tossed her purse into the front seat.

"Do you want to leave the keys with Rajiv?" Rose asked Birdie.

"Don't bother. Here he comes," Hannah said, pointing to the office.

They turned toward him as he walked across the cement lot. Pirate Pete trotted beside him, his pink tongue hanging from his mouth in a cheery manner. Rose looked at Jilly, worried at the stark pain and want she saw in her expression. Rajiv smiled his polite smile when he approached them, but his eyes darted back to Jilly.

"I wish you good luck," he said, sounding more like a hotel manager than any of them wanted. "And I hope you'll let me know how this saga ends. A note, perhaps?"

Jilly sharply turned her head away. He saw this and his face went still.

Rose caught a glimpse of the ferocity in his eyes that Jilly had talked about but that she'd never seen for herself.

"Rajiv, we'll miss you," she said, walking up to him and wrapping her arms around his neck. She hugged him warmly and was pleased to feel him hug her back.

"We all will," said Birdie, standing in line to deliver a hug of her own. Hannah followed.

He smiled at them gratefully, then turned his head to seek out Jilly.

On that cue the three of them went immediately into the car to give the two a chance to say a private goodbye.

"Come here," he said, holding out his arms.

She walked right into them and slipped her arms around him, burying her face in his neck.

"I'll miss you," he said in a strained whisper in Jilly's ear.

She looked up at him and saw that his face was filled with

sadness. She wanted him to tell her to return home—to him. How could he let her go like this? His silence, the very thing that had first attracted her to him, was painful now. She thought of waking up tomorrow and not finding him beside her and felt her eyes prick with tears.

"Damn you, you're ruining my makeup."

He reached out to cup her chin and bring her gaze back to his. He looked into her eyes, but she couldn't fathom what it was he was trying to tell her, if anything at all. It was maddening and heartbreaking at the same time.

"Look after yourself, Jillian. I really will miss you. I love you."

Her heart broke. He couldn't mean that and let her go, she thought with dismay. She moved close again to hold him tight. He held her tighter, squeezing the breath from her. A barking at her side separated them and she groaned as Pirate Pete jumped up on her leg, putting dirt streaks on her slacks. She let her hands slide from Rajiv's shoulders, feeling each millimeter of the separation, but kept her hands entwined with his. She looked down at the Pirate Pete, who was whining and jumping up at them for attention.

"Well, little guy, who's going to feed you now?"

He barked and his almond eyes sparkled with delight that he'd snared her attention at last. She reached into her pocket and found a bit of cookie. "Ready?" She tossed it in the air. Pete caught the cookie on the fly and swallowed it greedily.

"I'm afraid you've spoiled us both," Rajiv said. "We'll neither of us be the same."

She felt done in. "Goodbye, Rajiv." She kissed him lightly on the lips, pausing to breathe in his scent, then turned and quickly walked toward the car.

He stepped back, whistling sharply for the dog to follow him away from the wheels. Pirate Pete jumped and barked excitedly, ignoring Rajiv's orders and chasing the car out of the lot.

"Look back. Wave or something," Birdie murmured to Jilly in the front seat. "He's just standing there. It's too sad."

"I'm not looking back," Jilly said, staring at the road ahead with a fixed glare. "I can't. Go on, hurry. I'm only looking forward to my future."

The Embassy Suites was a tall, sweeping redbrick building in the Prairie style. Its professional landscaping and wide covered entrance welcomed guests with an impressive panache. The search had completed quickly and they'd decided to splurge for the weekend. They parked the car in the lot and carried their few bags up a winding hill back to the lobby, giggling as they tried to compare this hotel with the River's End. Beneath the jokes, however, they all felt a twinge of nostalgia for the charm they'd found in the small, friendly town, the peace in the gurgling river and the majesty of the forest that had provided them shelter during the past two weeks.

The inside of the hotel was designed to be an immense garden, lush with full-size trees and tropical plants in every conceivable corner. Glass elevators rode tracks on the outside of balconies.

"Now, this is more like it," Hannah said as she walked across the dark green patterned carpet toward the front desk.

Jilly followed, clutching her suitcase and turning her head from left to right to gaze at the decor. Then she saw it. While Hannah marched on, oblivious, Jilly came to a dead stop in the middle of the lobby. Birdie and Rose came up beside her and stopped, too. She could feel the heat of their presence as surely as if they were touching. They didn't say a word but stared straight ahead with pale faces.

There, nestled in a conservatory at the rear of the lobby, surrounded by glass walls like a crown jewel, was a large domed swimming pool. Through the thick green foliage Jilly could spy the azure water with light reflecting in the gentle waves, winking almost mockingly. The sisters stood shoulder to shoulder in silence and stared at the pool with blank expressions on their faces. The tension was palpable.

"There's a pool," Jilly said with dread, stating the obvious. Her mouth felt dry and she was fighting the urge to spin around on her heel and search for another hotel. She licked her lips and said in as casual a voice as she could muster, "I don't usually stay in hotels with pools."

"I don't think it's worth the money to pay for a pool," Rose said, her hands clenching her suitcase. Her voice was strained. "I don't swim anymore. I don't even know if I remember how."

"It's like riding a bike. You never forget," Birdie replied stiffly. Although she'd swum competitively for years to impress her father, she'd never gone near a pool for leisure. Then, clearing her throat, she added, "But we're on a budget. We can change hotels if you want. This one is pricey and the humidity and all..."

"Yes, the humidity is awful."

"Terrible."

"Come on!" Hannah called happily as she came back to them. Her dark eyes were dancing with excitement. "This place is so cool. Let's hurry and check in. I can't wait to use the hot tub. And there's a health club! This is so great."

Jilly turned to look at her sisters. When their eyes met they all saw in one another the real reason none of them wanted to stay at the hotel, though no one wanted to admit it.

Birdie flexed her shoulders. "It's only for one night. I suppose we can check in." She looked at her sisters for confirmation.

Rose's chewed her lip, hesitant.

Jilly glanced at her watch. It was eleven-forty-five. She had to meet her daughter for the first time at one. There wasn't time to drive around looking for another hotel.

"Okay, let's check in, then. These suitcases are getting heavy."

They checked into the hotel without fanfare and rode up in one of the exotic elevators to the fifth floor. Jilly's room was charming and spacious, in a hotel kind of way. She looked at the matched floral fabric of the curtains and bedspreads, the mint-green carpeting and peach towels, and longed for the cramped room at the River's End. But when she glanced at the little alarm clock on the bedside table and saw that it was twelve o'clock, all thoughts of hotels and Rajiv and anything else dispersed in a flash of panic. All she could think of now was her meeting with Anne Marie.

She stood in the shower for a long time while the soap and hot water sluiced down her hair, face and body. Closing her eyes she remembered that morning twenty-six years earlier at Marian House when she'd showered and laboriously shaved her legs on the morning of her delivery. She placed her hands on her flat belly, remembering how it had felt, swollen with her baby, her breasts full and aching, her skin stretched as taut as a balloon. That morning she'd wept because she'd known she was saying goodbye to her child. This morning she wept because she knew she was saying hello.

She stepped out into a cloud of steam and dressed with the care and attention to detail that she would have for an important television interview. Simplicity was the order of the day. She chose her best creamy silk blouse, straight black wool slacks and a pale rose silk sweater over them. In her ears she placed large pearls, the only jewelry she wore. She stared at her clean, scrubbed face in the mirror and saw the heightened color in her skin and eyes that always came from excitement.

She knew her daughter would think she was beautiful, but she didn't want her to find her mother glamorous. Over the past few weeks she'd grown accustomed to a more natural look and never wore foundation. A faint smattering of freckles emerged, a result of her morning jogs, making her appear younger than her forty-three years. She stroked bronze blush over her prominent cheekbones, added a bit of beige shadow over her vivid green eyes, and a dab of mascara. She needed the confidence that being well turned out always gave her. There had been too many impulsive moves and decisions in her life. This time, Jilly wanted everything to be well thought out.

She'd just finished washing black shoe polish from her hands when the telephone rang to inform her that her cab had arrived. Her sisters were waiting for her. There are times when there are simply no words to say. When all is quietly understood. This was one of those times. Jilly kissed each of them on the cheek, then left to meet her daughter.

She arrived at The Left Bank early. From the cab she searched the sidewalk in front of the charming restaurant for anyone waiting. After slipping a few bills to the driver, she stretched her long leg out from the cab, adjusted her dark sunglasses on her nose and then rose gracefully from her seat. She stood and stared at the glossy black door of the restaurant. This was a life-defining moment. She could either walk through that door to meet her daughter and reclaim her past, or turn away and bury the past forever. Jilly took a deep breath, dug deep and walked through the door.

The smell of delicious food rose up to meet her as she entered the cheery yet unpretentious restaurant. It was designed for ladies; sunny yet cozy, decorated with Provence patterns, murals of The Left Bank and black wrought-iron furniture. Conversation was humming, punctuated by laughter. She caught a few glances shift her way, cool and assessing. Jillian had worn her thick red hair pulled back into a chignon at her neck. Dressed in her black leather coat and her dark sunglasses, she knew she looked tall, sleek and polished.

"Can I get you a table?" asked a smiling woman in a black skirt and white blouse.

"I'm looking for someone. I believe we have a reservation.

Anne Marie..." She almost said Parker, but that wasn't right. What was her married name?

"Are you looking for me?" A voice sounded from her elbow.

Jillian jerked around. Standing before her was a younger, shorter, fresher, more exuberant version of herself. The beautiful woman's hair was a mass of thick waves that catapulted to her shoulders and was the same fiery red as her own. Her porcelain skin was as fair and her eyebrows as finely arched and dark. But her eyes were different. Instead of Jilly's brilliant emerald green, they were bluer, a turquoise color that seemed to reflect the warmth and vitality of her personality. Those eyes were round with anxiety now as they looked up at the cool, elegantly dressed, speechless woman staring back at her.

Her baby.

Her knees felt like buckling. "Anne Marie?"

The young woman broke into a heartbreakingly beautiful smile.

Jillian would have known her daughter anywhere, even if she wasn't wearing the bright red dress that flowed as only silk could from her slender shoulders down her enormously pregnant belly to her ankles. Looking into her eyes, she felt again the connection she'd felt when she first saw her through the narrow span of mirror in the delivery room.

"How do you do." Anne Marie held out her hand and tried not to stare at her birth mother's face.

Jillian looked at the outstretched hand with longing. Her child's hand. She'd never touched her baby. They wouldn't let her. She stared at the hand, feeling as though the leather straps were still holding her to the table. Anne Marie's smile slipped and she began to retract her hand. Jilly reached out quickly to grasp it. She felt an instant connection and had to force herself to let go. Her body, so well trained for grace, was choppy and stiff. She was desperately trying to act normal so Anne Marie wouldn't think that she was some weird, overanxious mother. How could Anne Marie know what it meant for her to just touch her daughter's hand?

"I hope I'm not late," Anne Marie said. She seemed a little nervous, smoothing the dress over her belly, looking at her shoes. "It was hard getting out of the house. Lauren wanted to come."

Jillian licked her lips but couldn't speak. She could only stare, grateful the sunglasses masked her eyes. "I've only just arrived. It's a lovely place. Very French."

"Well, you should know," she replied, seemingly relieved. Her eyes looked everywhere but at Jillian.

"Are you nervous?" Jilly asked kindly.

"Yes," Anne Marie replied while color bloomed in her cheeks. "I suppose I am."

"I am, too."

"Are you ready for your table?" the maître d' asked.

"Are we?" Jilly asked.

Anne Marie straightened her shoulders and gave her a long, steady, surmising look. There was no question that this was not a child but a woman, a mother, a force within herself. "Oh, yes," she said, then turned and took the lead with elegance and composure that did not go unnoticed by Jillian.

They were seated at a small round table for two covered in thick damask linen and brightly colored, Provence-style china. Jilly was pleased they were seated closely and would not be compelled to strain to hear each other's comments in a room already loud with chatting. Jilly removed her sunglasses and sat down. When she looked again at her daughter's face, she sucked in her breath and felt she might faint with shock. It couldn't be...

It was faint, delicate and not so visible when she was smiling. But when Anne Marie's face was still, as it was now while she read the menu, Jilly could very clearly see the unmistakable cleft in her chin.

Dennis's child.

Jilly's heart froze in her chest and her hands rigidly clenched the menu. *Anne Marie was Dennis's child.*

She felt the blood draining from her face as her breath came quickly. Jilly reached out for the glass of water, forcing her stiff hands to grasp the chilled glass and bring it to her lips. She thought of Birdie in the hotel. Of Hannah. She recalled Dennis's words, *She might look like me,* and shivered. God help her, her worst fear was realized. How was she going to handle this?

"The poached salmon is good," Anne Marie suggested, looking up from her menu.

Jilly cleared her throat and forced a smile. "Wonderful. Good. I'll have that," she replied, closing the menu. She was grateful for the interruption when the waiter approached with a basket of bread and a plate of butter. When he laid these on the table, he looked at them expectantly.

They both ordered poached salmon with Hollandaise sauce. Jilly ordered a glass of chardonnay. Anne Marie ordered iced tea. As he scurried off, Jillian told herself that she'd deal with this issue later. If she thought about the repercussions now she'd go mad. She owed it to Anne Marie, and to herself, to make this first private step as mother and child.

They struggled through halted sentences and stiff smiles while they waited for their food. When their dishes came at last, however, Jilly poked at her food and tried to lessen the tension by asking Anne Marie all about her daughter, Lauren, and her husband, Kyle. Anne Marie's eyes glowed and she visibly relaxed as she talked about those she obviously doted on.

Kyle worked at the local paper mill. Money was tight now, especially with the new baby coming, but they got along well enough. They lived in a small house in De Pere that they loved and were busy decorating. She talked at length about the vegetable garden they were starting that spring. Lauren was a dickens. She loved to laugh and was excited about having a new baby brother or sister. Jilly listened with wonder that her child had, in fact, turned out so well and was so *happy*.

When it was her turn Jilly spoke about the old Victorian house in which they'd grown up and what her sisters and parents were like, careful to speak in generalities. Jilly deliberately skipped over her past. She wanted them to start their relationship focused on the positives.

"I'd like to meet your sisters," Anne Marie said, opening the door to a possible reunion. "My aunts."

"They're all here, of course," she replied, eager to grasp this offering. "They'd love nothing more than to meet you, too. They hoped you'd feel this way, but we didn't want to all meet you at once. The Four Seasons can be a lot to handle."

"The Four Seasons?"

Jilly smiled. "That's what my father always called us when we were growing up. He lumped us all into one group. Lord, we were so embarrassed. Whenever we walked into a room together he'd call out, "Here come the Four Seasons." Looking back, though, I believe it gave us a strong sense of identity. It bonded us."

"But you said your sister just died?"

"Yes, she did. Merry, the youngest. She died earlier this month of lung complications."

"Then, how are there still four Seasons?"

"Ah, I see what you mean. My sister's daughter is here, too. Hannah. Your cousin. She's been officially inducted as the fourth Season."

"Well," Anne Marie said, looking at her plate, "that doesn't leave room for me, does it?" She said it as a joke, but once the words were out, they both recognized the hidden hurt at being the outcast.

"It's just an expression."

Anne Marie's cheery countenance shifted and Jilly braced herself, sensing that they were going to enter the murky territory they had avoided on the phone.

"Why did you give me up for adoption?"

The question had the power to bring her shoulders back. She looked around the room and pressed her knees tightly together under the table. Suddenly she felt choked. She brought a shaky hand up to cover her eyes and prayed she wouldn't break down. The old feelings of loss and desperation ripped through her as fresh and as powerful as they had so long before.

"You don't have to talk about this if you don't want to. I was only curious."

"I never gave you up," she managed to say, raising her eyes. Anne Marie's face was pale, revealing a smattering of freckles, so much like her own. Dabbing her eyes with the thick cotton napkin, Jilly managed to collect herself. "I surrendered you. That's the term used today and it's more accurate. You don't just give up your own baby."

Anne Marie leaned forward. "But why? My mother told me you were too young. Is that true?"

Jilly took a deep breath and nodded. "I was sixteen when I got pregnant. Seventeen when I had you. Just a senior in high school. A young senior."

"Then you weren't married to my father."

"No, of course not." Dennis's face flashed in her mind. "We were just children ourselves. It was so different back then. I wish you could understand. When a girl got pregnant, she was sent away. No questions asked. Being pregnant out of wedlock was a scandal. It was a stigma for the whole family. Being so young, the option of keeping you was never presented to me. From the moment I found out I was pregnant, everyone told me it was the best thing for the baby to be given to a family who wanted a child, that it was wrong of me, even selfish, to want to keep my baby."

"But why didn't you ever search for me? I used to wonder why you didn't at least try and find me."

"Oh, Anne Marie..." Her throat constricted.

"Don't misunderstand. I love my family. My mom and

dad, they've been wonderful and I wouldn't change anything. They *are* my family.'' Her eyes shone now in defiance. ''But sometimes, when I hear someone talk about how Lauren's eyes are like Grandma Marie's or how my cousin has Uncle Bob's laugh, I always feel a little left out, wondering where I got my nose, or where my laugh came from.''

''You can look at me and get a lot of your answers,'' Jilly said thickly, deeply moved. She glanced at the cleft, then as quickly moved away. ''But your laugh is like your aunt Rose's. High and like bells. It's music to my ears. And your red hair—'' She shrugged in the French manner. ''This is the Season trademark. When you see red hair, then you know it's from us.''

Anne Marie smiled, the light returning to her eyes. ''Lauren has red hair.''

''Does she?'' Jilly was extraordinarily pleased and her chest swelled. ''There you have it. Genetics will out.''

In the aftermath of that tense exchange they both reached for their coffees and sipped, needing a moment to regroup. Jilly studied her daughter's face. Her eyes seemed larger and her alabaster skin literally shone. At that moment, Jilly recognized the face of the infant that they'd held up in the hospital delivery room. When she saw her baby, even for that brief, fleeting moment, the mother in her saw *something*—in the eyes, in the features—that imprinted itself into her memory.

''I see so many things in you, Anne Marie,'' she said softly, tilting her head as she continued her perusal. ''The way you move your head a certain way, the breathiness of your voice, the manner in which you hold your shoulders back when you walk. They say there are blood ties in every family and I believe it. I'd like to tell you everything there is to know about me and my family—your family. Not to detract from the family that you already have, but to add to it.''

''I'd like that,'' she said, tears flooding those impossibly luminous eyes and making them even bluer.

The bill came and it seemed a good point to end their

lunch. They'd forged past the initial awkwardness well enough, yet the strain was beginning to show. Anne Marie looked at her watch and gasped with alarm.

"Oh, my God, look at the time. It's almost three o'clock. My mother is going to kill me. She has a bridge game and Lauren will be upset that I've been gone so long."

"I'd like to meet your mother. I don't want her to ever feel that I'm coming here to compete with her in any way. I'm just grateful to have found you, to have met you, and I hope to meet my granddaughter." It was a shameless begging for an invitation, but Jilly didn't care.

"When would you want to meet her?"

"As soon as possible."

Anne Marie seemed pleased rather than worried. "How about tomorrow? You're staying at the Embassy Suites, right? Well, there is a wonderful garden restaurant there that has a great brunch. Should we meet there, say, ten o'clock? I'll bring Kyle and Lauren. My mother, too. I think she's even more anxious to meet you. And please, would your sisters come?"

"You couldn't keep them away."

Jilly quickly settled the bill. Then, because she knew Anne Marie was in a hurry, declined a ride home and hailed a cab.

As she settled herself in the back seat and slipped her dark sunglasses over her eyes, Jilly felt shell-shocked and tired beyond thinking. Maybe after she lay down a while, perhaps when her muscles relaxed and her brain cleared, she could think again of that cleft in Anne Marie's chin and how that one sweet little dimple might be the bomb that exploded her family apart.

Twenty-Three

Jilly returned to her room, drew the curtains and collapsed on the bed. She lay staring at the ceiling, her mind stumbling over one immutable truth that she could no longer deny. Dennis Connor was her child's father.

Oh, the bitter irony of it. When she got pregnant she didn't know for certain who the father was and told herself it didn't matter since she wasn't going to get married or keep the baby. The father would simply slip into anonymity. Then years later, when the news came that Birdie was dating, then married, Dennis, she was stunned, unable to believe that fate could pull such a jest. Cruel fate! Even the possibility that Dennis could be the father had suddenly became another unsavory, dirty little secret. Then again, when she'd agreed to go on this search for Spring, she'd told herself Dennis couldn't possibly be the father. There had only been that one time with him. But God wasn't giving her a single break.

She sat up in the bed, untwisting the sheets that were corded around her legs like a snake. Raking back her hair, she took deep, cleansing breaths, clearing her head. "No more lies," she said, feeling the conviction deepen. That's what had gotten her into this problem in the first place. Yet she couldn't let Birdie walk into that restaurant tomorrow morning and be slapped with the truth. Birdie would take one look at Anne Marie and figure it out just like she had. If the tables were turned, she'd want to know the truth from Birdie herself.

She could hear her heart pounding in her ears and feel the blood draining from her veins. She imagined this was what it felt like to face a firing squad. She reached out, picked up the phone from the night table and dialed Birdie's room.

"Hello?"

"Birdie?"

"Oh, hi, Jilly. How's your headache?"

"Better, thanks."

"Good. Ready for dinner, then? Rose and I were just trying to pick out a restaurant."

"Birdie, listen, can we meet for drinks first? Just you and me? I'd like to talk to you. We could go to the lounge downstairs."

There was a pause. "Sure. I'll meet you there in say, ten minutes."

Jilly found a secluded table between a potted palm and the brick wall, ordered two glasses of white wine, then waited. The minutes passed in agonizing slowness as she tried to rehearse what she would say to Birdie. But nothing sounded right and she realized with dread that no matter what words she chose, they were going to hurt.

She heard the bell of the elevator and looked up to see Birdie step out and walk into the lounge. Jilly licked her lips and waved. Birdie's brows rose when she spotted her and a smile lit her face as she waved back.

"You look awfully serious," Birdie said, leaning forward for a quick kiss on the cheek. She looked at Jilly, her face clouded with concern. "Is there something you didn't tell us about Anne Marie?"

She waited until Birdie settled in her chair. "In a way. There's something I need to clear up with you."

Birdie leaned back in her chair. "I'm all ears."

Birdie was in high spirits. The thought that she was about to dash them brought a pain so raw in Jilly's heart that it hurt to breathe. There was no easy way to say this, so she decided just to begin with the truth.

"We've spent so many years apart, Birdie," she began, cushioning the blow. "I treasure the closeness we've found on this trip."

"I do, too."

"I don't want to lose it. That's why I've got to tell you something." Across the table Birdie's eyes intensified and her smile stiffened. The tsunami was coming and she saw it. Jilly's throat constricted. "Do you remember when we were at the motel and we talked about how you had a crush on Dennis?"

Birdie's face sharpened and she leaned forward slightly. "Yes?"

"You asked me if Dennis was the father of my baby."

The color drained from Birdie's face.

"I told you then that he wasn't, but that wasn't entirely true."

"He either is or he isn't." Her voice was low and cold. "Which is it?"

"I saw Anne Marie today. Birdie—" she clenched her hands tight "—she has a cleft chin."

Birdie sat motionless, absorbing the shock. All the spirit and joy was devastated by the wave of horror.

"You lied to me!" she cried out, her eyes bright with fury. "I asked you and you told me he wasn't the father. How could you? You lied!"

"I know I did and I'm sorry. I'm so sorry! I wanted to tell you the truth but what was I supposed to do? You were lying in bed after just having had a miscarriage. How could I have told you then?"

Birdie covered her face with her hands and rocked back and forth, shaking her head.

"It was wrong of me, I know that now. That's why I'm telling you. So you know the truth from me. But you have to know I lied to protect you, not hurt you.'' Jilly reached out to touch her, but Birdie recoiled as though her hand burned.

"I knew it!" she shouted to Jilly.

Jilly drew back, too taken by surprise to do anything but stare back at her fury. The people at the neighboring table looked their way with disapproving glances.

Birdie frowned at them, then leaned forward, lowering her voice to a strained whisper. "I always knew there was something between you but I wouldn't allow myself to believe it. Whenever you two were together I could feel the tension."

"What are you talking about?" Jilly cried, not understanding. "I hardly ever returned home. How many times could there have been?"

"I should've trusted my instincts."

"Birdie, there's nothing going on between Dennis and me."

"He's the father of your baby!"

"He doesn't even know he's the father. *I* didn't know until I saw Anne Marie!"

Birdie looked dumbfounded. She sat back in her chair and said, her face contorted with disgust, "That's great. Just great. And all this time we thought you were being so brave, so noble, keeping the father's name a secret. Now you're basically telling me you were a slut."

"You unfeeling bitch!" she cried out, shoving Birdie on the shoulder.

Birdie's eyes flashed with shock and fury and she shoved Jilly right back. "You slut!"

The couple at the next table tsked loudly and in a fluster rose with their drinks to find another spot.

Birdie and Jilly turned their heads to watch them pass, then stared at each other, shoulders hunched, eyes glaring and breathing heavily. Then their faces slackened and, for a moment, neither of them knew what to do or say.

"My God, what's happening to us?" Birdie said, slumping back in her chair and covering her eyes.

Jilly glanced around the intensely quiet lounge to see people staring at them with blank expressions. One woman sniffed disapprovingly, but the rest shifted back in their seats and turned their heads again. Gradually, conversation picked up in the lounge.

"Can I get you something?" a waiter asked. He'd quickly moved forward after the outburst.

"No. Thank you." Jilly's eyes were averted and she sat straighter in her chair. When he didn't move she lifted her chin and said in a clipped tone, "No, thank you."

"Okay. Just let me know if you do," he said in an over-cheery voice, ducking out.

Tapping her fingers on the table, she looked at Birdie, who sat slump-shouldered far back in her seat, looking down at her hands. Jilly leaned forward, weary and shaken, and rested her elbows on the table.

"I didn't mean to hurt you."

Birdie didn't say anything or move a muscle.

"What was I supposed to do?" she asked plaintively. "Not tell you? Let you walk in there tomorrow and figure it out for yourself like I did? I couldn't let that happen."

Birdie only closed her eyes.

"Or even if you didn't figure it out tomorrow, should I have kept this a secret? Dying inside every day wondering when you'd figure it out. I'd have to go away again. There's no way I could let Anne Marie become a part of my life, the family's life, for fear the truth would come out. And it would, Birdie. It always does. We'd just be trading one secret for another. Is that what we want? I'm trapped in this lie, too! Tell me, Birdie, what should I have done?"

"I don't know."

"I had to tell you. I should've told you years ago when we were kids."

"Yeah, you should have," Birdie said with a bitter laugh. "Then I never would've gotten mixed up with Dennis."

"Then you never would have had Hannah."

Birdie's face dropped and she looked lost. "I feel cheated. Lied to. Betrayed."

"How did we betray *you?*"

"You have a child. You and him. Together!" she blurted out, her face red with anguish.

Jilly stared at her sister, catching sight of the source of Birdie's pain. "This isn't about the child, really, is it?" she said slowly. "What's eating at you is that Dennis and I had sex. It's the old jealousy. You think we've shared some intimacy."

"And that's not betrayal?"

"No! He wasn't your husband. Get that through your head. Birdie, you weren't even in the picture then. How could we betray you? I had sex with a teenage boy named Dennis Connor when I was sixteen. Once, Birdie. Only once. Dennis wasn't the love of my life and I sure wasn't the love of his. He was just some boy I liked and let. Not your husband. Not even your boyfriend. Just some boy. There's nothing between us. Get over it!"

"I can't." She tossed her napkin on the table and rose to leave.

"Where are you going?"

"Away from you."

"You think you can just walk away from this?" Jilly called out after her. "I've tried that and it doesn't work. I'm your sister. You might never talk to me again. You can divorce your husband. But you can't just walk away. The truth always has a way of catching up with you."

Birdie didn't turn around. She just kept on walking.

Twenty-Four

~~~⊸⧉⊷~~~

The following day the weather was unseasonably warm. The hotel opened a few of the patio doors to allow the summerlike air to circulate through the garden restaurant. Beyond thick glass walls, the large swimming pool fooled them into thinking they were breakfasting on the veranda. The garden theme of the restaurant was carried to the hilt with ferns and plants everywhere and with waiters wearing forest-green aprons. Lauren ran around as if she was outdoors, from table to table, then to the wall, pressing her nose and palms flat against the glass and staring with fascination at the wavy water of the pool.

Lauren. Her granddaughter! Jilly couldn't look at the beguiling child, with her red-gold ringlets and luminous brown eyes, without feeling a wave of love unlike any she'd known before. She finally understood why grandmothers were so dotty about their grandchildren. She couldn't wait to spoil Lauren with candy and gifts, to hold her and smell her and kiss her—anything just to keep her close. Lauren was her second chance. She was so grateful to God and to Anne Marie for this unexpected gift.

The brunch had gone very smoothly, considering all the tension. Jilly sat between Anne Marie and her mother, Susan

Parker. She was a handsome woman in her mid-fifties and dressed to the nines in a scarlet suit with accessories to match. Across the table, Rose chatted valiantly with stoic Kyle, who looked as if he couldn't wait to get out of his suit. Beside them sat an equally glum Hannah. The poor girl was as upset and confused as Rose that Birdie hadn't come to the brunch. Hannah had sheepishly entered the restaurant and mumbled the message that Birdie had some patient emergency that needed her attention. While the excuse worked to smooth over any unpleasantness, it did not fool Jilly or Rose.

Jilly's smile was constant, despite the splitting headache that persisted after a restless night. While Susan and Anne Marie volleyed stories of Anne Marie's childhood, she offered polite and cheerful comments and questions. Mostly, however, she was slavishly grateful that Susan had the gift of gab. She did the yeoman's share of the work, keeping the conversation humming and not allowing for a moment of awkward silence to mar this reunion.

Yet it was annoying, too. Whenever Jilly tried to have a quiet word alone with Anne Marie, there was Susan, reaching up to smooth a hair from Anne Marie's face, or linking arms with her, or bringing up some tidbit from the past. She was determined to show Jilly that she and Anne Marie were closer than any mother and daughter could possibly be.

Jilly watched the performance and wished she could just put her arms around Susan and reassure her there was no need to fret. She was not there to snatch her child from her. She couldn't have even if she'd wanted to. All she wanted was the chance to be invited to their table once again.

When a tanned, fresh-faced young waitress delivered the bill, both Jilly and Susan lunged for it. Their fingers each rested possessively over the slip of paper.

"This is mine," Jilly said good-naturedly. "It's the least I can do."

"Oh, no," Susan exclaimed through a hard smile. Her eyes glittered, determined to win. "You're our guest."

"Don't be silly. Let me."

"This is our city. And I'm so delighted to be able to host such a happy reunion for my daughter."

She'd laid down the gauntlet. *My daughter.* Jilly heard the proclamation in those two words and knew that she couldn't challenge this woman's claim. No matter how much Jilly might feel like Anne Marie's mother, this woman *was* her mother. The woman who had lovingly raised and cared for Anne Marie. Jilly retracted her hand and tucked it neatly in her lap.

"Thank you," she said, meeting Susan's eyes. There was a moment's impasse and she hoped that Susan would hear and understand that she was grateful for so much more than brunch.

"Is that your other sister?" Susan asked as she placed her credit card on the bill. She was looking over toward the door with an animated expression. "She looks rather like you."

Jilly swung her head around to see Birdie standing at the entrance of the restaurant. Her heart soared; Birdie had come around after all. She swept to her feet to greet her, grinning from ear to ear. Looking across the table she caught Rose's eye.

In contrast, Rose's eyes had narrowed and her brow crinkled. She jerked her head toward Birdie with meaning. *Don't you see?*

Caught off guard, Jilly looked at Birdie again and saw that she was carrying something in her hands. Squinting, her breath hitched in her throat with stunned surprise. Instantly her hopes deflated. This was no visit of reconciliation. This was an act of duty. As co-executor of the trust fund, Birdie had come solely to deliver the time capsule.

Birdie spotted the party and began walking their way, her chin up and her back straight. She was dressed severely in a dark suit with chunks of icy diamonds in her ears. Birdie could look imposing on a good day, on a bad one, she was like a thundercloud rolling over a picnic. Her cool attitude swept across the room. As she approached the table, Anne Marie and Kyle stood up.

Jilly didn't have time to regroup. "Hello, Birdie. Glad to see you could make it."

She ignored Jilly and turned instead toward Susan Parker. "How do you do," she said, preempting Jilly's introduction. "I'm Beatrice Connor."

"Hannah's mother," Jilly added, trying to add a little warmth.

Susan remained sitting and raised a limp hand. "You're the doctor, then?"

Birdie's manner was frigid. She took the hand briefly before letting it go. "That's right."

Jilly felt a clammy cold surround her heart as she felt Anne Marie's presence beside her. She wanted to spare both Anne Marie and Birdie this moment, but there was no escape. Somehow, she found her voice. "And this is Anne Marie."

She saw Birdie's face pale as her gaze swept over the young woman. When a slow flush crept up her cheeks Jilly knew that she'd recognized the cleft in her chin. To Jilly's profound relief, she accepted Anne Marie's hand with cool grace.

"Anne Marie," Birdie said, her face barely moving to form a smile. "We meet at last."

Kyle stepped forward to shake her hand and mumble a greeting, but it was Lauren who shattered Birdie's icy composure. The little girl surprised everyone by running up and crashing against the pair of long legs, wrapping her arms around them.

"Hi!" she chirped as only a child could, and turned her head to gaze impishly up at the strange woman.

While Anne Marie and her family chuckled and made

comments about how cute that was, Jilly froze. Birdie coolly looked down at the little girl. She cracked a smile that did not reach her eyes as she studied the little girl that still clung to her leg.

"I see Lauren's introduced herself," Jilly said with faint cheer.

The little girl decided she'd had enough of this and ran off again. Kyle walked off to keep an eye on her, no doubt relieved to leave the women to themselves. Hannah sneaked away, too, and began engaging Lauren in a game of hide-and-seek in the palm trees.

"I don't know if Jillian told you about the time capsule," Birdie said in a formal tone now that the introductions were over.

"No, I haven't had time to do that," Jilly replied tightly. "Perhaps now isn't the time?" She was furious at Birdie. Jilly glanced quickly across the table at Rose, whose worried expression confirmed Jilly's guess. This was Birdie's way of stating that she would not give the money to Anne Marie. She was washing her hands of the situation as soon as her duty here was finished.

"I think this is as good a time as any," Birdie replied, gaining the upper hand.

Jilly's eyes flashed a warning. *Don't.*

Birdie stared back a challenge.

"Perhaps it *is* the right time," Rose said, stepping forward with a gracious smile.

Jilly glanced back at her, surprised.

Rose picked up a spoon from the table and gently clinked the side of a water glass. Kyle and Hannah looked up from across the room and she waved them over. "Won't you sit down?" she asked, including them all in her gaze.

Jilly and Birdie took seats at opposite sides of the table, apprehension on their faces. Lauren squirmed in Kyle's lap. Anne Marie sat beside her mother and Hannah beside hers.

They all turned to look up at the petite woman in an unremarkable dress with fabulous hair flowing down her back. Jilly wondered wildly what Rose was up to and sat erect, nervously clenching her hands in her lap. Rose bent to take the time capsule from Birdie, then strolled to Anne Marie's side.

"I'd like to tell you a story," she began in her melodic voice. Everyone shifted in his or her seat to listen. "It's about your aunt Meredith Season, who we called Merry. She was our youngest sister. The fourth Season. Not only in age, but also in mentality. She had an accident as a child and never progressed beyond the mental abilities of a girl of, oh, about seven or eight. Though, like most children, she could sometimes be very, very wise."

At this Anne Marie smiled and a light chuckle echoed in the room.

"We never acknowledged your birth openly," she said to Anne Marie. "This was a tragedy that hurt us not only individually but also as a family. It was a tragedy that each of us is very sorry about. It is also something that Merry never reconciled. She loved you in her child's way from the moment she knew you'd been born and asked for you time and time again.

"'Where is Spring?' she would say. That's the name that she gave you. Spring, after the season you were born in. She named a baby doll Spring and a night never passed for twenty-six years that she didn't sleep with it and kiss you good-night in the guise of this doll.

"But she knew the real Spring—you, Anne Marie—was out there somewhere. And she worried about you, loved you, and couldn't rest until you were found. So before she died, her last request to us, her sisters, was that we find you. And when we did, we were to give you her dearest possession—this time capsule."

Rose looked at the old worn and taped shoe box in her

hands. "You might wonder what value this time capsule has to you. This little box was put together by the three of us— me, Jilly and Birdie, when we were very young. I was only six, which would have made Birdie eleven and Jilly thirteen. It's filled with tokens of our childhood. All the little nothings that meant everything to us. What Merry is giving you, in this box, is the essence of who we are. Your mother and your aunts. She wanted you to have it so that you would always have the very best part of ourselves to call your own.

"We don't know what's in it, at least not all of it. We each put something special inside, but it was all very secret. As you can see, it's not been opened." She placed the fingertips of one hand lovingly on top of the box, then handed it to Anne Marie. "It's yours now. As your aunt I believe I can speak for all of us and tell you that in finding you, we have indeed found Spring."

Anne Marie accepted the box with reverence, her turquoise eyes overflowing.

Jilly was undone. Rose had said everything that she wished she could have said. She hated crying in public, but she knew she'd lost the battle as her lips began to tremble, then her shoulders started to shake. In a sudden gush, tears began flowing down her cheeks.

Anne Marie hurried to her side. They wrapped their arms around each other and wept. Jilly held on to her daughter, squeezing her tight, reveling in the feel of her child in her arms for the first time. How many times had she dreamed of this moment, never believing it would happen? "Thank you, Merry," she whispered.

Jilly! She heard her name whispered and looked over her shoulder, but no one was there. She heard the voice again, a child's voice. *Jilly!*

"Where's my grandchild?" Jilly asked, scanning the room, feeling a sudden unease.

"Lauren!" Anne Marie called into the sudden silence, walking quickly around the room.

Suddenly the room felt cold as they all realized that Lauren wasn't in it. At once, they all began calling her name with attempted calm. No one wanted to express the panic they all felt as they began to search around the tables and tall plants of the restaurant.

"Oh, she's probably just playing hide-and-seek," Susan said, but her face was white.

"I'll check the lobby," Kyle said curtly, jogging from the room.

"I'll check outside," Hannah volunteered and sprinted through the doors.

Jilly, Birdie and Rose stopped at different areas of the room and zeroed in on one another, their eyes wide with panic. In that frozen moment, they all shared one thought between them.

The pool.

Without a word, they took off on a run. It was a reflex action, driven by memory.

Jilly sprinted across the restaurant, her breath coming short. She heard again the high call of the birds circling around her. *Jilly! Jilly! Help!* Her feet hit the floor in time to her prayer, "Not again, not again, not again."

They sprinted through the lobby, Jilly in the lead, Birdie and Rose right behind her. Through the glass walls, between the foliage, she could see Lauren inside the conservatory tottering at the edge of the pool. Her hand was reaching into the water. In a heartbeat, she tumbled in.

"Lauren!" Jilly screamed. She had only once before known such blank terror. She scraped her leg on a chair as she rounded the corner, then pushed through the glass doors, hearing the pounding footfall of her sisters behind her. Kicking off her shoes she ran across the tile, slipping once, catching her balance, then going straight to the edge of the pool. With one flying leap, she jumped in after her.

The water felt as thick as syrup and her clothes grew heavy as she tried desperately to reach for her granddaughter. Two loud thumps echoed under the water as a large body jumped in to her left and another to her right. The turbulence caused a multitude of rocking ripples and a spray of bubbles that pulled her back from the small target of pink dress and white limbs flailing in the water.

It was her nightmare all over again. Jilly felt a great fury and an inner screaming, "I will not lose her. I will not let anything happen to this child, by God, I will *not!*"

With superhuman strength, she clawed through the water toward Lauren. Her breath was tight in her chest. She lunged downward, her hands reaching out through the veil of bubbles. She snagged a bit of cotton, tugged hard, then Lauren's small body was in her hands. She pushed her arms upward toward the surface.

Birdie and Rose broke the surface when she did. Rose grabbed hold of Lauren's trunk to help Jilly lift her out from the water. Birdie climbed up the ladder to cradle the child and carry her out and over to the terrace.

Jilly and Rose climbed from the pool and watched in silence as Birdie bent over the child and began checking her vital signs. She moved with quick precision, and for the first time Jilly saw her sister perform as a doctor. Jilly clung to Rose as Birdie administered CPR and she watched her granddaughter's chest move up and down in rapid succession.

In that millisecond of waiting, time stopped, rewound, then sped back at the speed of light to play a dark and murky scene for the Seasons.

It was the summer of 1969. The sky was cerulean. The Bahama Blue waters of the swimming pool were wavy as the mermaids frolicked from the deep end of their make-

believe world to the shallow end. But only two mermaids
swam today. Rose was piqued that Jilly wouldn't play and
kept calling her into the pool. "Come on, Jilly! We need
you."

But she wouldn't come. Jilly was changing now that she
was going into high school. She wasn't interested anymore
in their favorite game, or any game for that matter. All she
cared about were those stupid friends and the boys who
called and made her act all goofy. And Rose didn't like it
one bit. Jilly was talking to one of those boys now, stretched
out on a lounge chair, all slathered up with suntan oil and
listening to rock and roll.

"Jilly, get off the phone and play. Please? It's not the same
without you. Jilly!"

Jilly lifted her sunglasses to glare at her, then turned her
shoulder and went back to her phone call.

"I play! I play!" Merry called out from the ladder. "I
wanna play!"

"Get away from the pool, Merry!" Rose snapped back at
her.

Merry stepped back, pouting.

Rose dove under water toward the pool's drain for the
orange plastic ring Birdie had thrown in. Today Birdie had
made the new rule that the one who captured the magic ring
would be the queen of mermaids for that day.

Rose swam for it with all her might, wanting more than
anything to prove that she could reach the bottom and touch
the drain like her older sisters could. The pressure ached in
her ears and squeezed her lungs, but she felt a surge of elation
as she grasped the plastic ring in her fingers. Keeping her
legs tightly together to form a fin—a very important rule of
the game—she swam swiftly underwater back toward the
shallow end, making it only far enough to where she could
stand. Only Birdie could make it all the way to the shallow

end on one breath. She burst through the water triumphant, catching her breath and shouting, "Look, Birdie, I've got it!"

Still smiling, she searched for Birdie, eager to share her glory. She found her standing on the narrow strip of cement bordering the pool, anxiously inspecting a scrape on her foot. Rose felt the coolness of a cloud passing over the bright sun. Her skin prickled and she suddenly knew something was wrong. Her smile quivered as she pushed her long hair from her eyes and scanned the pool. Jilly was chatting on the phone. Birdie was bent over her foot. Merry... Where was Merry?

She looked over to the ladder, to where she'd last seen her baby sister. Merry wasn't there. She was about to turn her head when something caught her eye. A flash of movement under the water. Focusing, she saw a wisp of red hair and a snippet of pink dress.

Rose couldn't move. She couldn't even breathe. She felt frozen as she shivered in the cloud's shade. Overhead, she heard birds call. Only later did she realize it was her voice.

"Jilly! Jilly! Help!"

Birdie heard the cry for help and her head snapped up. Her sharp eyes instinctively searched the water. She spotted Rose standing stiff in the water, her arms stretched out toward the deep end of the pool. Following the trajectory, Birdie's gaze caught sight of a blur under the water. Even before her brain processed that what she saw was a body, she bolted to her feet and dove into the water straight for her target.

She dove too deep. She knew it the moment she hit the water and cursed herself for wasting precious seconds digging her way up and over to the tiny limbs motionless under the blue-green water. She swam her heart out, one stroke after another, and knew she'd reached Merry fast. Grabbing hold of her, she pushed her up, kicking strong legs hard, straining under the weight of her baby sister as she broke the water. She didn't know who took Merry from her hands, but it was enough to know that Merry was out of the water.

Jilly's hands shook as she grabbed Merry from Birdie's hands and pulled her out. She'd heard the call of her name and, irked, looked up to see Birdie dive into the pool. Instinct reared and she'd dropped the phone, leaping to her feet and running toward the ladder, scanning the water. Her heart stopped and forever after she'd recall the wavy image of red hair, blue water and white limbs.

What should I do, what should I do, she asked herself over and over in a blind panic as she lay Merry's body on the cement. Her sister's arms and legs flopped to her side like one of her stuffed dolls.

"Merry! Merry!" she called out, shaking her, desperate for her sister to open her eyes and say something.

"Turn her over!" Birdie shouted, climbing up the ladder. "Slap her back!"

Jilly did so. "Come on, come on…"

Merry's chest was not rising and falling. Her mouth was gaping uselessly.

"Call the operator! Get an ambulance! Run!" Jilly screamed. Birdie took off to the patio phone while Rose clutched herself and cried. Jilly gathered her baby sister in her arms, holding her tight against her cheek, rocking her, still patting her back. "It's okay, Merry," Jilly crooned, knowing in her heart that it wasn't. Tears fell down her cheeks as she stroked her sister's limp body and cursed herself. She should have watched her more carefully, she screamed inwardly. She was the eldest. She was in charge. It was her fault.

"Baby, baby, baby…just breathe."

"Just breathe," Birdie said to the little girl as she compressed her chest.

Lauren's small body heaved, then she coughed. Birdie quickly rolled the child to her side and held her close while she sputtered and threw up water. She was such a little one, she thought as she patted her back. Two? Maybe three years old? After she cleaned the child's mouth she gently turned her around again to check her vital signs. Lauren's big brown eyes stared back at her like a fawn's, confused and stark with fear. It struck Birdie how much she looked like Hannah. Right down to the adorable cleft in the chin.

She felt a sudden, overpowering love for her and realized in a flash that Jilly was right. It wasn't the child. This child was beautiful and innocent and all that she'd sworn the Hippocratic oath to protect. This child was not a stumbling block for her to overcome.

"Lauren! Lauren!" It was Anne Marie's voice in a high and strident panic.

"Mama," Lauren whimpered, reaching out. She coughed again.

"You're all right, Lauren," Birdie said, smiling, using her name. She lifted her up in her arms and turned to face Anne Marie, who was running toward them. "See, sweetie? Your mama is coming."

Anne Marie reached out for her child and hugged her tight against her chest, rocking from side to side as she cried. Lauren coughed again, rubbed her nose and blinked several times as she looked around with a dazed expression.

"She's going to be just fine," Birdie said in her reassuring doctor's voice. "She just took a little swim."

"Thank God," Jilly whispered, slumping against Rose.

Kyle and Susan came running into the domed pool area, followed by Hannah and a hotel manager. Worry was still etched on their faces.

"It's all right," Anne Marie called out, choking out a laugh. "This little dickens decided to take a swim." She was trying to put a cheery front on it, but panic still shook her voice and her grip was tight on her daughter.

Kyle swept Lauren into his arms and hugged her to within an inch of her life.

"We're sorry," Jilly choked out, emotion strangling her breath. "We're so sorry."

Anne Marie looked at her incredulously. "*You're* sorry? Whatever for?"

"For distracting you. For not paying attention to where Lauren was."

"Jillian!" Anne Marie exclaimed. "You have nothing to be sorry about. I am Lauren's mother. Watching her is *my* responsibility, not yours. It's not your fault. You saved her life!"

Jilly felt her strength ebb and turned to her sisters. This time, Birdie did not look away. Rose's eyes were red. Their hair was dripping, mascara was running down their faces and their ruined clothes clung to their bodies, exposing unflattering bra lines and bulges. She thought they had never looked more beautiful.

"We called an ambulance," the hotel manager said, wiping his brow. Two uniformed paramedics entered the pool area. Outside, the red flashing light of an ambulance reflected off the glass.

"She's okay," Kyle answered. "We don't need an ambulance."

"It won't do any harm to get her checked out, just so everyone can sleep tonight," Birdie said. "But don't worry. This little girl is just fine, aren't you, sweetie?"

"We'd feel better about it if you did, sir," the manager said.

Kyle nodded and Anne Marie reached over to carry Lauren, who had started to cry.

Her granddaughter was going to be fine, Jilly thought with inexpressible relief. But Merry hadn't been fine. They each knew it that day as they saw the paramedics rushing Merry into the ambulance. They each saw it on their mother's stricken face, in the unspoken blame in her eyes when she looked at them. They each understood it when they peeked into Merry's room weeks later to spy her lying listless and pale in her bed, surrounded by strange medical equipment, while their mother read at her side. They'd never talked about that day in the pool. Never allowed themselves to revisit the event in their private thoughts.

A nervous hotel manager and his staff hovered around them, offering towels and apologies.

"Yes, it's all right. We're fine, thank you," Jilly muttered, wrapping herself in a towel. She kept her eyes on her new family as they clustered together and followed the paramedics to the waiting ambulance.

"Come on, Jilly," Rose said, taking hold of her arm, taking charge. "Let's go upstairs to our rooms and dry off. You, too, Birdie. I'll order tea. Then I think it's time we talked."

Twenty-Five

After they'd showered and wrapped themselves in the hotel's thirsty white terry robes, a subdued Jilly, Birdie and Rose gathered together in Jilly's room. They quietly found places on the floral sofa and chairs ensemble by the window. An acid-hot sun was pouring in from the south, drenching them in light. Rose had ordered tea from room service.

"I'll never drink Darjeeling without thinking of Rajiv," opened Rose, setting her cup down on the table. Then, realizing what she'd said, she glanced quickly up at Jilly.

"It's all right," Jilly said, blowing on her cup. "I can hear his name without breaking into tears. Barely."

"Are you planning on seeing him again?" Rose asked.

"I don't know," she replied wearily, then sipped her tea. "I don't know that I can even think about him right now. My mind is...filled." She looked at her sisters from over the rim of her cup, then set it down in the saucer. "I know we're all thinking of Merry and what happened in the pool that day. We're all remembering it again, aren't we?"

They nodded and lowered their eyes. The mood deepened as they shifted in their seats. They all sensed that the unspeakable was at last going to be spoken.

"All those years I never allowed myself to think of it,"

Rose said in a hushed voice. "But it was always there somewhere, lurking. It was a punishing kind of thought. Blaming, you know?"

"I do," Birdie conceded. "I still wince whenever I remember grabbing hold of her little body in the pool. It's a searing pain. The image burns my brain, so I just reject it and push it out of my mind. I did that when she died, too. I just pushed it away. I couldn't mourn this death until I reconciled the first."

"We came close to talking about it in the attic," Rose reminded her.

"Thank God we didn't. Our instincts were right to back off. I don't think we could've handled it then. We weren't ready."

"I'm not sure I am now," Rose said. "Except that I want to. Even need to. I have to get past it so I can move on in my life."

"We all do."

Jilly wrapped her arms around her stomach, feeling for the first time in a long while the stabbing pains in her gut.

"Jilly?" Birdie asked, her eyes narrowing in study. "Are you all right?"

"It was my fault," she blurted out in a strained voice. "What happened to Merry was all my fault."

"It was not your fault!" Rose reached for Jilly's hand. "What about me? And Birdie. Don't you realize that this happened to all of us? We were all in the pool."

"I was the eldest. I was the one in charge!" Jilly lowered her face in her palms and shook her head. "I remembered it all today. I was on the phone! Fooling around with some boy. I wasn't paying attention. I didn't want to have to baby-sit when all my friends were out having a good time. I was mad at Mom and at Merry for making me take charge." Raising her face she said with self-reproach, "Mom was right about me. I was just so selfish."

Birdie hurried to her side. "Jilly, listen to me," she said, her voice wavering with emotion. She reached up to firmly remove Jilly's hands from her face. "It was not your fault."

"Easy for you to say. You're the one who saved her!"

Birdie's face contorted. "But I wasn't quick enough!" Her voice broke. "Oh, God, I wasn't there fast enough."

"Birdie..." Jilly breathed in disbelief. She never knew Birdie had felt any guilt about the accident. She'd always assumed that Birdie gloried in her role as the lifesaver, even to this day.

Rose looked up, her face pained, and she put her hands to her own trembling mouth. "No, Birdie, you *were* fast. You would have reached her in time. But... I didn't call out. To-day, when I saw Lauren in the pool, it all came back to me in a flash. I saw Merry in the pool again, under the water. I didn't do anything!" she blurted out in confession. "I couldn't move. I just froze."

"You can't blame yourself," Birdie said hurriedly. "You were only six years old. What could you have done?"

"Something! Anything! I should've done something in-stead of just stand there. I wasted precious minutes. Minutes that would have made a difference."

Jilly moved to wrap her arms around Rose, who was over-come with tears. "You did call out," she reminded her gently. "I remember. You called my name."

"Jilly..." Rose rested her head on Jilly's shoulder.

They hugged tightly, rocking, opening their arms to in-clude Birdie. They each felt so exposed they had to hold one another tightly as though bandaging one another's wounds. Together, they wept for Merry. They wept as they could not at her funeral. They wept for the sister they had loved and lost twice. Once to fate, another time to death.

Later, when they were reaching for tissues and wiping their eyes, Jilly felt drained but peaceful, the way a soldier might feel in the foxhole after the bombing had ceased. She flopped back on the small sofa and stretched her long legs out on the coffee table. Looking out the window she saw plump, white cumulus clouds in the beautiful blue sky. She thought of Netta.

"It's the theory of relativity," Jilly said in wonder, beginning to understand Netta's meaning at last.

"What?" Birdie asked, lifting her head.

"Relativity. This wise old woman I met on the plane tried to explain it to me. I didn't understand it then, but it's suddenly making sense. We each have our own version of what happened in the pool that day. And even though they are different, each one is valid. It has something to do with traveling at different speeds. I'm afraid I didn't catch that part."

Birdie's eyes lit up as she caught the gist of Jilly's meaning. "That's rudimentary physics these days. Basically it means there is no one correct view of the universe. We each see things from our own frame of reference."

"So then we're all right in what we remember of that summer day?" Rose asked, sitting forward.

"Or wrong..."

"Maybe if we'd understood this we could have helped one another," said Jilly. "Or at least understood one another better. That would have led to forgiveness." She thought of all the misunderstandings, the years lost to secrecy and silence. "We're sisters, after all." She looked at Birdie questioningly. *Aren't we?*

Birdie held her gaze and nodded. *Yes, oh yes.*

For a minute no one spoke.

"That wouldn't have changed the outcome of that day," said Rose, in her own line of thought. "No matter what we each remember of that day, none of us can change the immutable fact of Merry's brain and lung damage—though I'd give anything if I could."

"Nope. It happened, and we were never the same," said

Jilly. "That's what I meant about how our childhood ended that day."

"Only it was much more." Rose clenched her hands. "We changed after the accident. We grew up—I don't know—wounded. I know I became indecisive and afraid," she added almost inaudibly.

"I tried to make everything right," Birdie confessed. "As though I could somehow make up for what happened. I tried to be the perfect daughter. Then later the perfect wife, doctor, mother. Talk about putting pressure on yourself."

"I saw the way Mom looked at me," Jilly said in a dark tone. "I guess I figured if I was already a bad kid, then what the hell." Her eyes flashed. "Boy, did I show them. Weren't they proud of me? Especially Dad." She looked at Birdie. "You were the good sister and I was the bad sister."

"Oh, Jilly," Birdie said wearily, "can't we get past the competition between us? There is no good sister, no bad sister. There's only you and me. And Rose."

Jilly wondered if she really meant this. If so, then there was a chance for reconciliation. "And Dennis..."

Birdie looked at her squarely. "Yes," she said from her heart. "And Hannah. And Anne Marie."

Feeling a deep relief, Jilly nodded gratefully, hearing Birdie's acceptance and forgiveness. Before she could respond, a knock sounded on the door. They looked at one another questioningly.

"Oh, hell." Jilly hurried to answer the door, tightening her robe en route. A bellman stood at the door with a polite smile. "I have a package for Miss Jillian Season."

Jilly tipped him and returned to the group, her eyes wide with wonder. In her hands, she carried the time capsule.

"Oh my, what's that doing here?" Rose asked.

"Here's a note that came with it." Jilly tore open the note and scanned the contents. "It's from Anne Marie."

"What does it say?" They gathered close on the sofa.

I appreciate more than I can ever say that you gave this time capsule to me. I'll carry the sentiment of the gift with me always. But the contents are personal for you and your sisters and I'd be happier knowing that these treasures were safe with you. You've already given me the greatest gifts I could ever want: my own life and the life of my child.

She folded the note and tucked it in her pocket to treasure forever. Then she sat on the sofa and crossed her legs. "Let's open it."

Rose's eyes widened. "Now?"

"Why not? When's a better time?"

"Sure, why not?" Birdie said. "Who knows when we'll all be together like this again."

Rose looked at the time capsule with knitted brows. "I don't think we should just open it. I mean, this is important. Shouldn't we do or say something special?"

"You mean something ceremonial?"

"Yes. Some kind of ritual."

"Well," Jilly said, her mind whirling with ideas. "Let's bring another chair to the table for Merry. She's here. I can feel her. I've felt her presence all afternoon."

"I feel her, too," Rose said, getting up to drag an empty chair into their circle. That done, she sat down beside Jilly and tucked in her legs. "Okay. I feel better now. The circle is complete. The Four Seasons are all here."

Jilly handed Birdie a small butter knife from the tea tray. "Do a little surgery on this box, would you, Doc?"

Birdie looked at the pitiful tool, set it down, then went to her purse to pull out a small red Swiss Army knife. "Always be prepared."

"Typical," Jilly teased.

Birdie held up the knife. "For Merry," she said, then cut through the tape with the same skill and care that she would

use to perform a surgical incision. They all leaned forward
with anticipation as the tape peeled off the edges of the rag-
ged little shoe box. The white box had been painted in bois-
terous colors with flowers, mermaids, a sun and a moon, stars
and clouds in the free style of children.

"Who should open it?" Birdie asked when she finished.

"Rose," Jilly said firmly.

Rose's eyes gleamed appreciatively as she moved to the
edge of her chair. "Okay, here goes." With her delicate fingers she slowly, carefully, lifted the top of the box.

They all held their breaths and leaned farther to peek inside. A beige-colored cloth lay over the top of the contents,
wrapping it like a piece of tissue.

Jilly recognized it immediately. "My shawl!" she exclaimed, pulling it out. She fingered the soft chamois rag as
her mind hurtled backward in time. This had been her most
treasured possession as a child. Holding it, she recalled how
she'd made-believe the rag was her shawl when she was a
beggar woman in the Lower Kingdom clutching her child to
her breast. She slipped it around her neck, relishing the fragile softness against her skin.

Rose leaned forward and pulled out a crumpled tiara made
of sparkly blue-green paper. The pointed tip was bent but it
was still brilliant with color.

"That's my mermaid crown!" Birdie said, all amazement.
"I'd forgotten I'd put it in there." Her eyes were wide with
childlike wonder as she handled the fragile tiara about to
crumble into pieces. "I remember telling Mom to be careful
putting it in the box so that the sparkles would stay on."

She gingerly placed the crumpled tiara on her head. Short
red spikes of damp hair mingled against green sparkles. "I
loved this tiara more than any of my trophies," Birdie said
softly, looking at her sisters. "Mermaids was such a great
game, wasn't it? I mean, we really played."

"For hours and hours." Jilly reached out to gingerly touch

the bent point of the tiara. "And what about your treasure, Rose?"

Rose reached in and pulled out a small painted box that she instantly recognized. She'd painstakingly painted each intricate design on it. Birdie bent close as she opened it. Inside was her most treasured possession in the world at seven years of age—her very best collector's stamp. The one she'd hunted for, saved for and waited by the mailbox for. It still had the power to thrill her.

While Rose admired the stamp, Birdie reached into the time capsule to take out a photograph from the box. "What's this?" she asked, checking the back. In their mother's handwriting was written, *My mermaids and me.* Turning it, they saw another photograph of the four of them at the poolside, dressed in their tiaras and smiling big red-lipped smiles. Only this one was a close-up, and their mother had joined them.

Ann Season, with her red-blond hair and brilliant blue eyes, was crouched down beside Merry. One arm was wrapped protectively around her baby, the other clutched the metal pool ladder for balance. Jilly was flamboyantly perched high on one of the ladder steps, one arm around her mother's shoulders. Birdie was hanging off the other side of the ladder, one arm out as if embracing the world. Rose sat demurely on the top step, right below Merry, beaming at the camera with her wide-eyed innocence. The Season family resemblance was powerful—the varying shades of red hair, the pale skin freckled in the sun, the magnetic smiles. The one emotion that poured out from the photograph was joy.

It filled Birdie's heart with sadness. "I never saw this one. Who put that in here?"

"I've never seen it before, either," replied Rose. "It must've been Mother. She's the only one who could have. We gave her our treasures to put into the box and she sealed it."

Jilly took her turn to study the picture and felt a stab in

her gut when she saw her arm around her mother. They were so close then. When she was thirteen, her mother was her hero.

Rose dipped into the box again. All that was left were several pastel envelopes. On seeing them, Jilly and Birdie put their hands to their mouths and shifted back in their seats.

"Oh, God, I forgot about those," said Jilly, her voice soft. "I think I spilled out my guilt to write that and sealed it away."

"But we didn't seal the guilt away," Jilly said. "That's what I've been realizing ever since this search began. It's like memories. They're always there, like these letters, sealed inside of ourselves. Come on, we've gone this far. We might as well open them."

"I don't remember these," Rose said, perplexed. "I remember everything else, but not these. What are they?"

"I can't believe that you of all people don't remember *this*," Birdie said. "It all started when Mom gathered us together to tell us that Merry was coming home from the hospital."

Jilly remembered the scene as vividly as though it had just happened.

The girls were seated on the living room sofa in a row, their legs hanging over the edge and their hands in their laps. They knew this was a very serious discussion and no one dared utter a peep.

"I want to explain to you what's happened to Merry," Ann Season told them in her most serious voice. She was sitting with her knees together and her hands clasped tight in her lap. Her face was pale and strained and her eyes were red. "Merry won't be coming back to us quite the same. She's had some lung damage from all the water she took in. She can breathe all right now, but..." Her voice trailed away as she yanked a tissue out from the cuff of her dress and dabbed at her eyes.

Jilly sneaked a glance at Birdie. Both wondered if their mother would make it through the discussion without dissolving into tears. She'd been crying a lot since the accident, long into the night, and nothing seemed to console her.

When she began again, the strain made funny lines on her smooth face. "Her brain is not the same, either," she said a bit shakily. "The water damaged that, too. She'll still be our own dear Merry, but she won't grow up the same as you will. She'll always be a little girl. Do you understand?"

"Will her body grow up?" Birdie wanted to know.

"Yes, but her brain will still be a child's."

"Merry is *retarded?*" Jilly blurted out as understanding slowly dawned on her. The word burst from her mouth, striking fear into her sister's faces. How could someone in her family be retarded? She wasn't born that way, how could that happen now?

Her mother bristled. "We're *never* to use that word in this house. Never! Is that understood?"

Jilly had a thousand questions in her mind, but she knew she'd never be able to ask her mother a single one. Not ever. They all nodded meekly.

"I still don't remember," Rose said, looking at the time capsule. "I must've blocked it out."

"After mother told us that Merry wasn't going to grow up," Jilly continued, "we decided to dedicate our own adulthood to Merry. The one we lost for her. Can you imagine?"

"That's so sweet, actually," Rose murmured, her eyes glistening.

"So we came up with the idea of the letter."

"Not a letter, actually," Birdie interjected. "More a form letter. That was my idea," she said with a self-deprecating laugh.

"Let's do it." Jilly reached for the envelopes, handing one with Birdie's name on it to her, then one to Rose, and kept her own. The final one was of the thick Crane's stationery that their mother had always used. It was addressed To the Four Seasons in their mother's handwriting.

"Oh, boy," Birdie said, looking at it. "I sure didn't expect to see that in here."

"A letter from Mom?" Rose asked, incredulous.

"Let's hold off on this one," Jilly said with an edge in her voice. She set it down on the table, far away from her.

Then she opened her own letter. She saw in her own handwriting a simple sentence, like the form letter Birdie had described. Seeing it, she recalled the care and precision she'd undertaken to write it. Jilly laid the single sheet of paper on the table for her sisters to see.

I want to be an actress when I grow up. I dedicate this to you.

"I remember now," Rose said, deeply moved. She hurried to open her own and lay it on the table.

I want to be an explorer when I grow up. I dedicate this to you.

Birdie looked at the two dedications side by side, then smiled in bittersweet recollection. She opened hers and set it down beside the others.

I want to be a mother when I grow up. I dedicate this to you.

Jilly looked at Birdie with new eyes. "A mother? That's what you wanted to be? I would have thought a doctor or an astronaut or something like that. You had such big dreams."

"I know," Birdie replied in a far-off voice. "But this was my greatest dream." She looked at them and shrugged lightly with a crooked smile. "So? I always wanted to be a mother."

Jilly wondered if she would have made fun of Birdie's dream, had she known, or perhaps teased her for picking something so unimaginative. Probably. Now that she was a mother, she understood better. "I guess your dream came true."

"But I almost lost it. I'm very lucky. Your dream came true, too, Jilly. You became an actress."

"Rather cryptic, wouldn't you say? I started acting about the time I wrote that."

"I forgot that I wanted to be an explorer," Rose said with a self-deprecating laugh. "Me of all people. The one who never even left our family home." She looked away from them. "I guess I never fulfilled my dream."

"But you did!" countered Birdie. "You explore the world on the Internet. You collect stamps from every country. You have the heart of an explorer, Rose."

"Absolutely," Jilly agreed. "And tomorrow is your greatest adventure."

"DannyBoy," Rose whispered.

"We'll be with you every step of the way," Birdie said.

"Come on, Rose," Jilly urged, seeing Rose's slender shoulders begin to slump. "Lead the way! We've come a long way together on this journey. You said it yourself. We can't just go back to the way things were. We've come home at last and like good ol' Odysseus we have to slay the enemies. Pull back the arrow and let fly at that fear and indecision."

"But I'm not that brave."

"Yes, you are," Birdie said with emphasis, picking up the slip of paper with Rose's childlike handwriting spelling out her dedication. She handed it to Rose.

I want to be an explorer. I dedicate this to you.

"Hoisted on my own petard," she joked, laughing at herself. This was her dedication to Merry. She felt an overpowering resolve not to let her sister down a second time. She bent to pick up the other two pieces of pale blue stationery from the table. She handed one to Jilly and the other to Birdie, then looked at them with challenge sparkling in her eyes.

"If I can do it, so can you. In 1969 we dedicated our

futures to Merry. It's 1999. Let's renew our dedication starting this very moment.''

They held their dedications out so that they all touched in
the circle between them. ''To Merry!''

They talked and talked until Rose's head was bobbing to
her chest, yet each knew that they hadn't even scratched the
surface. The topic of Merry's near-drowning had only been
broached. They hadn't yet had time to individually process
it. That would take much more time and many more conversations. But for tonight, they were exhausted.

''I've got to go to bed,'' Rose said, stretching her arms
high into the air. ''I'm falling asleep here. And I've a busy
morning.''

''Me, too. Hannah's probably wondering where I am.''

''Okay, let's call it a day,'' Jilly said. She yawned noisily
and dragged herself up from the sofa to walk her sisters to
the door. ''I'll see you both tomorrow, then. What time are
you meeting Danny?''

''Nine-thirty.''

''Okay,'' she said, yawning again. ''I'll be ready, I pray.
God, I'm exhausted. We've been through the mill.'' She
leaned forward. ''Good night, my honeys.''

They kissed on the cheeks and Jilly knew that no matter
what pain or sorrow might erupt as they worked through their
problems, their connection as sisters was indestructible. They
were family. Shared blood ran through their veins. All this
she understood in her sisters' touch.

''Go ahead, Rose,'' Birdie said as Rose left the room. ''I
want to ask Jilly something.'' She waited while Rose padded
down the hall to her room, then turned to face Jilly again,
her face pensive. She closed the door and leaned against it,
staring at her feet.

Jilly knew this moment had to come and welcomed it.

When Birdie lifted her head, Jilly saw a fragility there she'd not seen before.

"I'm sorry, Jilly. I was horrible to you yesterday."

Jilly's mouth opened in a gasp. This was far more than she'd expected to hear. "You weren't horrible. You had a shock. You were reacting."

"Overreacting. I do that." She looked upward and closed her eyes. "Jilly, I was so angry at you. And Dennis. I couldn't see past the red haze in my eyes. What frightens me more than anything is to realize how uncontrolled it was. I was blinded by rage. After I left you, I called Dennis to tell him that it was over between us. I wanted to punish him like I wanted to punish you."

"Oh, Birdie, you didn't."

"Let me finish. I tried to call him, but he didn't answer the phone." She shook her head. "Thank God for small favors. When I think I could've ruined everything with one swipe of my tongue. But the anger still boiled and this morning I wanted to prove to you and the world that I was still in control. I was going to do my duty—just to show I could—then get in the car and never see you again. And I was damned if I was going to give this child of yours and Dennis's a penny of Merry's money." She took a deep breath and ran her hand through her hair as she collected her thoughts.

"Then Lauren fell into the pool." She released a short laugh of wonder and shook her head with disbelief. "It was déjà vu. I was eleven years old again, given a second chance to save Merry. I was holding that child in my arms and all my training clicked in. It was like I'd spent a lifetime preparing for this one moment. I was zoned. It was exhilarating." She looked again at Jilly and her expression shifted from triumphant to reflective.

"But when I saw her face, I suddenly realized that this wasn't Merry. It was Lauren. Little Lauren, with her own

face and mind and soul. This was yours and Dennis's and
my family. I felt a connection with her that was blood deep.
Visceral. All I knew was that I loved her and I had to save
her. You were right, Jilly. This anger I felt wasn't about the
child at all. It's inside me and it's poisoning so many of my
relationships. It leaves so little room for compassion.'' She
reached up to wipe a tear from her face. ''That's no way to
live. I have to get over it. I may need some help, I don't
know. But I realized something today dredging up all those
murky memories. I can't change the past. I can't take the
hurt back. But I can soften it if I can just learn how to accept
it.''

Jilly reached up to wrap her arms around her sister.

Birdie held her tight, and she spoke in a rush. ''I don't
want to lose you, Jilly. Not again. I just can't. That's the
bottom line. You're my sister and I love you and I don't care
what I have to deal with, I'll do it. But I *won't lose* what
we've found again.''

''We won't,'' Jilly replied, holding just as tight. ''We
won't. I promise. We love each other, and that'll get us
through.''

''I love Dennis, too,'' Birdie said, moving away and mop-
ping her face with her palms. ''To be honest, it's going to
be hard for me to reconcile that you and Dennis have a child.
It's going to take time for me to get used to the idea.''

''Of course it is. This whole thing is going to take a lot
of time. Months, even years. For all of us. Dennis doesn't
even know yet.''

''That's another thing. I want to tell him.''

''Absolutely. Whatever you want to do.''

She nodded, setting it straight in her mind. ''And I don't
want the family to know yet. Not even Rose.''

''More secrets, Birdie? Is that a good idea?''

''There's a difference between privacy and secrecy, Jilly.
This affects our lives, mine and Dennis's. It affects our mar-

riage. And this affects Hannah. We'll know when the time is right to tell her.''

''What do I say when Anne Marie asks who her father is?''

Birdie smiled wearily and shrugged. ''I don't know. That's for you and Dennis and me to work out later. Okay?''

Jilly nodded in agreement. ''Okay. I guess we've covered enough ground for one weekend.'' She looked at her sister, worried. Her face looked so pale and frail. So unlike Birdie. ''Are you okay, really?''

''I'm pretty good, considering.''

Jilly chuckled. ''I feel pretty raw. Do you want to sleep here tonight?''

Birdie shook her head ''No, Hannah would worry. I'd better go. Good night.''

Jilly opened the door, but privately she wanted to close it and tell her to stay. She didn't want her to leave yet. There was still so much more they needed to say.

''Good night, Birdie. Sleep tight.''

''Don't let the bedbugs bite.'' Birdie smiled her crooked smile and in that moment Jilly took heart catching a glimpse of the feisty eleven-year-old again with bangs in her eyes.

''If they do, hit 'em with a shoe.'' Jilly closed the door, smiling.

Jilly was gathering the teacups, bits of paper and tissue from the coffee table when she saw it. She paused, stooped over the table with her hand outstretched. Mother's letter was still lying where she'd placed it against the lamp, partially obscured by a napkin carelessly tossed. In the excitement, they'd forgotten all about it.

Setting down the cups, Jilly reached to pick up the letter and brought it close. Her mother's Palmer Method handwriting on the envelope sparked a pang of recognition. To her mind, the loops and swirls were unlike any other woman's.

She weighed the letter in her hand as she wondered whether to call her sisters back so they could read it together. She stepped toward the phone, then stopped, deciding it was much too late, and they were much too tired for more drama tonight. They could wait until morning.

But she could not. They'd forgive her, she thought as she slipped her finger under the seal. The old glue gave readily. Tugging out the cream colored paper, she couldn't imagine what Mother might have written to her daughters thirty years ago. Please God, she thought as she opened the letter, don't let it be an accusation.

To my daughters Meredith, Rose, Beatrice and Jillian, I'm sorry.

I should have been there. I never should have left children to watch children. I hope by the time you read this, you will be able to forgive me, my darlings. I doubt I'll ever be able to forgive myself.

I love you,
Mother

Hours later, Jilly lay in bed rereading her mother's letter through blurred eyes.

"Oh, Mother, there's nothing to forgive!" Jilly exclaimed in anguish and frustration. Except perhaps for the silence. So much had been left unsaid between them. Why hadn't her mother told her that she'd felt this guilt? Or at least that she didn't blame them for letting Merry get hurt. What good was it to scribble it all down on a piece of paper and seal it away in a box? Nothing was solved and they had all suffered.

She could only imagine the guilt her mother felt. It was no wonder she drank so much. It was the only way she could escape. *Poor Mother,* she thought, clutching the letter to her heart, torn apart by the years lost. So many years wasted in heartache and misunderstanding. She missed her mother with a vengeance, wanted her back so she could say all the things she should've while her mother was alive. It might have made such a difference in both their lives.

Jilly cried in the darkness, for what might have been and for what was. When she was done, she calmly wiped her eyes, accustomed to the tears she allowed to flow freely now, then smoothed out the wrinkles from the letter with her fingers. Closing her eyes, she brought the letter to her lips and imagined she was kissing her mother good-night.

"Tell you what, Mom," she said, folding the letter neatly and tucking it under her pillow. "I'll make you a little deal. Just between you and me." She smiled, feeling in her heart that her mother heard. "I'll forgive you all your secrets—if you'll forgive me all of mine."

Twenty-Six

$\sim\!\!\infty\!\!\ll\!\!\infty\!\!\sim$

The following morning, the Season sisters woke up knowing their lives had changed. They were forced into motion by the mundane realities of having to pack up their things and check out of the hotel, but that only served to punctuate the one big reality.

The quest was over. Anne Marie had been found. Merry's last request had been honored, and in doing so, she had at last been mourned and the past laid to rest.

Jilly lay in bed a few extra moments and stared at the textured ceiling, considering all this and wondering what path her life would take now. She'd come flying, driving, swimming over miles and years to reach this dawn. Her future was just beginning.

When I grow up, I want to be an actress. I dedicate this to you.

This was the future she'd dedicated to Merry when she was a child. Her sisters thought she'd achieved this dream. More's the pity. She thought of the seventeen-year-old girl who left Wisconsin, swearing she'd survive. She'd created a make-believe character complete with wardrobe and props. But it was all pretend. She'd been living a lie.

One truth emerged from all the deception, however. She'd

given birth to a daughter, who in turn gave birth to another daughter, and so the cycle continued. That was *real*.

The secret to survival was in seeing the world through the eyes—and heart—of a child. That was Merry's lesson to her sisters. To treasure life, and most of all, to love. Simply, unconditionally and with joyful abandon. To love without demanding or expecting anything in return.

Jilly decided to rededicate her future to Merry on this fresh new morning. She'd work to discover new truths in her life, rather than deception. Rose had told her, "When I act brave, I am brave." Wasn't this the purest form of acting? To call on one's inner strengths even when afraid or unsure? To be true to one's own convictions. She would be this very best kind of actress, she vowed.

Birdie's arms arced as she cut through the cool pool water. She'd been swimming for more than half an hour, stroking back and forth across the length of the hotel's pool. Her soft arms were shaky and it was a struggle to keep herself afloat but she wouldn't stop—couldn't. The need to keep going drove her mercilessly on.

She'd awakened early after a fitful night. She had dreamed again of being in a pool, swimming and swimming and not being able to catch her breath. Behind her lurked all the mistakes she'd made over the years, and if she could just make it to the other side she knew she could climb up, catch her breath and be safe. But danger was right behind her, like a ghost shark snapping at her heels. So she pushed and clawed most of the night and awoke with her sheets tangled around her like seaweed, feeling like she was drowning, gasping for breath.

She'd climbed from her bed with a savage churning inside of her. Dressing quickly, she went down to the lobby shops and found one clothing store just opening up. She picked a swimsuit from the rack, paid for it, then went straight to the pool without slowing her pace. She hadn't swum in a pool in twenty years, not since her father died. After that, she didn't see much point. She'd only swum for him, to triumph in the water for him.

This time, she was swimming for herself. She pushed hard and steady, ignoring the pain building up in her shoulders. Was it madness or did she feel that with each stroke some of the pressure and poison was leaching out into the dark water? As she completed lap after lap she forced herself to keep on kicking, to keep on reaching out. She had to reach the other side of wherever it was she was going. Water slapped her in the face. She swallowed some and coughed, crying now, but she plowed on through the cool, unforgiving water.

"Birdie!"

She jerked her head up and her arm flopped into the water. Was it her imagination, or had someone called her name?

"Birdie!"

Dog-paddling, she turned in the water and saw Dennis. *Dennis!* She felt a surge of joy and with new energy began swimming straight for him. Now her swimming had a focus. To Dennis. Her arms felt like lead and her muscles screamed in pain, but if she could just reach him she knew she'd be safe. Her nightmare would be over.

His arms reached out and helped pull her up like a clumsy seal from the water. He wrapped her in a towel and brought her close, holding her tight against his chest. Her legs felt wobbly and she shivered, but she clung to him. As he held her, she let go at last and sobbed, knowing he was strong enough to withstand the tsunami wave.

"You're here," she said at length with a shaky voice.

"I came up last night. I had to be here. I didn't know what hotel you were at so I stopped after two, checked in, then started looking for you again this morning."

"Dennis," she said, pulling back to look him in the face. "Anne Marie...she's your child."

His face revealed his shock and he looked off across the pool for a long while. Then he looked at her warily. "How do you know?"

"Jilly told me." When she felt his arms tighten in anger she said quickly, "To spare me. She knew I'd have figured it out myself. Anne Marie has a cleft in her chin like yours."

Dennis's eyes were intense as he struggled to digest the news. "Are you okay with this?"

She shrugged. "It's been hard. But yeah, I think so."

"And Hannah?" His eyes darkened with worry.

"She doesn't know. She won't know until we tell her. Jilly's agreed."

"Good," he said with relief. He paused, then shook his head with a short laugh. "It's a lot to take in all at once. I worried about this all along, worried what you would think if she turned out to be my child. When you told me on the phone that you were going with Jilly to meet her, I knew I had to come. I couldn't just sit at home and wonder what was going on up here. But now I don't know what to say."

"It's something we have to handle, together."

His brain seemed to process this and his face sagged in relief. "I'd like that, Birdie. I want that." Then his dark eyes shone with intensity and he said in a low voice filled with emotion, "But first we have to talk about us. Our issues are *not* about my past. Our problems are about our present. Between you and me."

She nodded, eager to show she was willing, more than willing, to talk. They sat down together at a white garden table by the pool. She wrapped the large towel around her shoulders, looked into his brown eyes and shivered. He glanced at her spiky short red hair and smiled. And they began to talk, slowly and awkwardly at first, then with feeling. They talked and listened, their gazes locked and their ears attuned. When Dennis reached out to hold her hand, Birdie felt a sudden warmth and knew they were going to be all right.

When I grow up, I want to be an explorer. I dedicate this to you.

Rose read the small slip of paper, then took a deep breath and tucked it back into her coat pocket. "Oh, boy, Merry," she whispered. "Stick by me now."

She and Jilly had entered the parking lot of the mall and circled near the west entrance where Danny had agreed to meet Rose. Most of the shops weren't open yet and Danny thought they'd be able to find each other more easily without a crowd. She looked outside the window as Jilly pulled into a space several rows back. Few cars filled the lot and there was no one standing at the door.

"How're you feeling?" Jilly asked.

"Like I'm going to throw up." Then, seeing the worry on her face, she said, "Not really." She'd been so nervous she couldn't eat and she had been repeating like a litany all morning, "I'm brave, I'm brave."

And what a morning it had been, she thought as she leaned against the door. Jilly and Hannah had spent over an hour cajoling her to put on a hint of blush and a whisper of mascara. Then Birdie shocked them when she came into the room holding hands with Dennis and asked them if they could drive Hannah home. Birdie was going home with Dennis on his motorcycle.

"Do you see him?" Jilly asked, turning off the engine.

"I don't see anyone," Rose replied, anxiously peering out the window. "Oh, God, is this what it feels like to be stood up at the altar?"

"We just got here and it's not even nine-thirty yet. Take a deep breath, honey."

Rose took her literally and began breathing deeply.

"Relax, Rose. It's not like a blind date. You *know* him."

"That makes it worse. I already know I like him. But will he like me? Will he think I'm pretty?"

Jilly faced Rose squarely. Her face was no longer jovial but serious. "You're beautiful. Yours is a quiet, even regal beauty. The kind that men marry and that other women admire. You know, all my life I wondered why Daddy never gave you a nickname."

"Oh, I know why," Rose said, blushing faintly. "It's because I'm so shy and plain."

"No," Jilly replied, looking at her intensely. "He was right not to give you one. You have a rare purity that stands alone, like a rose. A nickname for you would have been equivalent to gilding the lily." Jilly cupped her sister's chin and looked into her eyes. "If this guy doesn't see how beautiful you are, dump him. You deserve the best."

"It's just that I always believed there was someone special out there for me. I hope and pray it's Danny." Rose's eyes widened. She clutched Jilly's hand and pointed. "There's someone there."

Jilly swung her head toward the mall and saw a figure stepping out from the entrance.

"That's him," Rose said on a breath. Her hands went to her hair, smoothing the long locks that fell like water down her back.

"How do you know? You can hardly see him from this far away."

"I know."

The man in the distance was average height, slender, with brown hair worn short. He was wearing khaki pants and a light brown jacket. She watched him peer out over the parking lot. Drawn to him, Rose unbuckled her seat belt and put her hand on the door handle. Beside her Jilly undid her seat belt.

"You go on," Rose said, stopping her with a hand on hers. "I don't need you now."

"But, what if…"

"Really, I don't want you here. I love you, but try to understand. This is something I have to do alone."

"Are you sure? You don't really know him. I'll stay here for a little while, just in case you change your mind. What, five minutes?"

"He isn't some stranger. He's Danny. And besides…" she said with a smirk. "What can happen in a mall over coffee and a cinnamon bun? Go on now. I'll call you on the cell phone if I need you."

"Call me in exactly one hour to tell us when to pick you up. Sooner, if it doesn't go well."

"Don't worry." Then Rose smiled. "But thanks."

Jilly leaned forward and kissed her cheek. "Have fun." Then, pulling back, she added, "But not too much fun."

Rose stepped out into the morning air, then closed the door with a confident swing. At the sound, Danny looked her way. He stood still, watching. She lifted her hand and offered a brief wave. His hand came up to wave back and she saw that he carried a single red rose.

She walked toward him with slow, steady steps, as he did toward her. With each step she saw more of him. He had the look of a country boy. His body was lean and wiry, his face was tanned and weathered, and his hair was tawnier than brown and fell loosely at his temples. His shirt was a pale blue, open at the collar. Closer still, she saw only his eyes. They were the same pale blue as his shirt and they shone out from the tan as though backlit.

He was searching her face with the same intensity and she didn't shrink back from his scrutiny. His eyes were filled with wonder and appreciation and the gentleness of spirit that she immediately recognized. It was DannyBoy. She could have picked him out from a crowd.

Walking toward him, she felt sure that this was what it felt like when people talked about dying and heading toward heaven—just walking toward the light.

Jilly had one more stop to make before ending the quest. She drove out of Green Bay toward Du Pere to visit Anne Marie once more before leaving town. The directions were clear and the streets well-marked. It wasn't long before she pulled up in front of a small yellow brick bungalow with pale blue shutters. Even though most of the houses on the block looked the same, Jilly would have picked this house out as Anne Marie's even without directions. This house had window boxes spilling over with freshly planted annuals and a white picket fence bordering it. A wreath of dried flowers hung on the door.

Anne Marie answered the door and Jilly was relieved to see that the bloom was back in her cheeks. Lauren didn't hang back behind her mother's skirts as she had the first time they'd met. She ran into Jillian's open arms to deliver a kiss. Kyle was at work and Susan was at home, so the atmosphere was more relaxed.

Jilly spent a pleasant hour looking at photo albums of Anne Marie and Lauren while they sipped coffee. It was just long enough to tie and knot the tenuous bonds they'd established. They didn't have a relationship yet. That would take time, effort and honesty. But they did have a beginning.

When she gathered her purse to leave, Jilly sighed a private sigh of relief that Anne Marie didn't ask about her father. She would, someday, and when she did Jilly would work with Dennis and Birdie on the next step of this reunion. They all needed to proceed slowly.

"You'll call me right away about the baby?" she asked before leaving.

"Of course. You're the grandmother."

Jilly smiled and knew it would happen. She saw the commitment in her daughter's eyes.

At the door, Jilly hugged her daughter, then reached into her purse and pulled out a long white envelope. "My sisters and I talked and we want you to have this," she said, placing the envelope into Anne Marie's hand.

"What is it?"

"A legacy that is meant to go to you. You can open it after I leave. We can't begin to tell you how valuable the time capsule was for us and we're so grateful you returned it. We want you to know you're a Season, too. Don't ever forget."

Turning to leave, Jilly felt a sense of completion. By giving Anne Marie the remainder of Merry's trust fund money, the Season sisters had fully honored Merry's last wish. At the curb Jilly turned to wave once more. Anne Marie was standing on the front porch with Lauren, waving. Jilly's heart captured the sight to tuck away and bring out at lonely moments, like the photograph of Anne Marie as a baby that she had been given today.

As the Land Rover drove away, she looked through the rearview mirror for a final glimpse. She saw Anne Marie pull the check out from the envelope, bring her hand to her heart, then swing her head toward the car.

Jilly grasped the wheel tight and grinned from ear to ear. Birdie was right, she thought as she made her way back. Being a mom *was* the greatest dream.

Twenty-Seven

A month later Jilly stood at the black wrought-iron fence that bordered the small, redbrick house overlooking the sleeping town of Hodges. Her hand rested on the cool metal as she gazed up at the window on the second floor that was filled with light. She guessed Rajiv was already in bed. Was he thinking of her, she wondered? They'd shared some remarkable moments in that bed.

There was enough vanity still beating within her to suppose he had wondered what had happened to her, or where she was now. Perhaps he even missed her as much as she discovered that she missed him. Or, he could be over her already. That thought sent her heart pumping every last drop of vanity from her pores.

She wasn't young anymore. She thought she might even be a year or two older than him. She wasn't wealthy, either. She didn't have an exciting career or even that elusive something known as potential that had lured men to her in the past. She was simply herself, Jillian Season.

But her identity was hard-won.

She looked again at the light in the window. He's probably just reading a book and not wasting a moment thinking about her, she thought, and wondered for the hundredth time that day what she was doing coming back here.

Except she couldn't stay away. She loved this little place. The garden had exploded with color since she'd last been here. New leaves rounded the craggy branches of the ancient trees. Moonlight dappled through them as the branches waved gently in the evening breeze.

She loved him.

She held her breath and pushed open the heavy gate. It creaked loudly in the quiet night. One of these days she was going to have to oil that darn gate, she thought with a cringe. Predictably, there followed a high yip from the shadows.

"Pirate Pete? It's me."

She heard a low, throaty growl.

"Pete, stop that! Come here, boy," she cajoled in a loud whisper.

The little dog walked stiff-leggedly toward her, his growl rumbling in his chest. When he caught her scent, however, his ears flattened with delight and he sprang forward wagging his tail and whimpering.

"Such a homecoming! Did *you* miss me at least? I missed you, too." Buoyed by the dog's welcome, she rose again and made her way along the bumpy, uneven walk toward the back door. She passed thin patches of grass and weeds that threatened to choke out the tulips and hyacinth in the garden. Reaching the porch she saw that a flowerpot had been filled with geraniums, but it drooped sadly. The place looked forlorn and not well tended.

Jilly brought her knuckles to the door and knocked. A moment later the light turned on in the kitchen. She smoothed out her hair when she heard footsteps approach, licked her lips when the lock clicked and sucked in her breath when the door swung open.

He looked thinner. His dark hair was cut shorter and was tousled. A single dark lock fell over his forehead. He stood motionless with his hand still on the handle, blinking as one just awakened from a dream.

"Jillian?"

She shrugged and smiled crookedly. "I'm back."

He let go of the door and pushed the hair from his face. "So I see." Then, dropping his arms, he said, "I was hoping you'd come back."

"You were?"

"You know I was. I never wanted you to leave me."

Exasperated, she tossed her hands up in a futile gesture. "Then why didn't you tell me that before?"

"You weren't ready to stay. You had things to get done. We both knew that. Besides, there is an ancient saying that translates to something about how you can't hold on to what is not yours. Jillian, to stay was your decision to make."

"It's true. It was too soon. Rajiv, so much has happened! I met my daughter. She's lovely and I'm so lucky. Then I had to go home to take care of business details and help clear out the family house. We're all moving on. We had a lot of decisions to make." She looked at her hands. "I had a lot to make."

"What did you decide?"

She bent to pluck a wilted bloom from the geraniums. Its pungent, spicy smell permeated the air. "It's not so much what I decided as much as what I came to understand about myself. I realized I wanted to tell you all about what was happening to me. More than anyone else. That was strange for me, you see. I've never had this kind of relationship with a man before. I've never shared my private self. Sure, I married three times. But each time was for a reason that had nothing to do with love or commitment. Not even friendship, really. I was infatuated, perhaps even thought I was in love at the time, but in retrospect it was more of a business deal. I needed someone to handle my finances or to promote my career. I never allowed myself to get involved emotionally or let anyone get so close that I could get hurt.''

''And now?''

''And now… I want to be with you and it has nothing to do with what I can gain from the arrangement. It's more what I can give to you. What we can give to each other.''

''That sounds promising,'' he said, stepping closer.

''Well,'' she said, bringing her fingers up to toy with the buttons on his shirt. ''That's not entirely true. I do want some things.'' She looked up. ''I want to see your face first thing every morning and the last thing every night. I want to hear your voice at my ear and feel your skin next to mine. I missed you, Rajiv. I love you.''

He closed his eyes and sighed, then, opening them, moved forward to encircle her in his arms.

''I don't know what that really means,'' she hurried to add, pulling back a bit. ''I don't know that I ever want to marry again. I don't know that I'll be any good at this love thing. But I do know this.'' She cleared her throat and looked in his eyes. ''I'd like a room, please.''

He chuckled and drew her closer. ''How long will you be staying this time?''

''Longer than I ever have before.''

His eyes filled. Rajiv stepped back to open the door wide. Then, with a proper hotelier's nod, he ushered her into his home.

Before closing the door behind them he said, ''I think that can be arranged.''

Epilogue

It was a perfect day for a wedding.

Summer had arrived and with it an exuberance of spirit that matched the blazing reds, yellows and pinks of the Season rose garden. The sisters pulled together all their creative resources to stage an utterly romantic Victorian garden party complete with an enormous white tent, white linen and yards of thick white ribbons swirling around pale pink and white rose arrangements. It was a tour de force eclipsed only by the loveliness of the bride herself.

At the appointed hour the violins began playing Vivaldi. The small crowd of guests hushed and turned their heads toward the rear porch, festooned with swags and more roses. Jillian's face beamed as she began her slow, graceful descent down the porch stairs into the garden.

Mrs. Kasparov beamed and waved her gloved hand as she passed. This was the last event for the Season family in the old Victorian. Next week, the house would belong to a new family who would carve out their own memories.

The great-aunts and cousins clustered together with their spouses and children, presenting a formidable family support. Jilly loved them more than ever for their open-armed welcome of her daughter and family. She easily spotted Kyle,

tall and proud, carrying Lauren in his arms. Lauren's eyes lit
up and her little legs pumped with excitement when she saw
Jillian. Beside them, Anne Marie shone with the radiance of
motherhood. In her arms she nestled her newest daughter.
Seeing the infant's pink face and red peach-fuzz hair, Jilly
felt she'd come full circle. They had called the new baby
Spring, a gesture that had touched Jilly and her sisters more
than they could ever express. Merry would have been so
thrilled.

Then she saw his face, handsome and strong, with eyes
burning just for her. The heat of a blush pinkened her cheeks
as she thought, *So this is what it feels like to be in love.* At
last. Rajiv was her lover, her confidant, her best friend. As
she walked across the final length of green grass toward him,
she couldn't imagine life without him at her side.

He offered her a deep, knowing smile as she passed him
on her way to the rose arbor where the ceremony was to take
place. Father Frank was standing under it, smiling as she
approached. She took her place to the side, then turned to
watch Birdie follow her, resplendent in the same celadon-
green silk dress that she wore. Birdie strolled as regally as a
queen, her broad shoulders back, her red hair shining and her
glittering blue eyes settled firmly on Dennis.

There was a pause in the music and once again an antic-
ipatory hush settled over the group. Jilly raised her eyes expectantly toward the porch. The house door opened and a
collective sigh whispered in the summer breeze as Rose
stepped into vision.

Jilly's eyes stung; she'd never seen a more beautiful bride.
Rose seemed to have stepped out from another time in the
antique Victorian gown of white satin and chiffon. Her hair
was pulled back from her face by a pearl-encrusted headband
and cascaded down her back like a sheath of red-gold silk.
In her hands she carried a bouquet of white roses. Her
greatest adornment, however, was the joy and love radiant

on her face as she proceeded on the arm of Mr. Collins toward her soon-to-be husband, Daniel Hinds. Her DannyBoy.

How fitting that the wedding should take place here in Merry's garden, Jilly thought. Merry had planted her flowers in the soil that had long ago filled the swimming pool, transforming what had once been a site of tragedy into a site of life and beauty and hope.

The reading chosen for the ceremony was a verse in Ecclesiastes that had always been a mainstay for the Season family. Jillian closed her eyes as the priest read the familiar words.

"All things have their season: and a season for every purpose under heaven.
A time to be born, and a time to die. A time to plant, and a time to uproot.
A time to kill, and a time to heal. A time to mourn, and a time to dance.
A time to scatter stones, and a time to gather them. A time to embrace, and a time to refrain.
A time to search, and a time to give up. A time to keep, and a time to cast away.
A time to tear, and a time to mend. A time to keep silence, and a time to speak.
A time to love, and a time of hatred. A time of war, and a time of peace."

Jilly's gaze traveled to her sisters and she thought how those words had never rung as true as they did now. Life was a cycle of change—and oh, how they'd changed. And how much they were still the same. She was not fooled into thinking that, now that she had found her daughter, and each of them had revisited the dreams of their youth, the cycle was completed. Quite the contrary. Another cycle was just beginning, as the four seasons followed one another in perpetuity. Listening to the couple exchange their vows, Jilly thought how hard they'd each toiled in the spring for this one summer of their lives. A summer rich with promise for each of them. With luck it would ripen into a fall laden with the harvest of their hard work and dedication, then at some point darken again in a winter of doubt, sadness and tragedy. Winter was part of the cycle. Whatever came her way, she prayed she'd persevere with faith that another spring would bloom.

The bride and groom kissed while everyone applauded and shared the high of the moment. Rose turned to face her sisters first over all. It was a glorious moment. In that look all their memories of the past and present dazzled, swirled and danced through their minds, their hearts, directly into their souls.

Jilly, Birdie, Rose and Merry were united forever by bonds that transcended time. They were sisters. They were the Four Seasons.

Two delightful romances from
New York Times bestselling author

DEBBIE MACOMBER

Damian and Evan Dryden.
Brothers and confirmed bachelors...

As a teenager, Jessica Kellerman was wildly infatuated with
Evan Dryden. Now, ten years later, she's truly in love—with his
older brother, Damian. But everyone believes she's still carrying
a torch for Evan—including Damian!

Mary Jo Summerhill is in love with Evan Dryden. But her
background's blue-collar, while Evan's is blue blood. So three
years ago she got out of his life—and broke his heart.
Now she needs his help...and desires his love.

"Debbie Macomber is the queen of love and laughter."
—Elizabeth Lowell

Available February 2001 wherever paperbacks are sold!